Louise Allen has be~~~ ~~~~~~~~ ~~~~~~~~~ fictional, for as long a~ ~~~~ ~~~~~ ~~~~~~ ~~~~~ and places evoke pow~~~ ~~~~ ~~~~~~~ ~~~~~~~ her time between Bedfordshire and the north Norfolk coast, where she spends as much time as possible with her husband at the cottage they are renovating. With any excuse she'll take a research trip abroad—Venice, Burgundy and the Greek islands are favourite atmospheric destinations. Please visit Louise's website—www.louiseallenregency.co.uk—for the latest news!

Don't miss these other Regency delights from Mills & Boon® Historical romance's bestselling authors!

REGENCY
Pleasures

Louise Allen

MILLS
BOON

All the characters in this book have no existence outside the imagination
of the author, and have no relation whatsoever to anyone bearing the same
name or names. They are not even distantly inspired by any individual
known or unknown to the author, and all the incidents are pure invention.

Harlequin Mills & Boon Limited, Eton House,
18-24 Paradise Road, Richmond, Surrey TW9 1SR

REGENCY PLEASURES © Harlequin Books S.A. 2011

The publisher acknowledges the copyright holders of the individual works
as follows:

A Model Débutante © Louise Allen 2005
The Marriage Debt © Louise Allen 2005

ISBN: 978 0 263 88731 0

052-0211

Harlequin Mills & Boon policy is to use papers that are natural,
renewable and recyclable products and made from wood grown in
sustainable forests. The logging and manufacturing processes conform to
the legal environmental regulations of the country of origin.

Printed in the UK
by CPI Mackays, Chatham, ME5 8TD

A Model Débutante

To the Fufflers
For all the support and laughter

Chapter One

February 1816

Miss Talitha Grey shivered delicately and risked a glance downwards. A single length of sheer white linen draped across her shoulder and fell to the floor at front and back: beneath it her naked skin had a faintly blue tinge. Tallie strongly suspected that it was marred by goose bumps.

With a resigned sigh she flexed her fingers on the gilded bow in her left hand and fixed her gaze once again on the screen of moth-eaten blue brocade that was doing duty for the skies of Classical Greece. Perhaps if she thought hard enough about it she could imagine that she was bathed in the heat of that ancient sun, her skin caressed by the lightest of warm zephyrs and not by the whistling draughts that entered the attic studio by every door and ill-fitting window frame.

Tallie exerted her vivid imagination and summoned up the distant sound of shepherds' pan pipes floating over olive groves to drown out the noise of arguing carters from Panton Square far below. She was con-

centrating on conjuring up the scent of wood smoke
and pine woods to counteract the distressing smells
of poor drainage and coal fires when a voice behind
her said peevishly, 'Miss Grey! You have moved!'

Taking care to hold her pose and not turn her head
Tallie said, 'I assure you I have not, Mr Harland.'

'Something has changed,' the speaker asserted.
Tallie could hear the creak of the wooden platform
on which Mr Frederick Harland had perched himself
to reach the top of the vast canvas. On it he was
depicting an epic scene of ancient Greece with the
figure of the goddess Diana in the foreground, her
back turned to the onlooker, her gaze sweeping the
wooded hillsides and distant temples until it reached
the wine-dark Aegean sea.

There was more creaking, the muttering that was
the normal counterpart to Mr Harland's mental processes and then the floorboards protested as he walked
towards her. 'Your skin colour has changed,' he announced with a faint air of accusation.

'I am cold,' Tallie responded placatingly without
turning her head. Frederick Harland, she had discovered, took no more and no less interest in her naked
form than he did in the colour, form and texture of a
bowl of fruit, an antique urn or a length of drapery.
When in the grip of his muse he was vague, inconsiderate and sometimes testy, but he was also kindly,
paid her very well and was reassuringly safe to be
alone with—whatever her state of undress.

'Cold? Has the fire gone out?'

'I believe it has not been lit today, Mr Harland.'
Tallie wished she had thought to insist on a taper
being set to the fire before they had started the ses-
sion, but her mind had been on other things and it

was not until the pose had been set and the artist had clambered up onto his scaffold that she realised that the lofty attic room was almost as chill as the February streets outside.

'Oh. Hmm. Well, another ten minutes and then we will stop.' The boards groaned again as he walked back to the canvas. 'In any case, I need more of that red for the skin tones, and the azure for the sky. The cost of lapis is extortionate…'

Tallie stopped listening as he grumbled on, his words indistinguishable. A slightly worried frown creased her brow as she resumed her own thoughts. At least in this pose she did not have to guard her expression, for she was standing with only a hint of her right profile visible from behind, her long, slightly waving, blonde hair falling free to midway down her back.

Her feet were bare. A fine filet of gold cord circled her brow, its trailing ends forming a darker accent in her hair, and the linen drapery revealed her left side, the curve of her hip, the swell of her buttock and the length of her leg. All of which normally delightful features were now unmistakeably disfigured by a rash of goose bumps.

Still, at half a guinea a sitting she could hardly complain, for Tallie had no option but to make her own living and the guineas from Mr Harland paid the rent. The fact that she was engaged in an occupation that was entirely beyond the pale for any lady, and which would be regarded by almost every right-thinking person as scarce better than prostitution, did not concern her.

She entirely trusted Mr Harland's intentions towards her, for it was not even that he was *making* himself behave in an entirely proper manner. No, she knew he was entirely uninterested in not only her but, apparently, all females. She had heard that some men preferred their own sex, but this did not appear to be the case either. It seemed that his mind was filled with a single-minded obsession for his art and it allowed no room for any other strong feeling.

The second ground for Tallie's lack of concern about her employment was that she was well aware that no work of Mr Harland's in which she featured was ever likely to grace the walls of an exhibition. It was not that his obsession for the classical ran counter to the modern taste, as the excitement at the news that the Elgin Marbles were to be exhibited showed. No, it was simply that his canvases were too vast and his perfectionism too obsessive to allow him ever to finish one, let alone submit it to critical judgement.

The Diana picture was the fourth in which Tallie had featured: each had reached a stage of near completion when the artist had flung his brushes from him with a cry of despair at ever realising his inner vision. They were stacked away now and from time to time he would attack one of them again for a day or two, then give up in frustration.

It was fortunate, both for the artist and for Tallie, that he was not only the possessor of a modest inheritance, but also had a flourishing and lucrative business in portraiture, an occupation he despised as mere craftsmanship. On three days a week he indulged his classical passion. For the rest of the time he painted Society portraits in the rather more salubrious studio on the first floor of the ramshackle house. It was a tribute to his work that the *ton* were prepared to make the journey to the shabby house in the decidedly unfashionable street just off Leicester Square to have their likenesses taken.

Tallie was mentally casting her accounts in an effort to decide whether she could see the winter out without replacing her hair-brown walking dress and pelisse or whether her other, publicly acknowledged, occupation required her to make an investment in a new outfit.

This financial review was more than enough to account for the crease between her brows, but the frown vanished to be replaced with an expression of real anxiety at the sound of the knocker thudding four floors below, soon followed by the sound of a number of male voices echoing up the uncarpeted stairwell.

With an exclamation of impatience at the interruption, Mr Harland cast down his palette with a clatter and, clambering down from his post, flung open the attic door.

Tallie ran to his side and out onto the tiny bare landing, clutching her flimsy draperies around her. Clearly up the stairway from below she could hear the voice of Peter, Mr Harland's colourman. Peter inhabited the ground-floor rooms with his pots and jars, his bags of pigments and flasks of oils and there magically ground vivid colours out of strange materials.

'Mr Harland doesn't receive clients on Wednesdays, gentlemen. Tuesdays and Thursdays are his days. You can't go up there now, sir!'

'Dammit, I wrote to say I would call to arrange my aunt's portrait and I have no intention of trailing back another day at Harland's convenience.' The drawling voice was arrogantly dismissive of the colourman's protests. 'Are you saying he is not here?'

'Yes, sir, I mean, no, sir, he is here, but he—'

'Perhaps he is with someone?' It was a new voice, carrying easily up to Tallie far above. A coolly sardonic, rather bored voice that made the previous speaker sound affectedly high-handed.

'The man has just said that Harland does not have clients on a Wednesday, Nick. Step out of my way, fellow, I have no intention of standing here bandying words with you all afternoon.'

'But the master's working with a model, sir! You can't go up there!' From the rising note of Peter's voice, the speaker had pushed past him and was already on the stairs.

'What? A female model? Now that is more the thing! Come on, you fellows, this should be good sport.' The voice had lost its drawling arrogance and held a note of excitement that made Tallie's chilled skin crawl. They were coming up, and it appeared that there were several men in the group.

Tallie had disrobed in a room on the floor below, having learned from experience of the effect that the dusty attic had on her small wardrobe, and her only covering was the fragile length of linen. She cast round wildly, her heart thudding. The attics, although essentially one large open space, rambled around corners made by the construction of racks of canvases and piles of dusty props, and in one corner, shielded by the largest rack, there was a large cupboard with a door to it.

'I will hide in the closet,' she said urgently to the artist, who was exclaiming in irritation at the interruption. 'Whatever you do, Mr Harland, do not let them know I am here or I will be quite ruined.'

He nodded distractedly. 'Yes, yes, into the closet

with you. I wonder if any of the gentlemen would care to buy an historical canvas?'

Tallie did not stop to argue, but ran on bare feet across the splintery boards. She whisked round the corner of the racking as the voices outside neared the attic and jerked open the cupboard door. The key that had been on the outside clattered to the floor.

Tallie scrabbled for it, but it was nowhere to be seen. With a sob of frustration she abandoned the search and pulled the door to behind her. The closet was lit by a tiny window, begrimed with dirt and cobwebs, but sufficient for her to see that the space contained nothing in which she might cover herself and nothing to wedge the door with. Not, she realised despairingly, that wedging it would have done any good for it opened outwards.

The men had reached the attic now. Through the warped boards that framed the closet she could hear at least four voices. The arrogant man and the sardonic man she recognised from their voices far below; their companions had equally well-bred tones and in them she could recognise a kind of febrile excitement at the thought of what they were going to find in the studio.

Tallie felt quite ill with apprehension and scrabbled to pull her linen draperies around herself in some gesture towards a decent covering. Her fingers closed on air and chilled skin. The length of fabric had gone. Wildly she cast around the little closet as though three yards of white cloth could be hiding in an empty space, then she recalled the slight tug at her shoulder as she had hastened around the racking.

Harland's voice was clearly audible as she stood there, shivering with cold and fear, her ear pressed against the door panels. He sounded flustered. 'Gentlemen, as you can see, I am alone, but really not in a fit state to receive. However, now you are here, what can I do for you, Mr Hemsley? Something about a portrait of your aunt, I believe you wrote?'

'Alone?' The owner of the arrogant voice—Mr Hemsley, she deduced—appeared to take no notice of the artist's question. 'Your man said you had a model up here.'

'He is mistaken. I was working from the nude earlier, but—'

'Nude, I'll say! See here, you fellows!' This voice was younger, excited.

'Take care, my lord! That platform is not very stable!' So, one of them had climbed up to the canvas.

'Bloody hell.' It was Hemsley, his voice strangely flat with what even Tallie in her innocence could recognise as lust. Then the excitement came back to his tone. 'I'll bet she's still here, Harland, you dog. Come on, men, yoicks and tally-ho!'

'For heaven's sake, Hemsley.' The sardonic man sounded utterly uninterested. 'How much longer do you intend hanging around in this squalid attic? Oh, very well, if nothing will satisfy you but to search, let us search. I will look over here, you and the others take the rest. Doubtless we will discover some large spiders, a dead starling or two and any number of mice.'

The voice was getting closer as he spoke. Tallie thought wildly of seizing the door handle and holding on if he tried to open it, but the possibility of being dragged out into the open in such an undignified way only added to the horror. The approaching footsteps halted. From the far side of the attic there was the sound of boisterous searching, excited cries and the occasional 'Do be careful of those canvases, gentlemen!' from the agitated artist.

The footsteps resumed, rounded the corner of the racking if her straining ears were correct, and stopped outside the closet. Tallie turned her back on the door, moved as far away from it as she could and, wrapping her arms around her shrinking body, awaited the worst.

Her hair fell on either side of her bowed head giving her the fragile illusion of shelter and anonymity. But even that vanished as the door creaked open, sending light from the studio flooding into the small space. It defeated the glimmer from the closet window and spilt the shadow of a man across the floor beside Tallie's feet.

He did not move. Tallie could hear his breathing, steady and even, but she had also heard the sudden catch in it when he had first seen her. He was under control again now, standing there silently watching her. She could not drag her eyes away from the long shadow.

The unseen regard felt as though it was burning into her back. Tallie was well aware of just what he was seeing and a wave of scalding humiliation washed up her body. She was going to be sick, she knew it.

Oh, get it over with! she screamed silently. *How can you torture me like this?* At any moment he was going to call out and the whole pack of them would be there, leering, touching, jeering. Like an animal at bay she turned in upon herself, her mind too frozen with terror and shame to allow her coherent thought.

The shadow at her feet shifted. The man moved

and something touched her shoulders lightly. It was a hand resting warm on the shrinking skin. The soft whisper of cloth brushed down her back and over her buttocks. Tallie choked on a scream and his voice— very soft, quite dispassionate—said, 'Here, your wrap was caught on a nail. Be very quiet and everything will be all right, I promise you.'

I promise you. She believed him. The hand was lifted, but she realised he was standing very close just behind her, close enough to whisper in her ear without the sound penetrating outside, close enough for her to feel the warmth of his breath. There was the sound of a long indrawn breath and Tallie had the strange sense that he was inhaling the scent of her. When he spoke again there was an edge to the controlled voice, the merest hint that he was finding her proximity un-settling.

'I am putting the key in the lock on the inside; as soon as I am gone, turn it.' No, she was imagining it: he sounded practical, aloof, unaffected by the sight of the naked girl shivering before him at his mercy.

The door shut, cutting off the bright light. He had gone, leaving the tiny space feeling vast and empty. Over the sound of her own pounding heart she had not heard him move. The voices of the other hunters sounded suddenly loud outside. 'What are you about, Nick? Run her to earth, have you?'

'That closet is locked.' He seemed to be speaking rather louder than necessary and Tallie, wrenching herself out of her frozen state with an effort, twisted the key in the lock, the sharp click masked by the noise outside. 'The key was outside,' the man Nick said.

Oh, clever, Tallie thought as her legs gave way

under her and she sank slowly down the wall until she was huddled on the floor. *The closet is locked and the key was outside, so it couldn't have been locked from the inside. All perfectly truthful and all perfectly deceiving.*

'Gentlemen, gentlemen, will you not come down to the first floor, where you will be more comfortable, and we can discuss the question of Lady Agatha's portrait, Mr Hemsley.' The voices, the excitement dying out of them now their hunt had ended in disappointment, receded down the stairs as the men followed Mr Harland.

Tallie stayed huddled on the floor until her breathing settled a little and the wave of nausea subsided. Then she realised that she was so cold that she could hardly move. With agonising slowness, like an old woman recovering from a fall, she clawed her way up the wall until she was on her feet again. The sharp noise of the key in the lock as she turned it made her jump, but with ears straining she pushed the door open and tiptoed out into the cold attic. Far below she could just make out voices. Mr Harland had them all safely in his first-floor studio, thank goodness, probably offering them the good Madeira he kept for clients.

Tallie crept down the stairs to the next floor and into the near-empty bedchamber that she used to change in. The water in the basin on the washstand was icy as she rinsed her dusty fingers, but the blessed security of her clothing as she pulled it on warmed her from the inside, even though the old wool dress was chill from the room. The scent of the jasmine water she habitually wore touched her nostrils. In the absence of her body heat it was a faint ghost of an aroma.

Her hair snagged and tugged as she pulled the comb through it, but she had to braid it tightly and pin it up so that her hat covered the pale blonde shimmer of it modestly. To an onlooker familiar with the detail of ladies' fashions, the bonnet that she set on her now-subdued hair would have seemed surprisingly elegant in contrast to the shabby gown and pelisse. The straw was the finest pale Luton plait and the trimming, although modest enough, was of elegantly pleated grosgrain ribbon.

Safely and respectably dressed at last, Tallie ventured out onto the landing and peered over the rail. In the hall beneath she could see the tops of the hats of four gentlemen, a variety of well-tailored shoulders and the bare heads of Mr Harland and Peter, who had poked his dishevelled grey head out of his workshop door as the visitors left.

The last man paused and Tallie could hear his voice clearly. It was the sardonic tones of the man the others had called Nick, the man who had found and protected her hiding place. 'Good day, Mr Harland. I trust we have not caused any of your household too much disturbance.' The cool voice did not sound as though it was overly concerned, but Tallie was left with a strong impression of a gentleman who regarded his companions' behaviour with fastidious distaste.

'Thank you,' she whispered, unheard. She felt she had been rescued by him as surely as though he had plucked her from a burning building.

But he had not been unaffected, she knew. This man was no Frederick Harland, impervious to the female form. The sudden, soft sound of that intaken breath when he had opened the closet door and seen her, the very control of his stillness, told her that. The sensation that he was inhaling the scent of her body was a disturbingly sensual memory that shivered through her.

Her mind probed the hideous scene that would have followed if one of his companions had been there and instead decided that it was simply too horrible to think about yet. She needed to be safe at home with a hot cup of tea, a warm fire and some reassuring feminine companionship.

Frederick Harland came up the stairs, a look of surprise on his face when he saw Tallie standing there fully clothed. 'Are you going already, Miss Grey?'

Tallie knew him far too well to be surprised that he appeared to have already forgotten the peril she had been in. 'The light is going, Mr Harland,' she said simply. He gave an exclamation of irritation and continued up the stairs to the attic studio. With a sigh Tallie followed him. 'Did the gentleman have an interesting commission for you?' She needed her money for the day's sitting; although he never prevaricated when asked, or quibbled about how much she told him he owed her, the artist seemed to vaguely suppose money was of as little interest to her as it was to him and always had to be reminded.

'Hardly that. A Society dowager, Lady Agatha Mornington. Her nephew Mr Hemsley is paying for it. He doubtless sees it as an investment,' Mr Harland added suddenly, showing a surprising awareness of those around him.

'How so?' Tallie asked, pulling on her gloves. Mr Harland's portraits were hardly dagger cheap.

'He is none too plump in the pocket and I have

heard from reliable sources that he has taken out a post-obit loan on his aunt's life. He is no doubt investing in a portrait because he needs to keep her sweet so she does not change her will.' He noticed Tallie was holding her purse and the discussion about money jogged his memory. 'And how much do I owe you, Miss Grey?'

'Two guineas, please, sir. Today, and three days last week, if you recall.' She took the coins with a smile and thanks. 'Do you think Lady Agatha knows he has a post-obit on her? Would she not be upset to think he was borrowing against her death?'

'She would cut him out, I should think,' the artist replied, beginning to scrape down his palette with a frown of concentration. 'He is a wild rake, that one. He'll end up having to rusticate to escape his debtors if he doesn't have some luck soon.'

'How dreadful that anyone could regard the death of a relative as good fortune,' Tallie observed, thinking that any relation, even a formidable dowager, would be pleasant to have in one's life. 'Who were the other gentlemen?'

'Um? Pass me that rag, would you be so kind? Oh, Lord Harperley and young Lord Parry.' Tallie bit back a gasp. She knew Lord Parry's mother and it was even possible that his lordship would also recognise her, for he had seen her once or twice. She swallowed and made herself concentrate on Mr Harland as he continued. 'I did not recognise the quiet gentleman. He may have been abroad, he had a slight tan.' Tallie smiled inwardly—trust Mr Harland to notice skin tone and colour. 'Striking-looking man,' he added dispassionately. 'I wonder if he would sit as Alexander.'

Tallie said her goodbyes and slipped downstairs, leaving Mr Harland musing aloud on his chances of enticing a member of the *ton* to model for him naked and brandishing a sword. As she stepped out onto the narrow street she found that she too was musing on that image and was finding it alarmingly disturbing. *Home and tea for you, Talitha*, she reproved herself. *And time for some quiet reflection on a narrow escape.*

Chapter Two

The walk back to Upper Wimpole Street where Tallie lodged was not inconsiderable, but even with two guineas in her purse she was not tempted to take a hackney carriage. As she walked briskly through the gathering gloom of a late February afternoon she tried to put the frightening events of the afternoon out of her mind by contemplating her finances. She only succeeded in making herself feel even lower than before.

Talitha Grey and her mother had found themselves having to eke out a life of shabby gentility when her father died suddenly five years previously. James Grey had left them with no assets other than some shady investments, which proved to be worth less than the paper they were printed upon, and a number of alarming debts. With Mrs Grey's small annuity and Tallie's one hundred pounds a year they managed, although Tallie's modest come-out was perforce abandoned and her mother sank rapidly into a melancholy decline.

When she followed her husband to the grave three years later, Tallie discovered that the annuity vanished with her mother's death and she was faced with the very limited options open to a well-bred young woman with little money and neither friends nor connections.

A respectable marriage was out of the question without dowry or sponsor. The choice appeared to be between hiring herself out as a lady's companion or as a governess. Neither appealed: something behind Tallie's calm, reserved countenance revolted at the thought of any more time spent entirely at another's beck and call, cut off from all independence of action or thought. She had loved her mother and had never grudged the fact that her entire life since her father's death had been devoted to her, but she had no intention of seeing the rest of that life disappear in the same way in the service of those to whom she had no ties of blood or affection.

Tallie had reviewed her talents once again with a rather more open mind. All that it seemed that she possessed was a certain aptitude with her fingers and good taste in the matter of style. Donning her last good gown, she had sallied out and had called upon every fashionable milliner that she could find in the *Directory*.

The famous Madame Phanie dismissed her out of hand, as did several others. It seemed that impoverished gentlewomen were two a penny and could be depended upon to give themselves airs from which their humbler sisters were mercifully free. But just when Tallie was about to give up, she found Madame d'Aunay's exquisite shop in Piccadilly, not four doors from Hardin, Howell and Company, the drapers.

Madame was graciously pleased to interview Miss Grey and even more gracious when she had a chance to view Miss Grey's work. Tallie joined the hard-working team in the back room. But one day, having heard a paean of praise of a particularly fetching Villager bonnet that Tallie had produced entirely by herself, Madame was moved to call her out of the workroom to discuss with the customer the minor changes to the trimmings that were required.

Word spread that Madame d'Aunay's establishment boasted a young lady of charming manners and gentility who was an absolute magician with a hat, especially one to flatter a lady on the shady side of forty. Soon Tallie had her own clientele. Madame charged a handsome supplement to send Miss Grey into private homes for personal fittings, and, as Madame, once Mary Wilkinson of All Hallows, was a sensible woman, she paid Tallie a good portion for herself.

But it only just made ends meet. Tallie sighed as she climbed the steps to the front door of Mrs Penelope Blackstock's private lodging-house for young gentlewomen in Upper Wimpole Street. It was not like her to be so despondent, but it was beginning to dawn upon her lately that she was never going to earn enough to do more than scrape by and even that depended entirely on her ability to keep working. And now she had received an all-too-clear warning that one of her sources of income was perilous indeed. If Lord Parry had recognised her, then even her respectable employment would be in jeopardy.

'Tallie! You must be frozen.' Mrs Blackstock's eighteen-year-old niece Emilia, usually known as Millie, appeared from the parlour at the sound of the key in the door, her head wrapped turban-fashion in

a shawl. 'Do come in and get warm by the fire. Aunt
has just made some tea and we are toasting muffins.'

Thankfully Tallie dropped bonnet and pelisse on
the hall chair and followed her in, pulling off her
gloves as she did so. All the residents of the household, with the exception of Mrs Porter the cook and
little Annie the maid of all work, were gathered round
the fireplace.

Suddenly Tallie's vision swam and she found she
could not find her way to her chair. Her sight was so
blurred she had to grip the edge of the table to steady
herself.

'Tallie dear, what is the matter? Are you ill?'
Zenobia Scott, the other lodger, leapt to her feet and
guided Tallie to her seat. 'You are frozen! Please, Mrs
Blackstock, may I ask Cook to bring a hot brick for
her feet?'

'I'll go.' Millie was already on her way and Tallie
found herself a short while later wrapped snugly in a
blanket with the blissful heat of one of the bricks that
Cook always kept on the back of the range in the
winter glowing by her feet.

She curled her fingers tightly around the teacup and
smiled gratefully at her friends, thankful as always
for having found this cheerful feminine sanctuary.

'Have you walked all the way home, Talitha?' Mrs
Blackstock asked. 'I do wish you would not; it is so
cold out there, and dark now. What occurred to upset
you so? Has some man offered you an insult?'

'No, not exactly.' Tallie made herself think. She
could hardly pretend now that nothing had happened—and in any case she badly wanted to talk
about it—but although the other women knew she sat
for Mr Harland, they had no idea it was in a scan-

dalous state of undress. They knew how she had begun to sit for the portraitist and had unthinkingly assumed that the supply of Society ladies who required
someone else to model their less-than-perfect or preg-
nant figures was constant. But Tallie had failed to tell
them that after the first commission, undertaken at the
behest of one of her millinery customers wanting a
portrait to remind her husband of her pre-childbirth
slenderness, she had succumbed to the temptation of
far more lucrative modelling.

'I was at the studio,' she began, 'and a party of
gentlemen arrived unexpectedly and insisted on coming up. They guessed Mr Harland had a female sitter
and began the most dreadful hue and cry, looking for
me.'

'How dreadful!' Mrs Blackstock and her niece said
in one voice. Millie, a ravishingly pretty blonde with
a lovely figure and a charming, though light, singing
voice, was employed as a dancer at the Opera House.
Despite all popular prejudice about her profession,
she maintained both her virtue and an endearing innocence, whatever lures gentlemen threw out to
'Amelie LeNoir'.

'Did they discover you?' Mrs Blackstock added
anxiously. She kept a concerned eye on her three
young ladies, although hard experience since she had
been widowed had taught her that no lady of limited
means could afford to be over-nice about her employment.

'No, fortunately the ones who were making such a
hunt of it were diverted and all was well. But it was
frightening and I was so very cold...'

Mrs Blackstock clucked. 'Make sure you have a
good dinner tonight, Talitha dear, and go to bed early.

My goodness, just look at the time! Millie, if we are to take out those curl papers and dress your hair for this evening's performance, we must bustle!'

She swept her niece out of the room, pausing to pat Tallie's shoulder as she went.

Zenobia shifted her position to regard her friend closely. Three years older than Tallie, she was a governess who chose to live independently and to go out to households daily. She had a small but appreciative clientele amongst those rare families who took the education of girls seriously and who wished to have their children's regular learning with their own governesses supplemented by Miss Scott's tuition in Italian, German and, in two radical households, Latin.

'Well?' Zenobia demanded abruptly. Years of dealing with children had given her a sure sense for prevarication and careful half-truths. 'Who was he?'

'He? Who?'

Zenobia rolled her brown eyes ceilingwards. 'The man, of course. The one who was *not* hunting you.'

'How did you…I mean, what makes you think…?'

'Your choice of words was odd, that is all. And I know you very well. There is something about you, some little suppressed excitement. Come on, tell Zenna.'

'But I did not even see him, Zenna,' Tallie protested. 'Only his shadow on the floor. You see, they all came trooping up and I ran and hid in the closet, but the key fell out, and my draperies, er…'

'Tallie,' Zenna said, her face a picture of appalled realisation, 'you do not mean to tell me you were posing *unclad*?'

'Um…yes. But you see, Mr Harland is utterly immune to any interest in the female form. Why, I am as safe with him as I am with you; no one will ever see or buy his classical canvases, for they are never finished and, besides, they are vast in size.'

'Well, one group of men appears to have seen all too much,' Zenna retorted grimly. 'Just how many of them were there?'

'Four. But even if they saw me again, they would never recognise me from the picture, for the pose was from the back.'

A little whimper escaped Zenna's lips. 'But what about this closet you hid in? Did none of them find you there?'

'Well, yes, one of them opened the door. But he did not see my face and he was a perfect gentleman. He gave me my drape back and the key, and told the others that the door was locked so they went away.'

The whimper became a moan. 'You were in a closet, with no clothes on and this man came in?' Tallie nodded. 'And he did not say anything, or touch you or…?'

'He caught his breath,' Tallie admitted, a *frisson* running down her spine again at the recollection of that soft sound.

'As well he might,' Zenna said grimly. 'By some miracle you appear to have encountered the only safe man in London.'

'Well, he saved me,' Tallie admitted, 'but he did not make me feel safe.' Zenna's rather thick brows rose interrogatively. 'His voice was so…so cool and sardonic, as though he did not care what anyone else thought. And he is…powerful somehow.'

'How on earth can you tell?' Zenna demanded, attempting to pour some cold water over what she felt were becoming dangerously heated imaginings. 'You did not see him, did you?'

'No, he just emanated this feeling. I can't describe it, but I suppose power is the best word. And Mr Harland wanted to ask him to pose as Alexander the Great.'

'Goodness. Well, if he looks anything like the representations of Alexander that I have seen, he is an impressive man indeed. What a fortunate thing you did not see him,' she added slyly, 'or you would be imagining yourself in love with him.'

'Oh, nonsense.' Tallie laughed and tossed a cushion at her teasing friend. She was suddenly feeling better. Alexander the Great indeed!

The next morning, refreshed by a good night's sleep, undisturbed by dreams of hallooing gentlemen and Carthaginian generals, Tallie woke to a sunny day, feeling considerably more optimistic than she had for some time.

'Better?' asked Zenna over the breakfast table. They were alone, for Mrs Blackstock was out marketing and Millie was tucked up in bed—as she rightly said, beauty sleep was essential in her profession.

'Mmm.' Tallie spread preserve on her toast with a lavish hand and contemplated the advertisements on the front page of the morning paper. 'How much money would it take to set up in one's own shop, do you think, Zenna?'

'As a milliner?' Zenna bit thoughtfully into a forkful of ham. 'Rent for the shop—and that would need space for a workroom, redecoration and fitting it out. Girls for the workshop, materials. A lot of money.

Not as much as I would need for a school, but a lot. You would need a loan, or,' she added with a wicked twinkle, 'a protector.'

'I suspect that was how Madame D'Aunay got started, by prudently investing a farewell present from such a person,' Tallie confessed. 'But I have absolutely no intention of taking a lover so I can borrow money for a hat shop from him!'

Zenna choked back a gasp of laughter. 'It would certainly be a most original reason for abandoning the path of virtue. What are you doing today? I have the two Hutchinson girls all day and I plan to go for a nice walk in Green Park with them, conversing in Italian throughout.'

'That does sound pleasant, they seem such an amiable family from what you have told me. I have rather a pleasant day too, for I have hats to deliver to both Lady Parry and Miss Gower and they are quite my favourite clients.'

However, Tallie found it was hard to maintain such a cheerful mood. In the morning sunshine the hair-brown walking dress and pelisse were every bit as unsatisfactory as she had thought the day before. There was nothing for it but to purchase a dress length and make a new gown, for she really could not feel that she looked the part to be calling upon Society ladies. She looked in the windows of Hardin and Howell as she passed them and regretfully decided that the Parthenon Bazaar was likely to prove more suitable for her budget. Some economies were possible: if she did not take a hackney to her clients' homes but walked instead, that would save a few shillings.

Tallie was soon regretting the decision, for she had three hatboxes to collect at the milliners. Although her first call at Bruton Street was not far and the boxes were light, they were unwieldy, and the sight of a young lady carrying any parcel—let alone three hatboxes—in the street was sufficiently unconventional for her to attract several impertinent stares.

Feeling increasingly flustered, Tallie was tempted to change her plans and call at Miss Gower's in Albermarle Street first, for it was closer. But Miss Gower was eighty-three and would not be pleased to be disturbed before eleven o'clock. No, it would have to be Lady Parry and her two hats.

Tallie turned cautiously round the corner from New Bond Street, thankful that her destination was almost in sight. Inelegant though it was, she had found that, by balancing two hatboxes on top of each other and then holding the ribbons of the third twined in her fingers, she could just manage. It did nothing for her vision forward, however, and she was already getting a crick in her neck from peering around her pile of gaily striped boxes.

The collision happened just as she reached the entrance to Bruton Mews. For one startled moment she thought she had walked into the wall, for the obstacle she had hit was certainly solid enough and equally unyielding. One hatbox was driven into her diaphragm, making her whoop for breath, the top one fell off and rolled into the road and she managed to drop the other at her feet.

Doubled up, making unseemly gasping noises and with her eyes streaming, Tallie was conscious of an immaculate pair of boots in front of her. Rising out of them were well-muscled legs in buckskin breeches.

Her eyes travelled upwards past a plain waistcoat revealed between the flaps of an equally plain riding coat, past a crisp white stock to a firm, well-shaven chin and the enquiring and frankly appreciative gaze of the owner of these altogether admirable attributes.

It was too much. Coming on top of yesterday's shock and the knowledge that she had made a serious error of judgement in deciding to walk, Tallie found she was swept with an irrational wave of anger. How dare this man stand there, looking cool, calm and assured and openly scrutinising her while she made an exhibition of herself?

'Look what you have done!' she gasped indignantly as her breath returned. 'Just look at that box in the road!'

Before the man could respond to her attack, a carriage clattered out of the mews rather too fast and drove straight for the gaily striped cerise-and-white hatbox lying in its path.

'Oh, no!' Tallie took a hasty step forward to try and snatch it up by its trailing ribbons, only to find herself unceremoniously yanked back onto the footway. She struggled against the grip on her arm, but to no avail. The carriage's nearside front wheel caught the box and rolled it over, flipping the lid off. Lady Parry's exquisite new promenade hat fell out into the mud of the gutter and came to rest there like a wounded bird of paradise.

'Ouch!' Her arm hurt and at her feet the result of hours of work and the product of the finest materials lay, its curling feathers reduced to a sodden mass.

The man released her arm without apology. 'It appeared to be preferable to have the hat under the wheels of the carriage than to have you in that position.' He stepped into the road and picked up the hat, dropping it into its box and handing that to Tallie before removing a large white handkerchief from his sleeve and rubbing the mud off his gloves with it. 'My valet insists on checking that I have a clean handkerchief before I go out; how gratified he will be that for once it was needed.'

Considering that she had collided with him and harangued him, he sounded politely unconcerned. He also sounded, to Tallie's incredulous ears, hideously familiar. No, surely not—it couldn't be! Tallie felt her jaw drop and she covered her confusion by groping in her reticule for her own handkerchief.

'Yes, of course, you are quite right, I am so sorry, sir,' she managed to stammer as she pretended to wipe her eyes. 'I must suppose I walked into you, sir. I do apologise.' She was blushing, she knew she was, the wave of heat was rising up her throat, try as she could to control it.

'You did, but it is of no matter. Can *all* these be yours?' He gestured at the tumbled boxes, one dark brow raised.

'I was delivering them.' Tallie was certain that she was crimson. Her mind hardly seemed to be functioning at all, but somehow she had to end this encounter and remove herself and her hatboxes before something triggered his memory. Because with every word he spoke she was more than ever convinced that this was Nick—Mr Harland's Alexander the Great— the man who had found her hiding naked in the closet.

He never saw your face, you never spoke, she told herself frantically.

'Hmm. I hardly imagine your employer will be very happy about that,' he observed dispassionately, glancing at the boxes that Tallie had gathered up and were now piled beside her feet, each with at least one unpleasant stain on it.

Tallie glared at him, her anger returning as common sense asserted itself. Of course he would never recognise her—as far as he was concerned she was a humble milliner's assistant, someone of a class so far removed from his as to be virtually invisible. 'No, she will not be happy,' she agreed between gritted teeth. 'Have you any idea how much that hat that just fell out costs?' She knew she should not be addressing a gentleman in such a way, let alone one who had behaved with such chivalry to her the day before, but instinct screamed at her to keep him at a distance. She picked up the hatbox and held it, an insubstantial barrier between herself and all that maleness.

He lifted the lid of the box she was cradling in her arms and looked in. It brought him very close to her; close enough to see that his lashes were quite ridiculously long and dark for such a masculine-looking man, close enough to smell a peppery cologne with a hint of limes and certainly close enough to see a flash of wicked amusement in his dark grey eyes as he looked at her flustered and indignant face.

'Madame Phanie's establishment?' he enquired.

'No, Madame d'Aunay's.'

'Ah. Five guineas, then.'

This was so accurate that Tallie was betrayed into speech. 'How on earth do you know that, sir?'

She was answered with another lift of that expressive brow. 'One receives bills from time to time, my dear,' he drawled.

'Oh!' Tallie was furious with herself for asking and even more so for blushing hectically again. Even if he was merely referring to hats bought by his wife or sisters, her response to the remark showed clearly that she thought he meant he had been buying hats for a mistress. 'Well, I made it and it took *hours* and now it is quite ruined—and if you had not stopped me I could have saved it.'

'So it is all my fault?' he enquired drily. 'In that case I had better pay for it.' Before Tallie could respond he reached into his pocket, drew out a handful of coins and counted five bright guineas into her hand. Then he set the lid back on the ruined bonnet, stooped to pick up the remaining hatboxes and placed them carefully in her arms. 'Good day, my dear. And next time, ask your employer to send you in a hackney.'

Chapter Three

The man called Nick strode off up the street towards Berkeley Square without a backward glance, leaving Tallie standing staring after him. Then she realised that she was attracting no little attention. A kitchen maid, her head just visible through the area railings, stopped shaking out a rug to stare open-mouthed; a footman in livery raised supercilious eyebrows as he strode past bearing his employer's messages; a hackney carriage driver called out something that was mercifully unintelligible to Tallie and a very smart matron, her maid at her heels, fixed her with a look of scandalised outrage.

With a gasp Tallie clenched her fingers around the coins and walked on as fast as she could with her unwieldy burden. To be seen on the street taking money from a man! No wonder people stared—she must have appeared no better than a common prostitute. Tallie almost turned tail, then realised she must at least call upon Lady Parry and apologise for her tardiness and for the damaged hat.

Feeling that everyone was staring at her and expecting at any moment to be accosted, either by some buck with a proposition or an outraged householder ordering her from his respectable street, Tallie finally reached Lady Parry's door. It was opened with merciful promptness by Rainbird the butler. He allowed a faint expression of surprise to cross his thin face at the sight of the flushed and flustered milliner standing before him with her pile of soiled hatboxes.

'Miss Grey! Have you been in an accident? Please, step inside at once.' He stood aside to let her in and snapped his fingers imperiously to the footman, who hurried forward. Tallie relinquished her boxes gratefully and regarded the butler with an expression of rueful apology.

'I am sorry to arrive in such a state, Rainbird, but I dropped the boxes in the street.'

'I will ring for the housekeeper, Miss Grey. You will want to wash your hands and have your gown brushed before you see her ladyship, I make no doubt.' Rainbird approved of Miss Grey, and had so far unbent as to remark on one occasion to Henry the footman, 'A milliner she might be now, my lad, but she's a lady for all that she has come down in the world. You just observe her manners: always easy and polite to staff. That comes from breeding and consideration and there are many with a hundred times her income who will never manage that naturally.'

Tallie was just gratefully accepting his offer when a small dark lady wearing a most fetching cap with floating ribbons and a jonquil morning dress, which almost made Tallie forget her woes, emerged into the hall. 'Miss Grey, good morning. I thought I heard your voice.'

'Good morning, my lady.' Tallie bobbed a neat curtsy, conscious of the snapping brown eyes assess-

ing her appearance. 'I must apologise for arriving in
such a state, ma'am, but I had an accident with the
boxes.'

'I was just about to send for Mrs Mills, my lady.'

'Excellent, Rainbird. You run along with her, Miss
Grey, and come down when you feel quite comfortable again. There is no hurry.' Lady Parry vanished
as abruptly as she had appeared and Tallie surrendered herself into the care of the housekeeper who,
despite tutting about ruinous mudstains, restored the
tired old gown to as good a condition as Tallie could
hope for with sponge and badger-bristle brush.

Her cheeks cooled by a splash of water, her hands
rinsed and her hair tidied, Tallie hurried downstairs
and tapped on Lady Parry's morning-room door.

'Come in, Miss Grey, and let me have a look at
you.' Kate Parry was a widow on the wrong side of
forty with a son of twenty, a tidy personal fortune and
apparently boundless enthusiasm for whatever took
her fancy. 'Sit down and have a glass of Madeira. No,
show me no missish reluctance, you have obviously
had a shock and coddling your insides with tea or
ratafia will not help at all.'

She peered closely at Tallie's face. 'Have you been
crying, my dear? Were you hurt?'

'Oh, no, ma'am, only I had the breath knocked out
of me for a moment.' Tallie took a sip of the strong
wine, choked a little, then took another. It was certainly soothing to her nerves. 'It made my eyes water,
you see.' She hesitated. Rainbird had placed the two
hatboxes for Lady Parry upon a side-table, having first
carefully spread a sheet of the morning paper to protect the polished surface from the mud. 'I am afraid
I dropped your new hats.'

'How provoking for you! And has your handiwork been spoiled? I do hope not. Never mind, it is more important that you were not hurt. We will look at the hats in a moment: you drink your wine and tell me all about it.'

Thus encouraged by Lady Parry's warm interest, and perhaps rather more by the unfamiliar glow of the wine, Tallie began her tale.

The foolish decision to walk was easily enough admitted to, and, although Lady Parry shook her head, she did not lecture. She was quite well aware of Tallie's circumstances, having taken care to draw her out, little by little, during the year that she had been visiting Bruton Street. As a matter of course Kate Parry took considerable interest in most people who came her way, but she found herself particularly in sympathy with the reserved young woman who created such elegant hats for her.

Tallie was as discreet about her own affairs as she was about her other clients, but from the little she did let drop, careful study of the *Landed Gentry* and a thorough gossip with her old friend Miss Gower, Kate had a clearer picture than Tallie would ever have suspected. Tallie would have been even more surprised to discover that Lady Parry had a scheme in mind for her, but it was not something of which she had the slightest inkling since, for it to come about, something had to happen first to which Lady Parry looked forward with sadness.

She thought about it now and gave a little sigh before fixing her attention on Tallie's misadventures once again. 'So you were attracting some unwelcome attention?' she prompted as Tallie broke off.

'Yes, but by the time I realised how foolish it was to be walking I was halfway here, so there was no advantage in turning back. Then—' She broke off, took a deep breath and resumed. 'I walked straight into a gentleman. And I dropped all the boxes; the one with your special promenade hat rolled into the roadway—and I was quite...' she searched for a ladylike expression, failed and blurted out '...winded.'

Lady Parry suppressed a smile. Poor Miss Grey, it must have been most upsetting for her, but the scene itself sounded not a little amusing. 'Who was he?' she enquired, attempting to sound suitably grave.

'I have no idea,' Tallie said, then flushed. She could hardly say she knew his first name only—what would Lady Parry think?

'An elderly gentleman?' It was said with a wicked twinkle, which Tallie did not fail to notice.

'No, ma'am. About thirty, perhaps, or a little younger?' Tallie speculated, wrinkling her straight nose, which Mr Harland always compared favourably to those of the best Greek statues.

Enchanting, Lady Parry thought, watching the play of emotion on Tallie's face. *To have a daughter like that! So attractive, so intelligent. And she would so repay dressing well...* 'And did he assist you?'

'Yes, ma'am, although he stopped me rescuing the box from the road until it was too late and a carriage struck it.'

'Yet this gallant gentleman displeased you, and for more than his tardiness with the hatbox, I imagine?' Now Tallie was blushing in earnest. 'My goodness, Miss Grey, whatever did he do? Did he take some liberty with you?' It might well have occurred, for the sort of man who would think nothing of fondling a kitchen maid if she took his fancy would probably be equally free with an attractive young milliner if the chance arose, and he certainly appeared to have ruffled the normally calm and self-controlled Miss Grey.

'No. Not if you mean did he try and kiss me or make an improper remark, ma'am. But…but when I was cross because of your hat, he looked in the box and guessed how much it cost and he *paid* me for it, in guineas, right there on the street!' She swallowed. 'And people saw him.'

'Dear me, that was a thoughtless thing for him to have done,' Lady Parry exclaimed. 'No wonder you are so angry with him.' Now what had she said? The girl was as pink as a peony.

'Yes, but I should not be angry with him, it is very ungrateful of me and I am sure it was just thoughtlessness.' Tallie was finding herself more confused by the minute about how she regarded Nick. Gallant and quick-witted rescuer or heartless rake, not above trifling with a respectable working girl?

'I do not think that having the courtesy to pick up your boxes entitles him to sufficient gratitude for you not to be angry at such an imprudent act on his part as to make you the cynosure of all eyes on a public street.' Rather out of breath with the effort of such a convoluted declaration, Lady Parry sat back and watched Tallie with interest. There was more to her distracted mood than she was revealing, she was sure of it.

Tallie rummaged hastily in her reticule for her handkerchief. There really was nothing more she felt she could safely say, for the turmoil of her feelings increased the more she thought about the encounter.

To have seen the man who only yesterday saw her

naked body...to feel such anger when she knew she owed him a considerable debt for his tact and quick thinking and that in any case the reaction was out of all proportion to his offence just now... And she was making a positive exhibition of herself in front of her kindest and most influential patroness.

'I beg your pardon, ma'am,' she started to say when there was the sound of the front door opening and footsteps in the hall accompanied by male voices.

'Oh, good,' Lady Parry said, 'William is home. I have absolutely no hope that I will succeed, but I intend asking him to escort me to Lady Cressett's soirée tonight. I declare the wretch knew I was going to ask him, for he made himself scarce just before I came down for breakfast! Would you be so good as to pull the bell for Rainbird, Miss Grey?'

Tallie did so, remaining standing in the shadowy corner by the bell-pull. She had glimpsed young Lord Parry on occasions, but only fleetingly as they passed in the hallway. She had no real fear that he would recognise her from the picture yesterday, but she had no desire to come to the notice of *any* of the men who had seen it. In any case, it would be most unbecoming of her to put herself forward.

Rainbird entered and informed Lady Parry that their lordships had gone into the study. 'Would your ladyship wish a message conveyed?'

'Yes, please ask them both to come in, Rainbird. My nephew must be here as well,' she added for Tallie's benefit.

'I will wait in the hall, ma'am; you will wish to be private.'

'Not at all, Miss Grey, please, come... William, my dear boy! And my favourite nephew as well. Now that is fortuitous, you may both escort me this evening.'

William, Lord Parry, was twenty years old. Born to a large fortune and rather girlish good looks, he had grown up, much to his mama's relief, a thoroughly nice, unspoilt young man, if a touch young for his age. A suitable wife would mature him, she was sure; in the meantime she was happy for him to sow his harmless wild oats under the apparently careless eye of his guardian and her trustee, her nephew Lord Arndale.

William grinned disarmingly at the rallying note in his mother's voice. 'Escort you, Mama? Er…I think I am engaged; in fact, I feel sure I am.'

His companion followed him into the room and came across to take Lady Parry's hand in his. 'Aunt Kate.' He bent to kiss her cheek, a tall dark man in immaculate riding wear. 'I hope I find you well this morning, ma'am? I am happy to inform you that William has absolutely no engagements of note this evening and will be delighted to escort you to whichever concert of ancient music you have in mind.'

Lady Parry laughed, ignoring her son's outraged protestations. 'No such thing, you wicked man. I would like you both to come with me to Lady Cresset's soirée. I can promise absolutely no ancient music and several tables set out for cards.'

Tallie stood stock-still in her corner. Lady Parry's nephew was none other than the man she had just collided with in the street, the man who had protected her yesterday in the studio. To her horror she realised that Lady Parry had remembered her and had turned on the sofa to look for her.

'Miss Grey, do, please, come and sit down again.'

Tallie hung back in the shadows. 'Miss Grey was kindly engaged on an errand for me and has had a distressing accident in the street.'

Both men looked in her direction and Tallie realised there was nothing for it but to emerge. She stepped forward, keeping her eyes down and her hands clasped in front of her.

'Nicholas, this is Miss Grey. Miss Grey, Lord Arndale, my nephew. I believe you have met my son on occasion before now.'

Tallie dropped a neat curtsy without looking up. Was she blushing again? Her heart was certainly pounding. 'Lord Arndale, Lord Parry.'

William Parry stepped forward with the eagerness that typified him. 'I say, Miss Grey, are you hurt?'

'No, no, not at all, my lord.'

'Perhaps if you were to move, William, Miss Grey could resume her seat,' Nick Stangate observed drily, watching his cousin with suppressed amusement. 'I believe this was your chair, Miss Grey?' He indicated a bergère armchair on which a reticule lay, its drab plainness in startling contrast to the charming toile upholstery fabric.

'Thank you, it is, my lord.' So, this unusual young woman must be the lady milliner who had been concerning his Aunt Kate to the point where he had felt it necessary, as Lady Parry's trustee, to take a hand and make some enquiries himself. He should have realised when he ran into her in the street just now and scattered her hatboxes. Doubtless he would have done if his mind had not been preoccupied with another young woman altogether.

Nick took a seat beside his aunt, which had the

effect of bringing him opposite Miss Grey. She was certainly well spoken, and elegant in her deportment and appearance, despite the dreadful gown, unflattering coiffure and downcast eyes. Her present demeanour was in startling contrast to that of the angry girl who had scolded him in the street. She was sitting quite still now, seemingly composed, yet he sensed a desire to burrow backward into the chair cushions out of sight.

'But what happened?' William was persisting. 'Are you quite sure you are not injured, Miss Grey? Perhaps we should send for the doctor, Mama.'

Despite the self-effacing meekness of the slender figure in front of him and the fact that she had spoken hardly a word, Nick was quite certain he knew exactly what the young woman's problem was. It was not often that his conscience pricked him, but he felt its unfamiliar sting now.

'I believe Miss Grey is wounded in spirits, not in her person. She collided with a gentleman in the street and had the misfortune to choose one who was not only so slow that he allowed her possessions to be crushed under the wheels of a passing carriage, but who then had the impertinence to recompense her for the damage in a way that was, I believe, very ill judged.'

He felt a stirring of interest as Tallie's eyes flew to his face. There it was again, that mixture of spirit and—could it be—fear flashing out from behind the subdued front she was presenting.

'Ill judged!' she snapped, then appeared to recollect herself. He found himself both intrigued and amused. 'Yes, my lord, you are correct,' she added softly, and he realised her eyes were on his face, reading what little emotion he allowed to appear there. 'Although I am sure the gentleman's actions sprang from a genuine desire to make amends and not from the wish to—shall we say, tease—an inferior.'

'*Touché,*' he murmured, enjoying the emerald flash of her eyes. *So, Miss Grey, you are prepared to duel, are you?*

'Nicholas,' his aunt demanded, 'are you the gentleman in question?'

'I have to confess I am, Aunt,' he admitted, turning slightly to meet her indignant look. 'And I am justly reproved by Miss Grey. I had no idea that she was a young lady kindly undertaking an errand for you. I mistook her for a milliner's girl—'

'I *am* a milliner's girl, my lord,' Tallie said in frigidly polite tones. So, Miss Grey was not attempting to presume upon her patroness's friendly treatment. And she was certainly not going to toady to Lady Parry's nephew. How refreshing. He let his gaze linger on her face as she continued. 'If you will excuse me, Lady Parry, you will wish to speak in private to their lordships, I am sure. I will take the undamaged hat upstairs and leave it with your dresser. I will naturally make every effort to have the other one replaced within the week.'

She stood up, dropped another curtsy to Lady Parry, picked up the hatboxes and walked briskly to the door before Nick could get to his feet and step past her to open it. As she reached for the door handle it turned and Rainbird stepped into the room.

'Mr Hemsley is here to see his lordship, my lady,' he announced. Nick stopped where he was with an inward flash of irritation. Damn Hemsley; he was showing not the slightest sign of becoming bored with

William, despite Nick's persistently accompanying his cousin to every gambling den and sporting venue that Hemsley invited him to. He had made no attempt to fleece William while Nick was there. Possibly Nick was misjudging him and he was not the Captain Sharp he suspected, but he rather feared the combination of William's innocence and large fortune and Hemsley's financial embarrassment and lack of scruple was every bit as dangerous as he thought.

Either way, he was getting more than a little weary of chaperoning his cousin. Beside anything else, it was putting a decided dampener on the more sophisticated pleasures with which Nick Stangate normally entertained himself when in London.

Beside him his aunt nodded assent to the butler and Rainbird stood aside and ushered the visitor into the room.

Nick saw Miss Grey step back, but even so she could not escape coming face to face with the man who was entering the room. Why the devil was she blushing? Nick could see the colour staining her throat from across the room. Damn the man, had he murmured some remark? Could Hemsley not restrain himself from flirting with every woman who crossed his path? He schooled his face, resisting the temptation to take a hand. It was not part of his tactics to cross swords with the man yet.

'Lady Parry, ma'am! A thousand apologies for disturbing you...'

Flustered, Tallie found herself alone in the hall with Rainbird. 'I will just go up to Miss Hodgson with this hat, Rainbird.'

'There is no need, Miss Grey, I will have it taken up directly. May I call you a hackney carriage?'

This time Tallie had no hesitation in accepting, despite the very short distance to Albermarle Street where Miss Gower lived. She sat back against the squabs and contemplated the stained hatboxes on the seat opposite in an unsuccessful effort to keep her mind off those two unsettling encounters.

Infuriating man! If only she did not feel such a strong sense of obligation to Nicholas Stangate for the chivalrous way he had behaved yesterday, she could feel thoroughly and justifiably cross with him. And as for Mr Hemsley—well, he was just as much of a rake as she had imagined from what she had heard at the studio. The gleam in his blue eyes and the swift wink he had sent her as they passed in the doorway confirmed her in that opinion. A very good-looking rake, of course, if one had a penchant for that style of rather obvious blond handsomeness. And if one were prepared to tolerate such an insolent regard. Now she had been seen, but not recognised, by three of the four men from the studio; she closed her eyes and gave thanks once again for Nick Stangate's chivalry.

The hackney pulled up in front of Miss Gower's dark green front door and Tallie jumped down with one box. 'Please wait, I will not be above ten minutes.'

Miss Gower had not been well for several weeks now and her maid had told Tallie that the doctor had forbidden any but the shortest visits, but even ill health was not enough to stop the indomitable old lady's interest in her appearance. Of all her little indulgences, pretty hats were perhaps her favourite, and the more frivolous the creation that Tallie could show her, the happier she was.

On this occasion, however, Tallie saw with dismay that the heavy brass knocker was wrapped in baize. She knocked gently and the door was opened by Smithson, Miss Gower's butler, whom Tallie suspected was nearly as old as his mistress.

'Oh, Miss Grey,' he said lugubriously. 'The mistress cannot see you, I am afraid. Very poorly she is this morning, very poorly indeed.'

'I am sorry to hear that, Smithson.' The old man looked so shaky and distressed that Tallie wished she could give him a hug, but she knew he would be scandalised. 'Will you tell her I called and that I sent my best wishes for her recovery?'

'No hope of that, Miss Grey. No hope of that. Doctor Knighton called yesterday and warned us all.' He sniffed. 'Slipping away...slipping away.'

Tallie hesitated. 'Should I leave her new hat, do you think, Smithson?'

'Yes, please, Miss Grey. I will put it on the stand next to her bed so she can see it. That will give her so much pleasure. Is it a pretty one, Miss Grey?'

'Very,' Tallie assured him. 'Her favourite pink ribbons, and ruched silk all under the brim, and just one pink rose tucked above the ear.'

'Oh, she'll like that, Miss Grey.' The old man took the box in both tremulous hands.

'Goodbye, then, Smithson, you will let me know when...when she gets better?'

Thoroughly depressed, Tallie gave the driver Madame d'Aunay's direction and climbed back into the cab. One could hardly hope that a frail old lady would live for ever, but Miss Gower had seemed so indomitable and had had such a love of life that it seemed impossible that the years would ever catch up with her.

'Well, that will teach you to refine upon encounters with gentlemen and worry about what they think and say,' Tallie scolded herself out loud as the cab turned into Piccadilly. 'There are much more important and serious things happening than your foolish adventures. Poor Miss Gower, and without even any family to support her now.'

Chapter Four

Tallie spent a week engaged in exemplary hard work at Madame d'Aunay's, activity that entirely failed to distract her mind from worrying about Miss Gower or, when all self-discipline failed her, brooding about Lord Arndale. She was dwelling upon him, she told herself, because he had proved so infuriating. It was nothing to do with their encounter at the studio and most certainly had not the slightest connection with the fact he was an extremely attractive man.

As she had feared, Lady Parry's special hat proved beyond rescue, so it had to be entirely remade from scratch. Faced with the sale of it twice over, Madame was not moved to scold Tallie for the accident and instead recommended her personal service to a certain Mrs Leighton. 'A cit, of course,' she confided, 'but newly married and her husband is as rich as they come and denies her nothing. I expect her to spend at least as much as Miss Gower ever did and I would not want you to suffer from the loss of a client.'

But Tallie was not concerned about the size of Miss Gower's orders, and her grief when she heard the news that the old lady had finally slipped away two days after her last hat was delivered was as genuine as if she had been a relative.

On Saturday evening the residents of the lodging-house in Upper Wimpole Street found themselves together in the parlour before dinner. Although they were each engaged upon some small task, Tallie sensed a palpable air of relaxation amongst all of them with the end of a busy week.

'This is pleasant to be all together,' Zenna observed cheerfully. 'Do you not go to the Opera House this evening, Millie?'

'No, the run finished yesterday and they are staging a masquerade tonight. The new production begins on Monday—it is called *The Lost Italian Prince* and is a very affecting melodrama.'

'And do you have a good part?' Tallie enquired. She was sorting through a pile of coloured silks, which had become, through some alchemy of their own, hopelessly tangled whilst untouched in a closed box. Millie was a rarity in the world of the theatre— a genuinely chaste young lady—and her aunt and her friends did their best to support her, while living in constant anxiety about the bucks and roués she inevitably encountered.

'Yes!' Millie glowed with pride. 'I have a speaking line all to myself and I sing in a trio in the second act. I play one of the village maidens who, with her friends, helps hide the Prince whilst he is fleeing his Wicked Uncle.'

'What happens in the end?' Mrs Blackstock enquired, looking up from the account book she was filling in at the other end of the table from Zenna, who was marking her pupils' French vocabulary work.

Millie put down the sheet she was hemming, curled up more comfortably on the rather battered sofa and prepared to explain the plot. 'Well, the Prince falls in love with this village maiden—only she isn't really, she's the daughter of the Duke in disguise because he wants her to marry this awful man—and when the Wicked Uncle—the Prince's uncle, that is, who is trying to murder him—finds where he is hiding, she sacrifices herself by throwing herself from the battlements in front of his troops and—'

The sound of the front door-knocker thudding with great force in a resounding tattoo brought each lady upright with a start, for one moment convinced that the Wicked Uncle himself must be at the door.

'My goodness, who can that be?' Mrs Blackstock demanded, putting down her quill.

'Someone's very superior footman, I should imagine,' Tallie replied, getting up to edge the curtain aside and peep out into the dark, wet street. 'That was a fine example of the London Knock if ever I heard one. It is too dark outside, I cannot make out who it is. Oh, yes, now Annie has opened the door I can see the livery. Why, surely that is one of Lady Parry's footmen! I wonder why she is sending me a message here, she always sends orders to the shop.'

Annie came in, her sharp face flushed with importance. 'There's this footman, mam, and he's brought this letter for Miss Grey, mam. Cor, he is tall, mam.'

'Thank you, Annie,' Mrs Blackstock said repressively. 'Wait and see if Miss Grey has a reply for him.'

Tallie turned the letter over in her hands, then, realising that she was never going to find out what it was about until she opened it, cracked the seal in a shower of red wax and spread out the single sheet.

'But how strange!'

'What?' Zenna demanded at last, when, after the one exclamation, Tallie fell silent.

'Why, Lady Parry asks me to call at ten on Monday morning upon a personal matter. Annie, please say to the footman that Miss Grey will be happy to call as Lady Parry asks. Can you remember that?'

'Yes, miss.' The maid closed the door behind her, mouthing the words of the message silently.

'What can it mean, Zenna?'

Tallie handed the letter to Zenna, who scanned it and handed it back with a shrug. 'I have no more idea than you, goose.' Her friend laughed. 'Perhaps she wants to set you up in your own millinery business, producing exclusive hats only for her and her circle of bosom friends.'

'Now that would be wonderful,' Tallie agreed, smiling back. 'But somehow I do not think it likely.' Rack her brains as she might, she could think of no plausible explanation for the mysterious note and she could not help but feel a twinge of apprehension at the thought of another visit to Bruton Street so soon. What if she met Lord Arndale again? 'I wish tomorrow were not Sunday,' she said with a little shiver. 'I hate mysteries and being kept in suspense.'

Sunday did indeed drag, despite Matins at St Marylebone Church and a damp walk in Regent's Park. By mid-afternoon Tallie was disgusted to find herself apprehensive and, as she described it to Zenna, 'all of a fidget'.

'But what on earth is the matter with you?' her friend enquired, looking up at Tallie quizzically from her position on the hearthrug where she was burning her fingers roasting chestnuts. They had the parlour to themselves and had settled down to an afternoon of comfortable relaxation before the chilly walk to church for evensong.

Tallie considered confessing that her wild imagination was conjuring up images of Lord Arndale denouncing her to Lady Parry as an immoral and wanton young woman who posed nude for artists, but the words would not form on her lips. 'I am afraid I may have done something to displease Lady Parry and she is summoning me to say that she no longer requires my services,' she blurted out at last.

'What nonsense,' Zenna stated. 'Ouch! Oh, do pass that bowl, Tallie—these are so hot.' She dropped the nuts into the dish and gave the matter some thought while she sucked her fingers. 'Even if you *had* displeased her, surely she would write to Madame d'Aunay, not ask you to call?'

Not if Lord Arndale had told her such a scandalous story, Tallie thought miserably. Lady Parry was too kind to spread such a tale abroad, but she would certainly not tolerate continuing contact with such an abandoned young woman.

Zenna twisted round on the rug and studied Tallie's face thoughtfully. 'Has this anything to do with that incident at the studio the other day?' she demanded.

'Oh! How did you guess? Zenna, I met the man who found me in the closet—I would know his voice anywhere. And he is Lady Parry's trustee and nephew and he came to the house when I was there last.'

'And did he cry, ''There is that beautiful woman I

saw in a state of nature the other day''? Or did he quite fail to recognise you face on, fully clad, with your hair up and a bonnet on your head?'

'He did not recognise me then, I am sure of it. But, Zenna, he may have thought about it afterwards and something might have jogged his memory...'

'What nonsense. You told me you had your hair loose and it was falling around your face, did you not? It is a lovely colour, but not such an unusual shade that he could recognise you from it—and you look very different with it up, in any case. Besides, I somehow feel it would not have been your hair he would have been looking at.'

Zenna got to her feet and took the bowl of chestnuts from Tallie's limp grasp. 'If you are not going to eat these, I most certainly am. Do you really think that he took so much notice of you? At Lady Parry's, I mean? He would have had to be made of stone not to take notice before, of course.'

'No, you are quite right, Zenna. I am being foolish. All he saw at Lady Parry's was a milliner, not a young lady, or an artist's model.'

'Ah, but you rather wish he had.'

Tallie made a face at her friend, but some treacherous part of her mind did indeed wish that those lazy grey eyes had looked at her and seen neither a naked model nor a humble menial, but the real young lady beneath those guises. *Stop it*, she thought. *He is dangerous*, and leaned over to take a still-hot chestnut from the bowl.

But a long night tossing and turning did nothing to calm Tallie's nervous apprehension. She dressed with care and penned a note to her employer explaining that she had been called away for the day unexpectedly and sent little Annie off to deliver it, keeping her fingers crossed that Madame would not take exception to this rare absence.

Tallie took a hackney carriage, reluctant to risk arriving either late or windswept on Lady Parry's doorstep, but even a safe and punctual arrival did not make her feel any better.

Rainbird opened the front door with his usual stately demeanour, although a spark of something more than welcome showed in his eyes as he regarded the shabby visitor. 'Good morning, Miss Grey. Her ladyship asked me to show you through to the library.'

Tallie followed across the hall to a door she had never entered on her previous visits and was startled when Rainbird opened it and announced with some emphasis, 'Miss Grey.' It was not treatment she was used to and Tallie looked around the room with interest as she entered.

The first person she saw was Lord Arndale standing by a heavy mahogany desk set in the window embrasure. He had apparently been leaning over studying a document spread before the other occupant of the room and had glanced up at Rainbird's announcement. Tallie's heart gave a hard thump at the sight of him and she looked in confusion at the other man, a complete stranger to her.

The two could hardly have been a greater contrast. Nick Stangate towered over his seated companion, broad shoulders filling his riding coat, everything about him seeming to exude life and ruthlessly controlled energy. The other man was more than twice his age, his hair scant and greying, his face thin and of an unhealthy shade. His eyes, though, were sharp and intelligent and Tallie almost stepped back as he fixed them on her face.

There was no sign of Lady Parry and, in the few seconds of silence as the two men regarded her, Tallie felt the colour ebbing out of her face. Why she should feel she was on trial in some way she had no idea, unless it was her guilty awareness of her scandalous secret.

As Mr Dover rose to his feet Nick Stangate straightened up and studied the young woman who had been shown in. The same shabby gown and pelisse as before; the same rather elegant bonnet, but this time she looked as though she had passed a very indifferent night. He stopped speculating as his companion spoke.

'Miss Grey, good morning. We have not met: I am James Dover, Miss Gower's attorney at law. I believe you are acquainted with Lord Arndale, who is her executor?'

Now, what the devil had there been in that introduction to cause her to go white to the lips? Nick stepped forward and took her hand. 'Miss Grey, you have gone quite pale. Are you unwell? Please, sit here.'

She did not resist him as he urged her gently into a chair. 'I am sorry, my lord, I am being foolish. It is just that meeting a lawyer brought back the memory of the last encounters I had with members of Mr Dover's profession. You must forgive me, sir,' she added, turning to the older man. 'I mean no disrespect, Mr Dover. The situation when my father, and then my mother, died was…difficult.'

Nick realised that he was still holding her hand lightly in his. Her wrist felt cold under his fingers and she looked up to meet his eyes. Hers were candid, green and intelligent. He realised that although she must be deeply puzzled she had asked no questions. Her reticence was refreshing and also disconcerting. 'I am sorry we alarmed you, Miss Grey, your pulse is racing.' Her gaze dropped, and on an impulse he added, 'For a moment I thought you had a guilty secret.'

There was a silence. Then her eyes flew back to his face and to his surprise Nick saw the colour staining her throat, rising up to her cheeks. Without meaning to he had touched a raw spot and some hunter's instinct in him stirred. Instinctively his grasp on her wrist tightened and she pulled her hand free, leaving Nick staring down at her bent head in wild speculation. He thought he had found out all there was to know about Miss Talitha Grey. Had his investigators been so careless as to have missed a scandal?

With a rustle of skirts his aunt swept in. 'I am sorry to have kept you all. Good morning, Miss Grey. I do hope you did not get wet—it is a perfectly dreadful morning is it not?'

'Indeed, my lady,' Tallie agreed. She stood up and bobbed a curtsy. Nick saw her hand go to the wrist he had been grasping. Had he hurt her? She had made no protest. 'On days like this one wonders if spring will ever come,' she added politely.

'Do sit down, everyone.' Lady Parry took the chair next to Tallie, and regarded the men. 'You have introduced yourselves? Excellent. Well, Mr Dover, you had better explain to Miss Grey, who is doubtless wondering what on earth this is all about, why she has been asked to come here this morning.'

Mr Dover inclined his head, adjusted his spectacles, coughed and flattened the document before him with one hand. Nick, to whom none of this was new, watched Talitha from under hooded lids. Her first reaction was going to be very instructive.

'Miss Grey, as I told you, I was the attorney at law to Miss Gower and, with Lord Arndale here, it falls to me to administer her will.' He paused and regarded Tallie benevolently. 'I have to tell you that you are remembered in that document.'

'Oh, how very kind of Miss Gower!' To Nick's surprise he saw her eyes were filling with tears. Why had he thought her so composed that she would not give way to emotion? She hastily pulled her handkerchief from her reticule. 'I beg your pardon.' She dabbed her eyes, tried to speak, tried again and with an apparent effort managed to say, 'I will treasure any keepsake that she has left me; I was very fond of her.'

Nick chuckled softly to himself. If she thought she had inherited a pretty ornament or a book or two, Miss Grey was in for a surprise. He was startled as she shot him a reproachful glance. She was not going to pretend she was not affected by the old lady's thoughtfulness, the expression said as plainly as though she had spoken, even if his lordship found a milliner's gratitude for a trifling gift amusing. He absorbed the reproof silently. What very expressive eyes she had...

'It amounts to rather more than a keepsake, Miss Grey,' the lawyer said, smiling at her. 'I am happy to tell you that you stand to inherit fifty thousand pounds.'

'But...but that is...'

'Several thousand pounds a year if invested prudently. I must congratulate you.'

'I was going to say "impossible",' Tallie stammered. 'There must be some mistake, surely? Lady Parry?'

Appealed to, Lady Parry shook her head, laughing kindly at Tallie's confusion. 'No mistake, my dear. Miss Gower knew of your history, as I do. You must forgive us for looking into the past of such an unusual young milliner as you are. You must also forgive us for a little plot to restore you to the sort of life to which you were born and bred. It gave Miss Gower such pleasure to think of the difference this would make for you.'

Tallie looked from one face to another, her gaze skimming hastily over Nick's, set in an unhelpfully bland expression. She finally settled on the lawyer. 'But, Mr Dover, is this legal? I am no relative of Miss Gower's—surely someone else has a better claim to her fortune?'

'She was so devoid of relatives that she had to borrow me from my aunt to stand in as a nephew and executor,' Nick remarked, reaching the decision that she was as genuinely incredulous as she appeared and liking her for the lack of any sign of pleasure at the inheritance. No grasping little miss, this one. 'You are cheating no one of their dues.'

'But her servants, her friends...'

'Her servants have been left well provided with generous annuities and her few close friends such as myself have all been left keepsakes—pictures, jewellery and so forth.' His aunt leaned across and patted her hand. 'None of us need her money, my dear Miss

Grey. It is quite all right. This is not a dream, and you are perfectly entitled to your inheritance.'

Mr Dover got to his feet and began to shuffle papers into a portfolio. 'You will need a day or so to recover from the surprise, Miss Grey, but I will write to confirm what I have said and you will doubtless be able to furnish me with the direction of your bank and your man of business.' He tied the cords around the folder and bowed to the ladies. 'Your ladyship, Miss Grey, I bid you good day.'

Lady Parry got to her feet. 'If I could just have a word, Mr Dover. There is the question of Miss Gower's house—the staff asked me for advice on several matters, which I am sure you are far better equipped than I to answer. Miss Grey, would you be comfortable here for a few minutes? There is something I would very much like to discuss with you.'

The door closed behind her, leaving Nick alone with Miss Grey. Now was as good a time as any to confirm what his agents had found out about this young woman who had so won the hearts of his aunt and Miss Gower. Was she all she seemed? And what was the guilty secret that made her blush so? He suppressed a stirring of interest, which he recognised as sensual. She was far from his usual type; possibly that other blonde in the studio had had more of an effect than he thought.

Tallie was unconscious of the regard bent upon her face. She found it difficult to concentrate on what she had just been told, it was too unbelievable. Instead she found her mind wandering to the *Peerage*, which she had rather secretively conned the day before. Nicholas Stangate, 3rd Earl of Arndale... The family seat in Hertfordshire, a town house in Brook Street. Unmarried, twenty-nine years old with no brothers or sisters…

'You do not appear very pleased by the news you have just received,' he remarked, sinking into the seat opposite hers and leaning back. Tallie looked at him: he appeared completely relaxed, but his gaze was anything but casual.

'I was not thinking about it,' she admitted. She waited for that dark brow to lift, and, as she had anticipated, it did. Despite everything she smiled slightly, liking the expression of dry humour.

'I have said something to amuse you?'

'No, it was just that I was expecting you to raise one eyebrow when I admitted to such odd behaviour—and you did.'

Both brows shot up and he grinned at her disarmingly, instantly subtracting years from his age as the cool reserve vanished. 'I am appalled that I am so predictable in my mannerisms. I can see that acquaintanceship with you will be a salutary experience, Miss Grey.' She dropped her eyes, suddenly conscious of how intimate the conversation seemed, alone in the room with him. 'Not only do you have a keen eye to depress affectation, but you have a mind above the acquisition of a fortune. Do tell me, how is it you can dismiss fifty thousand pounds with such ease?'

'Oh, no! I cannot do that.' Her eyes lifted swiftly. 'No, you misunderstand me, my lord. It is such a shock that it does not seem real. I cannot think about it without becoming confused, so I was just letting my mind wander until I felt more rational.'

'Then I think you should have a glass of sherry, which will restore the tone of your mind a little, and we can discuss it. You will have some practical affairs to consider almost immediately.' He saw her dubious expression as he reached for the decanter that stood on a table beside his chair. 'Now, what is disturbing you, Miss Grey? The thought of consuming wine at this hour of the day or my presumption in making free with my aunt's decanters? If it is the former, think of it as medicine for your shock; if the latter, rest assured that I take no liberties without my aunt's permission.'

Tallie bit her lip in vexation. Was she *so* easy to read that he could observe her every emotion in her face? 'Neither, my lord. It is simply that I do not feel that it is my place to be—'

'But what *is* your place, Miss Grey?' He reached over and handed her the glass before picking up his own. 'To your good fortune, and to your happy restoration to your natural position in Society.'

Tallie took an experimental sip and decided she liked the taste. It still felt very strange to be having such a conversation with a gentleman, let alone this one, but she refused to appear a simpering miss, so she retorted frankly, 'If I knew what that was, I might welcome my restoration to it, my lord!'

'I wish you would call me Nick.'

'Certainly not, Lord Arndale!'

'You could adopt me as an honorary cousin,' he suggested gravely. 'Miss Gower considered me as a nephew and, as you are her heiress, I am sure that makes us cousins.'

In spite of her efforts Tallie could not help but laugh. 'I beg leave to tell you that this is ridiculous, *my lord*. I stand in no need of cousins, only of a recommendation to a bank and to a respectable man of business who is used to managing the affairs of single ladies, and I am sure Lady Parry will be kind enough to suggest how I go about finding those.'

At that moment her ladyship opened the door and sailed in with her usual energy, smiling gratefully at Nick as he stood to offer her the chair he had been occupying.

'I see the two of you are getting on famously, which is just as I had hoped,' she announced, sinking down and smiling at Tallie. 'Now, Nicholas, pour me a glass of sherry and be off with you; Miss Grey and I have plans to make.'

He handed her the glass and began to stroll out of the room but halted by Tallie's chair. 'I will bid you good day, Miss Grey. I have every expectation of seeing a great deal of you in the near future.' Lady Parry appeared to notice nothing odd in his voice, but Tallie was left uncertain as to whether she had just received a threat or a promise.

Chapter Five

Lady Parry regarded Tallie silently for a moment, then remarked, 'My nephew is anticipating a suggestion I am about to make to you, Miss Grey—Talitha, if I may call you that. Do I have it correctly?'

'Yes, ma'am, I agree it is very unusual. I was named for a great-aunt. Please, do call me that or better, Tallie, which is what my friends call me.'

'Tallie, then.' Lady Parry hesitated, an unusual occurrence for someone so decided, then said carefully, 'You must forgive me, my dear Tallie, if you find me interfering.' She waved into silence Tallie's immediate protest. 'I told you that Miss Gower and I took pleasure in our little plot to re-establish you to what, if it was not for the sad and untimely demise of your parents, would have been your natural position in Society.'

'But, ma'am, even if my father had lived, I would not have expected one-twentieth of this fortune as my portion!'

'Perhaps not, but I am sure you would have been able to live a life of comfort and security and to make your come-out, would you not?' She waited for Tallie's nod of agreement, then pressed on. 'Now you find yourself all alone without the family to assist with your belated entry into Society and perhaps you are a little nervous of how to go on.'

'But I do not look to make a come-out, ma'am,' Tallie protested. 'I am much too old! I have not been able to give this any thought, but perhaps I should find myself a house, in a country town maybe, where I may live respectably with a companion—'

'And wither into an old maid?' Lady Parry interrupted. 'Nonsense! What a waste that would be. How old are you, child?'

'Five and twenty, ma'am.'

'Indeed, you do not look it, and you will look it even less when your hair is dressed and you are clothed as befits your station. There is not the slightest reason why you should not come out this Season, and even less why you should not find any number of most eligible suitors when you do. Not, of course, the young sprigs such as my son—they will all be too busy flirting with silly little chits just out of the schoolroom, as green as they are themselves. No, you will attract the slightly older men, those who are bored with vapid girls in their first Season and who look for character and intelligence as well as a pretty face and good breeding.'

Tallie blinked. This fairy-tale picture was so far from her imaginings that she could not believe Lady Parry was serious. 'But—'

'But me no buts! Really, my dear, are you attempting to tell me that you had resigned yourself to your life of industry and self-reliance; that you dreamed no dreams?'

'Why, no, ma'am, I mean, yes, I had resigned myself. What use are dreams when one must worry day to day whether one can continue to support a respectable style of living, however modest?' *Perhaps some dreams*, her conscience prompted her. *Perhaps some dreams about cool grey eyes and a lazily amused, deep voice…*

'Then you must learn to dream, Tallie. In fact, you must learn to make your dreams reality.'

'I would need a chaperon,' Tallie said doubtfully. 'I believe one can hire gentlewomen who arrange come-outs…'

'Shabby genteel, most of them,' Lady Parry said dismissively. 'What I was going to suggest was that you come here to stay with me and I launch you this Season. There, what do you say to that?'

Tallie felt her mouth fall open unbecomingly and shut it with a snap. 'Lady Parry…ma'am…I could not possibly impose upon you. Thank you so much for such a wonderful offer, but—'

'I have told you, Tallie, no buts!' The older woman leaned forward and took Tallie's right hand in hers. 'My dear, let me confide in you. I have no daughter, no nieces and I long for the fun of launching a débutante upon a Season. I want the company, I want to have a lively young person to shop with, to gossip with, to watch over and hope for. I want a daughter— and you need a mama. What could be more perfect?' Tallie stared at her speechlessly, feeling like Cinderella, whirled from her cold hearth into the glittering ballroom at the palace at the wave of a magic wand. 'Do say yes!'

Feeling as though she was stepping into space, Tallie whispered, 'Yes.' Then her voice returned to her.

'Oh, yes, your ladyship, if you are quite sure I would be no trouble…'

'I *want* you to be a trouble! I want to plot and plan and make lists and schemes. We must think of parties and dances and I must make sure all the most influential hostesses know about you. Vouchers for Almack's, drives in the parks. Gowns, a riding horse, dancing lessons… We will be worn out, my dear, never fear. Oh, yes, and will you not call me Aunt Kate?'

'I could never…' Tallie saw her ladyship's expressive face fall and smiled helplessly. 'If you really wish me to, ma'am… Aunt Kate. I will do my very best not to disappoint you and to be useful.'

'Then you may start by pulling the bell rope for Rainbird. Will you be ready to move here in a week, do you think? Ah, Rainbird, has my nephew left yet?'

'He is on the point of doing so, my lady. Shall I request him to step in here?'

Nick Stangate put his head around the door, sending a sharp glance from his aunt's animated expression to Tallie's stunned face. 'I see my aunt has outlined her scheme, Miss Grey.'

'And dear Tallie has accepted my suggestion,' Lady Parry responded gleefully. 'Will you drive Miss Grey home, Nicholas? You may tell her your thoughts on a suitable bank and man of business while you are about it.' Taking his assent as read, she got to her feet and enveloped Tallie in a warm embrace. 'Off you go with Lord Arndale and I will speak to the housekeeper about your room. I did not dare tempt fate by making anything ready before I had spoken to you.'

Dazedly murmuring her thanks, Tallie allowed herself to be swept into the hallway and out to where a groom was standing patiently at the head of a pair of match bays harnessed to a rakish high-perch phaeton.

Nick Stangate helped her up into a seat, which seemed dangerously far above the roadway, and swung himself up beside her. 'Let them go, Chivers.'

They wove through the traffic in silence for a few minutes, then Nick remarked, 'Stunned into silence by your good fortune, Miss Grey?'

'Yes,' she admitted baldly. 'It all seems like a dream—the money, Lady Kate's wonderful offer, a Season... And last week I was worrying about whether I could afford a new gown and—' She broke off, biting her lip.

'And?'

'And Miss Gower and thinking about how shallow it was to worry about such a little thing as old gowns or muddy hatboxes when someone for whom you have affection and respect is reaching the end of their life.'

'And you had no idea of her intentions towards you?' He reined in to allow an old-fashioned closed carriage to draw away from the kerbside, then let the bays ease back into a trot, watchfully negotiating the Bond Street traffic.

'Why, no, not the slightest hint. It is so improbable, so like a fairy story I still cannot believe it.'

There was a hint of laughter in his voice as he said; 'Miss Gower as the fairy godmother—yes, I can imagine her in that role, wearing one of those outrageous hats you used to make for her.'

'She liked them as pretty as they could be,' Tallie said defensively. 'I am glad she saw the last one I made for her; it was quite impossibly pink with as

much ruched silk ribbon as I could fit under the brim
and a big rose.'

'I saw it,' Nick assured her. 'She had it on the stand
by her bed and showed it off to all her visitors—' He
broke off, then added, 'Do you have a handkerchief?'

'I am so sorry.' Tallie scrabbled in her reticule and
blew her nose. 'You must think me a positive watering pot, I seem to be weeping on virtually every occasion we meet.'

'Not at all. No one can help their eyes watering
after a blow to the...er, middle, and to shed a tear at
the reading of a will is a most natural reaction, I am
sure.'

He sounded indifferent rather than sympathetic and
Tallie, who had began to warm to him for telling her
about Miss Gower's hat, frowned.

'So my aunt persuaded you to come and stay in
Bruton Street?' he observed as they crossed Oxford
Street.

'Yes,' Tallie agreed, flushing at the coolness in his
tone. 'Do you not feel that is a good idea?'

'I am sure it will be very much to your benefit.'

Was she imagining the slight emphasis on *your*?
'You feel I am not a suitable person for Lady Kate
to sponsor?' she asked, keeping the anger out of her
voice with an effort. 'You think perhaps I am not who
I purport to be? Or perhaps you object to my employment at Madame d'Aunay's?'

Nick shot her a hard glance. 'I know that you are
precisely who you say you are,' he replied. 'I made
it my business to find out. And I am sure that your
employment as a milliner has been entirely respectable.'

The furious retort that rose to Tallie's lips went

unspoken. *Of course* he had to check on her, he was his aunt's trustee. It was his duty to protect his widowed relative. How was Lord Arndale to know that she was not an adventuress, ready to prey upon Lady Kate's kind heart, or someone who would bring scandal to the household?

Then as they crossed Weymouth Street into Upper Wimpole Street her heart seemed to stop with a sickening jolt. But she *was* just such a person! She had kept her shocking secret about Mr Harland's studio because she had feared disgrace and being branded immoral. But what would be simply a personal shame to a young milliner would be an utter scandal if it was exposed in the household of a Society lady.

Tallie realised that Nick had asked her a question. 'I am sorry, you said something?' Was her voice shaking?

'I asked if I am correct in saying it is the house just here on the left with the green front door?'

'Yes.' Of course he knew the address, he must have been checking on all of her circumstances and connections. He would know all about the humble lodging-house and its inhabitants and the fact that they were women earning their own way in the world. Did he know about Mr Harland? Surely not, he would have mentioned something as scandalous as that.

Nick reined in the horses and half-turned on the seat to look at her. 'Are you quite well, Miss Grey?'

'Yes. Yes, of course, my lord.' He looked at her for a long minute; Tallie stared back defiantly, expecting to see that cold grey, inquisitorial look in his eyes, but all they revealed was a concern and a warmth that completely unsettled her. The events of the day had overwhelmed her other senses and perceptions; now she was aware of him again as a man, a disturbing physical presence and an unreadable intelligence.

Behind her she was vaguely aware of the front door opening, but her eyes seemed locked with Nick's.

'Tallie! Thank good...I mean, Miss Grey, you are home.' It was Zenna, sounding uncharacteristically flurried. Tallie turned in her seat, conscious of a strange feeling; part relief, part resentment.

'Zenna! Please will you give me a hand down? I am sure his lordship will not want to let go his reins.' Zenna hurried down the steps and stretched up a hand while Tallie jumped down. 'My lord, may I introduce my friend? Zenobia, this is Lord Arndale, who has kindly driven me back from Lady Parry's. My lord, Miss Scott.'

Lord Arndale raised his hat. 'Miss Scott, good afternoon. Miss Grey, I will send details of a bank that I can recommend; should you wish me to accompany you to their offices, I am entirely at your disposal.'

Tallie tried to order her thoughts and behave like a young lady for whom a banker was a necessary adjunct to everyday life. Beside her Zenna was waiting silently; Tallie could feel the waves of antipathy coming from her like the heat from a fire.

Startled, she glanced from Nick Stangate to her friend. He was sitting patiently awaiting her reply, his gaze resting on the two plainly clad young women. Tallie was beginning to be able to interpret his apparently indifferent regard; it appeared Zenna was able to do instinctively. There was assessment in those grey eyes regarding them—assessment and disapproval.

She collected her straying thoughts and said politely, 'Thank you, my lord, that would be most kind. Good day.' She dropped the slightest of curtsies and turned to mount the steps. 'Are you returning inside, Miss Scott?'

As the door closed behind them, cutting off the sound of Lord Arndale's carriage wheels on the cobbles, Zenna said furiously, 'Insufferable man! Is he the one who…?'

'Yes, Lady Parry's nephew, as I told you the other day. But why do you say he is insufferable?'

Tallie took off her bonnet and gloves and followed the still fuming Zenna into the parlour. His regard had certainly been cool, but Zenna's life as a governess had inured her to snubs and she had always seemed to shrug them off.

Zenna appeared flustered, then she said slowly, 'I really do not know, but something in his regard infuriated me. I could feel my hair rising like a cat seeing a dog!' She brooded for a moment. 'I have it: he disapproves of me as your friend, not in principle. He does not like seeing you on good terms with a humble governess.'

'Nonsense,' Tallie retorted. 'I am a humble milliner, if it comes to that.' Not for much longer, an inner voice reminded her. 'And in any case, what is it to Lord Arndale what company I keep?' Even as she said it, the thought intruded that as his aunt's trustee Nick Stangate had every legitimate interest in the company she kept—and that included Miss Grey's friends.

'Do have a care, Tallie, I am so worried about Millie; the thought that both of you might be the prey of rakes is too worrying to contemplate!'

'Lord Arndale's interest in me and my connections

has nothing to do with any amorous intentions, I can assure you.' Tallie allowed herself one flickering moment's contemplation of being the object of such desires and hastily suppressed the thought. 'I will explain it all in a minute—but do tell me what is so concerning you about Millie.'

Zenna paced around the room, too agitated to join her friend on the sofa. 'I walked back from the Langton house across the Park and there was Millie, with no female companion at all, arm in arm with this man.'

'He may have been a perfectly respectable admirer.'

'You know as well as I that, given her profession, Millie cannot hope to make a *respectable* connection with anyone of the *ton*! And this man is nothing if not a member of the most fashionable set—his clothes, his air, everything about him. If his intentions were respectable, why did he not welcome an introduction to one of Millie's friends?'

'He did not, then?'

Zenna flushed angrily. 'I was comprehensively snubbed; not that Millie noticed, it was very smoothly done and she is obviously too entranced by him to see what is under her nose.'

No wonder Zenna had reacted so strongly to Nick Stangate's cold and judgemental regard. 'Do you know his name?'

'A Mr Hemsley. Millie calls him Jack.' Zenna, who was finally sitting down on the sofa, caught her friend's look of alarmed recognition. 'You know him?'

'Oh, yes,' Tallie said grimly. 'He is an acquaintance of Lord Arndale and the Parrys, and he was the man who led the pack of them hunting for me in the studio. I saw him again when I last delivered hats to Lady Parry. You are quite correct to be worried, Zenna, he is a complete rake and I am certain can have no respectable reason for paying attention to Millie.'

'What can we do? Should we speak to Mrs Black-stock?'

They regarded each other dubiously. 'It might have been a chance meeting,' Zenobia said. 'I would not wish to upset Millie by questioning her judgement.'

'And we would be suggesting that she might be-have imprudently if we were to mention it to Mrs Blackstock...' Tallie's voice trailed away. 'We must keep a quiet eye on Millie. It is possible that, if his intentions are dishonourable, the realisation that she has attentive friends will deter him.'

Zenna nodded decisively. 'Yes, I agree, that is the best plan.'

An awkward silence followed their decision on what action to take over Millie's unsuitable admirer. Tallie knew Zenna would be expecting her to tell all about the mysterious request to call upon Lady Parry and she must be equally curious as to why Tallie was being driven home by the very man she was so wary of. But Zenna would not pry and Tallie found her own tongue stumbling over what should be a perfectly simple piece of news.

But it was not so simple, she realised. As the fog of shock and confused delight at the news cleared, things became more and more complicated and deli-cate.

All her friends were in very straitened circum-stances. They would greet the news of her good fortune with unenvious delight, she was sure, but her immediate, unthinking instinct to give money away and make life easier for them was fraught with difficulties.

How could she do it without appearing to patronise and putting them in a position where what had been a friendship of equals would be shadowed by inequality? An outright offer of money would wound the pride of any of them, but she did so much want to help lift the anxiety of making ends meet day after day from all three, just as it had been miraculously lifted from her.

'Zenna,' she began tentatively.

'Yes? Do you want to tell me about this morning? Has something unpleasant happened?'

'No, nothing unpleasant—far from it. But I have had such a shock my head is spinning and I hardly know what to think or do.'

'Lord Arndale has proposed?' Zenna enquired.

'Proposed? No! Certainly not! Why should he do such a thing?' Tallie felt so hot and bothered at the very idea that she completely lost her train of thought and simply stared at her friend.

Zenna shrugged. 'Just a fancy that crossed my mind.' Tallie regarded her, astonished, until she retorted, 'Well, he is quite extraordinarily goodlooking.'

'*Zenna!*'

'I might be a spinster governess, but there is nothing wrong with my eyesight and I can recognise an attractive man when I see one, even if I do not care for him,' her friend replied somewhat snappishly.

'Yes, of course you can,' Tallie apologised hastily. 'Do you really think him so handsome?'

It was Zenna's turn to stare. 'There appears to be something amiss with *your* eyesight, Talitha. But never mind Lord Arndale—what happened if it is nothing to do with him?'

'Dear Miss Gower who died the other week has left me a legacy in her will,' Tallie said cautiously.

'Oh, how thoughtful of her. What is it? A piece of jewellery or a small sum of money?'

'That is what I expected when they told me, but, Zenna—it is fifty thousand pounds.'

'Fifty thou…are you sure? Not fifty or five hundred?'

'That is what I thought at first, but there is no mistake. She has left me her entire fortune, beyond legacies to friends and servants.'

'How wonderful!' Zenna hugged Tallie hard, then sat back with a face radiant with pleasure at her friend's good fortune. 'What are you going to do now?'

'I hardly know, it is such a surprise.' An idea suddenly struck her and, without giving herself time to worry about details, Tallie said, 'I must make some sensible investments, of course. Zenna, you know you have always said your dream is to have your own school? Why do we not go into partnership and do just that?'

'I do not have any money,' Zenna protested. But Tallie saw the sudden flare of excitement in her eyes.

'Yes, but you have all the skills and know how a school should be run. I will provide the money for the house and so forth, you manage the school. And,' she added as Zenna opened her mouth to argue, 'I would hope to find somewhere large enough for me to make it my home as well, if you should not object.'

'Object? Object! Tallie, do you really mean it? How wonderful, there are so many things I want to try, so many new ideas about the education of girls—' She broke off. 'But you have not given this any thought yet, have you? You must do so, and take advice. And, in any case, why on earth would you want to live in a girls' school? With this fortune you can be a Society lady.'

'I am too old, Zenna, and I know no one.'

'Nonsense.' Zenna leapt to her feet and began to pace the room. 'Lady Parry would advise you.'

'She already has,' Tallie admitted. 'She has invited me to stay with her and make my come-out under her aegis.'

'Did you not agree? That is a marvellous opportunity, you could not hope for anything more fortunate.'

'Yes, I did agree, but now I think I must tell her I have changed my mind,' Tallie said slowly. Her conscience was pricking her very badly and she knew that, whatever her views might be about Lord Arndale's opinions, she owed it to her kind patroness to ensure that she brought not a whiff of scandal to her household.

She met Zenna's bemused gaze and blurted out, 'I must tell her about my work for Mr Harland. I cannot risk the scandal if anything came out, it would be a dreadful way to repay her kindness.' She did not add the other consideration, which had been looming large ever since she saw Lord Arndale's inimical stare fixed upon her friend.

If a respectable governess was not considered a suitable acquaintance for the newly wealthy Miss

Grey, what would Lady Parry make of a lodging-house keeper and an opera dancer?

'I must speak to her this afternoon,' she said resolutely. 'I will thank her for her kindness, but she will see that I am an unsuitable recipient of it. Better to do it at once, before she has the chance to make any further plans on my behalf.'

Zenna shook her head sadly. 'You must do as you think fit, of course, but it is such a shame that you will not make a come-out.'

'Never mind. Tomorrow we can start to make plans for the school—if that idea is still agreeable to you.'

'How can it be anything else? I cannot believe my good fortune—I declare I feel as dazed as you look, Tallie dearest.' She broke off at the sound of the front door opening. 'That must be Mrs Blackstock. What will you tell her?'

'Nothing yet, I think. I have no wish to embarrass our friends with the size of my inheritance, although I would value your advice about how I might help them at some point. I think perhaps tomorrow we can tell her of our plans and give notice. If she finds other tenants before the school is ready, we can always find lodgings together, or go to an hotel.'

'An hotel?' Zenna echoed, wide-eyed.

'Why, yes,' Tallie said recklessly. 'I can afford it, after all!'

This frivolity did not last much beyond luncheon. Zenna was distractedly making lists, breaking off to suck her pen, gaze into space and then resume her scribbling.

But Tallie was imagining how disappointed in her Lady Parry was going to be when she discovered that her protégée was so abandoned as to supplement her living by posing naked.

Chapter Six

Rainbird hid any reaction he felt at Tallie's second, unexpected, call of the day. 'Her ladyship is At Home, Miss Grey, and has no one with her at present.'

'Talitha! What a nice surprise.' Lady Parry put down the book she was reading and looked up with a pleased smile as Tallie was announced. 'Come and sit down by me.'

'I...I think I would rather stand, ma'am.' Tallie took a deep breath and said, 'I am very sorry to appear ungracious, Lady Parry, but I feel I should not have accepted your kind offer this morning and I thought I should come and say so immediately.'

'Why ever not? My poor child, stop standing there looking like a parlour maid who has broken the best Minton and sit down. There, that is better. Now, I know you must have had a shock this morning, but—'

'It is not that, ma'am. I had not considered what a difficult position I would be putting you in.'

'Because you have had to work for your living? If I do not regard it, be certain that Society will not—

not when they learn of your family and fortune, and observe your ladylike deportment.'

'My friends, ma'am—'

'Your friends are more than welcome in my house, Talitha.'

'Lady Parry,' Tallie said with some emphasis, feeling she was being swept along faster than she wanted, 'my only friends are a governess, a lodging-house keeper and an opera dancer. I do not believe you could have been aware of that fact when you made your kind offer just now.'

'I have never met a governess who was not respectable and I am sure if the lodging-house in question is where you make your home, its proprietress is bound to be most acceptable.'

'The opera dancer is her niece and lives with us,' Tallie persisted.

'And is she a nice girl?'

'Very. And despite what the world thinks of actresses and performers, she is a modest, virtuous and respectable young woman into the bargain.'

'There now, so where is the problem?'

'You would not object if I were to continue my friendships?'

'Certainly not. Your friends are most welcome in my home whenever they wish to call upon you.'

'Thank you, ma'am. But not everyone will be of your opinion.'

'By everyone, I assume you mean my nephew?'

'Er…I…' Tallie had no wish to tell tales or to sound in any way critical of Lady Parry's family.

'And which of your friends has Nicholas been viewing with that chilly eye of his?'

'Miss Scott, the governess.'

'Foolish boy—he has always been overprotective. And has he set eyes upon the young lady from the opera yet?'

'I believe not.'

'He will,' his fond aunt prophesised cheerfully. 'At least, he probably already *has* met her if she is pretty. Never mind, Talitha. Whom I allow under my roof is my decision. Once Nicholas gets to know you better he will soon cease to worry.'

'That is not all, Lady Parry.'

'I thought we had agreed that you would call me Aunt Kate?'

'You will not wish me to when I tell you about the other matter, ma'am,' Tallie said, feeling ready to sink now that the moment for confession was upon her. 'I am not just a milliner, I have been earning my living in another way as well.'

'I know,' Lady Parry said calmly.

'You know? But, ma'am, you cannot…I have been sitting for an artist!'

'Indeed. Mr Harland, a most talented gentleman, I believe.'

'But, Lady Parry, how could you have discovered what I have been doing?'

Her ladyship held up a hand to silence Tallie as Rainbird appeared with a tea tray.

'Will you pour, my dear?' She waited while Tallie handed her her cup with a hand that trembled. 'A macaroon? No? You must not become so agitated, Talitha. I called upon Mr Harland a while ago as I am considering having my portrait painted. I observed a canvas and asked who the model was, for I thought I recognised her.'

'He told you?' Tallie was aghast, both at the

thought that the compromising classical paintings had been displayed in the studio and that Mr Harland had been so indiscreet as to reveal her name.

'He was immediately very embarrassed at his slip. I am sure it was only because I said I thought I knew the model.'

'And you are not shocked, ma'am? The fact that I was sitting for an artist at all, let alone the way I was…dressed.'

'Admittedly it was not the way in which one would normally wish an unmarried lady to be depicted, but under the circumstances I feel we should disregard it.'

'Circumstances?' Tallie said weakly.

'I can tell Mr Harland is a most respectable person and I am sure that his slip in revealing your name would not be repeated.'

Tallie was so taken aback that for a moment she could not find the words to continue.

Finally she ventured, 'But, ma'am, if it should be found out once I am launched in Society, it would reflect upon you. After all, I am of no account, but you are a leading member of the *ton*.'

'And have more than enough credit to carry off any little indiscretions of my protégée,' Lady Parry said with a chuckle. 'And it will not be long before you too are a figure in Society, mark my words. A fortune the size of yours is more than enough to cover up any number of indiscretions. Now then, you are still going to be able to move here in a week?'

'Yes, ma'am,' Tallie stammered.

'Aunt Kate, please, my dear Tallie. Goodness, is that the time? I am due at Lady Fraser's in an hour, and be seen in this gown I cannot and will not! No, there is no need for you to rush off, this is your home now. Just ring if you need anything.' Lady Parry sprang from the sofa on which she had been decoratively draped, fluttered across to drop a kiss on Tallie's cheek and was out of the room before the younger woman could do more than gasp,

'Goodbye.'

Tallie got slowly to her feet, too bemused to pull herself together and leave. She had been steeled to explain why she was an inappropriate person for Lady Parry to take under her wing and had found both her anxiety for her friends and her scrupulous confession about Mr Harland swept aside.

Which meant that in a week's time her former life also would be swept away and she would be making her come-out as a young lady of fashion. Her money worries would be about how to invest and spend it, not how to make enough to afford a new pelisse.

Tallie stood by the window and stared out at the fashionable street life bustling below her. She untied the ribbons of her bonnet and tossed it onto the sofa as though freeing her head would help her think, but things still seemed just as unreal and unbelievable as they had before.

'Back again, Miss Grey?' a voice behind her enquired. Tallie stiffened, but did not turn. He had entered without her hearing. 'Come to confess your secret?' Lord Arndale's voice sounded as uninterested as if he had enquired whether she had just returned from walking in the park.

Tallie felt the breath catch in her throat. She wanted... What did she want? Why had she had hardly a coherent, calm thought since this man had found her in the attic studio?

She found her voice suddenly. 'Confess? Yes, that is precisely what I have been doing, my lord.'

'You have?' Despite everything Tallie felt her mouth curve into a smile. So, she had managed to surprise the imperturbable Nick Stangate, had she?

'Yes, my lord.' Emboldened by the fact that she could not see his sardonic expression, Tallie wondered if it was safe to tease him further and decided against it. 'It appears that Lady Parry was already aware of the matter that was troubling me.'

'And?' He was coming closer; Tallie could see his reflection blurred in the window glass. How could she ever have said he made her feel safe?

'Lady Parry appears to feel I am refining too much about it. She does not regard it.' How her voice was staying so steady she had no idea. Nick Stangate was standing at her shoulder, just behind her.

'And do you think I would share her opinion?' He had lowered his voice. It sounded faintly menacing in the quiet room.

'Without wishing to appear rude, my lord, your opinion does not concern me. But then you are Lady Parry's trustee, not her guardian, are you not, my lord?'

Had she overstepped the mark? It appeared not: there was a faint noise that she realised incredulously was a muffled snort of amusement. Then he was still.

'What scent are you wearing, Miss Grey?' The question was so unexpected it was all she could do not to spin round.

'Jasmine,' she replied. Was it her imagination, or was he so close that she could feel his breath on her nape?

'It reminds me of something,' Nick said slowly.

'No—somewhere, a place. But somewhere cold, dusty...'

'Really? How strange: I have always thought it a summer smell.' Then Tallie realised what he was re-membering—the faint traces of her scent on her chilled, naked skin in the attic room. And he was standing as he had then, close by her left shoulder, close enough to touch, close enough to smell her fear and her perfume.

Talitha turned so swiftly that Nick had no oppor-tunity to step back, even if he had wanted to. He stopped racking his memory for a trace of an elusive perfume as a far more intrusive sensation than curi-osity flooded through his body. Simple desire. Damn it, why had he not realised the feelings that Talitha Grey evoked in him for what they were? It was not suspicion of the secret she openly admitted to him she was hiding. It was not even the perfectly natural protectiveness of his aunt that would mean he would take a sharp interest in any new acquaintance of hers.

His habitual honesty with himself answered his own question. He had been rather too preoccupied with another blonde young woman for him to have thought more clearly about this one until she had achieved this insidious effect on him.

Not that the two women were more than superfi-cially similar, of course. That exquisite nymph hud-dling in the dirty attic closet was shorter than Miss Grey. Her hair had waved in tresses shot through with varied shades of gold, unlike the straight, pale gilt severity of the coiffure so close in front of him now. And she had quivered with fear, unlike the tense

fierceness that this young woman showed in the face
of his curiosity or disapproval.

Nick shook himself mentally. He had allowed his
imagination to drift too often to that naked girl. She
had proved a damnably uncomfortable preoccupation,
so uncomfortable that he had been tempted to go back
to the studio and ask for her name and direction. A
natural fastidiousness had stopped him; to do so felt
like an extension of Jack Hemsley's behaviour.

But how had he been so blind as not to appreciate
the delicious feminine charms now standing so close
to him? That reproof about not noticing a 'milliner's
girl' was deserved. And how had he failed to look
beyond that frightful pelisse to the charming figure
beneath? Lord Arndale ruthlessly suppressed thought
of just how Miss Grey would appear clad only in that
length of sheer linen and smiled into the defiant green
eyes.

'Naturally I bow to my aunt's good judgement. Can
we not call it a truce, Miss Grey? After all, immediately after you heard of your good fortune we seemed
to be on good enough terms, did we not?'

Yes, he had allowed himself to relax with her, succumb to the image she presented of the innocent
young lady forced to fend for herself by harsh circumstances. And he had let her lull his suspicions at
the way she had reacted to a confrontation with a
lawyer. The sensation of her pulse fluttering under his
fingers returned and he clenched his fist to banish the
frisson.

Talitha nodded with apparent reluctance, but did
not let her eyes drop from his. They were standing so
close that she had to tilt her head back at what must
have been an uncomfortable angle, yet she made no

move away from him. Nick was suddenly struck by
the fancy that she was attempting to hold his attention
away from something else, something she was desperate to hide from him.

He broke the eye contact, abruptly stepping back
and sweeping the room in a comprehensive glance.
Nothing.

'Satisfied that I have not been stealing the silver?'
she enquired icily, stooping to pick up her bonnet and
tying the ribbons with a jerk. 'The truce did not last
long, did it, my lord?'

'The truce will last just as long as I am satisfied
you are hiding nothing that will embarrass or harm
my aunt,' he replied, trampling firmly on a desire to
rip open that bow, toss the bonnet to one side and
kiss the anger off her face. Then the image of those
green eyes fluttering closed in passion, that firm
mouth softening beneath his, that delicately curved
body yielding in his arms crashed into his mind with
the force of a blow and he turned abruptly on his heel
to hide the shock of arousal.

'I will ring for Rainbird. I regret that I am unable
to drive you this afternoon, but he will call you a cab.'

'Thank you, my lord. Perhaps before you leave you
would be so kind as to give me the direction of the
bank you were going to recommend to me. I have no
need to take you up on your kind offer to escort me—
Miss Scott will do so, I am sure.'

Nick strode to the bureau and, pulling a sheet of
paper towards him scribbled a few lines. When he
turned, Talitha was standing closer to him, her hand
held out for the note. 'Miss Scott? Ah, yes, the governess.'

'Indeed. My friend to whom you were introduced

this morning. Doubtless your investigations will have unearthed the full list of her extremely respectable clients. Lady Parry has been so kind as to say that all of my small circle of friends are welcome here while I am staying with her.' She tucked the paper into her reticule and added, 'In addition to Miss Scott, there is Mrs Blackstock, the lodging-house keeper, and her niece Miss Blackstock, who is an opera dancer.'

'Are you attempting to provoke me, Miss Grey?' Nick was conscious that his strong desire to kiss Talitha Grey until she was whimpering in his arms was rapidly being replaced by the need to shake her until her teeth rattled. 'An *opera* dancer?'

'Certainly, my lord. I am surprised your researches did not uncover that fact,' she replied placidly, slipping past him as Rainbird opened the door. 'Possibly you know her as Amelie LeNoir. Thank you, Rainbird. Good day, my lord.'

Nick threw himself down in the nearest armchair and stared at the closed door. *Damn it!* A little milliner with gilt hair and green eyes and a secret had undermined his self-control, his carefully maintained lack of emotion and his utter confidence that he had his world, and that of each of his dependents, firmly where he wanted it.

And no bad thing either, he told himself, his sense of humour returning as rapidly as it had left him. Bear-leading his cousin, assisting the failing Miss Gower, ruthlessly checking up on his aunt's new protégée—he would turn into a sanctimonious straightlaced Puritan if he carried on like this. *You need some fun, Nick Stangate*, he told himself. Whether having Miss Talitha Grey in the Parry household would prove to be fun, exactly, remained to be seen. It was certainly not going to be dull. And if that young lady thought she was going to keep any secrets from him for very long, she was seriously mistaken.

That small stiletto thrust about the opera dancer had been neatly delivered, he thought appreciatively. Presumably it was intended to repay him for the remark about buying hats, which she had risen to all too easily.

Amelie LeNoir. Could she really mean that she was friendly with an opera dancer? Presumably, if she was the niece of the lodging-house keeper, she shared the same house—unless she was in some man's keeping. No, even Miss Grey would not openly profess friendship with a kept woman. A virtuous actress would be a novelty—and possibly a means by which to tease Talitha Grey.

In a very short time he was becoming addicted to the stimulus of provoking the flash of green fire in those wide eyes. He would seek out Miss LeNoir and in the meantime he must have a word with his enquiry agent. Neither Miss LeNoir nor Talitha's secret had featured in the expensive reports that had arrived at regular intervals, systematically setting out Miss Grey's career from respectable gentry childhood through reclusive poverty with her dying mother to hard-working self-reliance. Lord Arndale disliked incompetence almost as much as he disliked not being in command of all the facts: Mr Gregory Tolliver was going to have some explaining to do as to why a Society matron knew his target's secrets and he did not.

Chapter Seven

The next day Zenna accompanied Tallie to see first Mr Dover the solicitor and then to Martin and Wigmore, the bankers Nick Stangate had recommended. Tallie found herself expected at both sets of offices and at both of them found herself making decisions and issuing orders, which, if she gave herself time to think about it, seemed the stuff of fairy tales. Eventually they emerged blinking into the watery sunlight on the corner of Poultry and Queen Street, an obsequious clerk at their elbow to hail them a carriage.

'We were received with the most gratifying degree of attention,' she observed to her friend once they were alone and the cab was crawling down Cheapside towards St Paul's. 'But I still cannot believe that I was sitting there, making decisions about bank deposits and gilts, and being lectured on the absolute necessity to make my will.'

'You and your money were what was receiving the attention,' Zenna retorted. 'What a lowering thought that men who would have scarcely noticed us yesterday hung upon your every word and wish today, simply because of your acquisition of wealth.'

'That is the way of the world, I suppose.' Tallie looked sombre for a moment, then smiled wickedly. 'But reprehensible though it may be, I fully intend to enjoy it—we have been prudent and sensible too long, Zenna. We deserve a holiday!'

'We? But I have my plans for the school to draw up and house-agents to see, as well as my pupils to attend to,' Zenna protested.

'You cannot do both, not efficiently at any rate. Zenna, why do you not give notice to the parents of your pupils and concentrate on the school. No, hear me out.' She raised a hand as Zenna opened her mouth. 'This school is an investment—a joint investment—is it not? Then I should be investing in your time to set it up, and you should be concentrating on house-agents, and interviewing teachers and drawing up a curriculum and so on.

'Stop frowning, Zenna!' She laughed at her friend's dubious expression. 'I understand all your scruples. We will talk to Mr Dover and ask him to draw up a partnership agreement, then all will be set out and fair. Now agree, do, because I have lots of other plans I want to discuss with you.'

'Very well,' Zenna agreed with the air of someone being persuaded to do something they wanted to do, but felt they should not. 'I will be guided by Mr Dover, he does seem a very rigorous lawyer and will make sure I am not taking more than my fair share in this agreement.'

Tallie nodded decisively. 'And I have had another brilliant idea for investing my money. It concerns Mrs Blackstock. What if I should buy a town house or two? She could run them as select boarding-houses.

I am sure she would soon be making a handsome profit for me and thereby a good income for herself.'

'An excellent idea,' Zenobia approved, grabbing the hanging strap as the cab once again jolted to a halt. 'What a crush! I had not realised the City would be so busy. What about Millie? I confess, I have not observed Mr Hemsley in her company again, but I know she is receiving notes from someone, for she blushes and hides them under her table napkin when the morning post arrives.'

'That is difficult,' Tallie agreed, peering out of the window. 'Why, no wonder the street is in such chaos, some yokel is driving a herd of sheep through! But I do not think it will be any faster to get out and walk, so we had better stay where we are. I had thought that if Mrs Blackstock was busy with the new boarding-houses, Millie might stay at home to help her. But she loves the stage—it is not as if she is doing it because she needs the money. Then I thought of giving her a dowry in the hope of attracting some respectable person to marry her, but I cannot think of a tactful way of doing that, so I confess I am somewhat at a stand.'

'Hmm. No doubt something will occur to us. What are you doing this afternoon? Shopping?'

A roll of banknotes had been burning a hole in Tallie's reticule for the past hour, but she wanted to take Zenna shopping with her when she went. Tallie had a plan to buy her friend some clothes so she could be invited to parties too. That was going to take some tact and cunning and Zenna was engaged that afternoon with pupils.

'I must go shopping tomorrow, for I cannot arrive at Lady Parry's with my wardrobe in the state it is. I am sure she will recommend me to all the right modistes once I am with her, but until then I need your advice, Zenna. Are you free tomorrow? Because if you are, we can look at house-agents as well.'

Zenna agreed, attempting to look as though she would enjoy the experience. She produced her tablets and began to add to her endless lists, while Tallie brooded on the interview with Madame d'Aunay she had resolved on having that afternoon.

She had already written to her employer, apologising again for her absence, giving a carefully edited account of her change in circumstances and informing her that she would be stopping work as soon as she had finished the hats on which she was working. She expected Madame to be unhappy about this, but she was unprepared for the atmosphere that greeted her when she arrived at the shop that afternoon.

The first shock was the fact that Madame curtsied as she entered the salon and ushered her through to her inner sanctum, the elegantly appointed private room reserved for the best clients.

'I must apologise, Madame…' Tallie began, only to be silenced by the expression of forced affability on Madame's face.

'Do not mention it, Miss Grey. Naturally you will wish to dissociate yourself from this establishment immediately. I have your outstanding wages here.' She reached for an envelope, a slight flush staining her neck.

'Goodness, no,' Tallie protested. 'I have given you no notice, I cannot take that.'

'Very well, ma'am.'

Tallie blinked. Had her former employer called her 'ma'am'? 'The hats on which I am working—'

'Sarah will take them over, Miss Grey.' There was an awkward pause. 'I will naturally be sorry to lose Lady Parry's business, but—'

'But why should you?' Tallie felt distinctly disorientated.

'I understood that you would be living with Lady Parry, Miss Grey, and naturally assumed—'

'Oh, good heavens, no!' Tallie realised her former employer thought she would be making the hats directly for her patroness from now on. 'Obviously if Lady Parry needed a trim changing or something of that nature...but I am sure she will wish to continue purchasing her hats from you.'

'I see.' Madame looked even more uneasy. 'I believe you said you will be making your come-out this Season, Miss Grey?'

'Indeed, yes, and I will need several hats...'

'What a pity that this salon produces hats so much more fitting for the older lady,' Madame said expressionlessly.

'But...' Tallie gathered her wits together. So, suddenly she was an embarrassment to Madame: neither a lady nor an employee, but someone who might prove a liability if there was a scandal when she made her début. Society ladies might take exception to the fact that one of Madame d'Aunay's artisans had the presumption to move above her station.

She glanced towards the door into the workroom. 'The girls are very busy, Miss Grey,' the milliner said hurriedly.

'I am sure they are, Madame.' Tallie got to her feet. 'I must thank you for having given me a chance when

I needed employment: I will not forget that. Please be assured that I will do nothing to dissuade Lady Parry from continuing to buy hats here.'

She swept out, head held high before she saw whether she was receiving another curtsy or not. When she found herself on the pavement outside the shop she hesitated, unsure which way to turn along the crowded street, unable to think clearly about what she should be doing next.

Anger, sorrow and insecurity fought within her. Was it going to be this difficult with everyone she met in her new life?

'Miss Grey, good afternoon.' The cheerful voice at her elbow jerked her back to the present and an awareness that she was still standing on the pavement with passers-by flowing around her.

'Lord Parry. I do beg your pardon, I was wool-gathering.' Tallie pulled herself together with an effort and managed a smile. William was regarding her with unaffected delight and she was irresistibly reminded of a large retriever puppy. He seemed painfully young and, she suspected, was rapidly reaching the stage when young ladies were proving a mysterious, but irresistible, source of interest.

'May I escort you anywhere?'

'No, I thank you, but I was just going to…to walk home.' She supposed that would be the best thing to do. She hardly felt inclined to go window-shopping in her present distracted frame of mind.

'I say, that is rather a long walk, isn't it? Let me call you a hackney carriage.'

'I…no…thank you. I think I would like the fresh air.'

To her surprise, for in Tallie's experience youths

were often far too self-absorbed to take much notice of anyone else's emotional state, William shot her a sharp glance, tucked her hand firmly under his elbow and began to steer her towards the end of Berkeley Street.

'Are you feeling a little out of sorts, Miss Grey? Never mind, I know just the thing.'

'What, my lord?' Half-amused despite her battered feelings, Tallie meekly allowed herself to be guided along the crowded pavement.

'Ice cream. I will take you to Gunter's and you can have a nice lemon ice and a wafer and a cup of chocolate and you'll soon feel right as rain.'

Tallie suppressed a smile. Of course, food and the sweeter the better—the answer to distress for every very young person. 'That is extremely kind of you, my lord.'

They arrived at the fashionable tearooms in a slight lull and found a choice of tables available. 'Would you like to sit in the window?' William suggested. 'There is more to look at.'

And everyone can see us, Tallie thought, allowing herself to be seated. She could hardly feel that her presence in her drab pelisse was adding much lustre to young Lord Parry's carefully cultivated image. His clothing was immaculate, if a little on the exaggerated side when it came to cut, his hair was ruthlessly pomaded into elegant curls and his neckcloth, although lacking the exquisite folds achieved by a certain gentleman Tallie could think of, was highly creditable.

'I see you are admiring my neckcloth,' he confided, dropping his voice.

'I beg your pardon,' Tallie said hastily, 'I had no intention of staring...'

'Not at all.' He fairly glowed with pride and Tallie concluded that if his lordship *was* twenty years old his birthday must have been very recent indeed. 'My cousin Nick showed me how to tie it. I was trying for a Waterfall and making a complete mull of it, so he taught me this.'

'You are close to Lord Arndale?' Tallie enquired, moving her napkin to allow a water ice and a cup of steaming chocolate to be set in front of her.

William became quiet, obviously unused to discussing his feelings. 'He's the best of fellows,' he managed after some thought. 'Like a brother, only he doesn't lecture. Leastways, I don't have a brother, but I hear what the other chaps say and older brothers sound like the very de—are very strict. Always lecturing.'

'And Lord Arndale does not lecture you?' Tallie enquired, surprised. It seemed unlikely from what she knew of him that Nick Stangate would tolerate the foolishness of youth.

'No.' William took a large spoonful of vanilla ice and paused with it halfway to his mouth. 'He *looks* sometimes.'

'Looks?'

'Yes, just *looks*. And then you feel uncomfortable and wonder if whatever you are doing is a good thing. You know?'

'No, but I can imagine.' Tallie took a reviving sip of chocolate.

'You'll see, once you come and live with us.'

'Do you mind me moving in, my lord?' Tallie asked abruptly. This was an unlikely conversation to be having with a very young man who was virtually a stranger to her, but William with his natural confiding friendliness did not appear to find it so.

'No, of course not. It'll be like having a sister and Mama is having a wonderful time already. You will call me William, won't you?' He ate some more of his ice and demolished his wafer, then, with the frankness that Tallie was beginning to associate with him—so unlike his cousin—said, 'Are you feeling better now?'

'I…yes, thank you.'

'Good. What was wrong?' Then he blushed scarlet. 'Lord! I am sorry, it is just that it is so easy talking to you I just didn't think. Forget I asked.'

Perversely Tallie, who ten minutes ago would have walked on hot coals rather than reveal her wounded feelings, said, 'No, it is quite all right to ask. I had just had a very difficult conversation with Madame d'Aunay, who used be my employer.'

'Um?' William nodded encouragingly. 'Old tartar, is she?'

'It isn't that. She is embarrassed because a day ago I was a milliner and her employee; now she thinks she has to treat me like a lady and is afraid that if I make a scandal it will reflect on her business. I do not think I know *what* I am any more.' To her horror a lump appeared in her throat.

'Oh, I say!' William whisked out a large pocket handkerchief and, leaning across the table, held it out to her. 'You aren't going to cry, are you, Miss Grey…? I feel an absolute clod…'

Tallie ducked her head and shot a rapid glance around the still half-empty room. No one appeared to have noticed them. 'Thank you, William, I am quite all right, truly. And I'm not going to cry, it is just that I do not know whether I am angry or hurt or what I feel.'

His hand still hovered with the linen, and she put up her own hand to touch his wrist and silently urge him to put the handkerchief away. As she did so a movement outside caught her attention. Lord Arndale was watching them through the glass, one dark brow raised in chilly incredulity.

'Good afternoon.' He appeared at their table with what seemed to Tallie to be supernatural speed. Glancing at William's face, she saw he had turned as red as she knew she had. The pair of them must have presented a perfect picture of guilt surprised.

This was ridiculous. William might be an awkward adolescent, but she was five and twenty and a woman of the world. She was certainly not going to allow Nicholas Stangate to put her out of countenance.

'Good afternoon, my lord,' she said affably. 'Will you not join us? Lord Parry has been treating me to the indulgence of an ice. I can certainly recommend the lemon, although I believe the vanilla is equally delicious.' William was rapidly collecting himself, stuffing the handkerchief back into his pocket and rising to move around the table and offer his cousin his seat.

'Thank you, William. No, nothing for me.' Nick waved away the hovering waiter with a careless hand and regarded Tallie with what she could only interpret as scepticism. 'It appeared that my cousin, far from treating you to afternoon tea, had reduced you to tears.'

'Oh, I say…'

'Did it appear so?' Tallie took another tiny taste of ice and smiled. 'A mote of something flew into my

eye and Lord Parry was kind enough to offer me his
handkerchief.' She smiled warmly at the youth, who
blushed again, this time with pink-cheeked pleasure.

Lord Arndale was watching the byplay with little
sign of either belief or approval. Tallie decided it was
time to distract him from his cousin. 'I deserve a little
indulgence, my lord. I have spent the morning in the
City, paying close attention to Mr Dover and the gentlemen at the bank, just as you recommended me to.'

The dark brows snapped together. 'You went
alone?'

'Certainly not, my lord.' Tallie managed a tone of
modest outrage. 'Naturally I was accompanied by
Miss Scott, as I told you I would be.'

'Ah, yes, your governess friend.'

'And my business partner,' Tallie corrected gently,
watching him from under demurely lowered lashes.

'And what business might that be?'

'It is far too early to divulge the details,' Tallie said
repressively, dapping her lips delicately with the napkin.

'If you are going to plunge into dubious investments, Miss Grey, I must tell you as your—'

'As my what, my lord?' Tallie gathered up her reticule and smiled at William. 'Do you know, I think I
would like you to call me a hackney after all, Lord
Parry, if you would be so kind.' She waited until he
rose and went to the door before turning back to his
cousin, who was watching her with smouldering eyes.
'You may be Lady Parry's trustee and you may be
Miss Gower's executor, my lord, but you have no role
in my life.'

William was on the pavement, head tipped back,
obviously asking the driver of the hackney carriage

'I don't think I can drink anything, thank you. I am full of lemon ice and hot chocolate.' She tried not to think about the episode in Gunter's, but it kept insisting on being worried at, like a sore tooth. '*Why* should he think anything so foolish as that? William is five years younger than I am.'

'Perhaps he's jea—' Zenna caught herself and bit off the word. 'Perhaps he is just abnormally suspicious,' she said soothingly. 'Tell me all about Gunter's, I have always wanted to try one of their ices.'

Chapter Eight

'There was a time—can it be just a few days ago?—when my only worry was earning my living,' Tallie lamented as the hackney carriage made its way along Oxford Street. 'Now I have to worry about my position in Society—or lack of it; how to invest a ridiculous amount of money wisely; how to keep an interfering, autocratic aristocrat from discovering my secrets and how to persuade *you* to allow me to buy you a dress or two.'

'Tallie, I simply cannot accept expensive presents…' Zenna protested for the third time that morning.

'I am not trying to give you expensive presents—just one evening dress so we can go to parties together. *Please*, Zenna. I need your support. Lady Parry is so kind, but it is not the same as a friend my own age. And it would give me such pleasure to give you a present.' She smiled hopefully at her friend, who sighed and smiled back.

'Very well, and thank you, Tallie. It would be very pleasant to have a nice evening gown, I have to admit, but as for the other gowns you were talking of, that is far too much.'

'Business expenses,' Tallie said firmly. 'We can put them down as business expenses. You must have some good day dresses for interviewing teachers and parents. We are aiming at the highest quality for this school, are we not?'

Zenna began to protest that arguing with Tallie was more exhausting than trying to handle a room full of six-year-old boys when the hackney pulled up outside the Pantheon Bazaar and Tallie got to her feet. 'We will start here, then I thought Hardin and Howell, Stagg and Mantle's and Clark and Debenham's.' She smiled at Zenna, who descended onto the pavement looking apprehensive at this formidable list. 'Then this afternoon, Dickens and Smith...' She plunged into the shop pursued by Zenna, who was grimly resolving that, whatever else the day held, it was going to include a lengthy pause at Gunter's. A very lengthy one indeed.

At four o'clock that afternoon two very weary young ladies made their way up to Tallie's bedroom and collapsed onto the bed, scattering parcels and bandboxes on the floor as they did so. Behind them came the faint sounds of little Annie struggling up the stairs with still more packages.

'My feet!' Zenna moaned, pulling off her shoes and wriggling her toes with a gasp of relief.

Tallie levered herself up on her elbows from her position prone on the mattress and sighed happily. 'Mine too. Oh, thank you, Annie. Put them in the corner, please, and then please bring us some tea up.' She dragged the pillows up into a heap and sat back against them. 'A nice cup of tea and then all the fun of unwrapping everything.' She smiled at Zenna coaxingly. 'Admit it, Zenna, you did enjoy it a little bit, did you not?'

'Well…yes, I have to confess I did. Thank you very much for the gown and the slippers and gloves. It felt very good to dress up for once. But we do seem to have bought a vast amount of things—do you think you have almost everything you need now?'

'I should not think so for a minute,' Tallie replied, reflecting on the ladies' boudoirs she had glimpsed so frequently in her career as a milliner. 'Lady Parry would be very disappointed if she does not have the opportunity to supervise my shopping. No, this was just so that I did not feel too drab in the first few days. My old pelisse and walking dress are on their last prayers, all my stockings have been darned and both my pairs of gloves have got splits in the seams.'

She closed her eyes for a moment, letting the images of the day's extravagances swirl across her memory. 'It is fun to have a holiday and to be able to buy what one wants, but I am glad we have our business ventures to be working on, Zenna. I cannot feel comfortable with the thought of Society life. From what I have seen it is entirely composed of luxury and pleasure. I am sure I would soon become bored with nothing else to think of.'

Into the images of dress lengths and slippers, fans and feathers the picture of a tall, dark, elegant gentleman rose, quite unbidden. How did Lord Arndale spend his time? she wondered. In the company of actresses and opera dancers? At the card tables? At cock-fights and the prize-ring? She tried to imagine that coolly sardonic expression giving way to excitement, passion, anticipation—and failed. His lordship was undoubtedly a prime example of the indolent and aloof members of Society whose way of life she was about to sample. It would be satisfying to cause some emotion to cross those chiselled features or to provoke a response that was neither controlled nor temperate. A small smile caught at the corners of Tallie's lips. Yes, very satisfying indeed.

Two days later the indolent and aloof gentleman in question mounted the steps of the house in Upper Wimpole Street and found himself unexpectedly encountering almost the entire household.

Nick had spent a taxing morning with his steward, who had come up from the country estates with a formidable pile of problems and questions to be resolved, and later that afternoon he suspected he was going to have to have an equally long list of details to decide with Mr Dover before the final work could be completed on Miss Gower's will. That evening he fully intended leaving young William to his own devices, however dubious they sounded, and relaxing with a small group of friends over dinner, cards and several bottles of excellent brandy.

But he had been waylaid by his aunt and asked to call upon Miss Grey. 'You will tell her I will collect her in my carriage at ten on Wednesday morning, will you not, Nicholas dear? And if you can establish how many trunks she has, then Rainbird can organise the carrier.' She had stood on tiptoe to kiss his cheek. 'Thank you, dearest.' And she had rushed away in her usual whirlwind manner before he could enquire why a note would not serve the purpose just as well.

Now he was here, he might as well take the opportunity of smoothing over the friction from their last encounter. He could not really believe she had set her sights on young William Parry, but it had been bad tactics to let her see he was concerned. If she was the sort of woman who saw opposition as a challenge, she might attempt to attach the lad's interest simply as a game. And William was far too young to be breaking his heart over an older woman Nick decided, conveniently forgetting his own initiation into the arts of love at the age of seventeen by a beautiful, sophisticated lady more than ten years his senior.

The door was opened by a diminutive maid with a snub nose, freckles, an apron too large for her and an expression of alarm. 'Oh, sir! Miss Grey? Oh, yes, sir! I'll tell her you're here, sir, if you'll just wait in the front parlour, sir.'

She flung open the door to let him in, appeared to realise she should have asked his name to announce him, gave a scared squeak and shut the door again behind him. Nick found himself in a cosy, slightly shabby room with an indefinable air of comfort and femininity. The latter quality was enhanced by the presence on the sofa of an enchantingly pretty girl with large blue eyes and a mass of blonde curls. Tumbled in a pile by her side were undergarments of a most frivolous, intimate and dainty variety.

She bundled the lingerie under a cushion with what struck Nick as admirable quick-wittedness and got to her feet, placing a thimble and needle on the table beside her. 'I am sorry, sir,' she said, a faint blush colouring her cheeks. 'Annie is not yet trained as a downstairs maid and I am afraid she does not always remember to announce callers.'

'Nicholas Stangate. I called to see Miss Grey. May

I presume to guess I am addressing Miss Amelie LeNoir? I apologise for disturbing you.' It would not be the slightest hardship to disturb Miss LeNoir, he reflected, watching the artless pleasure at his recognition, the lovely figure in a surprisingly modest afternoon dress, the parted lips and soft curves. No hardship at all.

'Oh, how did you guess? Your lordship,' she added hastily, bobbing a curtsy.

'You were described to me,' Nick said simply, enjoying the deepening of the flush of pleasure, the flutter of the long lashes. For a man who had always favoured dark-haired women, his life suddenly appeared to be full of blondes. It made an agreeable change.

'I...I had better go and find Tal...Miss Grey, my lord. One simply cannot rely on Annie. Will you not sit down?' She gestured at the sofa, recalled her mending, hastily whisked it from under the cushion to under her arm and hurried out.

Nick grinned. The enchantingly fresh young woman who had just fluttered out was either an exceptional actress or that contradiction in terms, a chaste opera dancer, just as Talitha Grey had said. Instead of taking the proffered seat, he began to prowl around the room. It was a rare glimpse for a man into a feminine world that was not arranged for display or entertaining, but simply for a group of women to pass their daily lives in.

A neat stack of account books next to a spike impaling tradesmen's bills. A basket of laces, ribbons and artificial flowers by a sewing box and a large velvet pincushion studded with glass-headed pins. A pile of novels and some copies of fashion journals upon a shelf. A chessboard set out for the start of a game. He moved a pawn in an opening gambit and continued to look around. A quill stained with red ink lay beside an open exercise book.

Nick paused and flicked open a page of the lexicon next to the exercise book. Greek! The door behind him opened to reveal not Miss Grey, but her governess friend. 'Miss Scott, good afternoon. You have surprised me reading what I imagine must be your Greek lexicon.'

'Yes, my lord.' She stood there, regarding him from under level dark brows. He expected disapproval; instead, he found himself unable to interpret the assessing look in her eyes. 'I teach both Latin and Greek, besides the modern languages.'

'I had not realised you teach boys,' he remarked, more to make conversation than anything, and was surprised by the flash of irritation in her steady gaze.

'I do not. These days I teach only girls. Perhaps your lordship does not consider the female mind has the capacity for the ancient languages?'

'I had never given it any consideration,' he admitted. 'But I can see no useful purpose in it for a woman.'

'Beside the intellectual discipline, the improved understanding of modern tongues and of history and art?' she enquired frostily.

'Well, there is that, of course, but if a girl is to marry…'

'Not all of us do,' Miss Scott informed him. 'I see no reason why an unmarried lady should have her intellectual range diminished because of that. Nor why a married woman may not be educated.' Her expression softened slightly. 'No doubt you consider that a married woman has no need to use her intelligence on more than the ordering of the household? Not that housekeeping is as simple a task as most men appear to think it.'

Nick thought of his mother, smiling gently whenever any problem arose. 'Your papa will know what to do' was her inevitable response, and more recently, 'Whatever you say, Nicholas dear.' And his aunt, undoubtedly intelligent, vibrant, energetic—but quite content to place her business affairs entirely in his hands.

'There is no need for a lady to concern herself with difficult matters—' he began.

'But not all of us chose to be helpless pawns,' said another voice gently. Miss Grey walked into the room behind her friend. 'I believe you wish to see me, my lord?'

Nick took a step forward, found his foot entangled, glanced down and saw he was standing on a piece of fabric. He stooped to pick it up and found himself holding a garment he had no difficulty in recognising as a chemise. Neither young lady appeared prepared to help him out of his difficulty so he folded it neatly and placed it on the side-table. Keeping his face entirely bland, he looked up and found he had met his match in coolness in Miss Scott, whose expression showed not the slightest recognition that he had been handling a piece of intimate apparel. Miss Grey, on the other hand, appeared ready to give way to laughter. Her green eyes sparkled with amusement at his predicament and her lower lip was caught firmly between white teeth.

The thought of nipping that fullness between his own teeth struck him with a bolt of erotic heat. A flare of it must have shown in his eyes for instantly hers sobered, widened, and he wondered if she had read correctly the nature of his thoughts and was in tune with them. Then the moment of mutual awareness was gone and she was waving him towards the sofa.

'Will you take tea, my lord?'

'No, thank you. I have called simply with a message from Lady Parry.'

Talitha Grey answered the queries with a directness that reinforced his knowledge of her previously straitened circumstances. 'Trunks? Why, just the one, my lord, and a valise.'

'And several new bandboxes,' the governess added drily.

'Oh, yes. I was forgetting.' She turned to him, smiling slightly. 'I have been succumbing to the lure of shopping.'

'Indeed? In that case I am surprised you have had the time to attend to your new business venture.' He watched not Talitha but her friend and saw the look of surprise and speculation she directed at him. But to his disappointment the governess did not speak.

'Ventures, in the plural. Yes, when one has been accustomed to working for one's living, my lord, one can find plenty of time in the day for business. Shopping is hardly time-consuming.'

'I suspect you may modify your opinion on that after a short experience of my aunt's approach to the subject.'

Talitha merely smiled politely. It was intensely frustrating. Every time he spoke to her he had the impression that she was keeping a part of herself hidden from him and he only caught brief flashes of the real Talitha Grey. Now he had the question of her 'business interests' to add to the list for Tolliver to investigate.

It was not until Nick was halfway down the front steps that he caught himself wondering why he wanted to find out about that aspect of her life. She was being advised by Dover and by the bank; she was hardly going to do something imprudent. Nor was it his business if she did, as she had so frostily reminded him during that encounter in Gunter's.

He was not given to self-deception and he did not indulge in it now. Finding out about Miss Grey's 'secret' might have started out in his desire to protect his aunt. Now finding out everything about her had assumed an altogether different character. Nick Stangate smiled ruefully as he nodded to his groom and got up into his phaeton. This was becoming personal.

For Tallie, too, the encounters with Nick Stangate were beginning to feel very personal indeed. She felt gratitude, anger, fear and attraction in a disturbing mixture that was threatening to obsess her.

The degree to which she felt the various emotions he evoked varied wildly, depending on what he had just said to annoy or alarm her and also on those fleeting moments when their eyes met and locked and she felt as though a dentist's probe had touched a nerve. When it happened her heart beat rapidly, her breath caught and she felt a strange heated ache deep inside. Tallie told herself it was fear: fear at what he might find out about her, fear of exposure. But she was very much afraid that it was another raw, basic

emotion and one that young ladies, especially respectable unmarried young ladies, were not supposed to
feel.

She could only be grateful that for the first week
of her stay with Lady Parry in Bruton Street she did
not meet him once.

'Have you seen Nicholas lately?' Lady Parry enquired of her son at breakfast on the Wednesday after
Tallie's arrival.

'Hmm?' William put down the paper he was idly
conning and furrowed his brow in thought.
'Twice…no, three times. You know Nick, he just
strolls in when you least expect him. Now, when was
it? Oh, yes, he dropped in at Watier's when I was
playing cards with Hemsley and some fellows on Saturday. And he arrived at Jackson's Saloon just in time
to see me pop a terrific right over Jack's guard. That
was Monday afternoon…'

'Is Jackson the famous bare-knuckle fighter?' Tallie enquired. 'And you managed to hit him? My goodness!'

'Lord, no.' William blushed at her praise, but hastened to set her right. 'No one lands a punch on the
great Jackson unless he lets them. No, it was Jack
Hemsley.'

'Oh, I see. Still, I am sure you must be very good
to be admitted to Jackson's Saloon,' Tallie said encouragingly. 'Might I trouble you for the preserve?
Thank you. And you saw Lord Arndale for a third
time?'

'Er, yes. Last night.' William seemed disinclined
to explain further, but Tallie, convinced she was beginning to see a pattern, persisted.

'And where was that? I do enjoy hearing about all

these fashionable places. I can hardly wait until I am ready to be going about in Society,' she added artlessly.

'This wasn't the sort of place you would be going,' William said with a harassed glance at his mother. Lady Parry, however, had returned to her correspondence and was busily slitting envelopes with her butter-knife.

'Do tell,' Tallie encouraged quietly, giving William the sort of look designed to convince him he was an exciting rake.

'Well…it was a bit of a hell, if you must know. I was feeling rather uncomfortable actually.' William was blushing. 'Some of the young ladies there were… were…'

'Not ladies?' Tallie suggested. Bless the boy, he really was a decent young man.

'Exactly that.' He looked grateful for her tactful description. 'I wasn't sure how to leave, I mean, I'd been invited by one of the guests and it seemed rude just to walk away. And then Nick strolls in, looking bored to death, curls a lip and drawls that he's been looking for me all over and had I forgotten we were going to White's that evening? *White's!* As if I'd forget that!'

His eyes gleamed and Tallie recalled that the club in question was the most exclusive in town and certainly one which a mere youth would not have the faintest hope of joining. The honour of being invited to spend an evening there by one of the members must have been overwhelming.

'So you went with him?' William was positively glowing. 'I imagine Mr Hemsley was a little put out.'

'Well, a bit. But you don't argue with Nick, you

know.' It did not seem to occur to William that he had not told her he had been in the hell at the instigation of Jack Hemsley.

Tallie returned to her toast with a thoughtful expression. So, Nick Stangate was putting himself out to intervene every time William was in the company of the rakish Mr Hemsley. And he was managing to do so without his young cousin realising that he had a guardian angel at his heels. Very clever—and thoroughly admirable. She was sure that for a mature and experienced man about town, bear-leading an inexperienced youth must be a complete bore.

She took a bite of toast and wondered if Mr Hemsley was aware of just how closely his pursuit of a rich young lordling was being observed. She rather suspected he was, for he had not struck her as a fool, however unpleasant his character. Lord Arndale had better watch his back and take care.

It was one of his most admirable characteristics, she realised: taking care. He took care of William, of his aunt—and of naked models in garrets. She rather suspected that his irritating interference in her life was part of that too. She had become family, so she was going to be looked after whether she liked it or not. With a little shiver Tallie decided she liked it rather too much.

Tallie was soon able to test this new-found charitable feeling. His lordship was waiting for her that afternoon as she and Lady Parry came back into the house.

Chapter Nine

'Nicholas dearest!' His aunt kissed him thoroughly, stood back to scan him from head to foot, flicked an invisible speck from his lapels and announced, 'I like that coat. Now, I must go and change before the orphanage committee meeting. Tallie, you need to rest. Nicholas, we have been indulging in an absolute orgy. Goodness, is that the time…?'

'Orgy?' Tallie made herself look at Nick, only to be met with one of his blandest, most infuriating expressions.

She raised an eyebrow. It was difficult, but she had been practising in front of the mirror and was almost satisfied with the effect. 'Of shopping, my lord.' Carefully sweeping the skirts of her newest afternoon dress to one side, she sank elegantly onto the sofa. 'Will you not sit down, my lord?'

'Certainly.' He took the chair she had indicated and sat, legs crossed, one booted foot swinging gently, fingers steepled and just touching his lips.

Tallie tried not to look at his mouth and stared at his booted foot instead.

'Lobb's,' he said helpfully. 'That is a very fetching gown.'

'Thank you. Lady Parry's taste is excellent. I am much indebted to her guidance.'

'My lord.' Tallie stared at him. 'You forgot to say "my lord". Up to then you had managed to insert it in every sentence. You also forgot to raise that eyebrow again, although I can quite understand why—it is devilishly uncomfortable until one has the knack of it.'

Tallie glared at him, then her sense of humour got the better of her and she laughed. 'It is, is it not? You do it to such effect I thought it worth cultivating to depress pretension. But it gives me a headache if I practise for too long.'

'And what did I do that required depressing?' he enquired gently.

'Nothing,' Tallie admitted. 'I was practising, my lord.'

'There you go again! I have a perfectly good name, Tallie. Why not use it?'

Tallie. He had called her not just by her Christian name, but by the diminutive that only her friends used. It sounded different on his lips. She gave herself a little shake and said firmly, 'It would be quite inappropriate.'

'You call Lady Parry Aunt Kate, you call my cousin William. I did suggest to you once before that you adopt me as an honorary cousin.'

The idea of *adopting* anyone as large, sophisticated and self-reliant as Nicholas Stangate was a preposterous fancy. Tallie felt her lips quirk and saw an answering twist on his. 'Very well, Cousin Nicholas.'

'Thank you, Cousin Talitha.' So, she was Talitha

now. She fought with the fantasy of hearing him whisper *Tallie* while he...while he...

'I am glad I caught you at home,' he was saying, reaching for a slim portfolio. 'Most of the house-agents are in the City and other areas where it is un-suitable for you and Miss Scott to be going unaccom-panied. I have had my man of business assemble some particulars that should meet your requirements for both your projected schemes. If they are not to your liking he will find others. Meanwhile, if you or Miss Scott wish to view—' He broke off to get to his feet in response to Tallie positively leaping to hers. 'Cousin Talitha?'

'How did you find out?' she demanded. 'Who has been spying on us? Or have you been worming it out of Zenna?'

'Miss Scott is the soul of discretion,' he said, sounding far too soothing. 'I would not dream of *worming* anything out of your friend behind your back.'

'But you are quite happy to set spies on me—be-hind my back?'

'Only to protect you,' he said, still so reasonably that Tallie wanted to hit him. 'It is your choice which properties you select.'

'After they have been edited and approved by you,' she said furiously, pacing back and forth on the fine Oriental rug. She used to be calm, she used to hide every feeling, she used to be self-contained—what was he doing to her?

'Cousin Talitha, young ladies do not conduct busi-ness on their own account.' He was standing relaxed by his chair, one hand resting on the back of it, his eyes hooded to hide the gleam that betrayed his appreciation of the sight she presented as she swept to and fro.

Tallie came to a halt in front of him, glaring up into his eyes. 'I am not a ''young lady'', I am an independent woman. I have had to earn my own living and I intend to carry on doing just that. I will be for ever grateful to Miss Gower for her wonderful legacy and to Lady Parry for the opportunity to experience the Season, but by this time next year I need to know what I am doing and how I am going to spend the rest of my life. And I need to prepare now.'

'But you will be spending the rest of your life as someone's wife,' he said, smiling at her. And that d…d…*damned* eyebrow was quirked at her as though she was an idiot.

'Really, my lord? I am twenty-five years old. I have been earning my living as a milliner. I have nothing to recommend me…' He opened his mouth. Tallie swept on, 'And before you say that I have my fortune to recommend me I must tell you, sir, that I would go back to hat-making for my livelihood rather than marry a man who wanted me for my money.'

'You think that your fortune is all that you have to recommend you?' Nick took her by the shoulders and turned her so that she was facing the great mirror that hung over the fireplace. 'Look at yourself.'

Tallie looked. Looking back at her was a young woman of slightly more than average height, dressed in a fashionable gown of soft spring green that clung to full breasts and skimmed over a slender figure. Her eyes, just a little darker than the gown, were wide and her lips full and slightly parted. Her colour was high, white cheeks flushed with rose.

Behind her a tall man held her with hands that

rested firmly on each shoulder. In the glass their eyes met—hers wide and startled, his dark and hot as she had never seen them.

'If you would just let your hair free a little…' One hand left her shoulder to touch the pins that kept the gilt mass tight and disciplined.

With a gasp Tallie whirled round and found herself right against Nick's chest. 'No!'

'No?' He was not asking her about her hair. His voice was deep, dark, husky. His hands were on her shoulders again, pulling her inexorably against him. 'No?'

She should step back. She should say 'No'. She should…she should let him kiss her.

Tallie closed her eyes against the fire in his and stopped pulling back. The heat of him remembered from the studio seemed to burn her flesh through the fine muslin of her gown. The scent of him—male, exciting, overlain with a civilising veneer of sharp cologne—*that* she had not remembered.

Nor had she imagined how his mouth would feel when it came down on hers. How could she know what her first kiss would be like? She had not realised that his mouth would be both firm and soft, demanding yet tender. She had not dreamed that her lips, already parted in surprise, would open of their own accord under the pressure of his, that his tongue would slip caressingly, shockingly between them. And she had had not the slightest suspicion that a caress on the lips would make her breasts ache, would send strange, uncomfortable, wanton messages down—

Tallie jerked back gasping and instantly Nick released her. His eyes were dark, his breath was short, but the imperturbable mask of control was back. Then she made the error of dropping her eyes from his and became jarringly aware of just how unsuited for hiding the effects of male arousal the fashion of the day for tight trousers was.

It was probably impossible to blush more than she was already, Tallie thought wildly as she took refuge behind the chair. And she had thought Nicholas Stangate made her feel safe! She must have been insane. Insanely blind. 'My lord…'

'Cousin Nicholas.'

'That was hardly cousinly!' She could not look at him.

'Cousins may kiss. And adopted ones certainly may. I am sorry to have discomforted you, Cousin Talitha; it was just that you appeared to be quite blind to the effect you are undoubtedly going to have on a large proportion of the men who meet you. It is best that you are on your guard before some rake takes advantage of that enchanting modesty of yours. I thought a demonstration would be advisable.'

'Demonstration!' Now she did look at him, incredulity showing in both voice and expression.

'But of course. You are quite safe with me. I will go and leave you to rest as Aunt Kate advised. Good day, Cousin Talitha.'

Safe? *Safe?* She would be safer in a locked room with Jack Hemsley! At least she knew exactly what her reaction to any advance from him would be—a slapped face and a briskly raised knee would be a good start. But with Nicholas Stangate she also knew exactly what she wanted to happen, and she knew too he was the last man in London with whom it was safe to let her guard down. And to think that only a few days ago she had decided it would be satisfying to provoke a response from him that was neither controlled nor temperate!

Now it seemed she had fallen neatly into her own trap. He appeared capable of reining back his passion as it suited him. She was the one left palpitating with confused, humiliating desire.

Tallie was not left to brood on Nick Stangate for long. The next day Kate Parry finally announced herself satisfied with her preparation of her protégée for the start of the Season, but with one omission.

'Your hair, Tallie,' she announced, making her jump and almost drop the portfolio of properties Nick had left behind. Infuriatingly they all looked highly promising, both for the school and for the lodgings. Tallie had too much good sense not to use what had been laid out for her so efficiently, however she felt about the source of the information.

'My hair, Aunt Kate?' Tallie set down the portfolio and eyed Lady Parry cautiously.

'Yes, dear. Everything else is perfect. Your clothes and accessories are just as they should be, you have proved a quick study with your dancing lessons and I could not believe how rapidly you have soaked up all I had to tell you about Society and how to go on. That just leaves your hair.'

'But, ma'am, I like it like this. It is suitable.'

'It is certainly suitable for a hired companion. It is not at all suitable for a fashionable young lady. And definitely not for one who is going to make her come-out at the Duchess of Hastings's ball tomorrow night. Now, Mr Jordan is coming this afternoon to cut it for you.'

'Oh. I am very sorry, Aunt Kate, but I have arranged to take this portfolio of properties to Upper Wimpole Street and discuss them with Zenna. I had not realised you had other plans.'

'Why not send a note round and ask her to come here? She might enjoy watching Mr Jordan at work.'

'Will he not object to an audience?'

'Tallie, he is going to be here as your employee; besides, he is bound to want to make a good impression on you by being as obliging as possible.'

'To me? But why?'

'Dearest, I keep trying to impress upon you that as the possessor of a fortune you are a very eligible *partie*. You are sure to take and it will do him good if you recommend him to other ladies.'

Tallie found this hard to believe, almost as hard as she found it to believe Nick telling her she would find herself the target of numerous amorous advances. But she could not bring herself to refuse whatever her kind friend wished her to do, so she obediently scribbled a note for Zenna and dispatched it with a footman.

To her surprise Zenna was not at all adverse to watching her having her hair styled, even tossing aside the portfolio of houses with a careless, 'I will look at it this evening.'

So Tallie submitted to the scissors so expertly wielded by Mr Jordan. She was prepared to dislike him, for she had never come across anyone quite so affected as the stick-thin coiffeur. She was convinced that he was wearing maquillage and his hands had certainly been manicured into an almost feminine softness.

However, from the moment he set those delicate

hands on her hair he stopped mincing and became impressively professional. After an hour of brushing, pinning, snipping, curling and further snipping, he stepped back and gestured to the other ladies to admire the results. The response he got would have gratified the heart of even the most exacting artist.

'There,' said Lady Parry triumphantly. 'Now you are ready for your first ball.'

Nick Stangate accepted a glass of brandy from his cousin and leaned back in the chair by the fireside. 'Stop fidgeting at that neckcloth,' he advised as William peered in the mirror for the third time and prodded at the gold pin securing the crisp folds of palest lavender linen.

William came and took the chair opposite. 'How much longer can they be?' he enquired impatiently. Occasionally he squired his mother to dances, but he had never known her to take so long getting ready that the horses had to be sent back to the mews.

'As long as it takes for Aunt Kate to make her arrival at exactly the right moment,' Nick said lazily, swirling the amber liquid round and admiring the way the light hit it. 'She will wait until all the people she wants to impress are there and before it becomes too much of a squeeze.'

'But why?' William grumbled. 'She usually likes to get there early, all the better for a good gossip.'

'I think we are about to find out.' Nick got to his feet, forcing himself to do so slowly. He sauntered out into the hall with William at his heels and waited at the foot of the stairs, his head tilted so he could see the full sweep of polished mahogany treads.

His ears had caught the sound of bedroom doors

shutting. He did not have long to wait. Faintly the sound of Lady Kate urging someone to go on in front of her reached the men in the hall, then a vision appeared.

Nick thought he had been prepared for what he would see. But he was not prepared for this. A tall slender figure in a dress of silver spider gauze over white crepe appeared to be floating down the stairs, one white-gloved hand resting lightly on the rail.

Huge green eyes, serious with the effort of maintaining both poise and a sweep of fragile skirts; full red lips slightly parted with nervousness and, crowning it all, a crown of gilt curls falling from a severely upswept mass of hair. As she got closer he realised that her face was pale and the soft tendrils of hair that had been teased loose around her temples were quivering slightly.

Tallie looked exquisite, terrified and, for the first time since he had known her, achingly vulnerable. There was no sign of the fierce independence, the anger when he crossed her, the aloof calm behind which she could so disconcertingly vanish along with her secrets.

Nick felt his entire body tighten, harden, racked with desire and that desire warred with a fierce protectiveness. He wanted to seize her in his arms, carry her to the nearest bed—or the floor, or the sofa—or take her here and now in the hallway. And he wanted to stop any man, himself included, who so much as laid a finger on her.

For once in his life Lord Arndale found words beyond him and it was his inexperienced cousin who knew exactly the right thing to say.

'Tallie, you look absolutely gorgeous. May I have a waltz?'

Nick felt more than saw Tallie's gaze sweep over him and past him to William. He saw her anxious face break into a soft smile of relief at the frank admiration and then she was past him in a soft cloud of silk gauze and jasmine perfume before he could find his own voice.

'Thank you, William. I would love that; here, please, can you write it on my card?' Nick watched as his cousin lifted the little folded card with its minute pencil that dangled from her wrist and carefully inscribed his name. He was aware of his aunt arriving at the foot of the stairs beside him and he turned abruptly to greet her as Tallie raised one hand to touch William's lapel. 'That neckcloth is the best yet,' she confided quietly.

Was Aunt Kate regarding him with covert amusement? People did not as a rule laugh at Nick Stangate. He narrowed his eyes at her, but she simply smiled and whispered wickedly, 'Close your mouth, dear,' before stepping to one side to allow room for her dresser who was carrying the ladies' cloaks.

It took some time to fit the four of them into the carriage without crushing skirts, knocking tall silk hats or mangling the magnificent plumes that were topping Lady Parry's coiffure, but it was achieved at last.

Nick hoped the forced closeness might break the ice a little with Tallie, for he had begun to realise that a good part of her nervousness as she came downstairs was because of their last encounter. He had been torn between kicking himself for letting that kiss happen, a fervent desire to do it again and a rather cooler interest in what it had taught him about her.

Whatever the secret she was guarding from him so carefully, it did not involve an entanglement with a man. There was no mistaking the innocent shock as his lips had met hers. That had been her first kiss and he felt a strange sense of privilege that it was he who had given it to her. Was that just a glimpse of a man's feelings when he took his bride's virginity? The thought shook him so much that he shifted in his seat abruptly, knocking William's elbow.

'Sorry. Cramp.' The thought of initiating Tallie into the arts of lovemaking was so powerfully erotic he could only be thankful for the dimly lit interior of the carriage. But it was the word 'bride' that really shook him. Marrying a milliner-come-lady, and one with presumably disreputable secrets, was not in his plans at all. He had no need of a bride with a fortune, he was eligible enough to have his pick of whatever Society beauties crossed his path and his intention was to find a well-bred young lady who would fit neatly into his life, produce his heirs, ornament his drawing room and generally make life agreeable.

Nick gritted his teeth, crossed his legs with care and reviewed his tactics. Discover exactly what that secret was. That was the first thing. Deal with it, if that were possible, cover it up if it were not. And if it was really bad, remove Miss Grey from his aunt's household and set her up with her school and her lodging-houses and whatever other schemes she had in mind. Safely out of Society, that was the best plan. It would be the most comfortable solution for every-one concerned. And in the meantime, make sure that no one made her a declaration. The thought of a lurking scandal being compounded by the girl having a romantic entanglement with a member of the *ton* was too much.

In consequence he emerged from the carriage looking so grim that rumours began to fly around the ballroom that Lord Arndale had suffered a crushing reversal on the 'Change, that his favourite racehorse had died or that he was about to be called out by an enraged husband.

A little thought caused these speculations to be dismissed. Arndale was too sharp to be burnt by his investments, his racing stable was too well stocked for him to suffer greatly by the loss of just one animal and he was well known to conduct his *amours* with the utmost discretion and a scrupulous avoidance of the charms of married ladies.

It was a mystery and one that gained savour by the fact that he did not appear to intend to dance and instead stationed himself at his aunt's side by a pillar against which he leaned, arms crossed, regarding the dance floor with brooding indifference.

'He is *so* romantic,' one impressionable young lady remarked languishingly to her brother. 'Just like Lord Byron.'

'Dash it all, Lizzie,' he replied, shocked. 'You can't compare Arndale to that poseur of a poet! Byron's dashed bad *ton*—and he's putting on weight.'

The object of their attentions was watching his cousin circle the dance floor with Tallie in his arms and was doing his level best not to scowl. They made a very fetching picture, both blond, both tall enough to be striking and both with a natural grace, which made up for the fact that William was still inclined to fall over his feet on occasion and Tallie had never danced in public before.

He had no real fear that Tallie was going to try and attach William whatever she said to tease him, so why he should feel so thoroughly out of sorts he could not imagine. He had a plan to deal with the chit and that should be the end of it.

Lady Parry had attracted her usual group of bosom friends around her and from the hum of conversation he could tell she had done her work well to prepare for Tallie's first appearance.

Ladies were sighing at the thought of the well-born girl forced by undeserved poverty to work with her needle and skilful fingers to earn an honest living. It was rapidly borne in on Nick that his inventive aunt had done more than sow a few seeds and let natural sympathy do the rest. She had been engaged on some major embroidery.

'How dreadful that a parent's well-intentioned plan should go so frightfully amiss,' one dowager was saying to another.

'Indeed,' the other lady responded, unaware of Nick's sharp ears bent in her direction. 'To have tied up Miss Grey's fortune until she was twenty-five in order to deter fortune hunters was very wise, but then to have omitted to provide her with the means of support until she reached that age...'

Nick swivelled slowly to meet his aunt's eyes and was met with a look of calm innocence that almost charmed a grin out of him. '*Baggage,*' he mouthed silently before turning to see where Tallie and William had got to. The music had ended and she ought to be on her way back to her chaperon.

There she was, talking with William in a knot of

attentive gentlemen. Nick caught William's eye and jerked his head slightly in a signal to steer her back, but he was too late. The music struck up again and Miss Grey was being led out onto the floor by Jack Hemsley.

Chapter Ten

Tallie knew perfectly well, even if William did not, that she should have made her way back to Lady Parry and allowed her chaperon to approve her partners. And she was certain she should not had agreed when Mr Hemsley had appeared at her elbow and had begged the privilege of the next dance. But the sight of him had so flustered her that she had not been able to decline gracefully.

It was a quadrille and Tallie quailed somewhat at the thought of the complexities of the steps. They joined a set with three other couples and at first Tallie was too focused on setting to the right partner at the right moment to pay much attention to Jack Hemsley.

But after the first repeat her confidence came back and she relaxed. Mr Hemsley was fortunately behaving himself impeccably and, if she had not known just how despicably he *could* behave to a defenceless woman, she would have felt perfectly comfortable in his company. It was obvious he had not the slightest idea he was dancing with the model for the 'Diana' picture and she even doubted he recalled the mousy milliner he had winked at in Lady Parry's drawing room.

She was quite certain, however, that he had garnered every scrap of gossip about her fortune and circumstances and this dance was the opening salvo in his campaign to woo the new heiress. It would be amusing to thank him coolly after the dance and to refuse another. She had no sooner resolved on this admirably sensible course of action than the parting lines of dancers gave her a view of Nick Stangate watching her across the floor.

His disapproval was as palpable as if he had spoken and she flushed angrily.

Did he think that after kissing her and lecturing her he was now going to try and exert some form of control over her in the ballroom? Well, it was time he was taught a lesson, Tallie fumed inwardly. She would show him she was not easily taken in by rakes and fortune hunters and could perfectly easily handle the likes of Jack Hemsley.

She pushed away the knowledge that she had been hurt that evening by his silence when she came downstairs. If she thought about it she would cry, which was ridiculous. She did not need Nick Stangate's approval or admiration. She knew she was looking very fine. Lady Parry had told her, William's open admiration told her, the expressions of the people she met told her.

Tallie tried not to refine too much on the look on Nick's face as she had walked tremulously down those endless stairs. She had expected him to be pleased at the transformation, to smile, to show some warmth and admiration. Instead his face had set into stone, his eyes had glittered coldly and he had not even managed to make some token remark.

Her thoughts must have shown on her face for, as the last notes of the dance echoed around the room and she rose from her curtsy, Jack Hemsley asked, 'Have I displeased you, Miss Grey? Do not say I am responsible for that frown.'

'Was I frowning? I do beg your pardon. It is just the…the noise and the heat. I am not accustomed to balls, you see.'

'Then you must have a glass of lemonade and some air, Miss Grey.' He was guiding her from the floor with practised smoothness, one hand just resting under her elbow, smiling and bowing as they made their way through the throng.

'I am all right, really, Mr Hemsley. If I could just go back to Lady Parry.' It was difficult to know how to extricate herself without making a scene.

'In a moment, Miss Grey, you are quite flushed. I am sure there is a risk of you swooning if you return immediately to that crush and heat. Now just here… ah, yes.'

He pushed open a door and Tallie found herself in a little room, almost like a box at the theatre. It opened out onto a balcony overlooking the garden, although the windows were closed against the chill March night.

'I will just open this a crack, so, and if you sit here…' he patted a sofa encouragingly '…then you will not be in the draught, but you will have the benefit of the air.'

It all seemed very sensible, even innocuous. 'Thank you, sir.' Tallie sat down, suddenly aware of just how warm she was feeling. 'Perhaps if I was to drink some lemonade as you suggested, I will be able to go back in a moment.'

'Of course.' Instead of going out for the drink, he sat next to her and lifted her hand in his. 'Why, your pulse is racing my dear Miss Grey. I think I had better remain here for a moment just in case you feel faint. Put your head on my shoulder so...'

'Stop it!' Tallie struggled to stand up and found herself very effectively pinned against the upholstery. Mr Hemsley might affect the airs of a languid man of fashion, but the muscles under his coat were alarmingly hard as she pushed against them.

'Just one little kiss before we go back, my dear.'

Tallie freed a hand and swung it. It made satisfying contact with the side of his head, but left her gasping and clutching her wrist with the jarring pain. Hemsley's hands groped for her, found her hair and gripped in an effort to turn her face for a kiss.

Tallie wrenched back and felt pins and combs falling down. With a jerk of her knee she was free, on her feet, halfway to the door.

It opened and she found herself face to face with Nick, William at his back. She stopped dead, the carefully piled edifice of her coiffure broke free and hair cascaded down her back. Behind her Jack Hemsley swore, a sharp, vicious sound. In front of her she saw Nick pull William into the room and slam the door to behind him.

'Stop anyone coming in.'

William placed his back against the panels and stared at the scene. The sight of the shock and distress on his young face hurt Tallie more than anything else.

'You will name your seconds, Hemsley.' Nick sounded icily calm.

'Now look here, I know how this looks…'

'It looks as though you were assaulting Miss Grey.'

'Well, I wasn't. Thought she was going to faint—heat and so on. Brought her in here, opened the window, see. Wouldn't do a damn fool thing like that if I was going to tumble the girl now, would I?'

William straightened up from the door, his fists clenched. Nick put out a hand and stopped him. 'You will speak of Miss Grey with respect or I will not trouble with form and deal with you here and now.'

'You wouldn't do that—look, Nick old chap, it's all a misunderstanding, silly chit thought I was trying to—'

The blow landed with a satisfying thump right on the point of Hemsley's chin. Nick stepped forward, rubbing his balled fist in the other palm. 'Get up. I want to do that again.' He sounded as though he was asking the man to deal another hand of cards.

Tallie swirled round and stared at the wall. She didn't want to see what Nick was doing, didn't want to see the look on his face as he methodically began to take Jack Hemsley to pieces. And she did not want to see the disillusion on William's face as he realised what the man he thought was his friend was capable of with a young woman living in his house.

'Now get out. William, make sure he gets away from this room without anyone seeing him. And, Hemsley, don't even think of speaking of this, will you? Because if you do, I'll break your neck.'

Thank God, he hadn't killed him. Tallie wondered vaguely if she was going to be sick. Probably not, she concluded after a fierce struggle with her stomach. Was she alone? William had gone, and Hemsley. The room was quiet except for the sounds of music and talk and laughter penetrating the heavy door.

She put out a hand to the wall in front of her and just stood, head bowed, her hair shielding her face. Then she knew she was not alone. Someone moved behind her, so close she could feel his heat through her flimsy gown and hands turned her into the safety of soft linen, encircling arms, a strong comforting heartbeat.

'Nick.'

'What?' His breath stirred her hair. She felt a weight on the top of her head as though he had laid his cheek there.

'Just…Nick. I am sorry to have been so foolish, I really thought he was going to get me a glass of lemonade. He won't say anything, will he?'

'Not and expect to live, no. He is a coward and I am both a better shot and a better swordsman than he is.' There was a pause. 'Are you crying?'

'No,' lied Tallie, trying not to sniff. She felt so safe, so warm, so *cherished*.

'In that case, why is the front of my shirt becoming soggy?' Nick enquired.

Tallie felt his hand under her chin and her face was ruthlessly tipped up despite her efforts to resist. 'I have to tell you, Cousin Talitha, your nose is pink, but your eyes look absolutely enchanting swimming in tears. It is quite obvious that you did not pay the slightest attention to the warning I gave you the other day. I will just have to repeat it.'

This time the kiss was not so gentle, not so careful. Tallie found her lips parting under the onslaught of his, then gasped as his tongue invaded ruthlessly. Her body appeared to understand exactly what that intrusion meant, wanted more, was telling her to react in ways that were new and shamingly wanton in order to incite him.

She felt her own tongue darting to meet his, to caress, challenge his, flicker daringly into the heat of his mouth. Her body arched against him, soft against the answering hardness. Her breasts ached, her loins ached, she ached...

There was a knock on the door.

When William peered round, he found Tallie lying back against the sofa cushions looking flushed and Nick on one knee on the carpet gathering up hairpins.

'Has he gone?'

William nodded. 'I followed him. He went out through the back; no one saw him. I brought you a glass of lemonade, Tallie.'

Tallie forced a smile for him, her heart aching at the look of distress on his face. 'Thank you, William, I am quite all right, truly.'

'What can I do? Shall I fetch Mama and send for the carriage to come round to the back?'

'No.' Nick's voice was sharp. 'The ball has hardly started, Tallie cannot simply vanish like that. It will cause talk. Help me find all these pins and then go to the kitchens and ask for some rice powder.'

'Rice powder? I can't just—'

'You are Lord Parry and a guest. If you ask them for a bucket of earthworms, they'll give it to you. Tallie, how many pins were there?'

Tallie racked her brains. 'Twelve, I think, and two combs.'

'I can find ten, that will have to do. William, have you got a comb?'

Tallie found herself perched on the edge of the sofa

while Nick combed, cursed and muttered through a mouthful of hairpins. Eventually she felt the weight of her hair lift and put up a tentative hand. 'Nick, it's wonderful! How did you learn how to do that?'

'I don't think I want to tell you,' he said. 'It would shock you. Well, Aunt Kate will be able to tell something has happened, but I don't think anyone else will suspect more than overenthusiastic participation in a country dance. Now, where's William?'

He appeared on the question, flushed and more than a little put out. 'They looked at me as though I was mad,' he muttered, handing over a large jar.

Nick grinned. 'I want to powder Tallie's nose, not bake a batch of whatever one cooks with the stuff, you young idiot. Oh well, it will give the housemaids something to speculate about in the morning when they find it.' He drew a handkerchief out of his pocket, dipped it in the jar and turned to Tallie. 'Sit still. There, that's better, now you look less like a white rabbit and more like an overheated young lady.'

Tallie dropped her eyes, too embarrassed to meet his amused gaze. He stood up and straightened his cuffs, then dabbed at his grazed knuckles with the powdered handkerchief. 'William, go and tell your mother that Tallie is all right and will be out in a moment.'

There was a long silence after the door closed. Tallie got carefully to her feet and smoothed down her gown. Surely the moment she stepped outside the door people would look at her and know that only a few minutes before she had been locked in Nick Stangate's heated embrace, kissing him back with all the fervour she could. Surely *wanton* was branded across her forehead?

'Tallie,' he said softly, one hand on the doorknob.
'Yes?'

'Will you not tell me your secret?'

Tallie's eyes flew to his face. Of all the things he
might have said, this was furthest from her imaginings. 'No!' she blurted out. 'No! Was that why you
kissed me? You thought you would confuse and be-
fuddle me until I would tell you *anything*? No!' And
she was through the door and into the corridor before
he could stop her. Three hurried steps and she was
on the threshold of the ballroom. Tallie ignored the
footsteps behind her, took a deep breath, fixed a social
smile on her burning lips and, with pounding heart,
stepped calmly into the mêlée.

She made her way to Lady Parry's side and sat
down with a careful smile on her face. After one startled glance her chaperon handed her a fan and said
brightly for the benefit of their near neighbours, 'Talitha dear, how often did I warn you about the country
dances? You look a sad romp.'

'Yes, Aunt Kate. I am sorry, Aunt Kate.' Tallie did
her best to shrink back while around her amused
chaperons tutted and smiled at her overenthusiasm.

She was rescued eventually by William asking her
to accompany him to the supper room. He tucked her
hand firmly under his elbow, treated her as though
she was made of glass and scowled so forbiddingly
at any man who came near that they ended up in sole
possession of a table.

Tallie made herself nibble at a savoury patty and
relax in the hope that William would relax too. It was
rather like being escorted by a large, fierce dog.
'Where is Lord Arndale?'

'I'm not sure. I think he has left; he was certainly

looking like thunder when you came out of that room. And he was pretty short with me when I tried to ask him what he was going to do next.'

'What...what did he say?'

'Didn't make sense.' William's brow furrowed. 'He said it was time to take some precautions and at least he now knew what he was dealing with. Does that make any sense to you?'

'No.' Tallie shook her head. 'None at all, unless... William, he wouldn't have gone after Mr Hemsley, would he?'

'What, to call him out after all? No, not without me. He'd need at least one second, and I'm the only one he can involve without risking talk.' William offered Tallie a plate of sweetmeats and, when she shook her head, stood up. 'Let's get back, shall we? Do you think we can have another waltz without all the old biddies shaking their heads over us?'

Tallie followed him, just relieved at the thought of being in a safe pair of arms and having something to think about other than Nick Stangate. All the contradictions were back, tearing her apart, making her unable to think about him coherently, let alone know how to deal with him.

He had saved her again, this time with his anger and his physical courage rather than his quick wits and self-restraint. And he had aroused in her feelings and longings that she could hardly comprehend, let alone control. And then he had struck at her with that question about her secret. He had tried to trick her into an answer when he must have known she was at her most vulnerable, must have known that he himself had contributed to that vulnerability.

Nick Stangate was ruthless and dangerous, and he

had most cause to be when he thought something of his was threatened. If he found out the truth about her, he would see it as a direct threat to his family, never mind how forgiving Lady Kate was inclined to be about it. And now he knew how she reacted to being in his arms, he had a potent weapon she had to make certain he never again had the opportunity to use against her. *Never.*

Chapter Eleven

The household in Bruton Street received no visits from Lord Arndale during the week following the Duchess's ball. Which was not to say that he was not making himself very much felt.

Tallie heard from Zenna that she was receiving particulars of houses almost daily. Then there was a visit from a very helpful clerk who offered Miss Scott his escort to any properties she might wish to view.

'He brought Lord Arndale's card with him,' she explained on a fleeting visit to ask if she might borrow a maid to accompany her. Lady Parry had agreed immediately, explaining that she had a parlour maid with aspirations to become a ladies' maid. 'It will be useful practise for her to learn how to behave when out with a lady.'

William reported bumping into his cousin in various clubs and once as he emerged from a house near Pickering Place. 'Asked him what on earth he was doing there. He gave me one of his poker-faced looks and said he was calling on his agent. Rum sort of place for an agent if you ask me.'

But, disconcertingly, Nicholas appeared at every

function Tallie attended. He did not ask her to dance or engage her in conversation, merely stopping long enough to give the appearance of normality before moving on to the card tables or another dancing partner.

Tallie moved rapidly from feeling relieved to being intrigued and then downright piqued—especially as she was beginning to enjoy a flattering amount of success with her come-out. The least Nicholas could do was to ask her to dance occasionally. When his parting shot at Lady Cressett's musical evening was, 'I am glad to see you are doing nothing indiscreet or unwise', Tallie was filled with an urge to do something quite outrageous out of sheer defiance.

Fortunately nothing occurred to her and the next afternoon she set off in the Parrys' carriage for a cosy evening in Upper Wimpole Street to discuss the lodging-house scheme with Mrs Blackstock.

She arrived early enough to spend some time with Millie before she set off for the Opera House and listened with interest to tales of backstage rivalries, Millie's excellent progress in her singing and the flattering number of floral tributes she was receiving.

Tallie caught Zenna's eye. She had confided her experience with Jack Hemsley because she wanted to put Zenna on her guard if she had any further contact with him. Now she raised an eyebrow and nodded slightly in Millie's direction. Zenna shrugged and a few moments later took the opportunity to whisper, 'I have not seen him around, but it doesn't mean she isn't seeing him at the Opera House.'

'Probably hiding his bruises,' Tallie said grimly, remembering the sound of those blows thudding home on flesh and bone.

* * *

By seven o'clock Tallie and Mrs Blackstock found themselves alone. Zenna had been invited to visit the family of one of her ex-pupils and Millie had departed for the Opera House in a hackney carriage.

'I'll just spread out the details of the ones we thought most suitable,' Tallie suggested, picking up the sheaf of house particulars. 'If I move these things off the table... Is this not Millie's reticule?'

Tallie held it up and Mrs Blackstock looked anxious. 'Oh, dear, it is, she must have forgotten it. Is her purse inside?'

A quick glance found the stocking purse nestling within, along with Millie's house key.

'I had better take a cab and go to the theatre,' Mrs Blackstock said with a sigh. 'She could borrow the cab fare back from another girl, I suppose, but knowing Millie she won't think of it until she's outside the theatre on her way home.'

Tallie looked at the older woman's tired face and got to her feet. 'No, I'll go. I haven't seen the new production yet and it will be fun to do so from backstage.'

Mrs Blackstock accepted the offer with gratitude, but insisted on coming out with Tallie until she found a respectable-looking hackney carriage and made sure that Tallie had Millie's stocking purse tucked inside her own reticule.

It took some while for the cab to make its way through the crowded evening streets from Upper Wimpole Street to the point where the Opera House stood on the corner of Haymarket and Pall Mall. Tallie had never been backstage before, but she knew where to find the stage door and the elderly man on duty there let her in willingly enough when she asked for Millie and tipped him a silver coin.

Tallie had to push her way through shabby, crowded corridors half-blocked with scenery flats and overflowing wicker baskets. Faintly she could hear the orchestra tuning up ahead and small knots of people hurried past, careless of whom they pushed aside in their haste.

Searching for someone who was not in such a hurry, Tallie turned into a quieter passageway. A door opened in front of her and a man wearing nothing but skintight inexpressibles, an obvious wig of red hair and a scowl stepped out. Tallie blinked at this apparition, unsure whether to scream or give way to giggles.

'John!' the man bawled, breaking off to glare at Tallie. 'Where in the name of Heaven is my fool of a dresser?'

'I have no idea, sir,' she replied, tearing her gaze away from his naked torso. 'Where is the chorus changing room?'

'Boys or girls?' he demanded.

'Girls!' Tallie said indignantly.

'Never can tell,' he observed obscurely. 'Down there, turn left, down the stairs, follow the cackling. John, you idle bastard!'

With her hands clamped over her ears Tallie hastened down the corridor in the direction of his pointing hand. There was no denying that the noise betrayed the location of the dressing-room, and when Tallie peeped round the door she could quite see why.

At least two dozen girls in various stages of undress filled the room, which was overheated, glaringly lit and reeked of perspiration, cheap scent and face powder.

At the nearest makeshift dressing-table to the door a dark girl in a thin chemise was clutching a post while another in pink fleshings that left nothing to the imagination hauled on her stay laces. 'Tighter, you silly tart,' the first girl gasped when the second stopped heaving. 'Tighter or I'll never get into the costume.'

'Fall out of it more like,' her friend retorted with a chuckle. 'That'll be a crowd pleaser.'

'Excuse me,' Tallie ventured when they both subsided panting, 'is Amelie LeNoir in here?'

'Millie? Yes, over there. Here, luv, just stick your finger on that knot while I do the bow. Ta. Millie!' She raised a voice trained to be heard from the front row of the chorus to the back seats in the gods. 'Visitor!'

Tallie extracted her finger from the tangle of stay laces and hurried over to where Millie's startled face appeared round a rack of costumes.

'You forgot your purse,' she explained, plumping down on a stool next to her friend. 'May I watch the performance from backstage?'

'Oh, thank you, Tallie,' Millie said warmly. 'Yes, of course, just take care you do not get in anyone's way—and you won't have to mind the language.'

Tallie settled down to absorb the atmosphere. Once her ears adjusted to the din and apparent chaos she began to pick out differences in costumes and to make some sense out of what was going on.

What had seemed to her first startled gaze to be Millie's state of near nudity was revealed as being a set of skin-toned fleshings over which a dress, apparently made of disparate pieces of fabric, was in fact held together by panels of pink net. It still revealed slender ankles and a quantity of Millie's well-turned calf.

Millie dusted her face with a vast powder puff and searched frantically through her cluttered table. 'Where's my lampblack? Jemmie!'

'Yes, miss?' A sharp-faced urchin appeared as though by magic.

'Where's my lampblack?'

'Suzy half-inched it,' the boy reported.

'Well, go and half-inch it back.'

'That's a boy!' Tallie gasped.

'Yes, I know. That's Jemmie. He's eight.'

'But you are all… I mean, half of you haven't got any clothes on and—'

'He's used to it,' Millie said calmly. 'Doesn't know any different. Thinks we're all his sisters in any case.'

A man stuck his head round the door. 'Overture and beginners! Shift your assets, you load of…' A chorus of abuse and thrown objects greeted this announcement and he ducked back through he door.

Tallie had a sudden vision of what Nick would say if he saw her now and had to suppress a laugh. He hoped she was being neither indiscreet nor unwise, did he? How would he categorise sitting in the middle of the opera-chorus dressing-room?

Millie was jamming a saucy hat on her head and picking up a beribboned shepherd's crook. 'Right. Here we go. I'm in the first scene with the other village girls.'

Tallie spent an exhilarating hour and a half being jostled, sworn at, deafened and shocked as she jammed herself into a corner of the wings and watched the performance. At last the final curtain came down and the cast rushed off, sweaty, exhausted and apparently ready to spend the rest of the night in a continuous party.

'Come on.' Millie caught Tallie's arm and dragged her along. 'I need to get changed before they let any of them in.'

'Who?' Tallie found herself acting as an impromptu dresser, unhooking Millie's costume and handing her pieces of cotton waste dipped in goose grease to clean off the make-up.

'We get the lot: the bloods, the peep o'day boys, a few flats, some pinks of the *ton*,' Millie said calmly. 'I don't encourage them myself, of course, but most of the girls have got followers.'

'They are going to let them in here?' Tallie squeaked. 'Can we go before that happens?'

'If I really rush.' Millie stepped into her petticoats and reached for a walking dress hanging on a hook beside her. 'Normally I'm never finished before they come in. So long as I'm dressed properly I don't mind. I just get on and do my hair and things.'

Tallie fidgeted with impatience, unable to see anything she could help with to finish Millie's toilette. The last thing she had expected was to be found in here by a crowd of amorously inclined men—judging from the very half-hearted efforts some of the girls were making to get changed, any man coming here this evening was not going to want to be discussing the finer points of the script.

'Where are my shoes?' Millie demanded, dropping to her knees and scrabbling under the table. 'Oh bother, I've kicked one right through...' She scuttled under the table in pursuit of her missing slipper, leaving Tallie by herself as the door swung open to admit a crowd of men.

They were in a dangerously boisterous mood, already half-drunk, clutching champagne bottles and more than ready to enjoy whatever favours the chorus girls were minded to share with them. Tallie retreated behind a rack of dresses, only to freeze as a very familiar voice reached her from the other side of the wall of mirrors.

'Why, Miss LeNoir! Charmed to see you. I did so enjoy your performance tonight.' Hemsley. Tallie pressed herself back against the wall, then realised that she could not abandon Millie, who was obviously responding with flattered delight to his compliments.

'Your voice goes from strength to strength,' he was confiding. 'I think you are wasted in the chorus. I happen to know someone who manages performances at Drury Lane. I know he would hear you as a favour to me. Why don't you let me drive you home this evening so we can discuss it? You don't want to be here with this rabble—it is unsuitable for an *artiste* of your talent.'

'Oh, thank you, Mr Hemsley, but I cannot drive with you this evening; besides, should you be out when you have so obviously been injured? Whatever happened?'

Tallie tiptoed closer to the end of the makeshift wall of mirrors.

'Footpads, my dear, six of them at least. I had my cane, of course, and I flatter myself I have a good right hook, but even so, it took me some time to—' He broke off, his drawling voice choking on the words as Tallie appeared. She glanced around, but the rest of the men were gathered round a giggling group of girls by the door; they would not be overheard.

'Why, Mr Hemsley, what a dreadful mess those villains made of your face!' If she had not been present when it happened, she would never have believed that mass of bruises was the work of one man. 'How heroic of you to beat them off.'

'Do you know Mr Hemsley, then, Tallie?' Millie asked innocently, her face lighting up to discover two of her friends were acquainted.

'Yes, indeed,' Tallie said earnestly. 'You have been having a hard time, Mr Hemsley, have you not? Such ill fortune to be attacked by footpads immediately after Lord Arndale beat you so soundly for attempting to ravish me.'

'What!' Millie gasped, running to Tallie's side to put her arm around her. 'You…you beast!'

It was obvious that Millie trusted her friend's word absolutely. She stood by Tallie like a fierce little cat defending its kitten against a dog. 'Take one step nearer and I'll scratch your eyes out, you libertine!'

'My dear Miss LeNoir,' Hemsley was making the mistake of trying to bluster. 'It was simply a misunderstanding—'

'On your part,' a cold voice said. Three pairs of eyes turned to find Nicholas Stangate lounging negligently against a clothes rail. A semi-clad dancer ran over giggling and put her arms around him. 'Not now, darling,' he said absently, giving her a pat on her rounded little rump. 'Off you go like a good girl.'

Tallie made a serious effort to steady her voice, then observed, 'If you hit him here it will start a brawl.'

'I know. Tempting, isn't it? I feel like a little excitement…of some kind. But we don't want to upset the ladies, do we, Hemsley? Why don't you run along while I take them home?'

Hemsley stalked to the door with as much dignity as he could muster. Nick did not even trouble to watch him leave and missed the look of murderous hatred he shot back at Tallie. *I will make you sorry for this*, those eyes promised. She shivered. She had made an enemy, a very bad enemy, and so had Nick.

Tallie turned back to look apprehensively at Nick. What was he going to do? What, more importantly, was he going to say in front of Millie and a potential audience of drunken bucks?

'Do you have your cloaks, ladies? Then if you are ready to leave, Miss LeNoir?' He escorted them firmly out, a broad shoulder turned to the romp in the main part of the room that was rapidly becoming raucous.

Nick appeared to know the labyrinthine passageways backstage with remarkable accuracy. 'You have an excellent sense of direction, my lord,' Tallie remarked slyly. Her nerves were getting the better of her, she wanted to throw herself into his arms. Directing jibes seemed safer.

'Not at all,' he retorted smoothly, taking the wind out of her sails. 'I just happen to be very familiar with this theatre.'

Oh really, Tallie fumed, allowing herself to be steered towards the stage door. *And which opera dancers have you got under your protection, Cousin Nicholas?*

There was a closed carriage waiting, its sides black with no arms visible. Millie settled back against the silk squabs with a sigh of pleasure and smiled prettily at Nick when he climbed in after them. He slid one of the shutters off an interior lantern and the inside of the carriage sprang into life.

'Thank you so much, my lord. I am very grateful to you. Tallie…Miss Grey was so brave to face up to Mr Hemsley like that. Why, I was quite taken in by him.' Her pretty face crumpled for a moment, then she regained her poise. 'I can see that I must be even more on my guard.'

Tallie leaned over to pat her arm and shot Nick a warning glance. Millie did not need any lectures on the dangers of her position.

He simply raised an eyebrow at her and said, 'Had you considered using your talents in any other way, Miss LeNoir?'

Millie smiled. 'I know I am not good enough to be a soloist. My voice is not strong enough.'

'For the stage perhaps you are right. But what about private parties, musical evenings, select gatherings of that sort? You would have to be very careful about what offers you accepted and you would need to employ a driver and a chaperon, but you could make an excellent living, I would judge, and be far less exposed to insult and unwanted attractions.'

Millie just stared at him, her eyes wide, then she clapped her hands together in delight. 'Oh, yes! Oh, my lord, thank you—it would be just the thing.'

'I can make some recommendations to start you off,' Tallie offered. 'Soon you will make your own reputation. And, Millie, I had been wondering what present I could make you—may I employ a chaperon for your first year?'

They dropped an ecstatic Millie off at Wimpole Street. Nick waited until he saw the front door close behind her, then rapped on the roof of the carriage with his cane. As the wheels began to turn, he said, 'Well?'

'I had no idea he would be there,' Tallie said defensively. 'I had no idea they would let any men into the dressing-room at all. I only went because Millie forgot her purse.'

'I know. I went to collect you from Mrs Blackstock's and she told me where you were.'

'Oh. I thought…'

'You thought I had gone to the Opera House on much the same errand as Hemsley, did you not?'

'I did not know what to think, only that I was very glad to see you!' Now was not the time to throw his familiarity with backstage in his face. Tallie searched round for another means of attack. 'Collecting me alone in a closed carriage is somewhat unconventional is it not?'

'We are in a closed carriage now, as you can observe. You may also have noticed that I am able to restrain my carnal appetites. If you can refrain from lowering the window and crying ''rape'', I think we can brush through the experience without having to resort to wedlock.'

Tallie reviewed a number of possible responses to this, including throwing herself into his arms, slapping his face or insisting on him stopping the carriage and getting out. None of these would approach his own standard of infuriatingly cool indifference and she badly wanted to surprise him. 'Well, that *is* a relief,' she said warmly.

Tallie had intended to provoke him, but she was not prepared for his reaction. Nick tipped back his head and laughed. He laughed without any restraint, a genuine, uninhibited roar of amusement, crinkling his eyes shut, stretching the long tendons of his neck as he threw his head back, removing every trace of constraint and control from his face.

She stared, torn between fury at being laughed at and fascination at the transformation. The carriage slowed, then stopped outside the Bruton Street house. Nick mopped his streaming eyes and regarded Tallie with a grin.

'Tallie, you are *enchanting*.' He leaned forward and planted a brotherly kiss on her cheek as the groom came to open the carriage door for her. 'Now in with you or Aunt Kate will be worrying.'

The groom might be standing there pretending to be invisible with an expression of well-trained indifference on his face, but his presence effectively silenced any retort that Tallie might have made. Always supposing she was able to think of one.

'Goodnight, my lord,' she said with a chilly formality that provoked an equally formal half-bow, marred somewhat by the fact Nick's shoulders were still shaking. Tallie swept up to the front door without a backward glance and was relieved that Rainbird was already opening it.

'Good evening, Rainbird,' she said brightly. 'Is Lady Parry in?'

'She retired early, Miss Grey. May I get you anything?'

'No, thank you, Rainbird. I will retire too—could you send my maid up?'

The minute she was in her room Tallie regretted that last request. Now she had to act with calm and dignity while Susan helped her undress, unpinned her hair, put away her jewellery. What she wanted to do was find another cushion and beat the stuffing out of it.

Instead she sat in her wrapper while Susan plied the hairbrush and calmed herself by mentally listing all Nicholas Stangate's numerous faults. *He is cool, he is manipulative, he is domineering, overbearing and suspicious, he kisses innocent young women, he makes me lose my temper and my self-control.* That was a satisfyingly long list.

Tallie bit her lip and decided in all fairness she should catalogue the few—very few—virtues Nick possessed. *He loves his aunt and looks after William with a great deal of tact. He rescued me from Jack Hemsley twice. He behaved with chivalry when he found me in the attic. He is highly intelligent. He has a sense of humour. He looks... He is very handsome. When he kisses me I want to...I want him never to stop. He makes me lose my temper because... because...*

Her thoughts stumbled to a halt. 'Thank you, Susan, that will do. I do not require you any further tonight.'

The fire flickered and crackled in the grate, hypnotically drawing her eye. Tallie gazed at the flames and let her mind go free. Why did Nick crack right through her painfully acquired poise, her calm common sense?

'Because I love him,' she said out loud to the room. *'Because I love him.'*

Chapter Twelve

The following morning Tallie found she had no idea what to do about her moment of self-revelation the night before. She had felt strangely calm afterwards and had simply gone to bed and slept. So far as she was aware she had not dreamed.

The odd calm persisted, but underneath she was disturbed. It was as though she was sleepwalking into danger, watching herself do so and yet unable to wake herself up. Something had to be done about it, of course, she quite realised that. Nick was certainly not in love with her and, even if he were, she was a most unsuitable wife for him.

The odd feeling persisted despite an expedition with Lady Parry to Ackerman's Repository. Although Tallie already possessed every gown she could ever imagine she would need, Lady Parry wished to get ahead of what she called 'the others' by procuring all the latest fashion plates now, so that a refreshed wardrobe could be paraded halfway through the Season.

'I am certain you will be receiving some offers soon, Tallie dear,' she remarked complacently as they embarked in the barouche for the Strand.

Tallie was staring absently at a thin individual in an overlarge greatcoat and battered beaver who was lounging against the railings near the house. He looked oddly familiar. She focused on Lady Parry. 'Offers, ma'am?'

'Of marriage. You are not sickening for something, are you, Talitha?'

'No, no…I beg your pardon. Who would offer for me?' Several gentlemen had appeared to enjoy her company, that was true. There were a number who always sought her out to dance, several who took her driving and more than one who had introduced the subjects of their family, country estates and interests in life into the conversation in a way that she supposed she should have recognised as being somewhat pointed.

Lady Parry rolled her eyes. 'Making all due allowance for modesty and inexperience—*honestly*, Tallie! Let me list a few—Mr Runcorn, Sir Jasper Knight, Dr Philpott, Lord Ashwell, the Reverend Mr Laxton…'

'Truly?' Tallie gazed at her incredulously. 'But…I had not considered marrying any of them. I simply had not thought of them in that way.'

Lady Parry shook her head at this folly. 'I will lay any odds you like that at least three of them come up to scratch by the end of the week, so you had better decide what you want to say to them.'

'No.'

'No? You want me to speak to them first? They will not necessarily approach me, as they know you are of age and I am not your guardian.'

'I mean, no, I do not want to marry any of them.' *I want to marry an infuriating man who does not trust*

*me, laughs at me—and for whom I am entirely inel-
igible as a wife.*

'Oh well, the Season is young yet,' Kate said phil-
osophically, gathering up her reticule and fur as the
carriage began to slow down in the Strand. 'You are
suffering a little from tiredness and nerves, I have no
doubt. We must buy some more hats—I find that is
always such a tonic.'

Nicholas Stangate awoke feeling decidedly cheerful, a sensation that lasted through a leisurely bath, a
careful shave, an excellent breakfast consumed in the
comfort of his bedchamber before dressing and two
cups of coffee.

It was at the point where the second cup was making its stimulating effects felt that he woke up enough
to consider just why he was feeling this good. A moment's reflection was enough to produce a vertical
line between his brows and a decided diminution in
his feeling of *joie de vivre.*

Miss Talitha Grey was proving a serious worry.
She might be enchanting to observe on her alarming
progress through Society. She might be delicious to
kiss and charming company for his aunt... But he was
now convinced that if Aunt Kate thought she knew
Tallie's dark secret, she was deceiving herself. One
blinding flash of revelation at the Duchess of Hastings's ball left him suspecting a far more unusual and
scandalous secret than any he had imagined. And if
he were correct, it could prove both dangerous for
Tallie and, at the very least, could cast a blight over
Lady Parry's position as a leading member of Society.

If she had only failed to 'take'! But Tallie had been
an instant success and, if he was not much mistaken,

would soon be receiving any number of offers. Had he known it, his list of likely candidates was the same as his aunt's, but Nick regarded it with considerably less favour.

Knight was a dull dog, Runcorn had a tendency to gamble, the Reverend Laxton was a prosy bore, Dr Philpott was only looking for a wife with money before retreating back to Oxford and his books and Ashwell was...Ashwell was probably perfect for her.

A title, a modest fortune, a nice little estate, bright, pleasant, responsible. Perfect. Nick kicked a boot across the room and contemplated a newly wedded baron storming into Lady Parry's house to demand why she had allowed him to unwittingly marry a woman with a shameful secret. It had to be stopped.

His aunt was delighted to see him arrive at the dancing-and-card party she was holding that evening, fluttering forward to kiss him on both cheeks. He looked down at her with a smile. 'You are very fine this evening, my love.' She put her head on one side and smiled back. 'What are you up to? You look positively smug.'

'Nicholas!' She rapped his wrist with her fan, then cast a swift glance round and whispered, 'I think Tallie is receiving her first declaration.'

'What? Who?'

'Lord Ashwell.' Lady Parry was positively glowing with pride. 'For him to come up to scratch so early is a triumph. A much, much better match than I could have hoped for. He is perfect.'

'Perfect,' Nick agreed. 'And where is this romantic interlude taking place?'

'The conservatory, I believe. He was steering her

in that direction just five minutes ago with considerable aplomb.'

We will see about that, Nick thought grimly. With a smile for his aunt he surrendered his place by her side to General Hepton and strode off in the direction of the conservatory.

So early in the evening it was deserted except for one couple virtually concealed behind a large potted palm. Nick advanced cat-like until he could see Lord Ashwell on one knee holding Tallie's hand, his head bowed as he made his declaration.

Tallie looked up and Nick saw her eyes widen and her chin go up at the sight of him. 'Go away,' she mouthed silently over her suitor's head. If he strode forward now she would know it was no accident that he had stumbled into the middle of the declaration, but a deliberate attempt to break it up.

Inwardly cursing, he forced a look of surprised apology onto his face, mouthed 'I'm sorry' and silently backed away out of the conservatory and into the reception room it opened onto.

The minutes seemed to drag by. Nick scooped a glass of champagne off a passing tray, agreed vaguely to make up a hand for whist later and bent an apparently attentive ear to the involved story concerning a bet on a curricle race being recounted by Lord Beddenton.

Lord Ashwell emerged from the conservatory so discreetly that Nick almost missed him, but he did not miss the droop of his lordship's shoulders, nor the lack of a smile on his face. He allowed him to get well clear into the room where the dancing was taking place, excused himself to Beddenton, snared another

glass of champagne and made his way into the conservatory.

Tallie was still sitting where he had seen her before, playing with her fan. She tapped it, let its folds
pour open, then flicked it closed, only to open it
again. He watched her calm face, her air of concentration, wondering at the reserve behind which she
could hide her feelings. Hide them most of the time,
he corrected himself. Since he had known her she had
appeared more transparent, more open. It seemed that
either he was learning to read her moods or in some
way he provoked her into revealing them.

How long had he been standing there watching her?
He realised he had no idea. Long enough to have
closed his eyes and repeated faithfully what she was
wearing, from the tortoiseshell combs in her high-
piled hair to the amber silk slippers just peeping from
beneath an over-gown of golden brown lace with a
pale yellow under-dress. The mix of golds brought a
flash of recollection: a picture of masses of golden-
gilt hair, shot through with deeper tones, waving over
the bared shoulders and back of that naked goddess
in the garret. Heat washed through him as he fought
for control.

He must have moved. Tallie's head came up and
she looked directly at him, her face expressionless.
She raised one eyebrow smoothly. It seemed she had
perfected the trick of it. 'Good evening, Cousin Nicholas.'

'Good evening. I apologise for blundering in just
now.'

A faint sceptical smile. 'I doubt if you ever blunder
anywhere, my lord.'

'You rejected him then.' He made it a statement.

'You asked him?' Her voice sharpened.

'I saw his face.' Nick strolled forward and took a cast-iron seat at right angles to her. The embossed ferns made an uncomfortable perch.

'I was sorry to hurt his feelings,' Tallie said. 'But I doubt they were deeply engaged. Thank you, no champagne.' He put down the glass.

'You think him insincere?' Nick let his surprise show in his voice.

'No. Not at all. I am sure he likes me very well and honestly believes that we would make a good match.'

'Then what is there to dislike?' It was suddenly important to know. 'He has breeding, a fortune, intelligence. He is kind…'

'Is that what you look for in marriage?' She swung round suddenly. It took an effort of will not to lean back away from her vehemence. 'Breeding, money, intelligence? *Kindness?*'

'Why, yes, they all seem admirable qualities.' Why was he on the defensive? Why was it his feelings that were the focus of attention now? She had just defined exactly what he had always felt he needed in a wife.

'You would settle for so little?' Tallie sounded genuinely curious.

'Little? It seems to me all one could want.' Suddenly he was not so certain. Her intensity seemed to slash open a hole in his philosophy. A void that ached. 'What do you look for?'

'Love, of course.' She stood, brushing against a jasmine in a pot and releasing a cloud of perfume from its early flowers, forced by the heat. 'I look for nothing more. I would settle for nothing less.'

'You could end up a spinster,' Nick said harshly, getting to his feet.

'Better that than compromise,' Tallie said calmly. 'Better that than mediocrity. And it is all I have ever expected, in any case.'

Something inside Tallie, some separate part of her that seemed to be watching the rest of her from a distance, registered surprise that she could regard Nicholas Stangate with such an appearance of calm. She was, after all, confronting the man she had only just realised she loved.

Tallie wondered if she had angered him, or even perhaps hurt him by attacking his views on what he would consider a suitable marriage. His grey eyes glittered like the interior of a newly split flint and there was colour on his high cheekbones.

'May I escort you back to the dancing, or were you expecting any other gentlemen?'

'No, not just now, thank you. I will have to go out and see if there are any I can lure in here,' she retorted, feeling the colour rise in her own cheeks. 'Aunt Kate tells me there are at least two more from whom I should expect a declaration within the next few days.'

A dark brow rose. 'Tut, tut, Tallie, a lady does not boast of her conquests.'

Tallie stood up in a swirl of tawny silk and lace. 'A *gentleman* would not provoke her into doing so.' She took a step forward, but Nick did not yield ground to her and she found herself standing almost on his toes.

His eyes dropped from the challenge in hers to linger appreciatively on the white slope of her breast and shoulders revealed by the low neckline of the gown.

The single heavy diamond pendant lying where the valley between her breasts began was moving in tune with her heightened breathing.

'That is a very fine stone. Have your admirers been showering you with diamonds?'

'Aunt Kate has kindly lent it to me, as she has all the jewellery I wear. I possess none of my own.'

'We must hope your admirers will make you some suitable presents.'

'I have told you: I do not wish to be on such terms with any of them that gifts of jewellery would be eligible.' It was becoming difficult to breath. The conservatory was really quite stuffy and the scent of the jasmine so close was positively overpowering.

'Look how it reflects the light.' He appeared to be taking no notice of what she said. He was still watching the many-faceted stone and the scintillation of light as it moved. 'Is it your heart that is making it jump and tremble so, Tallie?'

Before she could reply he raised his right hand and laid it gently, palm to skin against the curve of her breast between her collarbone and the neckline of her dress. Tallie started and stepped back, but his other hand came round to gather her to him and she was trapped, one palm at her breast, the other flat on her shoulder blade. 'Your heart is beating like a drum.'

Tallie made herself stand still, certain he was about to kiss her, telling herself that when he did she would have to move his hand and she could slip under it and away, knowing that she would do no such thing.

But instead of bending his head to take her lips Nick continued to hold her eyes with his while the thumb of the hand lying on her breast began to move slowly, insidiously stroking the skin just under the edge of her gown. She gasped, tried to make her legs move, but all that happened was that her eyes fluttered closed as the skilful caress slipped under the neckline.

She had been doubtful about the gown: the edge of the fabric was only an inch above the aureole of her nipples, but once she had tried it on she was reassured that the cut and fit were so good that there was absolutely no need to fear that sudden movement or bending would cause the gown to gape or shift embarrassingly.

But neither she nor the dressmaker had planned for seductive fingers. The ball of Nick's thumb found the puckered skin, then the bud of the nipple, and began to tease it. Tallie moaned deep in her throat, arching into his hand. Her breasts felt heavy, swollen. The sensation seemed to shaft through her. Her lips opened.

There was the sound of footsteps, a man's voice said playfully, 'Now where are you hiding, Miss Grey?' and then broke off abruptly. 'I do apologise, er…I will…' It was Sir Jasper Knight.

As the sound of hasty retreat faded, Tallie felt Nick's hand lift from her breast and his other hand release her. She opened her eyes slowly, knowing that anger on her part was completely unjustified. She could have stopped him at any time—but how could she face him now?

In the event he made it extremely easy for her. 'Oh well,' he said lightly, 'that's the second one routed.'

Tallie set her lips, drew back her hand and slapped Nick across the face with all the force she could muster. He made no move to avoid the blow, which rocked him back on his heels.

There was a long, difficult silence. Nick regarded

her with eyes that held an uncomfortable mixture of rueful apology and still smouldering desire. His left cheek bore the mark of her hand as graphically as if she had drawn it. Tallie knew she must be scarlet. Her lips felt swollen, although his had not touched them. Her nipples pressed against the silk lining of her gown, a humiliating reminder of her own arousal.

'Drink this.' Nick held out the neglected champagne glass. 'Then you had better go out—I suspect I show more evidence of this encounter than you do.'

Tallie gulped the wine desperately. There was a fountain in the corner: she dipped her handkerchief in it and dabbed her cheeks and temples.

'Tallie! Tallie dear, are you still here?' It was Lady Parry.

'Oh, God!' Nick swung round on his heel, but she was between him and the door. He stepped behind the potted palm as his aunt emerged into sight.

'There you are, dear. Whatever is going on? I saw Lord Ashwell come out looking most disconsolate, and then in came Sir Jasper—and came straight out again.'

'I did tell you that I did not want to marry either of them, did I not, Aunt Kate?' Tallie said, keeping her voice light as she stepped towards Lady Parry. She took her chaperon's arm and steered her firmly back towards the reception rooms. 'I just feel rather flustered. The encounters were rather difficult, you understand.' She did not look back. It felt as though Nick's eyes were burning through the back of her gown.

The next morning Tallie awaited Nick's arrival in Bruton Street with a sort of paralysed calm. She was quite certain he would come, for it would take a sang-froid even beyond what she believed he possessed to pretend that that encounter in the conservatory had not taken place.

He arrived at ten-thirty, which gave her time both to perfect what she was going to say and to develop a fine flock of butterflies in her stomach. Was he really going to believe that it was simply unmaidenly physical attraction that made her react the way she did in his arms or could he have any suspicion of the way she felt about him?

He arrived looking immaculate in cream panta-loons, Hessian boots and a tailcoat of darkest blue. He also looked infuriatingly cool and calm, not even a touch of colour staining his cheekbones as he was ushered by Rainbird into the drawing room. Tallie had no fear that the butler would hasten off to find her a chaperon; Lord Arndale was regarded as a son of the house.

He regarded her from a strategic position by the fireplace, one boot on the fender, a hand on the man-telshelf. She had not asked him to sit down which she now realised was a tactical error—he had the advan-tage of height.

'Good morning, Cousin Nicholas,' she said com-posedly.

'Good morning, Talitha.' So far, so good. 'Last night we—'

Tallie smiled and interrupted him. 'Last night we succumbed to a rather unfortunate physical attraction. I am sure it will not happen again.'

She was interested to see that he had not expected any such reaction from her. 'Are you? Well, I'll be damned.'

'Very likely, Cousin Nicholas, but I would be obliged if you would moderate your language.'

He ignored this crushing reproof. 'Physical attraction? Is that what you call it?'

'What would you call it?' Tallie asked. This was dangerous ground indeed.

'The same, but I hardly expected an unmarried girl to do so.' His expression was grim.

'Indeed?' Tallie got up and stalked towards the door. 'Well, my lord, I am not a girl, I am five and twenty, and I prefer the truth without hypocrisy. I have doubtless acted very imprudently, shockingly and in a downright unmaidenly manner. However, it was an interesting experience, which we can now forget all about.' She smiled sweetly and opened the door. 'It was most intriguing to see what all the fuss is about.' Nick took a long stride towards her, a noise alarmingly like a mastiff growling emanating from his throat.

Tallie, who was beginning to think she had gone somewhat too far in her efforts to disabuse him of the slightest suspicion of how she truly felt, was relieved to see Lady Parry in the hall.

'Ah, there you are, dear, I was looking for you. Nicholas! Excellent, would you care to accompany us to Mr Harland's studio?'

Chapter Thirteen

Mr Harland's studio. Tallie felt the blood drain out of her face and wondered wildly if she was going to faint. Then she saw Nick watching her speculatively and she rallied herself. 'Mr Harland, ma'am?'

'Yes, I have decided to have my portrait taken after all and I need to call to arrange terms and so forth. Do you mind accompanying me?'

'Oh,' Tallie managed feebly. 'No, no, of course not.'

'I am sorry, Aunt Kate,' Nick said, gathering up his hat and gloves from the hall chest. 'I had only dropped in for a minute. I have a business appointment now, otherwise I would be delighted to accompany you.'

Tallie's anger that he had considered 'only a minute' sufficient to discuss yesterday's encounter allowed her to put on her outdoor clothing and join Lady Parry in the carriage without refining too much upon where they were going. But once the carriage started her thoughts began to spin.

She had written to Mr Harland, apologising for having to cease her sittings and had received back such a carefully worded reply that she was reassured about his continuing discretion. Absence, and Kate's revelation that she knew all about her sittings, had lulled her still further.

Now she realised how dangerously she had let her guard down, even if Lady Parry knew her secret. What if Nick had been able to oblige his aunt and accompany them and saw something that linked Tallie and the naked Diana in his mind? Even a slight suspicion would be enough to spell disgrace.

The journey to Panton Square passed quickly, too quickly for Tallie, who was desperately trying to regain her composure. She held furs and muff for Lady Parry as she was handed down by the coachman, then descended herself. As she did so some instinct made her glance back to where the tiny square opened out into Coventry Street. A hackney had drawn up and a man was paying his fare—a thin man in an overlarge greatcoat. She shook her head, convinced she was imagining things. When she looked back both man and cab had gone.

The sound of the door opening behind her recalled her to the immediate problem and Tallie followed Lady Parry into the hallway of Mr Harland's house. Peter the colourman was standing holding the door, his best green baize apron in place, his scanty grey hair carefully brushed. On 'portrait days' he was always well turned out to greet clients. On the days when Tallie had posed for the classical works he had hurried back to his workshop, oil-stained apron flapping, knife or pestle in hand.

He helped Lady Parry with her things, then saw Tallie behind her. 'Miss Grey! This is a pleasure, miss. You'll be glad to know I've managed to get a nice consignment of mummy in at long last.'

'Good morning, Peter. I am pleased to hear that—supplies were getting very difficult, were they not?' Peter had sometimes allowed her to look round his workshop and had explained the contents of the jars and twists of paper that filled each shelf and spilled from every drawer.

'Mummy?' Lady Parry, always ready to be interested in something new, paused with one hand on the baluster.

'Yes, my lady. I'll show you.' The colourman vanished into his sanctum and emerged with a box, which he opened carefully. Inside were a number of fragile sheets of a flaking substance the colour of dried tobacco and a gnarled object which looked exactly like part of a human finger.

'Whatever is it?' Lady Parry asked, extending an elegantly gloved forefinger to prod it.

'I rather think it is a…a human finger.' Tallie swallowed. It had been fascinating to hear how artists ground up the remains dug from the hot Egyptian sands to use as a brown pigment. It was considerably less appealing to see it in the…flesh. She swallowed again. That had been an unfortunate thought.

'Oh, my goodness! The poor creature! What do you want it for?' Lady Parry withdrew her own finger sharply.

'It was only a part of a heathen, my lady, and been dead since the Flood, I daresay.' Peter shut his precious box carefully. 'It makes a wonderful deep brown pigment; nothing quite matches it. But the cost, ma'am, that is terrible. Lucky those rogues who broke

in last night didn't think to come down here—why,
I've got lapis and gold leaf—'

'You had burglars? What happened?' Tallie asked,
concerned. 'I do hope no one was hurt.'

'Nothing like that, I am glad to say.' It was Mr
Harland, alerted by the voices, coming down to greet
his new client. 'Good day, Lady Parry, this is an honour. Miss Grey, how very nice to see you again.' Tallie smiled despite herself. Frederick Harland might be
vague, inconsiderate and distracted when painting,
and he might profess to despise his portrait work, but
he did know how to charm his lady clients with every
attention.

He was ushering them up to his public studio and
reception room, a world away from the dusty
draughty attic where his great canvases would be set
up and where Tallie was used to shivering in flimsy
draperies.

'Was anything taken?' she asked as he drew up
chairs for them next to a series of empty display easels.

'No—a very strange thing, that.' The artist
frowned. 'They rummaged through the canvases—
fortunately damaged nothing—and that was all.'

'Possibly they were disturbed,' Lady Parry suggested. 'Or they thought you might hide your valu-
ables amongst them.'

'You are most likely correct, ma'am. Now, as I
understand you have decided upon a portrait and are
most graciously entrusting me with the task. I think
the first thing we must decide is the size and style of
the work. I will show you some examples…'

He proceeded to prop canvases on the easels. First
a head and shoulders of a formidable lady with grey

hair. 'Lady Agatha Mornington. I am about to begin varnishing this one.' Tallie started nervously; this was Jack Hemsley's aunt. Next, a three-quarters length of a young lady holding a child. Then a full-length canvas of a graceful figure in a clinging gown, one hand lightly resting on a classical pillar. It was a preparatory sketch only, but well detailed, and the face that smiled serenely back at the viewer was Tallie's.

'Ah, there is that delightful portrait I saw last time I was here,' Lady Parry said with pleasure.

'Yes, my lady. As you had already seen it, I thought there was no harm in producing it again, and I expect Miss Grey will be amused to see it once more. I will just fetch my notebook,' Mr Harland said and left the room.

'That…that is the picture of me you saw?' Tallie asked, hideous apprehension beginning to ball in her stomach. 'The one I sat for because Lady Smythe was expecting?'

'Yes, of course, dear. Were there any others? I do think it is nice that Mr Harland bothered to draw your face, even though in the finished work it is Lady Smythe, of course.'

'And that is the…costume you thought shocking?' The ball of apprehension was turning into lead shot in the pit of her stomach.

'It looks as though the petticoats have been dampened,' Kate said severely. 'One can see every line of your figure. And what is holding the bodice up—if one can call it a bodice—goodness only knows. Still, everyone knows Penelope Smythe thinks of herself as a dasher, and it must have hit her hard to have lost her figure, however temporary that state of affairs was.'

Tallie sank back in her chair aghast. So Lady Parry had not seen one of the shocking classical nudes, only this portrait. She should have trusted her instincts that her kind patroness was being too tolerant. Now what was she going to do?

Mr Harland had returned and he and Lady Parry were deep in discussion on the relative merits of head and shoulders and full length—three-quarters having been rapidly dismissed as neither one thing nor another. Eventually full length was decided upon, with a draped background. Tallie found it quite impossible to do more than keep an expression of interest on her face and then follow Lady Parry downstairs when her business was concluded.

Her head was spinning and she was conscious only of an overwhelming desire to throw herself on Nick Stangate's chest and confess all. As this was dangerous insanity she stood on the pavement in the light mizzle which had just begun to fall and tried to drag air into her tightened lungs. Then she saw the man.

'Tallie? What is it? You have gone quite pale.' Lady Parry hurried her into the carriage and began to rummage in her reticule.

'I think I…we…are being followed,' Tallie blurted out.

'*What?* By whom?'

'A man—he has just ducked back into an alleyway down there. I saw him getting out of a hackney behind us when we arrived here, and I saw him lurking outside the house when we went to Ackerman's the other day. And I am sure he has been around before— I thought him familiar then.' Tallie broke off and tried to speak calmly. 'I am sorry, Aunt Kate, I am probably imagining things.'

'Perhaps, perhaps not. There are any number of dangerous characters around,' Kate Parry said grimly. 'I will speak to Nicholas about it.'

'Oh, no! He will think me over-imaginative to worry about such things.'

'Well, *I* am worried, and he had better not suggest that I am over-imaginative,' Lady Parry retorted with a twinkle. 'And in any case Nicholas uses enquiry agents from time to time, he will know all about how to deal with this.'

An unpleasant thought crept into Tallie's mind. She knew Nick had had her investigated before she had joined his aunt. And he knew she still hid a secret from him. Was this man his, following her to discover that secret? If that was the case, then today he had been closer than he knew.

Nick was waiting for them when they returned to Bruton Street. They found him sprawled in an arm-chair with a careless elegance that took away Tallie's breath. He tossed aside the portfolio of papers he was reading and got to his feet as they entered the room. Tallie realised she had never been so conscious of how long his legs were nor of how easily he moved.

'A successful meeting?' he asked with a smile, which faded as he took in the anxiety on his aunt's face. 'What is wrong?'

'I think we had better talk about it over luncheon, Nicholas. Talitha and I will be down in a moment; will you be so kind as to tell Rainbird we will wait upon ourselves.'

* * *

Shortly after, Tallie sat down apprehensively and passed cold meats to Lady Parry at her side. She took a slice of bread and began to cut it into thin fingers.

'Aunt Kate?' Nick took a slice of beef, but did not start to eat. 'What has occurred?'

'Just a foolish idea of mine,' Tallie said defensively. 'The more I think about it, the more—'

'Talitha believes she, or perhaps we, are being followed.'

Nick's brows drew together sharply. 'By whom?'

'A thin man in a greatcoat and beaver hat.'

'I am sure it is just a coincidence,' Tallie murmured. His grey eyes turned to her face and he raised one brow.

'And how often has this coincidence struck you?'

'Four times,' she admitted. 'At least three I am certain of. I am sure I had seen him before—perhaps once, perhaps more—which is why I noticed him the next time.'

'Did he approach you? Try to speak to you?'

Tallie shook her head and Lady Parry added, 'I am certain he has some criminal intent. Perhaps he is trying to find a pattern to our comings and goings so he can break into the house. After all, look at poor Mr Harland.'

For a second the mask of calm enquiry that Nick was wearing cracked. His head turned sharply to his aunt. 'Harland? What has happened to him?'

'The house was broken into,' Lady Parry explained. 'It is dreadful how lawless the streets of London are becoming.'

'And what was taken?'

'Nothing apparently. They just searched amongst the canvases.'

'Interesting.' He said it almost to himself. 'Now that *is* interesting.'

'What shall we do about the man in the beaver hat, Nicholas dear?'

'Go nowhere without two of the larger footmen in attendance and tell the coachman to carry a blunderbuss. I will speak to Rainbird. I would not worry, Aunt Kate—if this man has any sinister intent, he will soon see you are well protected and shift his interest elsewhere.'

Lady Parry appeared to find this sufficient reassurance and began to talk cheerfully of her planned portrait. Tallie was not so sure. She made herself eat her bread and butter and sip a little from her glass while watching Nick from under her lowered lashes. She could tell he was thinking furiously, despite the flow of inconsequential talk he was maintaining in response to his aunt.

When they rose from the table he intercepted her. 'Tallie, I would like to speak to you if I may.'

She cast a hunted look at the dining-room door closing behind Lady Parry. She knew she should reprove him for using her pet name, but the sound of it on his lips was seductively sweet.

'I promise I am not going to kiss you,' he said infuriatingly. She narrowed her eyes in suspicion and he added, 'Or do anything else to take advantage of—what did you call it?—oh, yes, our unfortunate mutual physical attraction.'

'Good.' Tallie edged around the table. Despite his assurances she still felt safer with a width of shining mahogany between them. Quite whether it was Nicholas or herself that she was nervous of she was not prepared to examine. 'What do you want to talk about?'

'Will you reconsider telling me about your secret? The one you believe my aunt knows all about. Only I do not believe she does.'

'No, you are correct. She does not. I honestly believed it when I told you that, but I was wrong.' It was a relief to tell him some of the truth if not all.

'Tell me.' He sat down opposite her.

Feeling a little more secure, Tallie sat too. Her legs were shaking. 'Why?'

'Because I think it would be safer if you did.'

It was very tempting. Tallie stared into the grey eyes, but they did not hold the reassurance she was looking for. It would not take very much to make her blurt it all out—she could quite understand why people confessed to crimes when questioned. But the inimical gaze regarding her belonged to the man who did not trust her, did not approve of her friends, who wanted her out of his family's house and lives. The fact that she loved him did not make it any easier, it simply made the thought of the expression on his face when he discovered the truth harder to bear.

'No.' He looked a question and she said angrily, 'Why should I? You make it quite clear you do not trust me. You disapprove of my friends, you wish me gone from here. Why should I hand you a weapon against me?'

'Is this a war, then?' He raised a long-fingered hand and rubbed a hand over his face. It was an uncharacteristically weary gesture.

'It feels like one.' Tallie wanted to go round and stand behind his chair, massage his shoulders, gently rub his temples until that tiredness ebbed away and he relaxed. She clasped her hands tightly in her lap.

'I did not approve of your friends. I was wrong. I apologise. Miss Scott is an intelligent and principled woman. Miss LeNoir is a talented and virtuous one, and Mrs Blackstock seems eminently respectable.'

'Thank you,' Tallie said stiffly.

'If I do not trust you, it is your judgement I mistrust, not your motives. As for your presence in this house—' He broke off, pushed his hand through his hair and got to his feet, turning as he rose so that she could not see his face. 'It is my aunt's house, it is up to her who resides here. She enjoys your company very much. I believe she is proud of your success.'

'Why, thank you.'

'I try and fight fair,' he said ruefully.

Tallie almost fell for it. Then she caught herself. *Fight fair?* With enquiry agents investigating her? Fight fair when he had discovered that if he took her in his arms she trembled and responded to him with an utterly shameless ardour?

'Thank you,' she said again. 'But unfortunately I trust your motives as little as you trust my judgement, so I am afraid we are at a stalemate.'

'You will not tell me? Is it so very dreadful? You were prepared to speak of it to my aunt, and presumably would have done so if she had not said something that convinced you she already knew.'

'What I might discuss with another woman—and one who is my patroness—is quite different from what I might discuss with a man,' Tallie said, casting down her eyes in what she hoped might be mistaken for maidenly confusion. She glanced up through her lashes and saw Nick was regarding her with amusement.

'A very nice try, Tallie; however, I am not at all convinced by the shrinking maiden who is too shy to reveal her horrid secret to a man.'

'I most certainly am—' Tallie broke off, suddenly aware of the large hole her tongue was digging her.

'A shrinking maiden? Hmm. I am prepared to believe one part of that description, but not the other.' Only her determination not to give him any further cause for amusement stopped Tallie from an indignant retort. She glared instead. 'You realise you are effectively challenging me to discover the truth for myself?' he added.

'You could simply mind your own business.'

'But I am enjoying myself, Tallie,' Nick said, turning towards the door. 'You are proving an irresistible puzzle.' With a mocking bow he let himself out, closing the door gently behind him.

Tallie took an angry turn down the length of the room and back. Infuriating man! In an effort to stop thinking about Nick Stangate, she turned her thoughts to his aunt. She should tell Lady Parry the truth about her sittings. It was one thing to be innocently deceiving her, but now she knew Lady Parry did not know the true state of affairs she could not, in all conscience, continue the deception.

Best to do it now, confess while she was feeling determined. Tallie marched over to the door, flung it open and walked into a scene of chaos.

Chapter Fourteen

It was a testament to the quality and thickness of the doors that Tallie had not heard the uproar from the dining room.

A young woman in modest, travel-stained but respectable clothing was weeping unrestrainedly on a hall chair despite the housekeeper's efforts to calm her and wave smelling salts under her nose. William was standing back with the unmistakable air of panic of a man trapped by feminine emotion while his mother was alternating between anxious glances at the hysterical girl and attempts to con a letter she was holding. Lord Arndale, driving coat half-buttoned and hat and gloves in his hand, appeared to have given up trying to get out of the front door and was giving instructions to a footman who turned and hurried off towards the back stairs with unmistakable relief.

Rainbird, emanating disapproval of such a scene in the front hall, was trying to usher the entire party into the drawing room, but for once was being ignored by both family and staff alike.

Tallie decided she could either retire again, add to the chaos or attempt to be useful. With a sigh she

stepped into the breach and touched Lady Parry on
the arm. 'I think she might calm down a little, ma'am,
if there were not so many people. Shall I try and take
her into the morning room?'

'Oh, would you, Talitha dear? She just cries more
when she sees me.'

Tallie was by now making out the tenor of the
young woman's plaint, which appeared to alternate
between bitter self-recrimination that she should have
so let Lady Parry down and inexplicable references
to 'that monkey being the last straw'.

'What is her name?'

'Miss Clarke. Maria Clarke.'

'Come along, Miss Clarke…Maria. There's a good
girl. You come and sit down in a nice quiet room.
No, Lady Parry is not at all angry…yes, this way.
Mrs Mills, could you have some tea sent up, please?'

It took half an hour to calm the young woman and
at the end of it Tallie was no wiser. However, Miss
Clarke was red-eyed but subdued and had been sent
off with the housekeeper to lie down and rest.

Feeling as if she had just emerged from Bedlam,
Tallie emerged and found the butler surveying the
quiet hall with austere satisfaction. 'Where is her ladyship, Rainbird?'

'Packing, Miss Grey.'

'Packing? Is something wrong?'

'I could not venture to say, Miss Grey. However,
Miss Clarke, the young lady who was so afflicted, is
the companion to her ladyship's elder sister, the Dowager Marchioness of Palgrave.'

'I see.' Tallie saw nothing at all clearly, although
it appeared that some domestic disaster must have

struck the Dowager's household. Could it possibly involve monkeys, or was that simply hysteria? 'I do not believe I have met the Dowager,' she began cautiously.

'Her ladyship lives much retired.' Rainbird hesitated and unbent further, dropping his voice in case any menial should overhear his indiscretion. 'Her ladyship is considered…eccentric.'

Oh, dear, the monkey was probably real in that case. Tallie recalled hair-raising stories of Princess Caroline's menagerie. 'I had better see if there is anything I can do to assist Lady Parry. Have their lordships gone out?'

'Lord Arndale has gone to arrange her ladyship's carriage and outriders, Miss Grey. Lord Parry is, I believe, with her ladyship.'

As Tallie climbed the stairs she could hear William sounding plaintively defensive. 'Of course I will escort you, Mama, I would not dream of doing anything else, but can I not put up at the Palgrave Arms when we get there?'

'No, you cannot, William,' his mother was saying briskly. 'Goodness knows what we are going to find: monkeys could be the least of it. Remember last time?'

'Surely not another zebra?'

'Anything is possible with your Aunt Georgiana. At least she has got past the stage of unfortunate infatuations with pretty young men… Tallie dear, thank you so much for settling Miss Clarke. I must say I had not thought her the hysterical type, and after six months I was hoping she would prove ideal.' Lady Parry heaved a sigh and sat down on the bed. 'William, go and tell your valet to pack for at least four days. It took that long last time—and you are *not* putting up at the Arms.

'Tallie, my love, I am very sorry about this, but I am afraid I am going to have to go down to Sussex and see what can be done about my sister, Lady Palgrave.'

'Is she unwell, ma'am?' Tallie sat on the bed too.

'My sister, to be plain about it, is very strange—only, being a Dowager Marchioness, she is called eccentric. As a girl she was given to harmless but unconventional enthusiasms and regrettably her marriage proved unhappy, which only served to drive her further towards unsuitable obsessions. Her husband's death has left her without any restraining influence and with a fortune large enough to indulge whatever fancy enters her head.

'Her house is a menagerie of the most unlikely creatures, although fortunately now they are from the animal kingdom. There was a time when she was entertaining one unsuitable young man after another. All in pursuit of her money, of course—and I probably should not be telling an unmarried girl about it.

'Anyway...' she sighed again '...she swings between relative normality, when all that is required of her companion is to humour her, and really wild excesses. Apparently she has acquired a number of monkeys—quite large ones, according to the housekeeper's letter—and has established them in the guest bedrooms. I shall have to go and see what can be done to restore some sort of order.'

'Will Lord Arndale accompany you? I imagine he would cope very well with this sort of crisis.'

'And so he would. Unfortunately my sister has a

tendresse for him and is given to the most embarrassing displays of, er…affection.'

'Goodness,' Tallie said blankly, trying not to giggle at the thought of Nick being pursued around an animal-infested mansion by a middle-aged lady with amorous intent. 'I had better go and pack.'

'No, dear, it is very sweet of you, but I could not possibly inflict that household on you. You will be quite all right here with Mrs Mills and Rainbird and if you want to go to any parties while I am away, I will drop a line to Lady Cawston and Mrs Bridlington—their girls are usually invited to all the events you are. Or you could stay with your friends at Upper Wimpole Street if you do not feel quite comfortable here while I am out of town.'

'I will be perfectly easy here with Mrs Mills, I assure you, Aunt Kate. In any case, Mrs Blackstone and Millie and Zenobia are going to Putney for a few days. Zenna has found details of a house that sounds exactly right for the school and Mrs Blackstock has a cousin living nearby, so they are all having a little holiday. They went off this morning.'

'Are you sure you will be all right?' Lady Parry regarded Tallie distractedly. 'It hardly seems fair, but I could not possibly take you with me—one never knows *what* one might find.'

'Dear Aunt Kate, I will be perfectly fine, I assure you, and I promise I will send a note round to Jane Cawston or Sally and Lydia Bridlington if I wish to go out in the evening. Although I would not be sorry for a little holiday from parties myself. I will have a quiet evening or two and will doubtless be all the better for it.'

'If you are certain, dear.' Lady Parry smiled with

relief. 'I intend leaving as soon as possible. It will mean a late arrival, but the roads are good and there is a full moon tonight. As my sister rarely retires before three in the morning, I have no fear of arriving and finding the house in darkness.'

In a remarkably short time—a circumstance that Tallie had no difficulty attributing to Nick Stangate's forceful methods of organisation—Lady Parry's cavalcade set off. Tallie stood on the front step to wave goodbye to her ladyship's travelling carriage, Lord Parry driving his curricle and Nick astride one of his raking hunters.

He reined back at the kerbside, obviously desiring a final word, and Tallie came down to stand by the big horse.

'I will stay overnight at the Palgrave Arms, just in case the situation is beyond my aunt's capabilities to resolve, and will return tomorrow. If you need to speak to me, send word to Brook Street and I will come and take you for a drive.'

'Will you not call?' Tallie asked, puzzled. Nick was such a regular visitor to Bruton Street that it seemed strange that he would not come there directly on returning from Sussex.

'Given that you are alone in the house save for the servants, I do not think that you should be receiving gentlemen visitors.' He touched his whip to his hat and gathered up his reins, then hesitated. 'If there should be any problem while I am away…if you should feel in any way alarmed by this man who may be following you…send to Mr Gregory Tolliver, Pickering Place, off St James's Street.'

'Who is he?' Tallie asked, remembering William

mentioning meeting Nick leaving 'his agent's' house in that same location. How frank was Nick going to be with her?

'He is in my employ and will know what to do,' he said curtly, then unexpectedly leaned down and touched her cheek with his gloved hand before spurring the horse into a canter after the retreating carriages.

Thoughtfully Tallie climbed the steps and went into the house. So, Nick's agent—presumably the same man whom he had used to make his enquiries into her background—would 'know what to do' about the mysterious man. Which meant that Nick was confiding in him and was taking it seriously. A slight tremor of anxiety was replaced by one of irritation. Why could he not confide in her and tell her what he thought was afoot?

She answered her own question. *Because he does not trust you, Tallie*, she thought grimly. *You will not confide in him, so neither will he in you. Stalemate.*

The next morning Tallie was enjoying the novel sensation of having nothing to do, nowhere she was expected to be and no one to please but herself and was employing the holiday by trimming a promenade hat of Lady Parry's from last season. It was restful to be able to employ her old skills again, to concentrate closely on what her hands were doing rather than having to think or talk.

There was a knock at the door, which she ignored, then looked up in surprise when Rainbird brought a letter in. She was rather enjoying the solitude and regarded him with well-concealed irritation when the butler proffered the salver.

'The man is waiting for a reply, Miss Grey.'

Tallie turned the folded sheet over in her hands, then recognised the handwriting: Mr Harland.

Her hands froze, but her heart seemed to turn in their stead. Why should the artist be writing to her? Slitting the wafer seal with her sewing scissors, she found that his letter was lengthy enough to occupy two closely written sheets.

The artist had penned it in an obvious state of excitement to inform Tallie that he had sold all six of the large classical canvases in which she featured.

With an internal sensation of having eaten far too much ice cream, Tallie read on. *Please do not suppose that there is the slightest danger of the works being seen by London Society*, Mr Harland had written, obviously anticipating Tallie's anxieties. *The gentleman concerned tells me he is buying them to decorate his private rooms in his castle in the far north of Scotland. He has lately returned from the Mediterranean lands and wishes to have a tangible reminder of the classical landscape.*

Tallie blinked at the closely written sheet. It seemed likely enough, she supposed—but how had this Scottish patron heard of Frederick Harland, and particularly how did he know he had classical scenes for sale?

She opened the door and looked into the hall. As she hoped, it was Peter who had brought the letter and who was sitting patiently on one of the hard shield-back hall chairs, hat on knee, waiting for the expected answer.

'Peter? Could you come in here, please?' With the door safely shut on Rainbird, Tallie asked, 'Have you any idea how this gentleman who is buying Mr Harland's classical canvases came to hear that he had them available?'

'Why, yes, Miss Grey—he said he made enquiries for a painter of classical scenes at the Royal Academy. You know, Mr Harland talks a great deal about his ambitions for that style of art, even if he does not exhibit.'

'Oh.' That seemed plausible, but Tallie was still uneasy.

Peter appeared to understand. 'He is genuine, Miss Grey, I'm sure of that. Gentleman with a strong Scottish accent and his skin deeply tanned by the sun— he's been in the south, all right.'

Tallie turned back to the letter. The artist must want some sort of response from her, otherwise Peter would not be waiting.

As you know, none of the canvases is entirely complete and the purchaser—who does not wish to be named—requires to take them back with him in two weeks' time. In most cases the outstanding work is architectural or landscape and I have every expectation of completing these before he leaves. However, the last canvas, the 'Diana' scene, requires one more sitting from the live figure. While fully appreciating your reluctance to be further involved with my work, might I hope that you will oblige me on this one final occasion? To think that six major pieces of mine will be hung together in a fitting setting is a matter of such importance to me it gives me the hope that you may find yourself able to oblige me.

Tallie dropped the pages onto the sofa and stared blankly at Peter. 'Do you know what is in the letter?'

'Yes, Miss Grey. Mr Harland wishes you to sit for him one last time.'

Tallie's immediate reaction was simply to say 'no', but then the recollection of how grateful she had been for the money Mr Harland paid her, the gentlemanly manner in which he had always treated her and his intense belief and pride in his classical paintings made her hesitate.

'I do not know when I can sit for him, though,' she said. 'Lady Parry is away, but when she returns she will expect me to accompany her. It would be difficult to explain why I wished to spend several hours at the studio.' She bit her lip. 'I suppose this afternoon...?'

'Mr Harland is painting a portrait this afternoon and the gentleman in question will be attending the studio.'

'Oh, dear. Then I cannot say, for I do not know when Lady Parry will return—it could even be to-morrow.'

'Would this evening be convenient, Miss Grey?' Peter asked hopefully.

'But the light—surely that would be impossible?'

'Mr Harland has invested in some of the new oil lamps, Miss Grey—why, it is almost as light as day with those all lit up.'

Tallie bit her lip. It seemed that both circumstances and her own conscience were conspiring together.

'Shall I tell Mr Harland a time?' the colourman pressed.

'Eight o'clock?' Tallie suggested faintly. She could have an early dinner and take a hackney. Rainbird would suppose her to be going to Upper Wimpole Street, for she had not mentioned to him that the household was away.

In the event it proved almost too easy to evade difficult questions, for Rainbird had not been in the hall when she asked a footman to call her a hackney carriage. She remarked carelessly that she was going to meet friends and the sight of her evening dress and opera cloak was obviously sufficiently usual for the young man not to make the sort of more probing enquiry that the butler in his more privileged position would have had no hesitation in making.

Tallie checked nervously up and down Bruton Street but could see no one lurking suspiciously in the evening drizzle and she sat back against the squabs feeling slightly reassured. It appeared that her mysterious follower had gone—or she had refined too much upon a series of coincidences.

As they neared Panton Square, however, she discovered that her stomach was a mass of butterflies. Somehow there was all the difference in the world in sitting for Mr Harland when it was a routine matter of earning her living. Now—with no excuse other than a sense of obligation that she was certain any respectable lady would tell her was misplaced—she was creeping out alone in a cab, dressed up to deceive the servants and feeling thoroughly uneasy about the entire enterprise.

The hackney turned into Panton Square. *Too late to go back now*, she told herself firmly, paying the driver. She would insist that Peter found her a cab for the return journey before she left the house, she decided, glancing up nervously from returning her purse to her reticule as another cab drew up a little further down. But the short, middle-aged man who climbed down bore no resemblance to her sinister follower and she watched in relief as he opened an area gate and vanished down the steps after a word with the driver.

Once she was inside a sense of familiarity took

over from the nervousness and she climbed the stairs to the attic studio, feeling calmer. The artist had the large canvas already set up and his palette set and was busily adjusting the bright new lamps around the model's podium and the old blue screen.

'My dear Miss Grey, I cannot thank you enough,' he exclaimed, bustling forward to shake her hand. 'I understand how difficult it is for you now, but to be able to complete the canvases...to know that they will be fittingly hung, even if it is in remote and private rooms, not in a gallery...I cannot begin to explain...'

'I quite understand,' Tallie assured him. 'I will just go and change.'

'I have set up screens, in the corner.' Harland gestured to a set of old Spanish leather folding screens from which hung a length of white linen. 'With the new lamps it is so much warmer up here, I thought it would be more convenient.'

Tallie found the screened area contained a chair, a mirror and a clothes stand and began to undress. She had chosen the evening gown for its ease of removal and was soon draped in the linen and unpinning her hair. The gold filet hung from the mirror and within a few minutes Diana stared back at herself in the fly-spotted glass. Forcing herself to be practical, Tallie flicked her hair into the style of the portrait, gathered the linen around her as modestly as she could and went to stand on her mark.

After the first few, strange, minutes it simply became ordinary and familiar again. The attic still creaked, mice still scuffled in the corners and the familiar drafts penetrated even the warmth created by the powerful spermaceti lamps. The artist paced and muttered behind her, once hurrying down to twitch the hem of the linen drape, again to adjust the angle of the lights.

After an hour he observed, 'Splendid! Splendid. Now, Miss Grey, if you would like to take ten minutes to rest, then I believe another half-hour will see all complete.'

Tallie swathed the drape around her and turned, flexing her shoulders gratefully. 'How are the other canvases progressing, Mr Harland? Are you—?'

She broke off at the sound of thunderous knocking on the street door and froze, gazing at the artist in wild surmise. What was happening? It seemed just like that terrifying afternoon when Jack Hemsley and his friends had invaded the studio.

Harland threw open the attic door and once again, just like that nightmare day, Peter's voice rose up the stairwell. 'No, sir! You cannot go up there! Mr Harland is occupied.'

Tallie grabbed his arm. 'Who is it? Are you expecting anyone?'

'No! Get back inside, I will go down…'

But the sound of footsteps was clear on the stairs. Someone with a long stride was taking the stairs at the run. Frantic, Tallie spun round and began to flee across the dusty floor towards the only hiding place, the closet.

But she was only halfway there when the attic door crashed open behind her. She turned again, clutching the illusory protection of the linen drape around her and stared wild-eyed at the doorway where a man was thrusting the protesting artist aside with a peremptory hand.

Mr Harland staggered back and, trembling, Tallie braced herself for humiliation, disgrace and the ruin of her reputation.

Chapter Fifteen

His lungs heaving from the effort of taking four precipitous flights of stairs at the run, Nick Stangate stood in the doorway and regarded the goddess standing at bay in front of him. In the strong light she seemed bathed in a strange sunlight that gave her an ancient magic all her own and his breath caught in awe. Then he saw her wide, frightened eyes, the way her breasts rose and fell with her breathing, the courage that made her stay there, facing him down despite her terror.

He strode forward and seized her arm, forcing himself to ignore her nakedness, her nearness, holding her despite her frantic efforts to wrench herself away. 'Tallie, stop it! Listen to me, there isn't much time, Hemsley and a pack of his friends are on my heels—this is a trap.'

He saw Tallie turn her eyes on the artist, only for him to shake his head in furious denial at the accusation on her face. 'Good God, no, Miss Grey, I had no idea. Mr Laidlaw's offer seemed perfectly genuine—*he* seemed perfectly—'

'Later,' Nick snapped. 'Laidlaw *is* genuine. He's

Hemsley's cousin, just back from Greece, and he must have seemed the ideal tool for his purposes. Harland, where are the back stairs?' The terrified girl was struggling in his grip, he tightened it, one part of his mind recoiling at the thought of hurting her soft flesh, the other ruthlessly aware that he was going to have to force her to obey him for her own protection.

'There are none,' the artist wailed, then gave a startled exclamation as the knocker thudded again. He ran towards the door, calling 'Peter! Do not open it!'

'Too late,' Nick said grimly, 'they're in.'

Tallie tugged at his hand. 'Let me go, I must get dressed at least.'

'No time. Harland, can you hide her clothes, her reticule?'

'Yes, my lord.' He was already hurrying towards the screen. 'I have trunks full of old clothes, hangings for props...'

'Nick!'

'Quiet.' He dragged her towards the window, thrust it up and peered out into the darkness. The street seemed miles below; the attic of Harland's house was a clear storey above the other houses surrounding it.

'Thank Heavens for small mercies: there's a ledge.' It was narrow, shining with dampness, maybe crumbling, but it stretched across the width of the house just below the window line. He closed his mind to the possible dangers, focusing on the immediate one. 'Harland, close this after us—hurry, man!'

The artist thrust Tallie's evening cloak into a mass of multicoloured hangings, tossed her reticule and shoes on top of a bookcase and hurried towards them.

Nick began to climb out of the window, keeping a grip with one hand on Tallie. 'Come on.'

'I…I cannot. I can't stand heights…I…'

The sound of approaching voices was getting closer. 'Harland, get out there and hold them up as long as possible. I'll try and shut the window after us. Do nothing to draw attention to it.'

As the artist ran for the door, Nick forced himself to stillness, pulled Tallie close and folded his arms round her. She was quivering against him, her soft warm skin achingly vulnerable under his hands. He pushed up her chin and put all his power into his voice and his eyes.

'We are going out there and I will keep you safe. I will not let you fall. I will not let them find you. Do you believe me, Tallie?'

'Ye-yes.' He saw the terrified green eyes focus, her lips tighten. He could almost feel the effort of will it was taking her to control her fear. 'I believe you, Nick.'

He released her and ducked under the raised sash and out onto the sill. The drizzle had stopped, but everything he touched had a grimy, sooty dampness. He tugged at the cornice above his head, found it firm. He craned back, wondering if he could get them up on top of the cornice where the attic roof met the gutters, but there were no handholds. He reached in to Tallie with his free hand. 'Come on, out onto the ledge, face out and inch along to your right. There is a downpipe—hold that with your right hand and the edge of the window reveal with your left.'

'Don't let me go!' The panic was back in her voice.

'Just while I close the window. You can do it, Tallie, come on, show me.'

With a little gasp she took his hand and climbed

out, her naked limbs flashing white in the darkness. Then she was standing, groping with her free hand.

'I have got the pipe.' She swallowed audibly.

'Here is the window reveal.' He guided her hand to it. 'Now, hold on.'

Her fingertips seemed to cling to his for a fraction of a second, then she released his hand and he saw her fingers tighten on the rough brick. Nick shoved down the window, stepped across and flattened himself against her, his back to the drop, his hands gripping the same handholds above hers.

The sound of the door banging open and loud voices in the studio reached them clearly. Against his chest he could feel Tallie's breathing. Rapid, frightened. Then she whispered, 'It is all right, Nick. I won't panic, I will not let you down.'

The trust in her voice was so absolute it almost unmanned him as nothing else could have done. For a moment he closed his eyes, let his forehead rest against the wet brick. He found his voice and whispered, 'I know you won't, my brave darling. But I'm afraid we have to move: if anyone opens the window, they'll see us.'

Tallie wondered if she had heard him aright. It was difficult to think, let alone to hear properly. The blood seemed to be roaring in her ears, the sound of Nick's heart was loud where her face was pressed against him; on the other side of the window shouts and cat-calls marked the hunt in progress.

Below them, four storeys down, was the street, below that the spiked railings and the further drop to the unyielding flags of the area courtyard. Her naked back pressed against rough brick, her skin was crawling with cold and terror. But he had called her *my brave darling*. The poor little flickering flame of courage that had helped her get out onto the ledge burned stronger, then the rest of his words came into focus. *Move?* He wanted them to *move*?

She heard herself say, 'Yes, Nick', and, as nightmares do, this one shifted into new horrors.

He was edging carefully along the ledge, nudging her feet along inside his, his body arched out to give her room. He seemed to be holding on to something above their heads, she could feel the tension in his arms as they rose past her face. At first all she was aware of in their infinitely slow progress was pain; the bricks grazing her buttocks and shoulders, the grit on the ledge digging into her feet, Nick's body ruthlessly pushing her on, so hard against her that she could hardly breathe.

Then the cold began to numb the pain and fear took over. Under her bare feet she could feel how crumbly the ledge felt; pressed against him so tightly she was utterly aware of the strain on Nick's body and arms, the gasp of pain as he arched himself out to enable her to slide around the downpipe. Once, twice, his foot slipped and the jerk as he took the weight on straining arms froze her with terror.

It seemed endless, this nightmare; perhaps she would spend eternity on this ledge, her back raw, her feet frozen, crushed against the man she loved until even his strength gave out and he fell, leaving her alone as he plunged to his death far below.

He stopped suddenly; she felt his hand outstretched, groping into air. 'The corner,' he whispered. 'The ledge goes around and continues down the side of the building. If we go round, we will be out of sight.'

There was a moment where his body left hers, the damp night air striking icy on the one part of her that had been warm, then he was swinging her around the corner as behind them the window creaked upwards and loud voices echoed out.

'Not out here, not unless she's jumped.' The voice was unfamiliar, drunken, utterly uncaring.

'The bitch. How the hell did she escape?' That was Hemsley.

Faintly from inside the room she heard the indignant artist. 'Gentlemen, you have made a mistake. Someone dropped off a note for their mistress earlier, then left again. No one is here…'

'I am going to make Jack Hemsley sorry he was ever born,' Nick said close to her ear. Under any other circumstances his tone might have been considered politely conversational.

Tallie shivered. 'You are going to call him out?' she whispered back.

'Eventually.' Nick lingered over the syllables as though savouring them. His tone changed. 'Thank goodness for that, the moon's out.'

It was intermittent, still partly obscured by the clearing rain clouds, but Nick seemed pleased, which as far as Tallie was concerned was all that mattered now. She was keeping upright by sheer will-power and the strength of his body and she was so cold that she could feel nothing else at all.

Nick moved as though to turn his body and she gave a little cry.

'Shh. It is all right. The roof next door is lower

than this one and almost flat, just a few more inches and we will be over it and can get down.'

How would that help? Tallie wondered hazily. *How could you get off a roof?*

'I'm going to let you go for a moment, Tallie,' Nick said firmly. 'Just stay still, leaning back. It will only be for a second.'

Before she had a chance to protest he was gone. Terrified, her eyes tight shut, Tallie flattened herself against the wall and waited for the sickening thud from far below. When he spoke, his voice coming from the level of her ankles, she was so shocked that she lost her balance and tumbled straight off the ledge and into his arms.

'Shh, it's all right, my darling, I have you, we're quite safe, off that ledge now.'

Tallie made a huge effort and opened her eyes. She was cradled in Nick's arms as he walked across the flat leads of a house. She was also stark naked. The linen drape had vanished and her white skin was luminous in the moonlight. 'Oh!' Tallie tried to wriggle free, but Nick held her tightly.

'As soon as we are in the house you can have my coat, I promise. No one can see us, we are still too high up. Can you stand for a moment?'

Without waiting for an answer he set her on her feet, steadying her with one hand while he bent to tug at a trapdoor let into the roof. 'Damnation, it is bolted.' He tugged a knife from his boot top and attacked the edge of the trap. The wood splintered with a sound like gunshot and the flap hinged open. 'Sit down while I investigate—there can't be anyone sleeping up here or they'd have appeared by now.' He swung himself into the hole and vanished.

Tallie sank down onto the cold leads and peered into the blackness below. She was shivering uncontrollably now and it was very hard to focus and to think straight. Nick's voice came up to her in a clear whisper. 'Sit on the edge and drop, I'll catch you.'

Beyond caring what she was falling into, Tallie did as she was told and was caught neatly and swung to the ground. Nick had already stripped off his coat and began pushing her arms into it like a nurse dressing a clumsy child. It was blissfully warm from his body, but the cold went so deep her very bones seemed frozen and the shivering did not stop.

Nick forced the door with as much ruthlessness as he had opened the hatch and led her out onto a landing. Peering over the balustrade, she could see the staircase descending into darkness.

'Either all in bed, which seems unlikely, or out,' he whispered. 'Come on.' Tallie took a faltering step and felt her legs go. The next moment she was caught up in Nick's arms again and he was descending the stairs, step by cautious step.

When they reached the hallway she was vaguely conscious of him fumbling with the door lock, then they were out on the street and Nick was striding rapidly out of Panton Square, across Coventry Street and into the narrow mews entrance of Coventry Court. *Goodness knows what this looks like*, Tallie thought hazily, but no one raised an outcry. Nick whistled and a carriage emerged from the shadows.

'All right, my lord?'

'All right, Roberts. Drive us to Upper Wimpole Street, fast as you can.'

'No one there,' Tallie mumbled against Nick's chest. 'All gone…Putney.'

He lifted her onto the seat. 'What did you say?'

Tallie made herself focus. 'No one at Upper Wimpole Street. Gone away on a visit.'

'Hell.' The carriage door closed and she was vaguely aware of Nick in low-voiced conversation with the coachman. It all seemed a long way away. She wasn't even very cold any more, just numb and dizzy and very sleepy...

She was so warm, so blissfully warm. Tallie lay with her eyes closed, letting her sore and aching body relax into the softness of the mattress. Over her there was the comforting feel of linen sheets, the reassuring weight of bedcovers. She nestled her head into the goose-down pillow and sighed gently, letting the memory of why she had so much wanted to be warm, why she seemed to be bruised all over, come seeping back into her half-conscious mind.

The studio, Jack Hemsley—and Nick appearing just in time to save her. So strong, so reassuring, and he had called her *my darling*. Tallie drifted back to sleep, dreaming of Nick, dreaming of his arms around her, the steady beat of his heart against hers, his strength and his courage as he got them both safe along that ledge and to freedom.

When she surfaced again the early morning sunlight was flickering on her closed lids. She was still deliciously warm, wherever she was. This was definitely not her bed, although that was not an alarming thought. She allowed the idea to penetrate her waking consciousness and with the realisation came the awareness that while she might be warm all over, it was her back, her buttocks, her thighs that were warmest. And they were warmest because she was curled up against another naked human being. And the weight over her waist was not the bedcovers, but an arm.

Tallie's eyes snapped open onto closed green brocade bed curtains. Whoever she was curled up against was lying very still; their breathing was hardly audible. Tallie made herself relax and concentrate on what she could feel.

A long arm, still now but promising strength. A long body. A *male* body. Tallie might never have seen a naked man in the flesh, but she had seen enough drawings of classical nudes in Mr Harland's studio to have a fairly clear understanding of the male anatomy. And the scent of him. Nick.

Before she could give herself time to think, Tallie levered herself up on the elbow she was lying on and twisted round to face the man behind her. It was a confused and tangled manoeuvre. Somehow she ended up with both his arms around her and her uppermost leg over both of his.

It brought them so close together that she had to tilt her head back to focus on his eyes. Those grey eyes with their long black lashes. They held hers and she could not pull her gaze away. Fascinated, she saw his pupils widen, the dark flecks expand until his whole gaze was almost blackly intent on her.

He did not speak; she seemed to have lost the power to. His breath feathered her lips and she felt them part as though welcoming a kiss. Her tongue touched her sensitive upper lip and she saw the awareness of it in his eyes, knew from the change in the breath caressing her mouth that his lips had parted in response.

Nick's arms held her to him, encircling her but not moving. She was conscious of every point where the pads of his fingers rested lightly on her sore, grazed shoulders and the small of her back. The heat and the gentle pressure stung, but it stung with the reminder that she was alive, able to feel pain and pleasure; alive and with her reputation intact only because of the man who was holding her in his arms.

The embrace brought them breast to breast, just close enough for her nipples to brush the crisp hair on his chest. The sensation was incredible. Their breathing was enough to generate a teasing friction that tormented her nipples into hard peaks of arousal, made her breasts ache and grow heavy, made her want to arch into him, beg him to take her in his hands and caress her.

Waves of heat flooded through her, down to where her leg lay over his, her soft smooth skin of her inner thigh against his hard muscle. To the place where she was left in absolutely no doubt of just how aroused he was. She saw reflected in his eyes her own shock and excitement, realised just what an effort of self-control was keeping him still. If she in her inexperience throbbed with the need to move against him, draw him to her, surrender herself to him, how was he fighting the instinct to crush her under him, take her, make her his?

Her eyes stayed locked with his, despite the languorous feeling of surrender that seemed to drag at her eyelids. His breathing was harder, faster, the breath on her parted lips like fierce kisses, demanding, promising. Their breathing quickened. She was aware of the infinitesimal movement of his fingers as he widened his already spread fingers on her back and all the time she was aware of the heat and arousal and sheer overwhelming masculinity of his need for her.

Only his stillness and his silence kept her from moving, arching into him, urgent, begging for his caresses. Perhaps her own stillness was strengthening his resolve, perhaps in itself it was an incitement. Tallie did not know, could not read the dark grey eyes, hazed with passion. Passion for her.

Was that what it was? Only passion? Could he love her? Tallie tried to speak with her eyes, tried to fight the clamorous messages her body wanted to send him and replace them with a message of love, of trust.

She tried to free her mind, fight all her instincts that had taught her to guard her feelings, hide her innermost emotions in case she was hurt, exposed. The heat in his eyes was still there, but something else as well, something she had not seen before, something she could not read.

Tallie found she had a voice after all. Her lips moved but only the faintest whisper emerged. 'Nick.'

It broke the spell of his control. He moved, his breath hot on her mouth. His lips touched hers, his hands tightened on her back. Tallie gasped and arched towards him as though bonds had been released.

'Tallie.' His voice was ragged, hoarse, the voice of a man who has reached the end of his tether.

Chapter Sixteen

Nick brought his mouth down on Tallie's, felt the sweetness as her lips parted under his, the instinctive yielding trust to follow wherever he took her. A silent shout of triumph and possessiveness rose in him, overwhelming, extraordinary, beyond anything he had felt with any other woman.

The knock on the door, as discreet as only the most highly trained valet could produce, was like a cannon shot in his intensely sensitised state. Nick froze, the erotic dream he had been immersed in giving way to broad daylight and the appalled realisation that, despite his firm resolve, he was in his bed making love to an innocent virgin who had every right to expect his protection and his respect.

Wrenching his eyes away from Tallie's face, seeing the softness of sensuality being replaced with a sharp edge of awareness and alarm, he threw back the bed-covers and stalked towards the door. The soft gasp from the bed made him glance down and realise just what a betraying state of arousal he was in.

Nick seized his dressing-gown, praying that after the first startled glance Tallie had closed her eyes.

With the bed curtains partly drawn, she was at least sheltered from the door, he thought grimly, dragging the garment closed and tying the cord.

He yanked the door open to find no one outside, but a tray left on the table. He lifted it and brought it inside, flicking open the folded note as he put it down.

I apologise for waking your lordship but, as you intimated last night a desire to make an early visit to Bruton Street this morning, I thought it advisable. Matthews.

His valet was the only one of his household, other than Roberts the coachman, who had any idea that he had brought a woman home with him last night. With his usual tact Matthews had placed only one cup and plate on the tray, but the jug of chocolate was larger than usual and, instead of the single roll he would normally consume with it, there was a selection of sweet pastries. Matthews never showed the slightest inclination to judge his master, whatever queer starts he got up to. He was fiercely protective of his reputation amongst the other servants and would doubtless swear blind they were all hallucinating if they came in this minute and saw who was in his bed.

There was silence behind the bed curtains. Nick stood regarding them, suddenly conscious of the ache of passion denied competing with the appalling stiffness that racked his shoulder and arm muscles. He grimaced and flexed his arms, welcoming the distraction from his other discomfort while he pondered on what to do now and just what a mess he had got himself into.

The clock stood at quarter past seven. There was time to plan Tallie's return to Bruton Street with some care. He opened the clothes press and found a thin silk dressing-gown he used when travelling and extended an arm around the curtains.

'Thank you.'

At least she was still speaking to him. Nick cleared his throat. 'If you draw the curtain when you are ready, I have some breakfast here for you.' Again, a polite acknowledgment. 'Then we need to discuss what to do next.'

That was greeted by silence. Just how long did it take to put on a dressing-gown? But instead of pulling back the curtain Tallie emerged from the far side of the bed, the gown wrapped tightly around her, her bare feet shuffling so as not to trip over the trailing hem. She pushed back the weight of her hair with both hands, an action that caused her breasts to lift and thrust against the thin silk. Nick closed his eyes and turned abruptly to pour chocolate, wishing he kept a bottle of brandy in his bedroom.

Behind him Tallie cleared her throat and then asked in a voice of determined calm, 'What happened last night?'

She watched Nick turn, his eyes on the cup of chocolate, apparently intent on not spilling it. He set it on a table in the window embrasure and pulled out a chair for her. Tallie stayed standing, wondering if the pounding in her blood was ever going to calm down, or if the throbbing ache in places she had hardly been aware of before was ever going to subside.

Nick added the plate of pastries to the table and said abruptly, 'Please sit down. If you don't, I can't.'

She went to sit where he indicated and pulled the cup towards her, suddenly both hungry and thirsty.

The sweet warmth sank into her stomach and she sighed and sat back, sitting up again with a sharp gasp as her lacerated skin hit the wood.

'Your back is badly grazed,' Nick said shortly. 'I put basillicum powder on it; I do not think it will scar.'

'Thank you.' He was obviously not going to make this easy for her. 'What did happen last night? I need to know.'

'How much do you remember? My carriage was waiting, but when you told me Mrs Blackstock and the rest of the Upper Wimpole Street household was away I had to think where else to take you. I could hardly return you to Bruton Street to a houseful of servants, stark naked.' Tallie closed her eyes momentarily at the thought. 'And you were freezing cold to the bone, scarcely conscious. I did not trust anyone else to look after you, so I brought you here, warmed you up the only way I could think of. I did not intend to stay after you had got warm, but I must have dropped off to sleep. I am sorry.'

Tallie bent her head over her plate and crumbled a roll. 'It was not your fault, you must have been exhausted. But...' This was so difficult! 'I must know— did anything...happen? I mean, once I was here...'

Nick moved abruptly and stood up. 'You mean, was I not content with waiting until you woke up to force myself on you? Did I ravish you while you were unconscious?'

As soon as he spoke Tallie knew how insulting her suspicions had been. 'No, of course not! I just thought...everything is so muddled. I thought perhaps we had...and I had forgotten. And you did not force yourself on me.' She seized the cup and took a long gulp to hide her burning face.

To her amazement Nick laughed. She stared at him, forgetting how embarrassing it was to meet his eyes, uncertain whether he was mocking her. But no, it was genuine amusement. He came and sat opposite her again, leaned across and took her hand in his. 'Tallie, my dear, you may have been in a poor way last night, but I do flatter myself that when I make love to a lady she does at least recall the experience the next morning.'

'Yes, of course,' she said hastily. Doubtless he had made love to scores of ladies, none of them as insultingly gauche as she was being. 'And I am sure I would be aware, I mean I would feel…' Her voice trailed away and she took a desperate bite of roll. Probably it was impossible to blush any redder than she was now, not without bursting into flames.

Nick appeared to pull himself together, which, she reflected bitterly, was a good thing because just at the moment the self-sufficient, practical, sensible Miss Talitha Grey would be unable to deal with a kitten who had stolen her knitting wool, let alone the tangle she seemed to have got herself into.

'I had no intention of being in the bed when you woke,' he said firmly. 'I apologise for my reactions when you did—the result of only that moment waking up myself, which is, of course, an explanation, not an excuse. I should have been able to control myself.'

'You appeared to be making a very good job of self-control,' Tallie observed. It seemed that one passed some kind of barrier of embarrassment beyond which it was impossible to feel any more humiliated or shy than one already did.

'Not good enough. There are things we must discuss, but not now.'

'Oh, yes,' said Tallie eagerly, wondering why Nick seemed so taken aback by her response. 'How did Mr Hemsley know I was going to be at the studio and how did you know that he knew?'

He relaxed. 'I will tell you about that later. Now, the next thing is to find you some clothes, I can hardly take you back to Bruton Street dressed like that.'

'You could go back to Mr Harland's studio and ask him to give you my clothes back.'

'No, the place might be watched still. I will write and ask him to make a parcel of the whole lot and send them back to Bruton Street. Beside anything else, you will want your reticule back.'

'That is a good idea,' Tallie agreed. 'In any case, I could hardly arrive home in the morning wearing the gown I left in the evening before.' A thought struck her. 'My goodness! What will the staff be thinking has happened to me? I must send a note at once to say I am safe.'

'No need. I called on my way back here with you and simply told Rainbird that you had decided to spend the night with your friend and had desired me to pass on the message as I was passing. He immediately assumed it was Miss Scott to whom I referred.'

'That was very deceitful,' Tallie observed, secretly admiring his cool thinking.

'Indeed it was,' Nick said penitently with a poorly suppressed smile. 'I should have told him that you were in my carriage without a stitch of clothing on and I was about to take you to my bed.'

'It is a lowering and sobering thought,' Tallie observed gloomily, 'that I have sunk so far into immodest behaviour that I can find that even moderately amusing.'

'Indeed it is. I suggest that you write a note to the housekeeper, saying that as you had not intended to stay the night you did not take a valise with you and asking her to pack one with a change of clothes and a walking dress. Naturally you wrote this last night and I, being a heedless and careless man who had consumed one too many glasses of brandy, forgot to deliver it. I will therefore appear, willing to atone for my fault by delivering the valise personally and not troubling Rainbird to send a footman with it.'

Tallie smiled her agreement and finished her roll. Then she realised that there was only the one cup and refilled it, pushing it across the table to Nick. They ate and drank in silence, he staring rather blankly at the bookcase on the far wall, she marvelling that it was possible to be lying in a man's arms in the throes of passion one minute and calmly sitting eating breakfast with him the next.

Presumably marriage was like this. That was a dangerous thought. Tallie let her gaze stray across to Nick. Those long fingers idly playing with the sugar tongs were marked with cuts and grazes from last night's adventure. They were also the fingers that had splayed on her back, pressing her into his embrace.

The expressive mouth, now rather immobile and straight, had curved in amusement just now, had compressed in anger and determination in the studio last night, and in bed had caressed her lips with a tender, demanding expertise that made her tremble to recall.

And as for the glimpse of him as he strode from the bed to answer the knock at the door—that image was overwhelming. Clothed she could appreciate his fitness, his strength, his elegance. Naked he was magnificent. And frightening.

The frightening male animal suddenly put down his cup, ran his hand through his hair and stood up with a grin that banished all her heated imaginings. 'Right, now you get back on the bed and pull the curtains round. I will ring for water, have a shave, get dressed and go to Bruton Street. While I am away you can wash; I'll tell Matthews to bring up plenty of water. He'll make sure you are not disturbed.'

'Is it not rather early?'

'The sooner I get you out of here the happier I will be. Rainbird will be confronted by a man with a hangover who woke at six with a crashing headache and a bad conscience for not delivering your note. I will be on my way to my club for the hair of the dog.'

Tallie duly retreated into her hiding place and sat curled up against the pillows while Nick washed and shaved. It was all very interesting. It seemed he sang quietly to himself while washing, in a very pleasant tenor. The song he began with proved highly improper, a fact that appeared to dawn on him by the second verse, which was abruptly cut off and replaced by something unexceptional.

He also shaved himself. Tallie listened to the sound of the razor being stropped, the soap being whisked up into a lather, the rather strangled hum the song deteriorated into as he shaved, the swish of water as he rinsed the razor.

Matthews came back from the dressing-room at the end of this ritual for an earnest discussion on that morning's clothes and was disappointed by the decision over which waistcoat his lordship was determined to wear, and mollified by a compliment on the state of his Hessians.

'I'm off now,' Nick said eventually. 'Matthews will look after you, and mind you don't set foot outside this door.'

It closed behind him and Matthews remarked, 'There is fresh hot water in the ewer, madam, and I have taken the liberty of replacing his lordship's soap with something more to a lady's taste. The towels are on the chair. Is there anything further madam requires? I suggest it would be unwise to ring. I will return to the dressing-room in thirty minutes and tap on the door. If there is anything you require, I will then be able to fetch it for you.'

Tallie scrambled off the bed and pounced on the hot water and soft towels with delight. Her feet were black; goodness knows what the laundry maids would think of the state of Nick's bed linen. She pulled off the robe and tried to look at the state of her back in the glass. It looked dreadful and felt worse with the grazes stiffening as they healed, but it probably looked worse than it really was. No lasting damage had been done.

No damage except to her heart. If she thought herself in love with Nicholas Stangate before, now she was convinced of it. He was courageous, strong, intelligent, amusing. And the touch of his fingers turned her bones to water. But all those things were just the parts that made up the man. He was more than the sum of them, and she loved him.

And it seemed that he cared enough about her to rescue her from the difficulties she had got herself into, despite discovering in the process that her secret

was every bit as scandalous as he had always suspected.

Tallie allowed herself to dream a little, then applied
some chilly common sense. She was his aunt's protégée—of course he was going to look after her to
spare Lady Parry worry and embarrassment and to
protect the family name.

She got dressed again in the robe and wandered
round the room, studying how Nick lived in his most
private space. She did not open any drawers or cup-
boards, but studied the pictures on the walls, the
books on the shelves, the careless litter of banknotes,
invitations, seals and fobs on the dressing-table.

It was a comfortable, masculine, unplanned and
very personal room. Some of the books and pictures
looked as though they were old family possessions,
presumably from his country seat. Others were newer.
She kept coming back to an oil painting over the fireplace. It was a landscape that did not seem quite finished at first; then, as she stared at it, began to make
perfect sense. It was disturbing and she went close to
peer at the signature. Turner. It meant nothing and
she resolved to ask Mr Harland if he knew of him.

By the time Nick returned she was curled up in a
chair, her bare feet peeping out from under the robe,
a book of travel memoirs by a member of the East
India Company open on her lap.

He closed the door behind him and leaned back
against the panels, regarding her with a slight smile
on his lips.

'What is it?' Tallie asked, suddenly defensive.

'I was just thinking what a charming scene to come

home to this is.' He strolled over and looked to see what she was reading. 'Interesting account, that.'

'Mmm. I would love to travel, but as I cannot, I enjoy well-written descriptions.'

'Why can't you travel?' Nick enquired, bringing over the portmanteau he had put down by the door.

'Are those my clothes? Thank you so much. Why can't I travel? Well, it is not something single young ladies can do, is it?'

Nick shrugged. 'Doubtless your husband will indulge you, even if it is only to Italy and not as far as India.'

Tallie stopped, her hands on the buckle of the portmanteau. 'Husband? You have more confidence in my acquiring one than I have! Now let me see—how do you think I should go about explaining that I have modelled naked for an artist or have scrambled around the rooftops of London in a state of nature? And at what point during the proposal does one introduce the subject?'

Nick opened the dressing-room door and paused on the threshold. 'I'll be in here, knock when you are ready. You know, Talitha, you are so intelligent and so practical and independent that sometimes I forget just how young you are and just how sheltered your life has been.'

What on earth did he mean by that? Tallie blinked at the closed door, then shrugged, regretted carelessly moving her sore shoulders and began to pull garments from the bag. Both of them were in rather an odd mood this morning, which was hardly surprising considering what had happened last night, to say nothing of what had almost occurred when they woke. Doubtless Nick would be back to his habitual cool, infuriating, distrustful state by the end of the day and she could maintain a safe and comfortable distance from him.

Indeed, when she tapped on the door and he emerged from the dressing-room the mask was firmly back in place and Tallie wondered if she had dreamed those intense, burning eyes, the flashes of deep amusement, the unguarded sharing of thoughts.

He carried her empty portmanteau downstairs, his other hand lightly under her elbow. The hall was empty: presumably when Lord Arndale told his servants he wanted privacy, that was what he got. He lifted a long cloak from the hall table and swept it round Tallie's shoulders, pulled up the hood and ordered, 'Keep your head down.'

Outside his carriage was waiting, blinds drawn, and she was inside and it was driving off before she could catch her breath.

'Now,' Nick observed, dropping onto the seat opposite her. 'The trick is to drop you off at Aunt Kate's front door and be away before anyone inside realises you have not got down from a hackney carriage.'

This manoeuvre was carried out with apparent success and Rainbird opened the door to Tallie without any appearance that her arrival after an unplanned night away was anything out of the ordinary.

'Good morning, Miss Grey.'

'Good morning, Rai…' Tallie was overcome by an enormous yawn. 'Oh, I do beg your pardon, Rainbird! I am afraid I was up far too late last night, and you know how it is when you sleep in a different bed.' She stifled another jaw-cracking yawn with difficulty. 'Would you be good enough to ring for my maid? I think I will go and lie down.'

Tallie had just enough wits about her to remember the state of her back as she was about to be helped out of her gown and to dismiss the girl as soon as she had unhooked the bodice. Her grazes smarted as she lay down, but within seconds the familiarity of her own bed lulled her and she fell into a deep, dreamless sleep.

Chapter Seventeen

Tallie awoke with a start to a bustle on the landing and the unexpected sound of Lady Parry's voice. She tumbled out of bed and dragged on her dressing-gown before peeping round the door.

She was not imagining things. Lady Parry was just untying her bonnet strings and talking to her maid while the footmen carried her portmanteau into her room. She caught sight of Tallie's tousled head and sleepy eyes and hurried across.

'My dear! Are you not well?'

Tallie allowed herself to be bustled back into her room. 'I am quite well, Aunt Kate. It was just that I had a very tiring evening last night and found myself yawning my head off this morning, so I thought the best thing to do was to go to bed and catch up on my sleep.' Sooner or later she was going to have to confess the whole ghastly business, but she needed to be awake first.

'My goodness! What have you been up to while I have been away?' Lady Parry asked archly, her eyebrows rising at Tallie's answering blush.

'Oh, it is a long story, ma'am! I will tell you all

about it later. But how is it that you are back so soon? How did you find Lady Palgrave?'

Lady Parry made an ambiguous noise, waved her hands vaguely and subsided into a chair, gesturing Tallie to sit down opposite her. 'Really, in some ways it was better than I could have hoped, which is why I am back so soon. She was already out of sympathy with the monkeys, which had quite wrecked the Blue Bedroom, were attempting to eat the wallpaper in the Chinese suite, of which she is very fond, and had bitten her favourite footman. So she had got rid of them.'

Something in Kate's voice suggested that this was not quite such good news. 'How, ma'am?'

'By the simple expedient of opening the windows and letting them go. Two have already been shot by the gamekeepers on neighbouring estates and a delegation of villagers and the vicar arrived as we did, to complain about the remaining two, which had taken up residence in the church. The vicar was talking darkly about reconsecration—I let poor William deal with that.'

'How?' Tallie asked fascinated, forgetting her own troubles.

'He commandeered a basket of peaches from my sister's succession houses, drove up to the village, had the church doors opened and placed a trail of fruit from the porch to the lych gate. The curate proved to be a crack shot, apparently.'

'Poor things,' Tallie observed compassionately. 'It was not their fault; I am sure they were only acting according to their natures.'

'I quite agree,' Lady Parry said. 'I remonstrated with Georgiana and put it to her that she should not interfere with God's dumb creation. At least pretty poets can be expected to look after themselves. She did appear chastened and somewhat sobered, so I deemed it safe to come home. William was becoming somewhat restive.' She stood up. 'I must go and change. Are you ready to get up, Tallie? We can have a late luncheon. William has gone to find Nicholas, doubtless for some sympathy.'

Tallie agreed with as much enthusiasm as she could muster. Her stomach seemed to contain a cold ball of lead, but she knew she must tell Lady Parry all about her connection with Mr Harland as soon as possible.

As she walked downstairs, schooling her face into an appearance of calm, the front door opened to admit both William and his cousin. Thankfully they did not see her for Tallie stopped dead three steps down and had to stay there for a full minute while she regained her composure. Nick here already! He was obviously not going to waste a moment in telling his aunt what a cuckoo she had been harbouring in the nest.

When she finally made her entry into the dining room, William greeted her with enthusiasm and proceeded to regale his audience with tales of the horrendous experiences he had had to endure. This kept everyone harmlessly occupied for the duration of the meal.

When the footmen came in to draw the covers Nick remarked, 'I have some matters I need to discuss with you, Aunt Kate. William, could you do me a favour? You know that new bay gelding I bought at Tatt's last week? I am not sure it is fully sound. You have a good feel for that kind of thing—could you take him out for me this afternoon, give me your opinion?'

He could not have offered a more tantalising bait.

Glowing with pleasure at the compliment to his judgement, William made his excuses to his mother and hurried off to change.

Lady Parry was less easy to gull. She led the way into her writing room and sat down, regarding the two of them with a quizzical eye. 'Well?'

'I have a confession—'

'Aunt, there is something I have to explain—'

They broke off, then Nick said, 'If you start, Tallie, I will join in as we get to my part in events.' She stared at him, suddenly overcome with nerves and he smiled reassuringly. 'We had best get it over with, do you not think?'

Tallie nodded dumbly and took a moment to order her thoughts. 'You recall, ma'am, that I came to you and said there was something I felt I should tell you about? A reason why I should not have accepted your offer to sponsor me?'

Lady Parry nodded. 'Yes. You were concerned that you had sat for Mr Harland.'

'Indeed, I had sat for him, ma'am. But not just to assist with portraits he was undertaking. When you said you knew all about it, I thought you really knew what I had been doing.'

'Which was?'

Tallie took a deep breath. 'Posing naked, or only lightly draped, for classical scenes.'

Lady Parry gasped, her eyes widened and she stared back at Tallie, apparently bereft of words for once.

'Extremely tasteful compositions,' Nick interjected as neither woman appeared capable of speech. 'And Mr Harland, as I am sure you will realise, has always behaved with the utmost respect and propriety towards Tallie.'

'*Propriety?*' Lady Parry moaned faintly. Then her gaze sharpened. 'And how do you know about this, Nicholas?'

'I visited the studio with Jack Hemsley. He wanted to make arrangements to have his aunt's portrait painted. William was with us and some other young cub.'

'I was posing for a scene as Diana the Huntress,' Tallie added. 'When he realised that Mr Harland was painting from a model, Mr Hemsley forced his way in. Ni…Lord Arndale tried to stop him—'

'But failed,' Nick finished grimly. 'It turned into a hunt.'

'Not William, surely?' Lady Parry asked, obviously appalled.

'It was not real for the two youngsters,' Nick explained gently. 'They had no understanding that they were searching for someone real, someone who would be frightened. If William had found Tallie, he would have protected her, I am sure of it.'

'I hid in a cupboard,' Tallie pushed on, her voice wavering, desperate to get the tale told. 'I lost my drape running away, the key fell out of the door—all I could do was turn my back on it, hide my face and wait.'

'I saw the drape and managed to divert the others. Luckily I saw the key and was able to give it to Tallie so she could lock herself in.'

'You were wonderful!' Tallie said vehemently, suddenly finding her voice again. 'You saved me and you acted with such…such consideration, such tact. If that awful man had found me I do not know what

I should have done. And I have never thanked you for it, even this morning…'

Her voice tailed off as she saw Lady Parry's expression. 'I am afraid there is more, ma'am.'

'I presume you did not recognise Talitha?' Lady Parry asked Nick.

'No, Aunt. I did not know her then, of course, and her hair was down. I never saw her face.'

His aunt closed her eyes fleetingly, apparently considering just what he had seen. 'Go on,' she said grimly.

'I bumped, quite literally, into Lord Arndale when I was delivering your hats the next day. I recognised his voice, but I do not think he knew me.' Tallie looked questioningly at Nick, who shook his head.

'I must have been blind, especially as I cannot deny that my experiences of the day before were more than somewhat on my mind.' Tallie bowed her head, blushing.

'Someone in bare feet with their hair down is going to look different from when they are wearing shoes and have their hair up,' Lady Parry conceded in a calm voice that Tallie found more worrying than a storm of anger would have been. 'No wonder you were so upset when you arrived at the house, Talitha.'

Without thinking, Tallie nodded agreement. 'It is very difficult, feeling so desperately grateful to someone when you cannot thank them and at the same time being extremely angry with them.' She caught Nick's eye and warmed at the flash of understanding she saw in them.

'Indeed. Well, let me see if I understand how the situation stood when you joined my household, Talitha. You knew who saved you at the studio and also believed that I knew about your…unconventional employment. You, Nicholas, had no idea that Talitha was the model you saw?'

'You are correct, although I knew that Tallie had a secret that she had managed to conceal from my enquiry agent and also that she intended to tell you about it, for she informed me of that when I challenged her.'

'So, when did you discover the truth?'

'At Tallie's first ball. Jack Hemsley managed to lure her into a retiring room and attempted to kiss her. Tallie put up a spirited resistance and her hair came down—at which point William and I found them. As soon as I saw her from the back, I knew.'

Tallie stifled a gasp. He had known for *weeks* who she was?

'And my son?'

'He was too busy being furious and disillusioned with Hemsley—one good outcome of the situation—to make the connection between a glimpse of a picture weeks before and the lady living under his roof and his protection and now the subject of insult.'

'And do you think Mr Hemsley recognised Tallie?'

'I think he must have done; I cannot account for what happened afterwards otherwise. He was too afraid of what I would do if he talked. Then Tallie gave him added reason to hate her by interfering in his attempt to seduce her friend Miss Blackstock.

'You had been the cause of his humiliation twice,' he said to Tallie. 'And he had reason to dislike me too. He had guessed I was instrumental in foiling his attempts to fleece William—' he ignored his aunt's indignant gasp '—and now I had witnessed his rout at the hands of you and Miss Blackstock. But he was still too wary of me to do anything direct.' Nick got up and began to pace slowly up and down the room.

'I became concerned. He had reason now to want revenge on both of us. Together we had humiliated him and been the cause of separating him from William in whom he had invested many months of patient grooming before settling down to fleece him.'

'I never liked the man!' Lady Parry burst out, her carefully maintained composure vanishing. 'I tried to for William's sake and because his aunt, Agatha Mornington, always speaks so fondly of him. And she is not someone easily taken in.'

'She has been this time,' Tallie said. 'He has taken a post-obit loan out against her life.'

'Undutiful creature! What a revolting thing to do, to leech onto the fortune of one's relative in that manner. And doubtless he will be investing much time and trouble in ensuring she remembers him generously in her will.'

'Hence the portrait,' Tallie reminded her.

'A post-obit.' Nick regarded Tallie thoughtfully. 'Are you sure?'

'Mr Harland thinks so.'

'Well, well, that *is* a useful piece of information.' Nick's grim smile boded Jack Hemsley no good whatsoever.

'So then what happened?' Lady Parry demanded. 'Do come and sit down, Nicholas, you are making me positively jumpy and you are usually so restful to have about.'

He threw himself into an armchair, crossed his legs, and regarded his aunt. 'I set a man to follow Hemsley. And when I heard that Tallie thought she was being followed, I set a man to follow her as well. You were quite right,' he added, turning to look at her. 'Hemsley's man.'

'And Hemsley organised the burglary at the studio!' Tallie gasped, suddenly making the connection. 'All he wanted was another look at the pictures to make sure it was me, and to confirm that they still needed some work doing on them. Then he had someone go and pretend they were interested in buying classical scenes…'

'His perfectly genuine cousin Oliver Laidlaw, just returned from Greece and on his way back to Scotland.' Nick grimaced. 'He took some finding, Hemsley was keeping him close.'

'And in all innocence Mr Harland asked me to pose one last time to finish the paintings.' She looked ruefully across to Lady Parry. 'I had realised by then that you had no idea what I had been doing after all. I was going to tell you when you came back, but meanwhile I went to the studio yesterday evening to help Mr Harland.'

'Hemsley's watcher told him you had stepped into the trap and that I was out of town. Mine too reported to me what was afoot.'

'And you were able to rescue Tallie in time?' Lady Parry asked anxiously. Tallie noticed with relief that she was once again using the affectionate diminutive.

'Just,' Nick said. 'I got there only moments ahead of Hemsley and a pack of his friends, all drunk and primed for fun.' He hesitated. 'We had to leave by the window.'

There was a silence. Then Lady Parry said carefully, 'Wearing what, my dear?'

'Nothing, ma'am.' Seeing the older woman go pale, Tallie added, 'It was a narrow ledge, and it was raining and we were high above the rest of the houses. Lord Arndale was wonderful—if he had hesitated for a second they would have found me. As it was, it must have been very difficult for him to get me down safely.'

Nick made an impatient gesture with one hand. The bruises and grazes stood out starkly and he clasped both hands together out of sight. 'She was frozen,' he said directly to his aunt. 'Mrs Blackstock's household were all out of town. I could not bring her here with only the servants and not a stitch on. I took her home with me and made sure she was warm and unhurt.'

Into the silence that followed this confession Tallie said, 'I returned this morning properly dressed. The staff think I was with the Blackstocks.'

Lady Parry did not seem either as angry or as shocked as Tallie had imagined she would be. Perhaps her patroness was just stunned, which would be understandable. Tallie discovered that she had a throbbing headache, which seemed to have appeared out of nowhere.

'May I be excused, ma'am?' she ventured. 'I would like to go and take a little sal volatile. I find I have a headache coming on. I will be back directly.'

'Of course, dear. There is no need to hurry back. And, Tallie…' Lady Parry smiled at her '…please call me Aunt Kate again. I feel a hundred when you both call me ''ma'am'' so stiffly.'

Nick relaxed at the twinkle in his aunt's eye. So, they were not in such deep disgrace as he feared; he was glad for Tallie's sake. He got to his feet and smiled reassuringly at her as he opened the door to let her out. She blushed and dropped her gaze sharply.

Nick turned back to his aunt. She knew exactly what must follow from last night's adventures, even if Miss Talitha Grey appeared not to have worked out the consequences. How would she react when she realised? Not that it made any difference—she was as committed as he had been from the moment they had stepped out onto that nightmare of a ledge last night.

He began to pace again, filling in more detail than he had done in front of Tallie, outlining the decisions he had reached after a morning's hard and serious thinking.

Upstairs Tallie poured a few drops of sal volatile into a glass of water and tossed it back with a grimace. The thought of lying down on her bed was very attractive, but she could not just run away and leave Nick downstairs, doubtless on the receiving end of a lecture from his aunt. Once Lady Parry had recovered sufficiently from the shock of their revelations to react, she could not believe they were not both going to be thoroughly in disgrace and Nick did not deserve anything except her grateful thanks.

Rainbird was just closing the front door as Tallie reached the hall again and he placed an envelope on a salver before handing it to her. 'This has just arrived for you, Miss Grey.'

Recognising Zenna's handwriting, Tallie tore open the wrapper without ceremony and scanned the contents.

…absolutely perfect, Tallie dearest! I have taken the liberty of sending the details direct to your attorney, but naturally I could not say anything to commit us without your personal approval. Do, please come and see—I could not bear to lose such a perfect house…

Tallie glanced rapidly through the closely written pages. It was unlike Zenna to wax so enthusiastic, she must indeed have found the ideal home for her long-dreamed-of school. She was walking slowly towards the writing room as she read and stopped outside the partly open door to shuffle the pages back together before entering.

Inside Lady Parry was speaking and the words froze Tallie where she stood. '...not at all what you planned. A suitable débutante this Season—I believe that is what you said when we last discussed your marriage.'

Nick appeared to be moving around. His voice became louder, then unintelligible as Tallie strained to hear, unaware that Zenna's letter was crushed in her hands.

'Of course, about time as you keep telling me...set up my nursery...perfectly suitable...I had thought Lord Rushingly's eldest, perhaps. Invite her to Heronsholt in the summer, make up a house party...'

'Well, you have not had the opportunity yet to fix her interest,' Lady Parry observed, sounding a little concerned. 'Unless I have missed something?'

'...too distracted by this business, which is a mercy as it turns out...'

'I rather think she has not realised this all means she must marry you,' Lady Parry observed.

Who? Tallie shook her head, puzzled, confused and with a growing knot of dread tightening inside her. *Who?*

'Tallie?' Nick's voice was so close by the door that she jumped and dropped the letter. 'I do not think it has occurred to her for a moment just how compromised she is or what the consequences of that are.'

Tallie was on her knees, scrabbling to pick up the scattered sheets as Lady Parry said, 'Certainly, one could not imagine for a moment that the poor child would intend to make such a match.'

'She is not so ineligible,' Nick said coolly. 'Her birth is perfectly respectable, her fortune, now, is more than comfortable.'

'Of course not, and she is a dear child. But not what one would expect for an Arndale of Heronsholt.'

Tallie stayed on her knees, transfixed, waiting for Nick's reply.

'Needs must, Aunt Kate. There is really no choice in the matter.'

Tallie stood up, her knees shaking. Until that moment she had not realised that all she wanted in the world was Nicholas Stangate. Now, and for ever. Yes, she had admitted to herself that she loved him, desired him, admired him. The word 'marriage' had never entered her thoughts; somehow, while he was a part of her everyday life, that had not been a consideration.

'You fool,' she whispered to herself, backing away down the hall. Her mind churned. *How else could you have him? Be his mistress? Why, when the world is full of skilled courtesans, should he bother with you?* Hope answered her, desperate. *He is attracted to you. He kisses you, takes you to his bed. He risks danger for you.*

Tallie reached the foot of the stairs. Mercifully neither Rainbird nor any of the footmen were in sight. Her clear-sighted common sense trod firmly on her optimism. *Of course he kissed you, of course he took you into his bed. He is a man, is he not? You stood naked before him. What did you expect him to think, to do? And he is a gentleman. Of course he would protect you. He would have protected Zenna or Millie if he had found them in such straits.*

The writing-room door opened and Lady Parry emerged. Tallie whisked round and under the stairs just in time to avoid being seen. But she was careless as she stepped out again once her patroness's footsteps had died away.

'Tallie. May I speak with you, please?'

It was Nick.

Chapter Eighteen

'Tallie,' Nick repeated, 'if your headache is not too bad, I would like to speak with you.'

'Of course,' Tallie replied composedly. It was easy to seem calm. She felt as though she had just stepped off a cliff: it was a very long way down, time would pass until she hit the ground, nothing much mattered in the meantime.

Nick held the door for her and she stepped into the writing room again, sank gracefully into a chair and waited, her eyes unseeing on Zenna's letter between her clasped hands.

'I hope you managed to have a little rest since you got home,' he began politely. 'It was hard to have to explain everything to Aunt Kate so soon after it happened, but I think it was for the best.'

'Thank you, yes. I feel quite restored, and I am sure you are correct.' Tallie took a deep breath. 'It seems to me that I have never expressed my sense of obligation to you for the way in which you have acted towards me, both before you knew who I was, and since.'

She was not watching him, so she could not tell

whether the abrupt movement he made away from her chair was surprise, or simply embarrassment at her words.

'Thank you. But I do not look for thanks for acting in a way that any gentleman would consider appropriate under the circumstances.' His voice sounded as stilted as the words. Tallie began to pinch the letter into tiny, perfect pleats.

'I doubt that many gentlemen would have the initiative to put in place such a careful screen of watchers and informants, nor would many men have the courage to go out onto that ledge as you did.' She was managing, somehow, to keep her voice as calm and level as his.

'I did what seemed necessary at the time, including the breaking and entering. Which reminds me, I really must send a note to that householder to warn him that his attic is now unsecured.'

Despite everything, a little snort of amusement escaped Tallie and she looked up. 'I hope you do not mean to sign it?'

He smiled in return. 'No, I think that would be taking honesty a little too far. I will include some money for repairs, but I do not intend to add my seal.'

Nick came and sat opposite her, crossed his legs, steepled his fingers and regarded her over the top of them. 'My agent has collected your clothes from Mr Harland and has ensured that the canvases have been removed and stored securely. Hemsley will not be able to find any evidence to connect you with that studio now, however hard he tries.'

'Well, that is a relief,' Tallie said briskly, setting her hands on the arms of the chair and beginning to rise. 'Thank you for setting my mind at rest. How very efficient your agent is.'

'Please, do not go. Surely you did not think that was all I wished to speak of?'

His eyes were steady on her face and Tallie schooled her expression carefully to one of mild puzzlement. 'Why, yes. Was it not?'

'No. Tallie, you realise that after last night you have been completely compromised?'

'But no one saw me,' she protested. 'Except Mr Harland, who does not count, and your coachman, who I am sure will be totally discreet.'

'I am referring, not to our rooftop escapades, which by some miracle we did scrape through unseen, but to the fact that you spent last night in my bed. With me.'

'You put me there,' Tallie pointed out. 'And nothing happened.'

That maddening eyebrow lifted as he lowered his hands. Tallie saw his mouth was twisted into a wry smile and found herself hopelessly distracted by the subtle changes of expression those flexible, sensual lips could evoke.

'Your definition of ''nothing'' is an interesting one,' Nick observed evenly. 'For myself, I retain a very vivid recollection of how your body felt in my arms and how it felt to kiss you.'

Tallie flushed, but held his gaze. If he could recall how her body felt, she was certain she was branded scarlet at every point his naked frame had touched hers. 'You have kissed me before. Jack Hemsley kissed me, come to that. No one suggested I had been compromised as the result.'

'There is all the difference in the world between a

few kisses and being in a man's bed. Face it, Tallie, you are *ruined.*'

What was it she had said to him, days…weeks ago? That this struggle of wills between them felt like a war? What was happening now felt like a duel.

She took a moment to calm her breathing, then asked politely, 'In what sense ruined? For what am I now unfit? I am physically exactly the same. I have perhaps acquired a little more knowledge of certain matters that I did not have before, but those can stay shut up in my mind. So, please define ruined, Cousin Nicholas.'

Suddenly his control snapped. Nick brought both hands down hard on the arms of his chair and was on his feet in a fluid movement, which gave her a glimpse of what a lethal swordsman he would be.

'Damn it, Tallie. For marriage, of course.'

It took an effort of will not to press back into the illusory safety of the high-backed chair. Mentally Tallie rallied, raised her guard and riposted, 'Why? No one else knows. I am still a virgin. And in any case, I have never had any intention of marrying, so the entire matter is academic.' She saw him begin to open his mouth and added tartly, 'And kindly do not swear again.'

'Swear?' Nick's eyes narrowed dangerously. 'Of course not. I apologise. What I will do next, if you persist in this ridiculous pretence that nothing of any consequence occurred last night, is to put you over my knee and—'

'Inflict violence upon me?' Tallie enquired sweetly. Her mind and consciousness seemed to be existing on two levels. On top there was a dangerous enjoyment in sparring with Nick, provoking him, seeing how she could strike sparks from his temper. Underneath something was shrivelling, dying. The man she loved was telling her that his actions had made her unfit for marriage to anyone else. It could only be a matter of moments before he explained that—as any gentleman must—he would therefore marry her himself.

Nick stood glaring at her. 'No, of course I would not hurt you. It is just that you are so—'

'Irritating? I must be, to make you lose your prized self-possession, your *froideur*.'

He stilled, his eyes narrowed, regarding her. 'Is that what you think I prize? Self-control? Coldness?'

'Is it not? I heard it in your voice before I even saw you. Calm, controlled, slightly aloof, just a very little amused at the caperings and emotionalism of us lesser mortals. You need to know everything, be in command. No surprises for Lord Arndale. No messy emotion or ill-bred displays of temper.' Now even the fencing was no longer amusing. All she wanted was to hold him off, perhaps hurt him a little, just a very little to counterbalance the pain inside her.

It seemed she had succeeded. The grey eyes were like black flint, the sensual, mobile mouth a hard line. Tallie expected a stinging rebuttal. What she got were hands on her shoulders pulling her hard into a crushing, furious embrace. She struggled, stamped one slippered foot futilely onto leather boots, lifted a hand to strike out and found both captured and pinioned neatly between their two bodies, ducked her face away from the angry purpose in his and found that with his free hand he had grasped her chin and was forcing it up.

'Now *this*, Miss Grey, is a display of messy emotion and ill-bred temper,' he ground out before bringing his mouth down hard on hers.

Tallie struggled furiously, her lips a tight line against the onslaught of his anger and her own desperate desire to yield to him, open to him, let him do what he would with her. She closed her eyes, felt the heat beginning to flood through her, felt her legs begin to tremble and suddenly she was no longer struggling.

She had no idea whether he had sensed her capitulation or had merely decided the demonstration of mastery was sufficient. Tallie found herself released as rapidly as he had seized her and sat down. By some miracle the chair was behind her. Furious with herself for her weakness and with him for exploiting it, she dashed the angry tears from her eyes and glared back at him.

Furious grey eyes glared back. 'Now, Miss Grey, as we have both comprehensively insulted and offended the other, might I suggest we return to discussing what we came in here to resolve?'

'What *you*, my lord, came in here to resolve. As I thought I had made clear, there is absolutely nothing I wish to speak about, other than to reiterate my gratitude for your actions yesterday. They were, if nothing else since has been, the actions of a gentleman. No, that is unfair.' She held up a hand to silence him and continued in a manner of frigid politeness, which she could see was inciting him to even greater depths of anger. 'I must also be grateful for the manner in which you assisted me in telling Lady Parry a story that must have been very shocking for her.'

'I do not want you to be fair, Tallie, I do not want your gratitude, what I want is—' He broke off, one clenched fist poised to thump the table as the door opened.

'That horse is as sound as a bell. I cannot imagine why you thought—' William stood in the doorway, whip in one hand, hat in the other, regarding the two of them with some confusion. 'I beg your pardon. Have I interrupted? I could hear voices and I thought you would want your mind set at rest about the animal.'

'Not at all, Cousin William,' Tallie said warmly. 'I am delighted to see you. Do, please, come in and tell Cousin Nicholas all about his horse. I must go and write a letter.' His arrival had only put off the painful declaration she was certain Nick was going to make her sooner or later, but, although she reproved herself for being a coward, she could only be glad of the respite.

'We were just discussing Jack Hemsley's latest activities,' Nick said smoothly, ignoring Tallie's horrified expression. He moved across and placed a hand on her shoulder. Without an unseemly struggle she was effectively trapped. 'Cousin Tallie thwarted his attempts to seduce a friend of hers and it appears that two blows to his pride by one young lady was more than he could stomach. Added to that, it seems he realised that to attack the young lady living under my aunt's roof would be to attack me—and I have been acting in such a way recently that his dislike of me has grown inordinately. He hatched a plot to ruin Tallie, which fortunately misfired last night. I have been considering what to do about him.'

Tallie sank back into the chair and considered giving herself up to strong hysterics. Nick was blandly ignoring the furious looks she was shooting him while

William was reacting with predictable indignation. 'What to do? How can you even hesitate? Why, I will call him out, the bast—blackguard. Cousin Tallie is a guest under my roof, my mother's companion. This is outrageous!' He took an agitated turn around the room and swung round to face them. 'What did he do?'

'I really would prefer not to discuss it,' Tallie interjected hastily. If she had not been feeling so flustered she might have been amused at the confusion into which she had thrown William, who blushed and began to stutter at the thought he had embarrassed her. 'And, please, I could not bear it if either of you call him out. What if you were to be wounded?'

William looked hurt, Nick merely raised an eyebrow and remarked, 'Unlikely. No, we need to avoid any hint of scandal in dealing with Hemsley—Tallie's position in this household is too well known not to arouse suspicions if one of us openly challenges him. I have a better idea—one that I can thank you for, Tallie. Financial ruin is going to be a much more effective punishment for Jack than an uncomfortable dawn meeting on the Heath. Is Aunt Kate downstairs, William?'

'In the front salon,' he replied. 'I thought it was odd; she is usually in here at this time of day.'

Tallie glared at Nicholas through narrowed eyes. So, Lady Parry had tactfully removed herself while he made a declaration, had she? It was regrettable that she had to disappoint her kind patroness, but she was not going to marry Nicholas Stangate to satisfy anyone's ideas of what was the right and proper thing for a compromised young lady to do.

'Then let us consult her.' Nick opened the door for

Tallie and steered them both in the direction of the front of the house. 'If my memory serves me right, we will have the perfect opportunity for our retribution tonight.'

Lady Parry looked up with a smile that rapidly faded as she took in Tallie's tight lips, Nick's expressionless face and William's pink-cheeked indignation.

'We have just been telling William that Jack Hemsley has attempted to ruin Tallie.'

'Oh, dear.' Lady Parry fluttered a white hand and lay back against the sofa cushions. 'This is all very...distressing. You will not say anything, William dear, will you?'

'Of course not.' Her son looked indignant. 'Don't know what happened anyway, so I can't say anything. I just want to put a bullet in the man. Damn it, when I think I believed him my friend!'

'Language, dearest! You are not going to call him out, are you, Nicholas?'

'No. There is too much risk it would draw attention to Tallie.' Nick pulled over a chair and sat down. 'Am I right in thinking it is Lady Agatha Mornington's dress ball tonight?'

'Oh my goodness, yes, it is! I had quite forgotten, what with all the excitement of having to go down to Sussex and then poor Tallie's adventures. Were you thinking that Mr Hemsley would be sure to be there in attendance on his aunt and it would therefore be embarrassing for Tallie to see him?'

'Not at all. I was wondering if you felt rather too tired after your journey to go, that was all.' Nick sat twisting his signet ring round his finger with a vaguely abstracted air. Tallie eyed him cautiously. He was plotting, she was sure of it.

His aunt was even more certain. 'Out with it, Nicholas. What do you have in mind?'

'A punishment for Jack Hemsley that will ensure he is hurt where it will do him most damage—in his pocket and in his reputation. And it will ensure he will not dare to return to town for a good long while. If he can afford to, that is. But I am going to need all three of you to pull it off.'

Lady Parry sat up sharply, eyes sparkling. 'Wonderful! I have been wanting to box that young man's ears ever since I heard of his ungentlemanly behaviour.'

Nick turned to look at Tallie, who found that her hands were clenched into fists in her lap. The thought of turning the tables on Jack Hemsley was powerfully attractive. 'Tallie? Do you feel you can cope?'

'With anything,' she affirmed with emphasis. 'What do you want us to do?'

At ten that evening Nick smiled at his troops as their carriage drew up at the steps of the Morningtons' town house. In the light from the flickering flambeaux their faces were curiously intent and dramatic. 'All ready? Are you sure you know what to do? We cannot know the layout of the ballroom in advance, so we will have to improvise if necessary.'

'We will cope,' Lady Parry declared. 'After all, there are only so many ways one can arrange the room and Lady Mornington is not one to be endlessly seeking for variety and novelty. But poor Agatha! I do dislike being the one who reveals the depths of infamy her wretched nephew has sunk to.'

'Think how she is being deceived now, though,' Tallie comforted. 'And you did say she had some very pleasant nephews and nieces on the other side of the family from whom she has been estranged because she so favours Jack. How much better it will be if she has their loyal support and not that of a money-seeking rake.'

'I would not put anything past him,' William added grimly. 'If the moneylenders get impatient at having to wait too long for that post-obit to be repaid, goodness knows what he might do to get his hands on her fortune.'

Lady Parry gasped, but Nick said repressively, 'Your Gothic imaginings are frightening the ladies, William. Now, if we are all ready, let us draw the first covert.'

With butterflies in her stomach Tallie followed her patroness up the double staircase to the wide landing outside the ballroom. They had deliberately timed their arrival for when the receiving line would have ended and their hostess would be found inside with her guests. Kate stepped into the hot, noisy throng, nodding and bowing to friends. With her hand under Tallie's elbow, she steered her firmly past the young gentlemen who stopped to request a dance.

'A little later, Lord Dimsdale, we are on an errand at present... Good evening, Mr Hubbert, I am sure Miss Grey will give you a dance later, but just now we really must find our hostess for a few words.'

Tallie craned to see the other side of the room. Nick's dark head could be glimpsed in the gaps between sets of the country dance, which was boisterously under way. He was making steady progress up the room and suddenly Tallie saw his objective at the same time as Jack Hemsley saw Nick.

He turned abruptly on his heel and headed deeper into the onlookers towards the head of the room. 'Gone away,' she whispered to Lady Parry. 'Nick has successfully flushed him out of cover.'

'Good. Ah, there is poor Agatha Mornington.'

'And there is William, dodging into the retiring room and out of the other door to get ahead of Mr Hemsley.'

'This is very exciting… Good evening, General! Yes, indeed, *what* a crush.' Kate bowed graciously to the military man and bore down on their hostess, a formidable matron whom Tallie recognised from her portrait at Mr Harland's studio. 'Agatha! What a delightful dance! Have you met my dear young friend Miss Grey? Talitha, make your curtsy to Lady Mornington.'

Tallie bobbed neatly and shook hands, finding herself under a sharp and intelligent scrutiny. How had such a lady been taken in by her scamp of a nephew? she wondered. Presumably she was not the first doting aunt to be deceived by charm and address, and doubtless not the last.

Kate, with one rapid glance across the ballroom to where her son was converging with Jack Hemsley from one direction and Nick Stangate from another, turned slightly and began to stroll towards the head of the ballroom. Just a few steps away a small sitting-out area had been contrived with chairs and divided into two by a screen of potted palms.

'Agatha, my dear, I wonder if you can spare us a moment,' she said earnestly. 'Miss Grey has a favour to ask you.'

'Oh, please, Lady Parry,' Tallie interjected, obedient to her script. 'I would not want to trouble Lady Mornington by asking her about dogs when she must want to be talking to her guests.'

'Dogs? Are you interested in dogs, my dear?'

'Oh, yes, ma'am, and I was thinking particularly of buying a pug. Lady Parry says no one knows more about them than you and perhaps you could advise me where the best place to obtain one would be?'

She had been dubious when Lady Parry had told her that a discussion about pugs would be guaranteed to divert Lady Mornington whatever the circumstances, but it seemed that she had been quite correct. Tallie found herself seated and being comprehensively lectured and questioned.

'Well, yes, ma'am, I do enjoy walking...' There was Nick a few yards away. He had halted and was standing with his back turned, apparently deep in conversation with another man. That escape route had been stopped then; Jack Hemsley would not care to pass so close to Nick.

'I had no idea they would need so much exercise.' Lady Mornington was waxing lyrical about the boundless energy of pugs and the need for long walks whatever the weather. 'How very invigorating. I had rather imagined them to be lap dogs.'

Through the potted palms she could just glimpse William's blond head, then she heard him. 'Jack! I should have known I would see you here.' He sounded wary, but not unfriendly.

Hemsley's slightly deeper voice carried even more clearly and Lady Mornington turned her head slightly and smiled, obviously recognising her favourite nephew. 'Parry, old chap. Er...'

'Oh, look, I think I overreacted the other week at the ball, you know...' William was doing an admirable imitation of a callow youth in the throes of hero worship. 'I mean, I'm sure things weren't what they seemed... Thing is, I don't want to fall out with you...'

'Don't give it another thought. Tell you what, come to the prizefight in Bedford with me next week—we'll make up a party, what do you say?' There was relief and suppressed triumph in the affected voice and Tallie bit the inside of her lip in an effort to keep focused on Lady Mornington while watching Kate Parry out of the corner of her eye.

Lady Parry, who was dressed in an unusual shade of deep salmon to ensure she was visible, shifted her position and Tallie saw her nod. William must have glimpsed his mother through the palms and seen her signal, for his voice became a little louder and Tallie, hearing her cue, dropped her fan and dance card. With a murmur of apology she fell to her knees and began to hunt round under her chair, cutting off Lady Mornington in mid-sentence.

'That's a damn nice new curricle you've got, Jack,' she heard William say enthusiastically. 'More benefits of that post-obit loan you took out on your Aunt Mornington? Or has the old lady coughed up some more of the readies, seeing what a handsome portrait you commissioned of her?'

Tallie glanced up. Lady Mornington had frozen where she sat, her eyes riveted on the screen of palms. 'Wish I had your knack of turning old ladies up sweet,' William persisted loudly. 'What's the trick to it?'

Go on, Tallie willed Jack Hemsley. *Go on, boast about how clever you are.*

Chapter Nineteen

Jack Hemsley did not disappoint Tallie.

'Trick, old chap? Nothing to it. Old trouts like her will lap up any amount of honey, you can't pour too much on, trust me. Flatter her dreadful hats, take her driving in the park so she can wave to her ghastly friends, pet her God-awful pugs—they've all got something like that, if it isn't pugs it's a parrot—you can't fail. A bit of sharp work with the other relatives to put them out of favour and there you are—favourite nephew and all the dibs in tune.'

Lady Mornington surged to her feet. 'Excuse me, my dear,' she said with awful calm to Tallie, who was still crouched by her chair making a business out of picking up her fan. A terrible figure in puce, she stepped round the screen of palms. Kate pulled Tallie upright and the two of them followed apprehensively after her.

The scene that greeted them might have been a tableau from a melodrama. Lady Mornington, bosom visibly quivering with indignation, confronted her white-faced nephew who was pinned between his outraged relative, William—who was inconsiderately standing fast at his back—and an interested crowd of onlookers who, realising something was afoot, had turned to watch. Prominent amongst them was Nick and the man he had been talking to: the Honourable Ferdie Marsh, the worst gossip in London Society.

'Despicable boy!' Lady Mornington hissed, the plumes on her coiffure shaking. 'Lying, toadying, deceitful wretch! This is how you repay my kindness, this is how you serve your cousins, poisoning my mind against them! I shall change my will tomorrow morning, not one penny shall you get from me. In fact…' her eyes narrowed, regarding his pinched and furious face '…in fact, I will not risk leaving it to tomorrow. The Lord Chief Justice is here tonight—I am sure he will be only too pleased to draw up a codicil for me here and now.'

She swept round, magnificent in her fury, and her eyes fell on Tallie. 'And you, dear child, can help me find him. Are you acquainted with his lordship? Tall man, always looks different without his wig, I find…' She swept Tallie off without a backward glance. 'You shall have one of Esmeralda's puppies from the new litter. You are a good child and I am sure will look after it excellently well.'

'Tha-thank you, ma'am,' Tallie faltered, taken aback by this powerful self-control. 'Ma'am…I am so very sorry about what just…' She did not know whether to feel guilty or not. It was horrible for Lady Mornington to have Hemsley's character exposed before an audience, but perhaps it was much worse that she should be estranged from her honest relatives because of the greed of one unpleasant nephew.

Lady Mornington gave her a sharp look. 'I have been a foolish old woman,' she said briskly. 'Serves me right. His father, my younger brother, was just the same—should have realised the bloodline would breed true.'

'Is that the Lord Chief Justice over there, ma'am?' Tallie asked hastily.

'Indeed it is, you have sharp eyes. Now, off you go, back to Kate Parry and have a good time, child. I,' she added with a note of grim amusement in her voice, 'I intend to.'

Tallie hurried back, seeing William energetically dancing a boulanger with a pretty redhead and finding Kate just accepting a glass of lemonade from her nephew.

'Well done,' Nick said appreciatively. 'That was an entirely successful ambush. One cannot but admire Lady Mornington—did you notice the insinuation that she had to change her will immediately or she might not live to see the next day?'

'*Everyone* is talking about it,' Kate Parry said, fanning herself vigorously. 'And it is losing nothing in the telling, I can assure you. Tallie—is Agatha much upset?'

'Very cross with herself, I think,' Tallie said. 'And resolving to make amends with her other nephews and nieces. But I do not think she is sad, or greatly distressed.' She looked at Nick. 'Where is Mr Hemsley? Did he see us?'

'He has gone. Even someone with Jack's brass neck could not brazen it out in front of an entire ballroom full of people sniggering at him. There is no need to worry—he saw William and me and I am sure he has wit enough to know that we set out to entrap him, but I do not think he realises the part you and Aunt Kate played.'

'I am not frightened of him,' Tallie said scornfully, then caught Nicholas's eye and added ruefully, 'Not while I have you and William to look after me at any rate. I have to admit, I am not a match for someone like that without help.'

Nick bowed ironically. 'That is gracious, Tallie. May I solicit the next dance?'

It seemed they were on ordinary speaking terms again, and at least he could not launch into embarrassing lectures on how ruined she was or, even worse, make a declaration in the middle of Lady Mornington's dress ball.

'Thank you, Lord Arndale,' Tallie said politely, allowing him to lead her out onto the dance floor. 'What is it? I have lost track of the dance programme with so much excitement.'

'A waltz,' he replied, catching her efficiently around the waist with one hand and capturing her right hand with the other. 'You have to admit, my timing is perfect.'

'Perfect,' Tallie agreed hollowly as the music struck up and she was swept into the dance. *Perfect.* The last thing she needed was to be held in Nick's arms as the sensuous, exciting music took them. It was hard enough being with him and fighting to keep the yearning out of her voice, the love out of her eyes, without being so close to him that she could feel his warmth, smell the clean, sharp, indefinable maleness of him.

She needed to concentrate on thwarting any attempt to make her an offer, or, if she failed in that, to refuse him convincingly. As it was she could feel him gathering her tighter into his arms and could make no effort to draw away. Another couple brushed against her skirts and Tallie found herself touching his body, then he had released her again and all she was conscious of was the pounding of her heart and the glitter of his grey eyes when she looked up at him.

The music drew to a crescendo and stopped. Couples stepped apart, clapping politely and beginning to stroll off the floor, but Tallie found herself steered ruthlessly through the onlookers fringing the dance floor and into a deserted retiring room.

'My lord! What on earth are you about! Please return me to Lady Parry at once—she will concerned to know where I have gone.' Tallie tried to convince herself that the breathless catch in her voice was simply natural agitation and not the effect of being masterfully carried off in the midst of a crowded ballroom.

'You may return to her side the minute we have had this much-overdue conversation,' Nick said patiently, moving round to lean broad shoulders against the door panels.

Tallie eyed the only other exit from the room, a narrow window.

'And we are one floor above pavement level and, if I am not mistaken, that window will overlook the area, which adds another floor to the drop. If you feel you have overcome your fear of heights do, by all means, feel free to leave.'

Tallie glared. 'I have no intention of scrambling out of a window to escape you, my lord. You have only to remove your shoulders from that door and I will walk out.' Provided she could stay angry with him, it was easier to cope. Tallie stamped her foot. 'Will you please open that door, my lord!'

'Only if you stop calling me "my lord" every sentence...'

'Very well then, Nicholas, please—'

'And if you agree to marry me,' he finished.

It was not unexpected. She had been trying to avoid him putting that very question all day, but that did not make it any better. Every fibre of her being was screaming *yes*! Tallie raised both eyebrows haughtily. 'You will excuse me, *my lord*, if I find the warmth and sincerity of your offer less than compelling. I am, naturally, conscious of the honour you do me in making such a proposal; however, I must decline.'

'Tallie.' It was a warning growl.

'My lord?'

'I suppose you would like me to come and kneel down, clasp my hands to my heart and beg you to do me the honour?'

'That would certainly be an improvement,' she agreed, casting her eyes downwards so that he could not see the sudden resolution in them.

'Very well.' Nick straightened up, took two long strides forward and fell on one knee in front of her. He placed one hand on his heart and said, 'Miss Grey, may I solicit—'

Tallie whirled away and made a dash for the door. Her fingers were closing around the handle when he took her by the shoulders, spun her round and trapped her against the panels, one hand on either side of her head. It had been a mistake to forget just how good his reflexes were and just how fast he could move.

Now what are you going to do? she asked herself. *If he kisses you, you are done for and you know it.*

'Tallie. As we were discussing this morning when William interrupted us, I have thoroughly compromised you. There is only one outcome from that. You must marry me.' He sounded as though he were keeping the lid upon his patience with some effort.

'And as I explained to *you*, you may have compromised me, but nothing *happened*. No one else besides ourselves and Lady Parry knows about it. I *have* to do nothing whatsoever, and if you tell me that your honour is at stake or some such masculine nonsense, I give you fair warning, I will kick you.'

Frustrated grey eyes stared into hers. 'Why will you not say yes? I am hardly ineligible. You know you may acquit me of fortune hunting. Is there someone else?'

'No, there is not.' Where the breath to keep talking was coming from Tallie had no idea. She was not conscious of breathing at all and her heart was banging so hard she thought it must be visible through the fine gauze of her bodice. 'I do not wish to make a loveless marriage, it is as simple as that.'

'But—' Nick broke off, for once silenced. Then he said with a hint of a smile, 'I had rather thought that when I kissed you you were not averse to the caress. In fact, when I have held you in my arms you reacted with warmth.'

'I am aware that ladies are not supposed to enjoy such things,' Tallie retorted, wondering if the guardian spirit of Modest Behaviour was about to strike her down where she stood. 'But I can see that is nonsense, some tale put about to shelter innocent girls. After all, if married ladies did not enjoy it, why would they have affairs? I must confess that I find being kissed by you very…pleasant, and being in your arms is positively stimulating. However,' she hurried on as both Nick's eyebrows rose alarmingly, 'that does not mean

I want to marry you. Naturally I realise that now we have had this discussion you are not going to kiss me any more—and that is a pity because I do enjoy it and I would certainly not trust any other gentleman of my acquaintance in that way.'

'Well, that is frank speaking indeed.' The familiar cool expression was back on his face and she could not tell whether he was shocked, angry or even, just possibly, amused.

'I am afraid so.' Tallie tried to look penitent. 'I did feel ashamed of myself and then I realised that it is foolish to deny one's natural, er...appetites. Of course, one should not indulge them any more than one should drink too much wine or eat too much rich food, and one realises in the case of ladies that the penalties are somewhat more extreme.' Now, surely, she had shocked him sufficiently to put an end to any desire to marry her. She was certainly shocking herself.

'But within marriage you could indulge those appetites completely,' Nick observed. 'You know, Tallie, you are not managing to shock me, which is what I believe you are trying to do. Amuse me, exasperate me and try my patience, certainly. But I am hard to shock and quite alarmingly patient when I want to be. And I do not believe your assumption of the mantle of a loose woman remotely convincing. Now, be a good girl and say ''yes'' and we can go out and tell Aunt Kate and all will be easy.'

'No.'

'Tallie, you have failed to convince me you do not wish to marry me because you are a wanton...'

'Not a *wanton*,' she protested. 'Or at least, only with you. I like you kissing me, I have to admit it, but I would not have said so if you had not produced that as a clinching argument as to why we should marry. But liking kissing someone is absolutely no reason to think they would be the right person to marry. How many women have you kissed?'

'Me?' He removed his hands and straightened up, although he did not move back. 'I have no idea.'

'Did you enjoy kissing them?'

'On the whole, yes. Tallie, what *has* this to do with our marriage?'

'And how many of them have you married?'

'None of them!'

'Precisely my point,' Tallie said triumphantly. 'Just because you enjoy kissing someone, it does not mean you want to marry them. So that, my lord, is not a good argument. How else do you intend to convince me?'

'You enjoy sparring with me, do you not, Tallie?' He had his hands on his hips now, head on one side as he regarded her thoughtfully. His lips quirked and she fought the urge to either smile back or stand on tiptoe and kiss the corner of his mouth. She was proving a puzzle to him, a problem, and Tallie sensed that she was also becoming a challenge, almost an intellectual conundrum to be solved.

'Yes,' she admitted. *And how much fun it would be to be married to him, to stimulate that sharp brain and tease that flashing sense of humour.*

'You will not win, you know,' he observed.

'That is not gentlemanly of you.' Tallie tried a pout for effect. The only reaction that produced was a grin of sheer devilment.

'Are you a gamester?'

'No…no, I do not think so. I have never been tempted by games of chance.'

'Well, let me tempt you with a bet upon a certainty. I wager you will agree to marry me within two weeks of today.'

That seemed safe enough, she was not going to agree, whatever wiles he used. 'Marry you within two weeks or simply agree to do so?'

'Agree, I think. I see no point in setting myself any harder a task than I have to.'

'And if you win?' she asked.

'You marry me.'

'And if you lose?'

'What would you like?' He stepped back and smiled again at the innocent calculation her face betrayed.

'My own phaeton and a team of match bays.'

'Very well.'

Tallie gasped. 'Seriously? I never thought you would agree.'

'I have absolutely no intention of losing, so I can afford to be generous. Of course, if you want such a rig, you only have to marry me and you can have one anyway.'

'You are absolutely the most infuriating man I have *ever* come across.' Tallie reached behind her for the doorknob. 'Now, are you going to let me out of here?'

'Once we have sealed the bet,' he said and took her in his arms. His mouth silenced her protests and he made not the slightest attempt to restrain her, simply allowing the drugging, languorous, sensual slide of his mouth over hers and the insidious caress of his fingers on her throat and shoulder to hold her to him.

Tallie moaned softly and let her body mould to his

for a long, shuddering moment. Her lips parted and his tongue slid between them, so gently, so subtly that before she knew what she was doing her own tongue had begun to caress his in turn. He left her mouth and began to nibble the taut tendons of her neck. The blood was roaring in her ears so loudly that she hardly heard the question at first, then he repeated it, murmuring it as his lips teased and tormented the soft skin behind the curl of her ear.

'Marry me, Tallie.'

Tell me you love me, Nick, say it. Then I will marry you. Tell me...

'You stir my blood, Tallie. Marry me.'

Not enough. Oh, I want you too...but it is not enough.

'No.' Tallie pushed him away with both palms flat on his chest. 'No, and I am not going to kiss you again.'

Nick stepped back, his own hands raised in the fencer's gesture of surrender. 'I promise not to try— for tonight at least.'

Tallie caught a glimpse of herself in the mirror that hung on the opposite wall. 'Oh, for goodness' sake, just look at me!'

'I am,' Nick drawled. 'You look delightfully tousled and it provokes the most terrible desire in me to tousle you even more.'

'Well, you can't,' she retorted crisply, more to suppress her own longing to be back in his arms than out of any real fear that he would snatch her into them. She smoothed her hair, rescued some pins that were hanging on by their very tips, fastened the roses, which her maid had tucked into the knot at the nape of her neck, back with their comb and surveyed herself critically, managing not to catch Nick's amused eye as he watched her. 'It will have to do. Now, how are we going to get out of here unseen?'

'Through the window?'

'You certainly deserve to!' Tallie peeped round the edge of the door and saw with relief that a particularly noisy and energetic country dance was in progress with most of the onlookers' attention focused on the dance floor. She slipped out and wove her way through the chairs and pillars until she had put a respectable distance between herself and the retiring-room door.

'Cousin Tallie, may I ask you something?'

It was William, appearing at her side as though by magic. Tallie blinked at him, still too shaken by what had just taken place to focus properly. 'William? Not you as well? It is too much!'

Chapter Twenty

Nicholas sauntered casually out of the retiring room just in time to see Tallie turn from William, fumble in her reticule for her handkerchief and disappear into the sitting-room which had been set aside for ladies.

He laid a none-too-gentle hand on his cousin's shoulder. 'And just what have you said to Tallie to upset her?'

'Damned if I know,' William retorted defensively. 'All I said was that there was something I wanted to ask her and she said, "Not you as well? It is too much" or some such nonsense. Then her eyes filled up with tears and off she bolted!' He looked aggrieved. 'I only wanted to ask her to dance the boulanger. I know I'm not that good a dancer, but no one has ever burst into tears before when I asked them.'

Nick eyed the firmly closed leaves of the sitting-out-room door, a faint and uncharacteristic line forming between his brows. 'I suspect she thought you were about to propose.'

'Propose? Propose what?' William crooked a finger at a passing waiter, secured a glass of champagne, then choked on the first sip. 'Not *marriage*?'

'Hmm.' Was that what Tallie thought? That there was a family plot for one of them to marry her because she had been compromised and if she did not marry him, then his cousin would step into the breach?

He regarded William, who was coughing indignantly, and administered a sharp slap on the back. 'Stop that racket. Is it so surprising? I've been dinning into her the fact that she has been compromised and will have to marry someone.'

'Well, why isn't she marrying you?' William enquired in a whisper, casting a hasty glance round to see if anyone had noticed their conversation. 'You compromised her. And she's in love with you.'

'*What?*' Nick thundered, fortunately under cover of the opening chords of the boulanger, then dropped his voice hastily. 'Of course she isn't. If she were, she wouldn't have turned me down.' Or given me such an effective summing up of my thoroughly unsatisfactory character, he thought grimly. His mind flinched at the memory of her bitingly expressed opinions—cold, controlling, aloof, amused at the antics of lesser mortals. Apparently pleasant enough to kiss.

William gave an unmannerly snort of disbelief. 'The pair of you are going about like April and May, for goodness' sake!' Nick regarded him incredulously. 'Very well, not quite like that, I suppose, but one can feel it in the air when the two of you are together. A certain something.'

'What you can feel is irritation on my part and wilful bad temper and obstinacy on hers.' And enough erotic attraction to light kindling, Nick ruefully acknowledged. Could Tallie possibly be in love with him? Surely not, or why on earth refuse him?

He shook his head as though shaking off an irritating fly. William was hardly a connoisseur of the tender passions—paying him any heed on the subject was madness.

And if anyone was running mad it was Nicholas Stangate, Lord Arndale. He had given himself two weeks to change Tallie's mind and now he was even further from understanding that mind than he had been at seven o'clock that morning. Damn it, was it only that morning that she'd lain in his arms, in his bed? He felt his body tightening at the memory and trampled ruthlessly on the recollection of soft, warm, naked... 'Boiled fish.'

'*What?*'

God, he *was* losing his mind if that was the best he could do to conjure up the most unerotic thought possible. 'Never mind, I was thinking aloud. Best go and find Aunt Kate and tell her Tallie is not feeling well. She'll probably want to take her home.'

William began to weave his way through the guests. Nick was vaguely conscious of him leaving, but his eyes stayed on the closed door of the sitting-out room. Provokingly independent, charmingly outrageous, worryingly courageous. All those descriptions fitted Talitha Grey. Marriage to her would certainly never be boring. His involuntary smile faded at the memory of the handkerchief she had held to her eyes as she vanished into the room. He had never seen her cry before, surely? Oh, yes, he had, he recalled with a pang of conscience. Once when he had knocked the breath out of her and once when some sharp remark he had made had caused her eyes to fill with bravely suppressed tears. At the thought of her distress something tightened hard in the pit of his stomach. Had he been harassing her? Pushing her too far? Or was it just that the last twenty-four hours were enough to undermine the spirits of anyone, however resolute?

Tallie sniffed resolutely and waved away the sal volatile that Miss Harvey, a fellow débutante, was helpfully attempting to press into her hand. 'Thank you, no, I am quite all right. It was just that someone stood on my toe—so very painful! I quite thought he had broken it, and my eyes were watering. No, no, I assure you, you are most kind…'

Would the wretched girl never go away? Tallie wiped her eyes, smiled with more than a hint of gritted teeth and at last, thankfully, Miss Harvey turned away, only to swing round at the door with renewed offers of assistance.

'No, nothing you can do. *So* kind of you…' And it was kind, Tallie acknowledged to herself. And poor William had probably meant nothing more than to ask her to dance, or if she wanted a drink. Her nerves were on edge, she was overtired, that was all. In the morning after a good night's sleep all would be in proportion again. Nicholas would accept his *congé* with good grace, Aunt Kate would stop worrying and she could slip away down to Putney to see Zenna's proposed schoolhouse for a few days' peace and quiet. Then she could return and spend the last weeks of the Season enjoying herself before slipping quietly out of Society for ever.

'Talitha dearest, whatever is the matter!' It was Lady Parry, all of a flutter, waving aside the attendant and seizing Tallie's hands in hers as she plumped down on the sofa next to her.

'Nothing, Aunt Kate, I am just a little tired, that is all.'

'I should never have agreed to this madcap scheme of Nicholas's, not so soon after…after last night. You must be emotionally drained, you poor child. Come along, I have told William to order up the carriage; we'll send it back for the men later and they can stay and play cards and flirt to their hearts' content. Why they do not flag with exhaustion I do not know—I am quite worn out.'

'Possibly because you do not stay abed until past noon the next day, ma'am,' Tallie suggested lightly. She would raise the idea of a trip to Putney on their way back, then she could try to sleep, at least knowing that was settled.

Clucking under her breath at the indolent and dissipated ways of modern young men, Lady Parry swept Tallie out of the sitting-out room and scanned the crowds. 'Goodness knows where Agatha Mornington has got to—probably flirting with the Lord Chief Justice.'

'Surely not?' Despite herself Tallie was entertained at the thought.

'Well, they do say she had an *affaire* with him in their youth,' Lady Parry confided, then recalled to whom she was speaking and added firmly, 'All silly gossip, of course. Now, where has William got to?'

At length the ladies found themselves safely in their carriage, Tallie having found the opportunity for a rapid whispered apology to William. 'I am so sorry I was short when you tried to speak to me, I am just so tired this evening.' The effect of her green eyes, still swimming with unshed tears, was more than enough to reduce him to a stammered assurance that he had noticed nothing, nothing at all out of the way, and of course she must be tired.

Lady Parry disposing her furs, reticule and fan about her on the broad expanse of green velvet, was less easy to fob off. 'You poor child! What a dreadful couple of days you have had of it.' Although Tallie could not see her face, she was aware of a shift of mood, a sharpening of interest. 'Now, has Nicholas had the opportunity to speak to you?'

'Yes, ma'am.'

'And?'

'And what, ma'am?'

'Has he proposed to you?'

'Lord Arndale has kindly explained to me that I am ruined, hopelessly compromised and must marry him, yes.'

'And?'

'In the face of such a tender declaration I felt no compunction in declining,' Tallie replied, somewhat more tartly than she had intended.

'Oh, foolish boy! I had no thought that he could express himself so badly! What on earth is he about? When I consider how much address he has…'

'Possibly too much, dear ma'am. I think Lord Arndale expects the weaker sex to fall in at once with whatever he proposes, whether it is a walk in the park, the best place for their investments or his opinion on their marriage prospects. I, however, do not choose to dance to his lordship's tune and, as I have already explained to him, I have no intention of marrying and never have had.'

'But, Talitha, do consider…'

'I agree, dearest Aunt Kate, that I am indeed compromised. Should I be intending to marry, it would put me in the most delicate of situations for I would need, in all honour, to confess everything to a prospective husband. And,' she added with a wry laugh, 'I suspect he would remain a contender for my hand for not a moment after hearing that confession. But I have not the slightest desire to take a husband, so it does not arise.'

'Oh, Tallie, how can you not wish to marry? And Nicholas is the most eligible of men.'

'Why, certainly, ma'am, if one is concerned only with title, wealth, intelligence, looks and a ready address. I am foolish enough to wish only for a husband, be he ever so humble, who loves me and tells me so. I am most unlikely to find such a soul mate, and his lordship, to do him justice, does not perjure himself with false declarations of emotions he does not feel.'

'Oh, dear,' Lady Parry said dismally. Even in the fitful light cast by the flambeaux as they passed Tallie could see her shoulders droop. 'This is not what Miss Gower and I dreamed about for you.'

'You thought that I should marry Lord Arndale?' The words were out before she could help herself. Surely the two ladies could never have dreamed that their protégée would attach the interest of the eligible Nicholas Stangate, Lord Arndale?

'Well, you always seemed so...different, so independent.' Lady Parry was obviously struggling to articulate what the two friends had plotted so deviously. 'And Nicholas is inclined to be so cool and so much in command of everything. We thought—' she broke off in confusion '—we thought you would do him good, shake him out of that control, make him enjoy himself.'

'I would have thought,' Tallie said drily, 'that Lord

Arndale was more than capable of enjoying himself without any help from us.'

'You mean his mistresses and so forth,' Lady Parry remarked, apparently rendered indiscreet by the darkness. Tallie felt incapable of enquiring what *so forth* meant. 'Well, of course, but there too he is in control. By all accounts he is perfectly fair, very generous, but he needs shaking up a little in my opinion.'

'Well, I doubt if being turned down by me will be an adequate shock,' Tallie observed. It was a most peculiar sensation, having this intimate discussion about Nick in the dark. It was almost like talking to herself and it most certainly did not feel real. 'I must confess, Aunt Kate, I did overhear you both discussing his marriage plans. Being turned down by an eligible young lady would, I imagine, administer the appropriate salutary shock. Being spurned by a shockingly eccentric milliner is unlikely to do more than sting his pride.'

'Oh, dear.' Lady Parry sighed. 'I appear to have made a mull of everything.'

'Do not say so!' Tallie impetuously moved to sit next to her patroness and hugged her. 'I have had a lovely time, truly. And I could not have hoped for a warmer welcome than you and William have given me. It is an experience I will always treasure, but I am not cut out for this sort of life. If you will allow me, may I borrow the carriage to go down to Putney tomorrow to stay with Miss Scott? She thinks she has found the perfect house for her school and wants me to approve it.

'If I stay perhaps a week, then Lord Arndale will forget all this nonsense about having to marry me and

I can come back and finish the Season, if you will allow.'

'Of course you may have the carriage.' The vehicle drew up outside the house as Lady Parry spoke and she continued as the groom helped her down. 'And of course you must finish the Season. I cannot imagine how I am going to get along without you; I have had so much pleasure from your company.'

'And I from yours, dearest adoptive Aunt.' Tallie kissed Lady Parry on the cheek as they stood in the hall, blinking in the light of the many-branched candelabra that Rainbird had set on the side-table. 'Thank you so very much.'

Tallie managed to escape the next morning with her portmanteau without an encounter with Nicholas—who, as she had predicted to Lady Parry—had kept to his room until noon. Had Tallie known it, her haste to escape was quite unnecessary. His lordship was far too old a hand at games of cat and mouse to press his suit so soon after the ball. He partook of a leisurely luncheon before strolling round to Clifford Street to visit his tailor, then made his way to his club and passed a pleasant afternoon apparently immersed in the news-sheets and keeping half an ear open for gossip about Mr Hemsley's fall from grace.

His quarry, meanwhile, sank back against the squabs with a sigh, which might have been either relief or regret, and watched the bustling street scene as it passed. How long was it since she had counted every penny before considering whether to take a hackney carriage? Not so many weeks, and here she was taking for granted the luxury of a private carriage with liveried servants at her beck and call.

Tallie took a firm grip on her imagination, which was wistfully conjuring up images of a certain grey-eyed gentleman, and thought fondly of dear Miss Gower, whose kindness had led her to pluck an anonymous young lady out of her genteel poverty and establish her in comfort and elegance. The smile that curved Tallie's lips at the memory of the doughty old lady faded as she wondered how many other young women the City held who were forced to make their own way in a hostile world, most of them without the benefits of upbringing and education she had received.

The germ of an idea began to form as the carriage drove into the country near Little Chelsea; by the time it had reached the village of Fulham her eyes were positively sparkling. *Yes! This is what I can do...* Tallie knew next to nothing about the advanced theories of education that Zenna held so dear, but she did know what sort of start in life an impoverished young woman needed, and it was not just young ladies fallen on hard times who required help.

The pretty view of the Thames from Putney bridge passed unnoticed, and when the coachman drew up in front of the tall double-fronted house just off the High Street in Putney Tallie was so lost in thought that the groom had to cough to draw her attention to the fact that he had been patiently holding the door open for her for some moments.

'I am so sorry,' Tallie apologised, stuffing her tablets and pencil into her reticule and jumping down. 'I had an idea. Zenna! Have you been watching for me? I am sorry not to have given you more notice.' The friends embraced, then Tallie allowed herself to be shown into the house.

'What do you think of it?' Zenna asked anxiously. 'The country air is so pleasant, and it is not too far from town, I thought…'

'Is it big enough?' Tallie demanded, staring around her with furrowed brow.

'Big enough? But I was worried that you would think it too big!' Zenobia broke off, torn between relief and puzzlement. 'There are two wings at the back that do not show from the road. I had thought perhaps a dozen young girls and a dozen older ones. There is ample room for that and for classrooms and rooms for the assistant mistresses, a dining hall, a suite of rooms for me and servants' rooms. The kitchens are rather antiquated, but a new close range and a little work and they will be perfectly acceptable.'

'No, it needs to be bigger.' Tallie took her friend's arm and began to march towards the stairs. 'Can we manage to accommodate another dozen or so girls? Not fee-paying ones, but poor girls who would benefit from a good education? And a suite for me as well.'

'Well, there *is* room, we might have to do more work on the left-hand wing, I suppose.' Zenna dug her heels in and they stopped abruptly at the foot of the stairs. 'But who is going to pay for these girls? And why do you want a suite of rooms? Surely you are going to marry Lord Arndale?'

'I am going to pay for them and, no, I am not going to marry Nicholas or anyone else. I am ruined and I intend to devote myself to the education and advancement of deserving girls.'

Chapter Twenty-One

'Ruined?' Zenna squeaked. 'How? Who by?'

'Really, Zenna,' Tallie chided, starting to climb the stairs. 'Do you not mean ''by whom''?'

'You know perfectly well what I mean,' Zenna said fiercely, running to catch up. 'I suppose it was Lord Arndale, and why are you not marrying him? You might be…I mean…'

'Expecting a child?' Tallie stopped on the landing and surveyed the doors opening off it. 'This will need some redecoration, will it not? No, I am not in any danger of that. It appears that one can be quite effectively ruined without any of the supposed pleasures one might expect in the process.'

'Talitha Grey!' Zenna stopped dead in front of her and wagged a finger. 'Stop sounding flippant and as if you do not care. I know you better than that, remember. Why will you not marry Lord Arndale, for goodness' sake? You are in love with the man after all.'

'But he is not in love with me,' Tallie replied briskly. 'And I have no intention of finding myself married to a man who will be making the best of things by regarding me as a cross between an unpaid housekeeper, a hostess for his entertaining and a brood mare.' She paused and added with a rueful smile, 'And not necessarily in that order!'

'Tallie! I am certain Lord Arndale would never—'

'Oh, he would be perfectly charming, I am sure, and I would live a life enriched with every comfort and elegancy.' She broke off to push open a door. 'These rooms are very spacious for the second floor, are they not?

'The children would be a joy, of course,' she added somewhat absently, 'although I would prefer it if their father had married me because he loved me, not first and foremost because he had compromised me.'

They had arrived at the end of the corridor and Tallie started to climb the narrow stairs in front of her. 'Where does this go?'

'To the attics and down to the kitchens. Tallie, do stop and come and sit down and have some luncheon and tell me why you will not marry his lordship. What has upset you so?' Zenna regarded her friend's set face. 'Now, this minute, Tallie! Or I swear I will write to Lord Arndale and demand to know what he has done to you.'

Miss Zenobia Scott was not given to making threats she would not carry out. Tallie allowed herself to meet her friend's eyes for the first time that day and smiled ruefully, finding it difficult to prevent her lip quivering.

'Very well, Zenna,' she capitulated meekly, following her down the twisting servants' stair to the ground floor.

'Mrs Blackstock is staying with her cousin, but the

lady kindly lent me two of her maids so that I could stay here for a few days and assess the house better. The owner is proving so co-operative that I think he must be having trouble disposing of such a large establishment. That gives me hope we can drive a hard bargain.'

She tugged the bell-pull and spoke a few words to the maid who appeared in answer. 'There, something will be ready in ten minutes. Now sit down, Tallie, please, and tell me what has occurred.'

Taking a deep breath, Tallie repeated the tale she had told Lady Parry the day before. It was easier the second time round and without Nick there it was considerably less embarrassing. She was also far more frank with her friend about exactly what had happened when she awoke in Nick's bedroom.

'Oh, my goodness,' Zenna said weakly, her eyes round with shock. 'And his lordship did not…'

'No.'

'Goodness,' she repeated. 'I would have thought that his lordship is quite…er…that is, he is very…'

'Very,' Tallie agreed drily.

Zenna digested this for a moment. 'And he does desire you?'

'So it would seem. But then, most men appear to have very passionate desires. It means nothing in particular to them. It is certainly no basis for a marriage.' Tallie turned to her friend, suddenly fierce. 'I have no intention of sharing my husband with his mistress, however much Society may turn a blind eye to that sort of behaviour.'

'It appears to be almost expected in Society marriages,' Zenna agreed sadly. 'But are you so sure he does not love you?' She bit her lip, obviously searching for some hopeful comment. 'Perhaps he is shy and...no, perhaps not.'

'I cannot imagine the circumstances in which Nicholas Stangate would be shy,' Tallie said with a smile at the thought. 'Besides, he tried every argument to point out to me just how necessary this match is. If he loved me, surely that was when he should have told me?'

'You would think so, but men are unaccountable beings,' Zenna mused, breaking off at a tap on the door. 'That will be luncheon ready. We will serve ourselves, so we can continue talking.'

The meal was set out in a charming parlour at the back of the house, giving Tallie the opportunity to admire the garden.

But Zenna was not to be diverted. 'So how have you left things? Surely you cannot avoid meeting Lord Arndale if you are continuing to reside with Lady Parry?'

'He has wagered me that I will agree to marry him within two weeks of yesterday.'

'He is very sure of himself!'

'He is indeed, which is why I want you to promise me that you will not admit him here if he calls. A few days' peace will allow me to think about how I can best dissuade him from this.' Zenna looked doubtful, but Tallie persisted. 'Promise me, Zenna!'

'Very well,' her friend agreed. 'Beside our friends and tradespeople, I will admit prospective parents only.'

That provoked a laugh from Tallie. 'Come now, Zenna! Even for someone as confident as you, that is carrying expectation too far, is it not?'

'It is not impossible,' Zenna retorted, passing a

plate of ham across the table. 'I have confided my intentions to a number of people and I do think this house will prove suitable. Now, tell me more calmly about this idea of yours to admit young women of no means. How can we afford it?'

'I will pay their fees. We cannot take many, I quite realise that, but even a few who leave with the skills to manage their own small business, or become governesses or companions—surely that is better for them than struggling in poverty when they have the intelligence and the spirit to do better for themselves?'

Zenna looked thoughtful. 'Yes, you are right. Think what a difficult situation you or I would have been in if we had tried to make our own way in the world with no education.' She delved into her reticule for the set of tablets and pencil that inevitably accompanied her. 'This has given me much to think about and will change some of my calculations.' She sucked the end of her pencil thoughtfully. 'How many girls do you think we should start with?'

Tallie, who had begun by using her idea as a defence against having to think about Nick and how miserable she felt, found herself drawn deep into Zenna's plans and how they could be adapted to accommodate her 'special students', as Zenna called them.

Dinner time found the pair of them still hunched over the dining table surrounded by sheets of paper, Zenna's tablets long exhausted. Rough sketch plans of each floor with scribbled notes about alterations jostled with lists of everything from subjects to be taught to bed linen required.

They continued during the meal until Tallie spilled

gravy on Zenna's tabulated curriculum for the youngest girls.

'Enough!' she announced, mopping it up. 'I am too tired to concentrate any more. In fact, if you will excuse me, Zenna, I will go direct to my bed. I declare I had no idea that education would be such an exhausting undertaking.'

Her friend, who had been prepared to carry on talking until she dropped if that helped keep the haunted look from Tallie's eyes, nodded encouragingly. 'What a good idea. I will just make sure the maids have locked up and then I will not be far behind you.'

Tallie fell asleep instantly, hardly stirring when Zenna slipped into the other side of the big bed they were sharing.

But her slumber was racked with nightmares and she tossed and turned, muttering under her breath until poor Zenna seriously considered taking a pillow and the counterpane and trying to sleep on the chaise longue in the front parlour.

In consequence, it was two heavy-eyed young ladies who regarded each other over a very late breakfast. 'What were you dreaming about?' Zenna demanded bluntly, draining her second helping of hot chocolate and reaching for the pot to refill her cup. 'It was like sharing the bed with a basket of puppies.'

Tallie rubbed her aching brow and tried to recall. 'I was in class and you were telling me to write on my slate "I will marry Lord Arndale" one thousand times. And when I refused you turned into him and he shouted at me that I was ruined and must go and stand in the corner and disobeying him was no way to learn ancient Greek. And I would not do that either so he took me in his arms and...'

'Yes?' Zenna's chocolate cup tilted dangerously.

'...said he would have to kiss me until I could do all my irregular verbs.'

'I am sure I would never have learned mine if that was the penalty for disobedience,' Zenna observed dispassionately.

'Zenna!'

'Well, he is extraordinarily attractive, and if you do not want him...'

'I do want him! But not on his terms, so there is no use in teasing me—I am not refusing him on a whim.'

They both chased their sweet rolls around their plates in a desultory manner.

'I suppose I should sort out those papers from yesterday,' Zenna observed, making no move to do so.

'Hmm. It is a nice day; perhaps we should look at the garden.' Tallie too stayed sitting at the breakfast table.

Suddenly Zenna pushed back her chair and got to her feet. 'I know what will blow the cobwebs away. Come along, up to the attics.'

'That's more likely to cover us in cobwebs,' Tallie grumbled, but she submitted to being urged towards the back stairs and climbed up behind Zenna to the very top.

'There!' Zenna flung open the door to reveal light-filled, spacious rooms opening one after another. 'There is a mansard roof,' she explained, gesturing at the high ceilings and big windows. 'It is unconventional, but I thought of having my rooms up here.

There is room for both of us, in fact—a bedroom each, two dressing-rooms and a big sitting-room.'

Tallie nodded, catching her enthusiasm.

'But the space is not the best thing, just look at the view.' Zenna flung open a window and, ducking slightly, stepped out onto the leads. Without thinking Tallie followed her, then clutched the window frame with a gasp.

Because of the design of the roof there was a flat walkway, perhaps five foot wide, running around the edge of the roof before it sloped up steeply to its flat top. The edge was bounded by a stone balustrade at about waist height and, even with her back to the window, Tallie could see the wide view across the rooftops of Putney to the sparkle of the river beyond.

Careless of the height, Zenna perched on the balustrade and called, 'Come and see. It is quite safe, the stonework is sound.' She glanced back over her shoulder, and saw Tallie's face. 'Oh, I am sorry, I had forgotten about your fear of heights.'

'It is very foolish of me,' Tallie said firmly, making herself let go of the window frame and stand up. 'The view is indeed lovely and I think the rooms would be delightful.' Her stomach heaved, but she managed to fix a smile on her face, wondering what she could do to lure Zenna off the parapet and away from that dreadful drop.

In the event Zenna hopped off with as little concern as she would have shown getting up from a chair and leaned over, heedless of the effect on the elbows of her gown. 'Oh, look, a carriage has drawn up. Now who can that be?' She leaned further, oblivious of Tallie's squeak of alarm. 'Not Mrs Blackstock, for it is not a hackney carriage. I know—it must be Lady

Whinstanley, she was most interested when I told her about my plans and she has a house somewhere near.'

'You had better run down, then,' Tallie managed to say. 'It would never do to keep her waiting.' To her immense relief Zenna straightened up and ducked back through the window.

As the sound of her footsteps diminished down the stairs Tallie began to back into the room, eyeing the balustrade warily as though it might leap at her and toss her over. Then something stopped her. Quite what it was she could not decide, but the sound of Nick's voice calmly telling her she could step out onto that nightmare of a ledge at Mr Harland's house mixed with the hasty apology that Zenna had made when she remembered her fears.

Nick had had to put himself at great risk by having to coax and support her along that ledge. Zenna was doubtless regretting her plan for converting this lovely space into rooms because she knew Tallie was scared of the height.

She made herself step out again, clinging to the window frame as she had before. At least she was certain this was a genuine fear and she was not indulging herself in order to draw attention, or have a man protect her. Here she was alone and as terrified as she had been at the studio. But if she could only manage to conquer the fear enough to stand out here and admire the view with Zenna, that would be something.

She held on to the window and looked up, studiously following a bird in flight until it began to swoop down. That was all right; she could look at the tree tops. She dropped her eyes further and her stomach lurched with them, but after perhaps five minutes carefully gazing at the distant prospect she felt able to let go of the window and walk up and down the wide ledge.

This was so successful that she even let her eyes stray to the parapet and its broad top. It was far wider than any stool she had ever sat upon. How proud of her Zenna would be if she could sit on that or even just lean against it. Her stomach lurched again.

Tallie closed her eyes and began to pace up and down, repeating out loud, 'I will not give in, I will *not*.' She put out a groping hand and found the parapet, edged towards it and, with her face screwed up into a scowl of grim determination, eyes still tight shut, started to hitch one hip up onto the broad top as she had seen Zenna do.

The voice shouting 'No!' hit her almost at the same moment as the arms that seized her, dragged her round and off the parapet.

She screamed, opened her eyes and saw her worst nightmare, the wide view spinning around her. She was falling, helpless…

With another shriek Tallie hit the steep slope of the Mansard roof, her breath crushed out of her by the body that pinned her there. Hands pressed her face to a broad chest, fingers laced desperately in her hair and a voice, a familiar voice sounding utterly unfamiliar, repeated words that made no sense at all.

Tallie stopped flailing and trying to find breath to scream and heard incredulously what Nick Stangate was gasping into her hair, against her face.

'My love, my darling…no…I am sorry, I will not harass you any more, I promise, my love…only promise me you will never do anything like that again. Tallie, my heart, I will never come near you, if only you'll promise me...'

She gave up trying to push him away and reached to fasten her hands in his hair, forcing his head back so she could gaze incredulously into Nick's face. His eyes were wild, dark, his expression vulnerable as she had never seen it.

'What did you call me?' she managed to whisper.

'My love.' His voice was hoarse. 'Tallie darling, I never meant to hound you until you would do something so desperate...'

'You thought I was going to jump?' Of course, that must have been what it looked like. 'Oh, no Nick, I was just trying to sit on the ledge, like Zenna did. She was so disappointed that I might not want to share her rooms up here because of the height. I was only trying to conquer my fear.'

He slowly straightened his arms until he was standing with her trapped by them, her back against the near-vertical slope of the roof. He closed his eyes and Tallie saw the tension ebb out of him. 'Of all the damn fool, witless ideas,' he said, his voice shaking. Then he caught hold of himself and the grey gaze was furious on her face. 'You could have been killed, you could have become dizzy, fallen. You were all by yourself up here. It was the most hen-witted...'

Tallie swallowed and enquired meekly, 'Did you call me *your love*?'

'Yes.' The glare faded. 'Tallie, my darling, never, never do anything like that to me again. You have taken years off my life—in fact, I will probably wake up tomorrow with white hair.'

'Very distinguished,' Tallie murmured, the growing bubble of happiness welling up inside her, threatening to burst and leave her speechless. 'Did you mean it when you called me that?'

'Of course I meant it.' Nick touched a cautious finger to her cheek. 'Your face is dirty. Did I hurt you just now?'

'No, I do not think so. Nick, why did you not tell me? You made me all those arguments about why I had to marry you and never mentioned the one thing—the only thing—that matters to me.'

'I had no idea that I loved you,' he admitted, regarding her ruefully. 'Not an inkling. I knew I desired you, but that seemed to blind me to what else I was feeling.' He shook his head, apparently trying to explain things to himself as much as to Tallie. 'I knew I worried about you and you infuriated me and puzzled me. I wanted to protect you and I wanted to make passionate love to you—and half the time I wanted to shake you. How was I to know I was in love with you? I have never been in love before.'

'Neither have I.'

'Then you do love me? After what I've done to you? Embarrassed you in the street, pried into your life, disapproved of your friends, kissed you in the most improper way, compromised you...'

'...looked after me, saved my reputation, fought for me, made me laugh, made me want to behave in the most abandoned and outrageous manner?'

'Then why would you not marry me when I asked you, you little wretch?'

Tallie regarded him in loving exasperation. 'What, agree to marry a man who was lecturing me on how I was ruined and *had* to marry him? Marry a man whom I had just overheard telling his aunt all about his now useless plans to marry a well-connected nice young Society miss?'

'Ah, I can see that would be a consideration.' Nick regarded her steadily, all the amusement gone from his eyes. 'It would have been a terrible mistake, that nice young Society miss. I would have been bored in a month. What I want—what I *need*—is a beautiful, scandalous, argumentative milliner.'

'Is that a proposal, my lord?'

'That is a proposal, Miss Grey. Will you do me the honour of becoming my wife?' Nick stepped back, leaving her free, as though he did not want to constrain her answer any more than her person.

Tallie dropped a neat curtsy. 'Thank you, my lord. I accept with all my heart.'

The sensation that this must be a dream—an impossible, wonderful dream—was swept away as Nick swooped and caught her up in his arms, carried her through into the attic and, setting her on her feet, proceeded to kiss her with a thoroughness that even the most torrid dream could not conjure up. This was indeed real.

Tallie finally managed to free herself and hold him off with both hands hard on his chest. 'Nick, tell me truly, will your family be very shocked at such a misalliance? Because if they will be I could not bear to be the cause of any coldness between you.'

'My aunt loves you already, William adores you like a sister, my assorted great-aunts and great-uncles who have yet to meet you will congratulate me upon securing such a charming bride and my dear mama, who is nursing a collection of completely imaginary ailments in Bath, will dote upon you. And, besides, I have a clinching argument.'

Tallie regarded the twinkle in his eyes with some suspicion. 'And what might that be?'

'The economy of having a wife who can make her own hats. Why, I need give you but a fraction of the dress allowance I would otherwise have to.'

'You beast!' Tallie seized a cushion off the moth-eaten sofa, which comprised the furnishings of the attic room, and swung wildly at Nick with it. He retaliated with its companion and the space was instantly a snowstorm of dust and feathers. Almost unable to breath with giggles and sneezes Tallie landed a telling blow just as the door swung open to reveal Zenna, a look of horror on her face.

'Oh, no!' she wailed and promptly burst into tears. Tallie had never seen her with so much as a dampness in her eye; appalled, she dropped her cushion and ran to put her arms around her friend.

'Zenna dearest, what is wrong?'

'I thought…I thought I was doing the right thing letting Lord Arndale in,' Zenna hiccupped miserably. 'I thought he really loved you, and all the time he just wanted to ravish you and you had to beat him off…'

'Ravish her…!'

'Do be quiet, Nick, can you not see that Zenna is upset? We were having a pillow fight, Zenna darling, that is all. He does love me, we are going to get married.'

'Truly?'

'Truly.' Tallie regarded her friend's pink-faced embarrassment severely as she scrabbled in her pocket for her handkerchief. 'But what were you about letting Nick in? You promised me that you would not.'

'I asked him if he would send his daughters to my

school,' Zenna stated, blowing her nose defiantly. 'And he said of course he would—so that makes him a prospective parent. And you agreed I might let those in.'

'We would, would we not, my darling?' Nick enquired.

'Would what?' Tallie was too amazed at Zenna's duplicity to follow his question.

'Send our daughters here.'

'Our daughters? Oh!' Tallie gazed at Nick, the blush spreading up her face. 'You would like daughters?'

'Two daughters and two sons seems a reasonable sort of number to me, but naturally it is something I feel we should discuss at considerable length.'

'Excuse me,' Zenna said with some firmness, her schoolmistress expression back on her face, the effect only marred by a very pink nose. 'I should point out that this is a most improper conversation and that we should go downstairs, Talitha. I am sure his lordship will have many things to arrange and will be calling upon you on your return to London tomorrow. I will accompany you.'

Nick gave way with grace in the face of such a formidable front. His bow on the dusty threshold was a model of deportment and his face serious as he said, 'You are entirely correct, Miss Scott. Miss Grey, I will call tomorrow afternoon if you will permit.'

He then spoiled the effect, much to Tallie's delight, by seizing her by the shoulders and kissing her lingeringly on the lips. 'Darling Tallie, I adore you.' And he was gone.

Chapter Twenty Two

The new Lady Arndale sat up nervously against the pile of lace-trimmed pillows in her big bed. Her bed, her suite of rooms, her house. Heronsholt, hazy in the evening light, a mass of grey stone and warm red tiles, the impression of a classical frontage and a hint of more chaotic wings behind.

But Nick had given her little opportunity to study the house nestling in its woods overlooking a sweeping Hertfordshire valley. He had ushered her past a confusing number of bowing and curtsying servants, delivered her into the hands of the beaming house-keeper and announced that dinner was required within the hour.

When she had joined him in the dining room there was a full contingent of footmen and an impressive butler to face. Tallie sent a look of pure panic down the length of polished mahogany to where Nick was getting to his feet and met his eyes. They were steady, confident, approving. Her chin went up and she returned the look with a smile that was suddenly calm. Her footmen, her butler—and she was not going to be intimidated by any of them.

Nick was at her side, holding her chair and she smiled up at him. 'Thank you, my lord.'

'Thank you, my lady,' he whispered back. 'Tomorrow we will have three leaves taken out of the table and will dine in comfort.'

But tonight he wanted her to impress the servants, she could tell. He had told her all their names on the journey from London, a dreamlike journey after the equally dreamlike wedding ceremony and the wedding breakfast organised on a lavish scale by Lady Parry. Flashes of memory came back to her: Millie looking radiant as she sang at her first private engagement, Mrs Blackstock in earnest discussion with Mr Dover as she explained the problems of finding reliable servants for three lodging-houses and Zenna shamelessly cornering Society ladies and lecturing them on the advantages of an education for girls at her select new seminary.

Nick had dealt with her obvious inexperience of managing a large household and her nervousness about the staff not by referring to it, but simply by giving her the information she would need.

'Thank you, Partridge,' she had said firmly, turning to the waiting butler. 'You may serve now.'

But coping with the servants was one thing—that merely needed acting and a show of self-confidence until she acquired the real thing. Of all her new acquisitions, there was one that could not be dealt with in such a way. Her new husband.

Tallie swallowed, pulling the sheets up to her chin before she realised what she was doing and turned them down again. *He has kissed you countless times*, she chided herself. *You have been in bed with him,*

*for goodness' sake. He has seen you naked. You have
seen him, if it comes to that. Why so shy now?*

If Nick had not been so restrained and proper for
the four interminable weeks before their wedding, she
might not have felt so nervous. But he had acted with
the most scrupulous propriety, which unnerved her to
the point where she almost convinced herself he was
regretting the entire thing and was not in love with
her after all. Then she would catch his gaze, see the
passion burning in his eyes, hear the tenderness in his
voice and she no longer doubted him.

A board creaked outside the door to her dressing-
room. It opened onto a tiny lobby and then into his
suite. Tallie swallowed, folded her hands over the
crumpled wreck of the sheet edge and attempted to
look calm. There was a scratch on the panels and the
door opened to reveal her husband clad in a splendid
dressing-gown of heavy crimson silk, his feet disconcertingly bare.

'You look very small in that big bed,' he observed,
leaning one shoulder against the doorframe. 'Is it
comfortable?'

Tallie's voice vanished into a squeak. She coughed
and tried again. 'Very, thank you.' Why did he not
come in?

'I wondered if perhaps you were very tired and
would prefer it if I stayed in my room tonight.'

For a moment a ripple of relief ran through her.
She would not have to face the horrible possibility
that she might not please him tonight. Tomorrow she
would be rested, not so tense. A good night's sleep
would surely banish this quivering, feverish feeling
that had been spreading through her limbs ever since
she had placed her hand in his at the altar.

She opened her mouth to agree and heard herself say, 'Oh, no, Nick, no. I am not so very tired.' Before she could correct herself he was at the bedside, flipping back the covers to reveal her modestly clad in the long nightgown of fine cambric that she had nervously chosen to wear. With one hasty, appalled glance she had rejected the dozen or so outrageous pieces of nonsense that Lady Parry had encouraged her to buy and which her new maid had spread out for her choice.

'Very restrained,' Nick observed. 'How does it come off?'

'Er…over my head.'

'And are you very fond of this garment?' His long fingers were toying with the chaste satin ribbon which gathered the neckline.

'No. Why?'

In answer Nick simply took the neck edges in both hands and ripped the nightgown firmly from top to toe, leaving Tallie naked. Before her hands could grasp the edges again he bent down, scooped her up and strode back towards the door. 'I have been having the most improper thoughts about doing this since the first moment I saw you in Harland's studio.'

'You have?' Tallie gasped, wrapping her arms around his neck as they swept through both dressing-rooms and into the master bedroom.

'Hmm.' Nick's voice was a throaty growl of anticipation that sent an answering echo through her. 'And your hair…' He set her on her feet, tugged at the ribbon that was tying her hair back and swept the freed mass out over her shoulders with both hands. 'And that scent of jasmine has been haunting me.' He buried his face in her hair and Tallie found herself pressed against the warm sensual silk. It slid across her naked skin. She shivered and instantly Nick cupped her face in his hands and looked intently down at her.

'Are you cold? No? Then are you frightened?'

'Um, a little bit,' Tallie admitted. Nick seemed so big, so dominant, so possessive.

'Did Aunt Kate say anything to you?'

'Only that it would be all right and you were much too experienced to make a mull of it.'

'Oh, did she?' Nick said indignantly. 'And did you find that reassuring?'

'Not very.'

'Then let me assure you, Tallie, that I am not experienced in bedding virgins and I intend this to be the first and last time I do so. So we are going to have to muddle through this together and try not to make a mull of it jointly.' She suppressed a little snort of amusement and he smiled. 'That is better. Now, then, where were we?'

Fortunately that appeared to be a rhetorical question, for Tallie very much doubted that she could come up with a coherent answer. She burrowed closer against him as though to cover her nakedness with his robe and found that her fingers—quite of their own volition—were untying the knot of the sash. The edges fell apart and she was against Nick's body.

Tallie froze, absorbing sensations, recalling how it had felt when she had woken in his bed and was held in his arms. This was different. For a moment she was puzzled, then realised that, standing, she was pressed against Nick in a slightly different way. She could rest her head on his shoulder, which meant she could let her lips graze against the side of his neck where the pulse beat so hard. The strangely exciting friction of his chest hair against her softness was the same; she wriggled and caught her breath at the way his breath caught in turn.

And like this, tight against him, there was no mistaking the extent to which she had aroused him.

'Tallie,' Nick murmured against her hair.

'Mmm?'

'Let me kiss you.' She tipped back her head and his hands came up to her shoulders to push off the wreck of her nightgown. The fine cambric whispered to the floor as he bent to her lips and Tallie responded, opening to him, yielding to the demands of tongue and lips until suddenly this was no longer enough and the aching, throbbing feeling inside built into a clamorous demand that she could no longer pretend she did not understand.

Nick seemed to sense the change in her. He bent, caught her up in his arms, laid her on the bed. With one fluid movement he had shrugged out of his robe and was on the bed at her side.

Tallie swallowed, struggled to calm her breathing, still the turmoil that racked her. Then the world seemed to stop as she met Nick's eyes. She had thought she had seen love in them before. She had glimpsed admiration, desire, love. But what she saw now took her breath away. There were all those things in the deep grey gaze, but mixed with them was awe, tenderness, strength and an aching vulnerability.

'I love you,' he whispered.

'I love you too,' she answered and saw the vulnerability vanish, showing her the banked fires of controlled desire behind the gentleness. And suddenly she did not want him to treat her like a fragile butterfly cupped in his hands, for the desire was welling up in her too, threatening to overwhelm her. 'Love me, Nick. I will not break.'

Even then he was careful, controlled. She learned to surrender to him, to his clever hands, to his mouth, to the heat and strength of his body until her own was arching in supplication beneath his. When he entered her Tallie was already so tense with the passion he had been building for her that the momentary pain passed in a flash to be replaced with an explosion of sensation.

Tallie cried out, her hands locked about Nick's neck, her head thrown back on the tumbled pillows, her entire body and mind swept by a crashing wave of sensation.

Slowly, slowly she came to herself, marvelling at the weight of him capturing her so powerfully, so tenderly. Then she realised that he still possessed her, filled her, completed her and her newly awakened body quivered around him.

'Oh, my love.' Nick's eyes were on hers as she smiled tremulously up at him. 'My beautiful, beautiful Talitha.' And he began to move again, thrusting, possessing until she found that she was no longer just marvelling at the feel of him within her but that her body was responding, answering his. That extraordinary sensation was building again inexorably, even more overwhelmingly. She drowned in his eyes, convinced she was going to shatter now, break into pieces.

Then as her body convulsed around him again she heard his cry and saw, as her vision blurred, the expression of triumph and love and utter completion that transformed his face.

* * *

Tallie woke slowly, languorously. She stretched, reached out a hand as one or other of them had done at intervals throughout that incredible night—and found the bed empty. Her groping hand found only the warm rumpled hollow where Nick had lain. Tallie opened her eyes, blinking in full daylight and lay looking up at the underside of the bed canopy while she thought about just how new and strange her body felt.

It was as though every muscle was sleek and polished, as though her skin had been oiled and as if she should stretch and purr like a cat instead of simply sitting up in bed. She compromised, wriggling up against the pillows, arching her back and raising her arms in a long, luxurious stretch.

Her husband was standing across the room from the bed, reaching up to turn a small key in a hole in the panelling. As he heard her move he turned and smiled at her. Tallie felt her heart give a sharp beat. Loved and loving, that was how she felt, how she knew she would always feel with Nick.

'Good morning, my lady wife.'

'Good morning, my lord.' He had not troubled to pull on his robe and Tallie regarded him unashamed and admiring. 'What are you doing? That panelling is new, is it not?'

Nick turned back and opened what she could now see was a pair of doors above the dado level, then stepped aside to repeat the action on the next length of wall.

Tallie gasped. Revealed by the opening doors was a large oil painting, a scene of a classical temple with a nymph placing an offering before the altar.

'But that is one of Mr Harland's canvases...' She

swung her feet out of bed and ran to Nick's side as he opened one panel after another. 'And that, and that one and that is the Diana picture! Nick, have you bought all the paintings he did with me as the model?'

In answer Nick swept a hand around the room. The locked panels were open to reveal six scenes of the ancient world, each with the slender blonde-haired figure of the new Lady Arndale gracing it. 'It seemed the safest way of keeping them from prying eyes, and, when I saw them, how could I resist?'

He watched, hardly conscious of the smile on his face as he regarded his wife walking slowly around the room gazing up at the luminous pictures, her hands pressed to her flushed cheeks. Each image was lovely, but none matched the real woman he knew. For a moment he shivered at the thought of how he would be feeling now if she had refused him. To possess those still images and know that he had lost the one being who completed him as a person. Unbearable.

Tallie turned slowly to face him and he felt his spirits soar again, the unthinkable vanishing in the warmth of her smile. 'There is still one space.' She gestured at the central panel between the windows.

The half-formed idea he had entertained but never thought through came to his lips before he could check it. 'Perhaps you could…no.' No, the idea of his Tallie exposed to the eyes of any other man again, even the apparently sexless Harland, was unbearable. Then he saw her face and could not have felt worse if he had struck her.

'Tallie, darling, I am sorry, I would not have you go through that again for anything. I am a thoughtless beast.' He caught her in his arms, burying his face in her hair. *Damn it!* This business of being in love was far harder than he had ever imagined. You opened up your every thought and feeling to another and they to you—and that made it so easy to hurt them. He was aware of her slender body shaking against him. He had made her cry.

'Tallie, sweetheart… You are *laughing*.' She struggled to get her expression under control. 'You were teasing me?'

Instantly she looked all contrition. It was incredible the way she could hide every feeling or let down every barrier and expose her soul to him. 'I am sorry. It was just your face when you were contemplating it, and then instantly you came all over-possessive. I think perhaps people would expect a nice conventional portrait of both of us for the main reception rooms, but I have a much better idea for this wall.'

'Yes?' Nick said cautiously, telling himself that he had better learn fast how to deal with this infuriating minx of a new wife before she ran rings around him.

'It was Mr Harland's suggestion, and I have to admit that I have thought of it often since he made it.' Nick waited, hands on hips. 'He said, the first time he saw you—when I, of course, did *not* see you— that he would like to paint you as Alexander the Great. I found it a powerful image,' Tallie added reflectively.

'Alexander? I suppose I must be flattered, but you do not want a picture of a man in armour in the bedchamber, surely?'

'Oh, no, not in armour.' For some reason Tallie was edging away from him round the edge of the bed. 'In the antique style, carrying a shield and sword and wearing sandals.'

'And what else?'

'Why, nothing at all.'

'You little wanton! You expect me to pose naked for some da—blasted artist?'

'Why not? What is sauce for the goose…'

Nick stared at her. The thought that Tallie could think of him with quite the same physical admiration that he thought of her—in fact, *had* thought about the image Harland had conjured up with a no-doubt idle suggestion—that was powerfully erotic. He felt his body tighten and stir and caught the spark of wicked acknowledgement in his wife's eyes.

'Madam, this gander is not for plucking. And if you need any convincing about just who is master in this house, I am afraid I am just going to have to show you all over again.' He grinned as she dodged laughing away from his reaching arm and then tumbled of her own accord onto the big bed, stretching out her hands to him.

'Of course, my lord, if you dislike the idea we will say no more about it…'

Nick let himself be pulled down onto the bed then rolled Tallie over to hold her trapped tightly beneath him. 'For some reason, my adorable new wife, I suspect that this show of meek obedience is just that— show. I have no doubt that I am going to be cajoled, lured and tricked into Harland's studio.'

Tallie attempted a hurt pout and only succeeded in looking adorably flustered. 'Do you mind?'

'Not in the least. I fully anticipate years of enjoyment from your wiles, my love—and from attempting to take your mind off further schemes. Like this, my very dearest love…'

And Tallie, gasping with delight in his arms, could only murmur against his lips, 'I do love you so, Nick. So very, very much. And for ever.'

* * * * *

The Marriage Debt

Chapter One

The tall man in the frieze coat sat cross-legged on the hard bench, put his elbows on his knees, his chin on his clasped hands and thought. It required some concentration to ignore the shackles on his legs, the cold that seeped out of the damp walls, the rustles and squeaking in the rotten straw that covered the floor and the constant noise that echoed through the long dark corridors.

A few cells away a man was screaming an incoherent flood of obscenities that seemed to have gone on for hours. More distantly someone was dragging a stick across the bars of one of the great rooms, a monotonous music that fretted at the nerves. A boy was sobbing somewhere close. Footsteps on the flags outside and the clank and jingle of keys heralded the passing of a pair of turnkeys.

Long ago his father had said he was born to be hanged. At the time he had laughed: nothing had seemed more improbable. Now the words spoken in anger had been proven right: in eight days he would step outside Newgate gaol to the gallows platform and the hangman's noose.

One small mercy was that they had put him in a cell by

himself, not thrown him into one of the common yards where
pickpockets and murderers, petty thieves and rapists crowded
together, sleeping in great filthy chambers as best they might,
fighting amongst themselves and preying on the weakest
amongst them if they could.

Apparently his notoriety as Black Jack Standon was worth
enough in tips to the turnkeys for them to keep him apart
where he could be better shown off to the languid gentlemen
and over-excited ladies who found an afternoon's slumming
a stimulating entertainment. The sight of an infamous highwayman who had made the Oxford road through Hertfordshire his hunting ground was the climax of the visit to one of
London's most feared prisons.

He had hurled his bowl at the group who had clustered
around the narrow barred opening an hour or two ago and
smiled grimly at the shrieks and curses when the foul liquid
that passed as stew splattered the fine clothes on the other side
of the grill. He doubted they'd feed him again today after that.
It was no loss, he seemed to have passed beyond hunger after
the trial—if such it could be called.

Footsteps outside again, slowing. He raised his dark head
and regarded the door through narrowed eyes. There was
nothing left to throw except the coarse pottery mug and he
was not prepared to give up water as easily as food.

The slide over the grill rasped back and he squinted in the
beam from a lantern directed through the gap. It was probably daylight outside; all that filtered down into his cell was a
dirty smudge of light that hardly had the strength to reflect
off the rivulets of water on the walls.

They did not sound like society sensation seekers. One
man talking. No, two, low voiced and apparently arguing.
Suddenly moved to real anger at being exhibited like a caged
animal at a fair he swung his legs off the bench and took a

stride towards the door before the shackles jerked him to a standstill. The grill shutter slammed closed. All he heard was 'She'll never agree…'

With an awkward shuffle, the man they called Black Jack got back to his bench and hoisted his feet up again away from the foul straw and the rats who lived in it. *Better get used to being stared at*, he told himself grimly. In eight days he would walk out of here to die in front of a vast crowd. They expected the condemned to 'die game', defiant in their best clothes, a joke on their lips for the onlookers. They would have to do without the fine clothes, all he had was the ill-fitting ones he was wearing and not a penny-piece in his pockets to buy anything else.

So, he continued his inner dialogue, *Better get used to the idea and think up something witty to say*. Was it too late to save himself? Yes, days too late. If he had sent word when they first took him, the message might have reached Northumberland; help might have come. Or might not.

He had made this particular bed. Pride had kept him away for six years, pride was damn well going to have to get him through to the end. Meanwhile pride and a hard bench made for little sleep. He closed his eyes and let his mind drift. At least it wasn't raining, at least there was no mud and nobody was going to try and kill him for eight days. That was an improvement on the night before Waterloo. 'Count your blessings,' his old nurse was wont to say. The bitter twist of his mouth relaxed a little and he began to doze.

Katherine Cunningham looked up from her book in some surprise as the front door opened and she heard male voices in the hallway. A rapid glance at the mantel clock showed it still lacked half an hour before six: what was Philip doing home at this time in the afternoon?

She got to her feet and went to the door of the small back parlour of the Clifford Street house where she had been indulging in some snatched leisure for reading. With virtually no staff, it was easier to keep only the one small reception room in use; the rest were under holland covers with the exception of the room that Philip liked to call his study.

He was approaching it as she stepped out into the hall, Arthur Brigham, his friend from schooldays, at his heels. At the sight of her they both stopped dead.

'Good afternoon, Arthur.' She studied their faces. 'What on earth is the matter? You look as though the pair of you have seen a ghost.'

'Good…good afternoon,' the young lawyer stammered. 'I was… we were just going to look at something in Phil's study.' As he spoke he gave her brother a firm shove in the back, propelling him into the room before Katherine could get a good look at him.

The familiar wave of apprehension swept over her: now what was Phil up to? Drunk again, that would be almost inevitable despite the hour. But there was something else afoot, she could sense it.

'Philip, what is wrong?' She swept neatly through the open door before Arthur could close it, then stopped dead as she saw Philip's face. It was blotched—with drink, doubtless— but also with dried tears. The expression in his eyes was desperate and his mouth, so like hers, too feminine for a man, quivered. Something clutched at her heart. 'Phil! Sit down, quickly. Arthur, is he ill?'

Thank goodness for Arthur, she thought, kneeling beside Philip's chair and trying to get him to meet her eyes. He might be wild to a fault and perfectly capable of neglecting his studies or his duties in his uncle's law firm when it suited him, but he had none of Phil's fatal weaknesses for drink and gaming. And he was patient and loyal enough to keep hauling his friend home whatever the scrape he was in.

'You must tell her, Phil,' Arthur urged. 'She has to know sooner or later.' It seemed to Katherine as she knelt there that he could not meet her eyes either. The grip on her heart tightened.

'Oh God, oh God, I'm sorry, Katherine.' To her horror her brother burst into tears, his head on her shoulder. Ignoring the blasphemy, she patted his arm, stroked his hair until he suddenly jerked upright. 'We're ruined, Katy, absolutely ruined.'

'How can we be?' Somehow she could not get to her feet, her knees felt like jelly. She stayed there by his side, the wetness from his tears soaking the front of her old blue dimity gown. 'You said you had won at the races, you said you had won at cards and we could pay off that money you borrowed and everything would be all right.'

He buried his face in his hands. She caught the muffled words, 'Lost it again. Payment due.'

'What? All of it?' Philip was beyond listening to her, so she twisted to look up at Arthur. 'Arthur, what is he saying?'

'He went to a new hell in Pickering Place last night. Said I'd meet him there, but by the time I arrived most of the money was gone.' The young man shot her a look of mingled shame and apology. 'I couldn't get him to leave, Katherine, he was drunk as a judge, convinced it would only take one more throw of the bones.' He bit his lip, his eyes shifting under her horrified gaze. 'I did get him out eventually, before he actually wrote any vowels.'

'Small mercy,' she said bitterly. 'They would have joined all the other debts and the tradesmen's bills. But thank you for trying, Arthur. Where have you been today?'

'To the moneylender, to see if he could get an extension on the loan, some more money. But the old bloodsucker just laughed in his face, said he'd give him two weeks' grace, then send the bailiffs round.'

'Merciful heaven.' Katherine sank back on her heels, her fingers pressed to her lips. 'Philip!' She shook his arm. 'How much do you owe them?'

'Five,' he muttered, head averted.

'Five hundred... Let me think, what is left we can sell...?'

Arthur cleared his throat. 'Er, no, Katherine. Five thousand.'

The room swam. Surely she had misheard him? *'Five thousand?'* she whispered. 'Five thousand *pounds*?'

Philip nodded mutely.

'And there are all the other debts and bills.' Her stomach seemed to have risen so she could not breathe, would be sick at any moment. Katherine gulped air and clenched her hands until the nails bit into her palms. When she could speak, she said flatly, 'We must sell the house and the furniture, it is all we have left that even approaches that sum.'

'Can't.' The single word was choked out of Philip. Like an old, sick man he dragged himself upright in the chair and passed a trembling hand across his face. 'I've already sold them.'

'What?' Arthur's exclamation cut across hers. 'You've sold the house? How could you do that and Katherine not know?'

'Did it the month before Christmas when she went to stay with Great-Aunt Gwendoline, just before she died. Waste of time and effort that was,' he added. 'Never left us a brass farthing.'

'Philip, how could you?' Katherine shook her head, too buffeted at the rest of his news to scold him for his callousness as he deserved.

He shrugged. 'Anyway, sold it then. And the furniture.

Man I sold it to agreed to rent it back furnished. I paid off the worst of my gaming debts and kept some back for the rent, but that's gone now too.'

Katherine tried to get to her feet and found Arthur's hand under her elbow. 'Here, better sit down. Shall I ring for some tea?'

'Yes, thank you, Arthur. I think Jenny is in the kitchen.'

They sat in silence, all unable to find words. Mercifully Arthur showed no sign of wanting to leave, although Katherine realised he must wish himself anywhere but in the centre of this family crisis. She shot him a grateful look. Goodness knows how she could cope with Philip without his help.

Jenny, once Katherine's maid and now, since all but one of the other servants had left, their maid, cook and housekeeper rolled into one, put her head round the door. 'You rang, Miss Katherine?' Katherine swallowed, trying to get her tongue around a simple order for refreshment. Jenny took one look at their faces, said simply, 'Tea. Yes, Miss Katherine', and went out.

The silence stretched on. Philip scrubbed his handkerchief over his face and sat cutting and recutting a pack of cards that lay on his desk. Arthur simply waited, studying his clasped hands, and Katherine forced herself to try and make a plan, find some way out of this trap. But all she could see were doors slamming in her face however much her mind twisted and turned.

Jenny returned with the tea tray, put it down and left. Somehow the simple presence of this symbol of everyday social life woke Katherine from her trance. She poured tea, passed cups, insisted Philip drank, then began to ask the questions that were beating on those locked doors in her mind.

'What will the moneylender do if you do not repay him?'

'Send the bailiffs like he threatened,' Philip said dismally.

'But there is nothing to take. You say the house and furniture are sold, what is left?'

'The kitchen utensils, the china and silver, your clothes.' Arthur spoke when Philip lapsed into silence again.

'The very clothes off our backs? But none of that will make up five thousand pounds? What can they do?'

'Debtors' prison,' Philip choked out.

'Prison? No, oh, no, Phil, I cannot bear it if you go to prison!' Katherine stared white-faced at Arthur. 'Arthur, you must know how to stop that happening?'

'Nothing I can do.' He shook his head. 'And the money-lenders will soon find out who else money is owed to. They'll all see to it that it'll be prison until the debt is paid in full. They have a perfect right to do it.'

'But how can Arthur earn money to pay off the debt if he is in prison? And nothing I can do could ever hope to approach that amount.' Katherine felt sick again, sick and despairing. Then the quality of the silence that filled the room penetrated her frantic thoughts. 'What is it?' she demanded of the two young men. 'What are you not telling me? What can be worse than Philip going to prison?'

Philip buried his face in his hands again, tipping over the tea cup so the dregs spilled across the polished wood. Arthur got up and knelt by Katherine's chair, taking her hands in his. 'It is not Philip who would go to prison, it is you.'

'*Me?* Why should I go to prison?' It was some ludicrous, ill-timed jest. Some misplaced effort by Arthur to lighten the atmosphere.

'Because you signed the papers for the loan,' he said gently.

'No! I witnessed some papers for Philip, that is all.' Katherine got to her feet and took two rapid steps across the room. She wanted to wrench open the door and run, but her own reflection in the glass overmantel stopped her dead.

This morning she had got up and dressed in the old dimity gown, which was now still blotched with Philip's tears. She had arranged her heavy honey blonde hair in a simple knot and spared no more than a glance for her face. Now the big pansy-brown eyes were wide and drenched with unshed tears, her full lower lip caught in her teeth and her heart-shaped face white and strained. She had strayed into a nightmare and the nightmare was real.

Philip stood up and tentatively put his hands on her shoulders. She could see him in the glass; the features that were so feminine in her face merely showed the weakness on his. 'They would not lend me any more,' he explained. 'They seemed to feel you would be more reliable.'

'You tricked me into signing?' She spun round so she was facing him, his hands still on her shoulders. 'You lied to me?'

'I thought you might not quite like it…'

'I would have refused and you knew it!' Katherine had spent much of her twenty-four years excusing her younger brother, picking up after him, managing as best she could on their increasingly straitened means since the death of their parents. She had never let her occasional anger with him overwhelm her affection; now anger surged like a tidal wave, unstoppable.

'How could you? How could you lie and cheat just to gratify yourself? How could you risk everything, not just for yourself but for me as well? You are selfish, Philip, selfish beyond belief!'

He stepped back from the force of her fury, his face crumpling again. Philip had always traded on his looks, his charm, his happy-go-lucky attitude. To face criticism from the one person he believed would indulge him in anything rocked his entire world.

'Katy, Katy don't be like this.'

'Like what? Angry? Afraid? Oh, sit down, Philip, this will do us no good. Is there anything you can think of, Arthur? Anything at all?'

'I have been giving it some thought actually,' he said, his relief that her outburst was over apparent. 'The only thing for it is marriage.'

Katherine regarded him as though he was mad. 'To whom, pray? Our breeding is good, but Philip has no title, which is the only thing likely to recommend him to some rich cit wanting to marry his daughter to the gentry. And good blood is nothing in the face of huge debts, a reputation for heavy drinking and no title. And who do you think is going to want to marry me, pray? No dowry, on my way to the debtors' prison… I do not hold myself cheap, Arthur, but I cannot delude myself that I have any of the charms necessary to attract a husband blind enough to pay my debts as part of the bargain.'

Arthur looked distinctly uncomfortable. 'That was not quite what I had in mind, Katherine.'

She thought his meaning unmistakeable and felt the blood rise hot in her cheeks. 'If you think I am going to make myself some man's mistress in order to pay Philip's—my—debts, you must be mad, Arthur. Or are you offering me the position?'

'Good God, no! I mean, would be honoured, of course, but I have no money, trust fund doesn't pay up until I'm thirty…not that I wouldn't want…'

Katherine waved a hand at him. 'Stop it, Arthur. I did not mean it. If it comes to that, why does Philip not find some wealthy widow to squire about? One sees it all the time.' She did not wait for an answer to her bitter enquiry. 'But I am not selling myself: I would rather go to prison.'

'No, you would not,' Philip muttered.

'How do you know?'

'We were in Newgate this afternoon. There are debtors in there; it is hellish.'

'What on earth were you doing in Newgate?' Even the name made her shudder.

Arthur cleared his throat. 'Because I had an idea. We were finding you a husband.'

Chapter Two

He had been right. His display of anger in throwing his plate at the visitors had not been forgiven. The dark man raised his head as the familiar early evening sound of shuffling feet penetrated the heavy door. There was the thump as the stew pot was set down, a rattle as grills were opened to ladle out the disgusting slop in one cell after another, the duller sound of the water bucket grounding on the flags.

But the sounds reached his door and passed by. Resigned, he reached for the beaker and tipped it to his lips. A small trickle of water touched them. He was used to the taste now, grateful he could not see clearly the colour of it. Thoughtfully he ran his tongue round as much of the damp interior as he could reach and set it down again.

He had spent six years of living the life of a rake and an adventurer, the course he had chosen for himself in defiance of everything he had been brought up to respect. It had given him freedom, amusement, some moments of intense pleasure, some fear, much insecurity. He could have been said to have lived to the full those past years. Was it worth the price of his life? It seemed someone was calling in the debt and he had no choice. He had never been one to rail against fate: you changed what you could and put up with what you could not. Pride was all he had brought with him out of that old life, it was just going to have to be enough to see him out of this one.

The rats, who knew the prison's routines even better than he, skirmished in the straw, waiting for their dinner, which unaccountably had not appeared.

In the study of the house in Clifford Street Katherine stared at the two young men as though they had sprouted feathers and began to cluck. 'You went to Newgate prison to find me a *husband*?'

'Let me explain,' Arthur said hurriedly. 'I know the son of the Governor and he plays cards regularly with the Assistant Governor and some of the wealthier prisoners who can afford to pay garnish—that's the money for better food and accommodation and so on. So that's how I can get in and out of the prison.'

'I don't wish to get in and out,' Katherine said tartly. 'I want to stay out in the first place.'

'Yes, I know that. But me knowing the Assistant Governor and Christopher Hadden—that's the Governor's son—means that I can see how we can put my plan into operation. They are both in debt to me, you see. Not much, but Hadden's on a short string from his father and the Assistant Governor knows there'll be hell to pay if the old man finds out he's been involving him in deep play.'

Katherine sank back in the chair. This was like some insane dream. Any moment now she was going to lose all touch with reality and that was dangerous; she could not let herself sleepwalk into whatever desperate scheme the two young men were hatching.

'And your plan is what, exactly?'

'Well.' Arthur steepled his fingers and suddenly became an almost perfect copy of his uncle, a very senior and pompous family lawyer. Katherine stifled a hysterical giggle. 'You are aware of the situation as regards women's property?'

'I think so,' Katherine said dubiously. Not having any property meant she had given the matter little thought.

'Well, let me explain in detail,' Arthur continued. 'An unmarried woman is effectively the property of her father until she comes of age and marries, at which point she becomes the property of her husband and all her assets come under his control. With an unmarried lady who is of age, or a widow, then you do—subject to any trusts and so forth—have control of your own property.'

'Arthur,' Katherine said patiently, 'the entire problem arises because I do not have any property.'

'Yes, indeed. But the reverse also holds true. If you are under age, any debts you incur are your father's responsibility. If you are married, they are your husband's.' He paused significantly. 'Even debts incurred before the marriage.'

'So you think that by marrying someone in Newgate prison I will be able to pass my debts to my new husband?' He was obviously mad—she must just humour him. 'Why should anyone saddle himself with more debt? I assume you are talking about one of these card-playing debtors. It would only make their position worse.'

'I am not talking about them, Katherine.' Arthur's pose of legal dignity dropped away and he looked down at his hands, suddenly unable to meet her eyes. 'When a man dies without any assets his debts die with him. They do not revert to his wife.'

'But how do you know who is going to die?' she began, still trying to humour him in this insane game. Then what she had just said penetrated her consciousness. 'You want me to marry a *condemned man*?'

'It is the only way, Katy,' Philip suddenly burst out. 'Don't you see? The five thousand pounds would be wiped out at a stroke, as the gallows trap dropped.'

'Stop it! That is an obscene thing to say—how can you even suggest it?'

'Because it is the only way out,' Philip retorted. 'Can you think of another?'

'There must be.' But she heard the despair in her own voice as she said it. What choices were there to meet such a debt in so short a space of time? They had no assets, nothing to sell.

'But what could possibly induce a condemned man to such a course? What benefit to him would there be?' Even as she asked the question, she knew she was on the verge of agreeing; it did not take the exchange of looks between the two men to see they thought she was won round.

'Hard to say,' Arthur shrugged. 'I've heard of half a dozen cases from Hadden. I suppose in some of them the wife promises to take care of the man's dependents, but you can't afford to take on any more costs, which is why I have gone for the other option. It seems that for some of the most hardened cases—the ones with nothing to lose or the ones who like to make a show, like the highwaymen—it is a diversion.'

'In what way?'

'Someone new to meet, the wedding, getting out of their cell for a bit, being the centre of attention—all those liven things up when you are sitting, waiting to hang, with nothing to entertain you but counting rats and wondering what the ballad mongers are going to write about you.'

'And you have a convenient highwayman, have you?' This was not happening to her. This morning she had got up with nothing more on her mind than the fishmonger, who was becoming pressing over his account, and whether she could turn the cuffs on Philip's shirts yet again. Now she was discussing marrying a highwayman in order to avoid being sent to prison.

'Yes, Black Jack Standon. Notorious, but not a lout. No gentleman, mind you, but by all accounts he behaves well enough when he holds up stages. Good looking, the ladies say. He'll be expecting a lot of attention when he's turned off and, like all of them, he'll be a bit of a showman. I think he is our best bet.'

The hysteria which she was aware of just under the surface was threatening to break through again. *My late husband, Black Jack Standon the highwayman...*

Katherine fought it down. 'And just how is this all to be arranged, assuming, that is, that Mr Standon is willing?'

'You'll need a licence and then there's the Ordinary— that's the chaplain—to fix and his fees to pay. There's garnish to the turnkeys as well, but I've put it to Hadden and the Assistant Governor that, if they make all the arrangements, I'll forget what Hadden owes me and nothing about the gaming will get to the Governor's ears.'

'Damn good of you, Arthur,' Philip said with feeling. 'We'll go tomorrow, get it fixed up, put it to Standon. If he agrees, we can get the licence and the wedding can be the day after tomorrow.'

'I think I will go and lie down.' Katherine got to her feet. It was that or give way to the crazy laughter that was bubbling inside her. 'Please will you ring for Jenny? I have a headache.' As she reached the door she turned back. 'And however lightly you take that debt, I am not going to forget it. Somehow it will have to be paid back, however long it takes. I might be reduced to marrying a highwayman, but I am not going to be a thief.'

The man they called Black Jack stood blinking in the morning light of the Assistant Governor's office and wondered if bad food and water were making him hallucinate. Had he really agreed yesterday to marry some foolish spinster because she wanted to escape her debts? It seemed he had or he wouldn't be here. Goodness knows why, unless it was the instinctive reaction that any woman saddled with that dandipratt of a brother deserved some kind of help. And it passed the time more interestingly than sitting in his cell day and night and reflecting on his past sins. Of course, there was the other benefit that the young lawyer had drawn delicately to his attention. Or perhaps it would not prove to be a benefit; he would wait and see.

The more intelligent of the two young men who had made the proposition to him, the lawyer, was speaking to Mr Rawlings. The Assistant Governor frowned, then nodded. 'Very well, we will have the leg irons off him, no need to alarm Miss Cunningham, but the hand shackles stay.' There was further hurried speech. 'A bath and a shave? I think not, Mr Brigham!' More muttering. 'Er, yes, there is that. I had set aside one of the better cells; Mr Wiggens left it only yesterday, having cleared his debts. But it will have to be after the ceremony, I cannot detain the chaplain any longer than necessary.'

The dark man caught sight of his own reflection in a mirror hanging in one corner of the office and grimaced. The blushing bride would probably scream and run at the sight of him; he had not realised just how bad he looked and doubtless the smell was worse.

'Ah, Miss Cunningham, do come in.' Mr Rawlings was ushering in a tall, slender woman in grey, heavily veiled. A trim maid, wide-eyed with apprehension, was at her back. The woman lifted a hand and put back her veil and the dark man felt the impact as a catch in his throat. She was beautiful.

Huge brown eyes, wide cheekbones tapering to a pointed chin, a mass of dark blonde hair just visible under her bonnet—lovely, terrified, brave.

Katherine sent one searching look around the office and fixed on the man in chains at its centre with almost painful attention. It was hard to look at anyone or anything else. He was tall, broad shouldered, dark, with eyes that looked black. It was difficult to see the rest of his face under a heavy growth of untrimmed beard, but what she could see had a fading tan. She noticed with a strange pang that the skin under his eyes was pale: he was not well.

His hands were filthy and his wrists red raw where the shackles had chaffed. His clothes were quite simply appalling: a torn frieze jacket, buckskin breeches and a pair of muddy boots. If he was wearing a shirt, it appeared to be collarless and a ragged neckcloth, red with white spots, filled in the gap at his throat. She could smell him from across the room. Sweat and the smell of the prison that seeped into everything. She realised it was part of the air of this place.

Then his eyes met hers and he was quite simply a man in desperate trouble, a fellow human being that she and Philip were using for their own convenience.

'I wish to speak to Mr Standon privately.' Her voice sounded unnaturally calm to her own ears.

'I am not sure that is wise, ma'am.'

'I will speak to him,' she insisted, walking forward past the highwayman and into the far corner of the room. 'Mr Standon, please.' Her legs shook.

He followed her, stood with his back to the room, shielding her, and raised one eyebrow interrogatively. 'Yes, Miss Cunningham?'

Katherine regarded him, startled. He was so well spoken!

A gentleman turned highwayman? It happened, she had heard of cases. 'I want to know why you have agreed to this,' she said impetuously, keeping her voice low. 'What possible benefit to you can there be in it?'

The dark eyes held hers and laughter lines crinkled at the corners. 'It is an improvement on sitting in a dark cell for twenty-four hours a day.'

'That cannot be all,' she said impatiently. 'If you had some dependents I could promise to take care of, I would do my best by them, despite my circumstances—but my brother says you have no one.'

'I have no one who needs your help,' he confirmed and she wondered at the sudden grimness in his voice.

'Then why?' She was not going to be fobbed off—suddenly it was important to know why this condemned man should put himself out in any way for her.

The laughter lines were back, and with them a new note in the soft, deep voice. 'I have to admit that the prospect of tonight was a powerful incentive, Miss Cunningham. Once I had seen you.'

'What do you mean—"tonight"?' Her heart was beginning to thud. He could not mean…? No, surely not.

'A legal marriage requires two things Miss Cunningham. A wedding ceremony and the consummation of the union.'

Katherine felt the blood draining out of her face and the room began to swim. She staggered and his hand was under her arm. She blinked, steadied herself and withdrew from him. 'I must speak to my brother.' Turning, Katherine stalked across the room and took Philip firmly by the arm. 'Outside, please, and you too, Arthur. Excuse us, Mr Rawlings, Reverend.'

The corridor outside the office was deserted. Katherine turned on the two men, her voice shaking with outrage. 'You did not tell me this wedding would have to be consummated! What are you thinking of? How can I possibly give myself to a man I do not know, a convicted criminal? Am I supposed to retire to his filthy cell for the night? Is that what you expect? Because if that is the case, let me tell you, you are far and away out!'

'Katherine, please calm down.' Arthur took her hand. Furiously Katherine swatted him away. 'The moneylenders will have their spies in here. This is not an uncommon occurrence. If they can find grounds to contest the marriage and pursue their money, believe me they will.'

'And they promised me he will have a bath and a shave first,' Philip added, flinching at the look his sister sent him. 'And a nice cell…'

'A nice cell? And what does that consist of, pray?' She had to keep her anger fuelled or otherwise she was going to give way under the wave of fear and embarrassment that threatened to swamp her. 'House-trained rats and tasteful sackcloth hangings?'

'No, it is a proper room, Katy, like a room in a good inn, I promise you. It has just been vacated by one of the better-off debtors.'

Katherine took a few hurried steps away from them until she could rest her forehead against a bookcase that stood in the corridor. Behind her she heard Arthur say, 'Leave her for a moment.'

The tears welled up in her eyes and she blinked them back, but not before two escaped and ran down her cheeks. She scrubbed them away and tried to think. What was the alternative? To end up in this place herself with no prospect of release? Put like that, the choice seemed relatively simple.

She supposed a young lady should be prepared to die rather than surrender her virtue in such circumstances, but was it so very different from the young girls whose families married them off to men old enough to be their fathers, or to some dissolute rake for money or dynastic reasons? Like them, she would be married. And, for some reason she could not define, the condemned man in the other room made her feel ridiculously safe.

'Very well.' *Do it now*, an inner voice urged. *Do it while you have the courage of your anger.* Without looking at the two young men, she threw open the door into the office and went in to find herself in the middle of an argument between the prisoner and a very flustered chaplain.

'The name on the licence is incorrect, I cannot proceed.'

'That is my name.'

'Your name is Jack or John Standon.'

'That is what they call me.' The prisoner reached out a hand, fetters clanking, and laid it on the Bible which the chaplain had placed on the desk. 'I swear upon this book that what is written there is my true name.'

There was sincerity in his voice, which appeared to convince the clergyman almost as much as the oath had done. 'Very well, we will begin. Let us go down to the chapel.'

The ceremony passed like a strange dream for Katherine, who was aware only of the hand holding hers as Philip stepped forward to give her away, the tall presence next to her and the sudden shock of hearing his real name.

'Will you, Nicholas Francis Charles Lydgate, take Katherine Susanna Cunningham…'

'I do.' It sounded as though he meant it.

'With this ring…' the chaplain began, then paused, looking expectantly from one man to another. Philip and Arthur looked confused, then anxious. Katherine found her hand being released as the prisoner tugged the signet ring off his finger and handed it to the priest. It felt odd on her hand; warm from his, smooth and old from long wear. She glanced down, but the engraving was worn and unreadable. The fruit of some robbery?

Then her mind was jerked back to the present as he repeated, 'With my body I thee worship…' She shivered convulsively and the filthy fingers tightened around hers for a moment. Strangely reassured, she tried to force herself to concentrate on the rest of the ceremony; it was, after all, a sacrament and she should be suitably attentive.

The chaplain droned to the end and then began, apparently out of habit, 'You may kiss the—' He broke off at a warning cough from the Assistant Governor. Beside her the prisoner— her husband, for goodness' sake!—made a small noise that might have been a chuckle. Katherine found her hand lifted and her knuckles were brushed by his lips. The heavy beard obscuring most of his face felt strange on the soft skin on the back of her hand.

Before she could say anything, thank the clergyman even, Philip's hand was under her arm and she was swept towards the door. She heard Mr Rawlings say, 'At about eight this evening, then, Mr Cunningham?' and Philip's muttered acknowledgement before she was out of the chapel.

Chapter Three

'That went off very well, I think,' Philip announced when they were once again sitting in the old family coach and it began to move off up the Old Bailey.

Katherine simply gave him a long look and he subsided into sulky silence. *What has he got to sulk about?* she thought. *If he had said one word that showed he understood how devastating this is for me, it would help. At least Arthur seems to feel it as he ought.*

She gazed out of the coach window at St Giles's church. The journey home was taking longer than it might, for they only had the single pair of horses, which somehow her scrimping and saving allowed them to retain. Still, it was a useful punctuation in this unreal day. Time, perhaps, for some practical planning. Anything was better than dwelling on what she had just committed herself to.

The Assistant Governor had promised them a decent room. Well, she would take her own bed linen and candles. And he had promised that Mr Standon—no, Mr Lydgate—could have a bath and a shave. Not that that would do much good if he had to put those revolting clothes back on again. Now, where could she get some the right size? Philip and Arthur were striplings by comparison. Of course, John was the answer.

John Morgan their coachman turned general factotum was up on the box now, an impressive broad-shouldered figure in his old caped coat and cocked hat. He would be able to spare one outfit that would fit the highwayman, surely. He would have to go straight back to the prison as soon as she had packed a parcel.

Katherine fished in her reticule and found her tablets and a pencil. *Clothes, soap, shaving tackle*—Philip could sacrifice some of his—*candles*. She would take the bed linen and some food with her when she returned at eight o'clock. Should she take Jenny with her? She watched the maidservant covertly as she sat silent in one corner of the coach. No, better go in with John; Jenny had been horrified by what she had seen already, there was no point in making her spend a night in that place, always assuming there was somewhere suitable for her to wait the time out.

Making the list and thinking of practical matters had steadied her. When they reached Clifford Street, she found she could get down from the carriage and bid farewell to Arthur with every appearance of calm.

John leaned down from the box. 'Shall I take the carriage back to the mews now, Miss Katherine?' He always asked her for orders, much to Philip's irritation.

'Yes, please, John, I have another errand, but you had best take a hackney for that to save time. Can you come and see me when you have finished in the mews? I will have some things I wish you to take to the prison.'

'What things?' Philip enquired querulously as they climbed the steps to the front door. 'You are going back there tonight, what do you want to send now?'

'Soap,' Katherine replied briskly. 'A lot of soap. Some towels and, Phil, let me have your spare shaving tackle.'

'What, for that jailbird?'

'For the *husband* you have found for me. As I have to spend the night with him, I would prefer it to be without his beard and whatever is living in it.' She turned her back on him. 'Come along, Jenny. Is there anything else you can think of?'

'A comb,' the maid volunteered as they shut Katherine's door behind them. She looked at her mistress, her lower lip quivering. 'Oh, Miss Katherine, that it should come to this!'

'Yes, well, it has. Now stop it, Jenny, or you'll have me weeping too and I cannot afford to do that.' She began to search in drawers for towels. 'There, these will do. And some soap, a comb…'

'What are you going to do, Miss Katherine, when he's…I mean, when you're a…?'

'When he is hanged and I am a widow?' Katherine enquired, her tone harsh. 'I will find a small country town to move to with you and John and I will earn my living taking in pupils for foreign languages. My French and Italian are excellent and my German would be good if I applied myself a little.'

'And Mr Philip?'

'Mr Philip will have to find some employment himself, I am afraid, Jenny. I cannot think for all of us any more.' Something was falling on to her hands as she folded the linen towels, something wet making dark splashes on the fabric. She was crying. Blindly Katherine raised her hands to her face and found the tears were pouring down her cheeks. Her shoulders began to shake and she sank onto the bed, curling up and weeping as though her heart would break.

'Oh, Miss Katherine, don't now, don't, you will make yourself ill. Oh, it is so wrong that you have to go back to that terrible man tonight, so wrong…' Jenny, the same age as

Katherine and devoted to her mistress, had been struck almost dumb with terror at the sight of the unkempt, sinister figure of the highwayman. The thought that Katherine—slender, fastidious, chaste—was going to have to give herself to him was hideous. She wrapped her arms around her and cried too.

Eventually Katherine found the tears were stopping and sat up, sniffing and groping for a handkerchief. She found two and passed one to her maid and they sat curled up together on the big white bed, mopping their reddened eyes. 'It is not the highwayman I mind, Jenny,' Katherine ventured, surprised to find that was true. Tonight was a frightening prospect, but it would have been whoever the man was, and the setting made it worse. 'He was kind and not at all coarse in how he spoke to me or what he did. I think he was a gentleman once. He makes me feel safe somehow. Perhaps it is because he is so big!' She smiled at the maid's scandalised face.

'You know I always tell you the truth, Jenny.'

'Then why are you crying?'

'Nerves, I suppose, and the shock of that prison. And realising just how desperate our situation is. None of it seems real—and then it is all too real.' Discovering just how Philip had used and betrayed her hurt almost beyond anything. And she felt bad about using Nicholas Lydgate in their plans. True, he had nothing to lose and perhaps, as he said, there were some benefits. But he was a human being in the most dire of situations, literally at the door of death, and they were using him for their own ends. It left a bitter taste in her mouth; Philip would think her mad for refining upon it.

'Now, Jenny, pack those towels into a basket, put in the soap and the comb…oh, and this.' She plucked a book from her night stand. 'Then go and ask Mr Philip for the shaving tackle. Then find John and ask him if he can spare a shirt or

two and some breeches and a jacket for Mr Lydgate. I will
buy him new to replace them. He will know what else is
needed.' She sniffed resolutely and scrambled off the bed.
'Ask him to take a hackney and go as soon as possible, please.'

Alone at last, Katherine went to sit at her dressing table and
survey the damage her fit of crying had caused. Red eyes, red
nose and blotched cheeks—how she envied ladies who could
shed a decorative tear and all it did was to make their eyes
shine more brightly. When Jenny came back she would have
a bath, wash her hair and rinse it with jasmine water and then,
when it was dry, lie down and rest with cucumber slices on
her eyes—always supposing there was a cucumber in the
house.

Thinking about Nicholas Lydgate made her determined
that she was going to deliver her part of their strange bargain.
In the middle of that noisome hell-hole he was going to have
one night with a woman who smelt delicious and who went
to him willingly. Doubtless he would have preferred an experienced Cyprian, but she would just have to do.

Katherine realised she felt better. She was still terrified, but
the sense that she was behaving towards her stranger-husband
as she ought was calming, as was the realisation that she had
a plan of sorts for when it was all over and the immediate
threat of the debt was removed. Then the reality of what the
end of this meant hit her again: before the debt was due she
would be a widow and her husband would have gone to a
shameful public death.

The clock over the gate of the prison struck eight. Nicholas
Lydgate straightened up from the table where he had been sitting, reading the volume of poetry his surprising new bride
had added to the eminently sensible basket she had sent him.
Soap and Byron were both welcome, although he would

gladly have traded the entire works of the poet for an ounce of soap if that had been the choice.

Was she going to come? He would not blame her in the slightest if she did not. He ran one hand over his freshly shaven chin. Another luxury he had her to thank for, although the turnkey had stood over him while he shaved and had removed the razors the moment he had finished with them.

The door rattled, swung open and Mr Rawlings, a turnkey at his heels, looked in. 'Your wife is here, Standon, or Lydgate, or whatever your name is. I will come to collect her at eight in the morning. Ma'am.'

In fact it was her coachman, the man he had seen earlier, who came in. He shot Nicholas a suspicious glance, measured him up and down with critical eyes, then gave a sharp nod of approval before he dumped a hamper on the table and another large basket by the bed. 'You clean up better than I'd have suspected,' he remarked with a grunt. 'All right, Miss Katherine, I will be here all night if you need me.' This parting shot came with another hard stare at Nicholas as the door closed behind him, leaving Katherine standing alone just inside the threshold.

He made no move towards her as she lifted her veil from her face and untied her bonnet, which she placed on the bed. Then she simply stood looking at him, her hands clasped in front of her. Her face was calm and lovely, but he could see the hem of her gown vibrating with her trembling. There was a thud and a howl of rage from somewhere close by and she started, her face pale.

Nicholas took a quick stride. 'Here, let me take your pelisse. Come and sit down at the table. You have brought still more supplies, I see. I cannot tell you how grateful I am for the ones earlier; I hope I present a slightly less unnerving spectacle than I did before.' He felt he was talking too much, but, until she seemed willing to speak, he could not be silent.

She sat obediently and finally managed a small smile. 'Yes. I have brought food and drink and clean bed linen.' She reached out a hand and touched gently the raw marks on his wrists where the shackles had rubbed. 'And bandages with some of my own salve. Those must chafe horribly where your cuffs touch. If you take off your coat and roll up your sleeves, I will bandage them now.'

His immediate reaction was to refuse. She should not be sitting in a cell, tending to a felon's wounds. But she had to spend the night here, come what may, and it seemed to be helping her to have something practical to do. He stood up and did as she asked before sitting again and holding out his arms for her attention.

'Oh...' she bit her lip at the sight of the sores, but to his surprise it was compassion, not revulsion in her tone '...how can they justify such heavy, tight irons? It is cruel.' She unscrewed the lid of a jar of greasy green ointment and began to smear it on his wrists with light fingertips. The little shock of sensation he had felt when he took her hand in his in the chapel ran through him again. 'I am sorry, did that hurt?' He had not realised he had moved. 'It is mainly wood sage, chickweed and betony, but I have put in thyme as well.'

Her voice seemed stronger discussing the herbs. 'What does the thyme do? I thought that was a pot herb.'

'It is, but I like to put it in most things for the scent. It is supposed to be helpful for courage and against nightmares.'

'That will be useful.'

To his surprise she raised her eyes and looked directly into his. 'I do not think you are in want of courage, Mr Lydgate. Do you suffer nightmares? It would not be surprising in this place.' Her eyes dropped again to the bandage she was carefully wrapping around his right wrist.

'Waking ones only,' he rejoined, trying to keep his tone

light. 'Having the luxury of sleep in which to have a proper nightmare is rare here.' Her fingers quivered again as she tied the bandage off and took up his other wrist. He wondered if she could feel his pulse hammering. 'Will you not call me Nicholas—or Nick? That is what my friends call me.'

'And where are these friends, Nick?' Again those intense brown eyes met his.

'In France.'

'I see.' She finished with the bandages and began to tidy away her ointment.

'And what do your friends call you, Katherine?'

That produced another upward look and a flashing smile that showed even white teeth before she was serious again. 'Katherine. My brother calls me Katy, but I dislike that.'

Nick reached out his hand and tipped her face up. 'I shall call you Kat. Has anyone told you that you look like one, with your heart-shaped face and those big eyes?'

'No.' He could see from the emotions that flitted rapidly across her face that she was not sure she was flattered, then she decided she was. 'Very well, you may call me Kat.'

He let his fingers just pinch her chin before releasing her. 'Husband's privilege, Kat.' He could have kicked himself. Instantly the shutters came down and her hands tensed. How to retrieve it? 'Are you hungry, Kat? I confess I am. Why do you not set out the food you have brought and I will tidy away the other things?'

He had been about to say 'make the bed', but reference to that would hardly be tactful at the moment.

'Very well.' She stood up with her back, fortunately, to the bed and began to open the hamper. Nick threw back the lid of the other basket and pulled out sheets redolent of lavender and pillowcases edged with fine lace. For a moment he stood there, letting the feminine softness and sweetness sweep over him, then he stripped off the harsh blankets and made up the bed.

When he turned back the table was laid and she was watching him, a touch of colour staining her cheeks. But she had stopped trembling. Something within him knotted and he felt his loins tighten. *Damn it, have some self-control*, he snarled inwardly. She was frightened and adrift, cast there by her selfish brat of a brother; the last thing she needed was to be aware of how much she aroused him.

'This looks good.' He held a chair for her, then sat, reaching for the bottle of claret and the corkscrew. 'Why, you have even brought glasses.'

'I confess I did not look forward to whatever the prison authorities deem suitable in place of china and crystal.' Katherine smiled at him. 'And I asked Jenny to slice the meat; I did not think I would be allowed in here with a carving knife.' She began to heap meat on his plate—beef, ham and chicken—then spread butter on rolls and passed him two. 'Go on, eat, and do not even think about the food you have been eating the past days.'

The taste of good, simple food was like an explosion in his mouth. Nick tried not to wolf it down, not to gulp the wine Katherine kept pouring into his glass, but when he finally put down his knife and fork and reluctantly shook his head at her offer of another chicken leg, he feared he had exhibited little grace. She appeared unconcerned, however, sitting toying with a slice of chicken and some bread and butter. He caught her eye as she took a drink of wine and she smiled again. 'Dutch courage,' she admitted. 'Would you like some cheese, or Jenny's famous plum cake? Both together are good.'

Nick held out his plate wordlessly. After this meal, in this company, he felt if he died in his sleep tonight he would be content. 'Do you need it?'

Her nose wrinkled in puzzlement. It was a new expression to add to those he was beginning to learn, and emphasised the cat-look even more. 'Dutch courage,' he explained.

'Oh. Yes.'

'I should not wonder after your first sight of me. It frightened me when I saw myself in a mirror. Am I so frightening now?' Another woman would have prattled, or retreated into silence or rushed to reassure him. Katherine put her head on one side and contemplated him seriously.

'How frightening do you think it is for a virgin to find herself alone in a bedroom with a husband she has known for perhaps two hours in all?' She gestured to show it was a rhetorical question. 'No, I was not frightened of *you* then and I am not frightened of you, as a person, now. You made me feel…safe.'

This was not the time to preen himself because she had paid him a compliment. 'But you are afraid of me as a man? I will not hurt you, I promise you.'

Her answer was a little shake of the head and a rueful smile. 'Of course. It is just foolish shyness. Now, what more would you like to eat? There is another bottle of wine.'

They finished their meal and packed the hamper together, leaving the new bottle of wine to sip. Nicholas saw Katherine's eyes keep straying to the bed, then jerking back. He was having increasing difficulty keeping his mind off it himself.

'Tell me about yourself,' he asked abruptly. 'Where are your relatives that you find yourself in this coil?'

'I have none. None except my brother.' Her fingers were idly running up and down the stem of the wine glass in an unconsciously erotic glide. Nick crossed his legs and forced himself to concentrate. 'Our parents died some years ago. We were not well off, but we had enough with careful management.

'Unfortunately, Philip has a weakness for both drink and

gambling and the money just leaks away. We had to let all the servants go but John and Jenny; they only stay with us out of loyalty. Then last year, while I was away, Philip sold the house and the furniture without telling me. I only found out the other day, at the same time that he revealed that he had tricked me into signing the papers for a loan of five thousand pounds.'

'Hell's teeth! The bloody fool.' He did not apologise for his language and provoked a reluctant smile.

'Yes indeed. I know he is my brother and the head of the family, but I have to confess to wishing I could say exactly the same thing. But you see why I had to take this way out of my difficulties? I honestly believe I had no other choice but this or debtor's prison. Or to become a kept woman.'

Nick shook his head. 'No, no choice, and you should never have been put in that position. I had no idea from what he and his friend told me.'

'Ah, well, it is no good crying over spilled milk. Tell me…' she curled round in the chair '…what made you become a highwayman?'

'Nothing.' Nick made a sudden decision. He was not going to lie to her. 'Nothing made me a highwayman. I am not Black Jack Standon. I was drugged, tricked and framed and the devil of it is, I have not the slightest iota of proof on my side.'

Chapter Four

Katherine looked deep into the dark eyes opposite and read anger, frustration and truth. She was not married to a highwayman, she was married to Nicholas Lydgate who was falsely accused and was due to be hanged in five days' time. Fear ran through her, knotting her stomach.

'What happened? Who did it?'

'You believe me?' He sounded incredulous, as though he had not expected this reaction.

'Yes, of course.'

'Why? Why should you believe me, Kat?'

Katherine thought about it. 'Instinct? I trusted you from the beginning, I am not sure why. I look into your eyes and I see the truth. I am used to living with a weak man, one who lies and twists. I believe I can recognise a strong and an honest one when I meet him.'

Nick flushed, half-turned from her, running his hand over his face as though to smother some emotion her trust evoked. 'Thank you for that.'

'So what happened?' she prompted.

'I had just returned from France. I had been on the continent for some time and it was years since I had been in England. I went first to Aylesbury, hoping that an old friend was still there, but they told me he had moved away long ago. I decided to go to London, it seemed as good a place as any while I thought about what to do next.

'Just outside Hemel Hempstead the road runs over an area of rough grazing beside the river, called Box Moor. It had been a filthy day—wet, driving rain and cold with it. It got dark early and I was trying to decide whether to push on to King's Langley or turn off to Hemel Hempstead when I saw an inn ahead. Not much of a place, certainly not somewhere gentry frequent, and when I walked in I thought either they or I were drunk.'

'Why?' Katherine reached for the wine bottle and poured herself a glass without thinking. His voice was easy to listen to, strong yet well modulated. Nick removed the wine from her hand, topped up his own glass and put the bottle out of reach.

'They recognised me. For a few seconds people turned as if to greet me, hands were raised, the landlord reached for a tankard and began to draw ale without being asked. A pretty barmaid ran over and gave me a kiss.'

'But did they know you?'

'No, of course not. The moment I stepped out of the shadows into the light of the bar it all changed. Shoulders were turned, men went back to their cards and their pipes. Even the barmaid flounced off.'

'Then what happened?' Katherine was so engaged with the story and the wine was so warm in her veins that she forgot her reticence at being alone with Nicholas. It felt like being alone with an old friend.

'I asked for a room and stabling for my horse. The landlord was reluctant, surly even. If it had not been such a foul night, I would have walked out and found another lodging. I wish I had! But I persisted and eventually the girl showed me to a room. Not much of one, but it would do. I saw my horse settled and had a meal. The atmosphere was strange; they were uneasy, as though waiting for something, and people would slip out and come back in again.'

'Um, the privy?' Katherine suggested.

'That is what I thought at the time. Then it all went very quiet. The barmaid brought me a beaker of rum. It was to help me sleep, she said, because it was such a rough night.'

'You drank it and it was drugged?'

'It was. I made my way upstairs, wondering why my legs were so weary, but I put it down to the long ride. I pulled off my clothes, I think. I can remember falling on the bed, then nothing until I was shaken awake.'

'By whom?' Katherine swallowed with tension.

'A captain of dragoons, two of his men, the local magistrate and his parish constable. The magistrate had a bandage round his head and was in a towering rage. It seems he had just been held up at gunpoint on the Moor by Black Jack Standon, scourge of those parts, and had been hit on the head and lightened of his watch, card case and rings. The man had become such a menace over the past few months that the dragoons had been stationed in the vicinity to catch him and the magistrate put them hot on his heels.'

'But why did they think you were he?' Katherine demanded. 'A perfectly respectable traveller…'

'A man bearing a close resemblance to a tall, dark, black-eyed highwayman. And a man, apparently drunk on rum, slumped on a bed in a shady inn known to be one of Black Jack's haunts. My clothes and all my possessions had gone and I was dressed in the clothes you saw me in today. My horse had vanished and in its place was a distinctive black gelding with one white foot and a white blaze. Black Jack's horse. The barmaid put on a particularly good act, throwing herself on my chest and sobbing that I was not Black Jack. Naturally that looked as suspicious as hell.'

'But you told them who you were? Surely your friends…' Once again the light went out of his eyes, just as it had when she had asked him about his dependents. Katherine watched the strong line of his jaw tense before he answered.

'There is no one. Everything I had to prove my identity had gone. The trial was a foregone conclusion and so was the verdict.'

'So Black Jack escaped the dragoons. And all he has to do is lie low for another week or so…'

'Five days to be precise, as of noon tomorrow.'

'Why are you not angry?' Katherine demanded. Fury was building in her on his behalf. 'The coward might just as well have shot you in the back!'

Nick shrugged. 'Anger will not do me any good. He was caught like a rat in a trap and got out of it with some quick thinking. It was just his good fortune that I have no way of proving who I am. Most people would have been shown to be innocent within days; as it is, the hunt will be off—he could not have predicted it.' He looked keenly at her. 'Now, Kat, don't cry. Why are you crying?'

'Because I am angry,' she said, rubbing furiously at her eyes with her handkerchief and glaring at him, defying him to read any other emotion into her sudden spurt of tears. He looked back, an amused smile tugging the corners of what she was increasingly aware was a very sensual mouth. His eyes were dark and steady on her and she swallowed. He was a very attractive man. A very big, very masculine man and any minute he was going to…

'I think we should go to bed, Kat.'

She had been expecting it all evening, knew it was inevitable; still she could not suppress the little gasp of alarm.

'Kat, I said we should go to bed, not anything else. We can talk if you like or we can go to sleep, but that is all, I promise.'

'You don't want to—' Her voice failed her.

'Make love to you? Yes, of course I want to,' he said matter of factly. 'I am a man, you are a very attractive young lady who just happens to be my wife. But I have no intention of forcing an unwilling woman.'

'You would not be—I mean, I would not be.' Katherine swallowed. This was very difficult. 'We had a bargain. I am resolved to honour my side of it. How else can I repay you?'

'With a daily supply of plum cake for a week?'

'Do not laugh at me!'

'I am not, I respect your courage and your sense of honour. I should not have said what I did about the marriage being consummated. Of course it does not have to be: all that is needed is for us to be seen to have spent the night together.'

'But we are married, we are here and you said you wanted to.' Inwardly she flinched. Did she sound as though she was begging him to make love to her? Of course she was not, it could not be that making her feel confused and disappointed and hot inside.

'I have been doing some thinking.' Nick got to his feet and began to shrug off his coat. 'What if you were with child as a result? You will have a hard enough time of it as it is without carrying a highwayman's child.'

Katherine's internal turmoil took a new frightening swoop. 'I never thought of that.'

'Yes, well, it happens. Now please, Katherine, get into bed. I have been dreaming of a good night's sleep in a decent bed for weeks.'

'You have the bed then, I will sit up.' She felt as panicky as if he had begun to make love to her.

'Do you want me to undress you and put you to bed?' That glint was back in his eyes, the sensual drawl back in his voice. Katherine was in no doubt he would enjoy the tussle.

'There is no need,' she said with a dignity she was far from feeling. 'If you would just turn your back, I will get into bed.'

He did so, spinning his chair around and sitting at the table. Katherine scrambled out of her clothes and into the nightgown she had brought. She had chosen the flimsiest, prettiest one she had while she was still buoyed up with her determination to prove willing and to please him; now it seemed scandalous.

She pulled the pins from her hair until it tumbled down her back and slipped into bed. The sheets came up to her chin. 'I am in bed.'

'Good. Now close your eyes in approved maidenly fashion and I will join you.' He was laughing, the wretch. Katherine screwed up her eyes and reflected that if Nick Lydgate was getting some amusement from the evening it was no more than she owed him.

There was the sound of boots hitting the floor, the softer sound of clothes falling on a chair, then the covers moved, the bed dipped and he was beside her. Katherine felt his warmth, the touch of linen against her skin. Thank goodness he had retained his shirt. He smelt good; there was the familiar soap she bought for Philip, but under it a faint scent that could only be himself, clean, warm and relaxed.

'That is a devilishly pretty nightgown, Kat.' The straw mattress moved as he shifted to settle himself beside her. She opened her eyes just a fraction and saw he had snuffed all but two of the candles. 'You should not be looking. Oh!'

He caught her in his arms and rolled her against his chest, his face buried in her hair. 'My God, you smell good.'

'No! You promised.' Katherine wriggled.

'I am not going to do anything but hold you and enjoy the scent of you. Now stop wriggling, it is extremely provocative and I will either break my promise or fall out of bed if you persist. That is a very charming noise you are making—you sound like a cross kitten.'

Katherine subsided. Infuriating man…but he did appear to be as good as his word, he was simply holding her. She could feel his breath stirring her hair, but his arms were strong and unmoving around her and his hands did not stroke or caress.

This was a very strange sensation, being held by a man. She tried to sort it out. The bed was surprisingly comfortable and she had drunk a whole glass and a half of wine, so her head felt a little muzzy. Nick's arms around her, though unfamiliar, made her feel protected and safe. But his body—that was quite another thing. That made her feel anything but safe, yet she was not in the slightest bit frightened. Just shy and confused. He was hot and long and felt very hard and strong. She shivered, not from fear, but from a restless need to explore, touch…

'Try and relax and go to sleep.'

'I am relaxed.'

'No, you are not, you are quivering.'

'Oh. I am sorry.' She must stop thinking about how this felt, think of something else. It did not take much effort to find a topic. The story Nick had just told her came back in all its horrifying detail. It was as effective as cold water splashed in her face. This man who was holding her so gently was going to be executed in just a few days for a crime he did not commit. Anger stirred again and with it the beginnings of an idea.

'Nick?'

'Mmm?' He sounded half-asleep.

'What was the name of the inn? The one at Box Moor.'

'The Lamb, I think. No, the Lamb and Flag. Why?'

'Nothing.' She yawned. 'I just wondered.' And slept.

When she woke there was daylight in the room from a high barred window and she had no recollection of stirring in the night. They were lying as they had gone to sleep, but in a far more intimate tangle. With the colour rising to her cheeks, Katherine realised that her nightgown had ridden up around her hips and one of Nick's legs was over hers.

She felt him move and raise his head. 'Kat? Are you awake?'

'Umm.'

'We had better get up soon, I heard the clock strike seven.'

'Oh.'

'Are you usually this chatty in the morning?'

She smothered a snort of amusement. 'I do not know. I am not in the habit of waking up in bed with anyone.'

'I am glad to hear it.'

She felt him throw back the covers and his warmth left her. Grumbling, she burrowed down into the body-shaped dip in the mattress, eyes tight shut.

'You look like a cat who has finally managed to secure all of the sofa cushion,' Nick remarked. From the muffled sound of his voice he was pulling a shirt over his head.

'You let the cold in.'

'I am sorry. But you must get up now. There is some cold water on the wash stand behind the screen in the corner and I am gazing fixedly at the ceiling and a large spider directly above the bed.'

'Wretch.' Reluctantly Katherine opened her eyes and jumped out of bed. The water was indeed cold, and by the time she had washed and dressed she was well and truly awake. And the chill seemed to have settled in a hard knot in her stomach.

When she emerged, Nick was laying the remains of the meat and bread out on the table and had found the bottle of ale she had included. 'Are you as silent over breakfast?'

'No.' It was strangely difficult to look at him. Katherine wondered how she would be feeling if they had made love last night. She jumped as he pulled the cork from the bottle with a pop and made herself smile and take the proffered glass. 'Thank you. Did you sleep well last night?'

'So well. I should not have done with a beautiful woman in my arms. I should have lain awake in torment.' He laughed as Katherine frowned at him. 'You are very soothing.'

That was a mixed bundle of compliments to be sure. 'Beautiful' produced a warm glow. No one had ever called her that before. But she was not sure that being soothing was preferable to being the sort of woman who drove men wild with uncontrollable desire.

She sneaked a sideways look at him while he ate. His hair was too long and was decidedly untidy. Goodness knows what he had done with the comb. There was the night's growth of stubble shadowing his chin and his eyes, despite his protestations of a good sleep, seemed heavy and brooding. Good cheekbones, she decided, and a very straight nose.

Katherine wanted to get up and go and rub his shoulders, wrap her arms around him and hug him until that bleak look vanished. But what power had a hug to banish the thought of the cell he was about to return to?

They packed the hamper again, stripped the bed and folded the sheets. Katherine risked teasing a little. 'You are very domesticated.'

'It comes from being in the army.'

'Were you? Which regiment?'

'A cavalry regiment,' he said evasively.

'But surely there are some of your fellow officers in England, in London! Tell me some names and I will go to Horse Guards. Oh, Nick, why did you not think of that before?'

'Because I enlisted as a trooper, under a false name,' he said with a finality that warned her not to pursue the reason why. 'There, all packed.'

The clock began to chime. 'Nick...'

'Come here,' he said roughly, pulling her towards him by the shoulders.

Katherine went without conscious thought, wrapping her arms around him and tipping her face up to his. His mouth on hers was not gentle, not tender, it made no allowance for her innocence or inexperience.

Clinging to Nick's shoulders, swept along by his need, Katherine opened to him, instinctively parting her lips as he ravished them, meeting his thrusting tongue with hers. It was as though he needed to absorb her, press her to him until she left an imprint on his body.

He let her go as suddenly as he had taken her, staring down with eyes like dark flame. Katherine licked her lips, tasting him on them. Her hands went up to lock into the long hair at his nape and he put his own hands up to catch her wrists.

'Katherine...'

The clock struck eight.

Chapter Five

Behind her the sound of the key in the lock tore across her nerves.

'I will come back, I promise, Nick.'

'No, not to this place.' He took her shoulders again, so hard it hurt her. 'Promise me. Not the last day. Promise me that at least.'

'No. I will not promise and I will come back.' The door swung open. 'Goodbye, Nick.' She stood on tiptoe and kissed his set lips swiftly, then turned to the door.

'Good morning, Mr Rawlings. Good morning, John. John, everything is packed, I will just put on my bonnet.'

Nick stayed still as a statue by the door as John helped her into her pelisse and picked up the bags. She stopped at his side as she tied her bonnet strings. There did not seem to be any words so she reached up, touched his cheek and left.

John was a brooding presence at her side as they walked down the endless dark passages and out into the blessed sunlight and fresh air. He hailed a hackney carriage and bundled her inside before plumping down opposite her and demanding, with all the licence of an old family servant, 'Are you all right, Miss Katherine?'

'Mrs Lydgate,' she said firmly. It was the first time she had said it; it sounded rather well. Her coachman regarded her with much the same air her father had adopted when she came up with some excuse to distract him from a misdemeanour.

'John, Mr Lydgate behaved like a perfect gentleman and absolutely nothing happened. Now that is as much as I am prepared to discuss with you so you can stop looking like a cross bulldog.'

'Humph. If you say so Miss…Mrs Lydgate.'

'I was teasing you, John, please call me Miss Katherine. Now, has Philip taken the carriage out?'

'No.' He was still regarding her suspiciously as if he expected her to burst into tears at any moment. This was obviously not the reaction he had been anticipating.

'Good, because I need the horses putting to and for you to pack your bags. We are going into Hertfordshire today.'

Jenny was inclined to be tearful at her return and then as baffled as John by their mistress's brisk determination to leave London. 'Pack, Miss Katherine? But for how many days?'

'I am not sure. It cannot be more than three, I pray it will take no more. And Jenny, you know that old hat box we put up in the attic?'

'Yes, Miss Katherine.'

'Fetch it down, please.'

Jenny departed, shaking her head. Kate ran downstairs and into Philip's study. Now, where was the atlas? Yes, here it was, a volume of road maps. She conned the one for the Aylesbury and Oxford road carefully as it unwound in a long ribbon over several pages. There was Hemel Hempstead and there was Box Moor. Now, where best to stay? Her heart told her the Lamb and Flag, but her head counselled caution. Hemel Hempstead was large enough to hold several respectable inns and, more importantly, magistrates.

She lifted the volume and started to leave, then turned back. She had better leave Philip a note to say they had gone away, although as he was not even here to meet her on her return, she felt a chilly hardening of her heart towards him. She pulled a sheet of notepaper towards her, dislodging several bills as she did so. *Oh, Philip! Was it possible to stop loving your own brother? How many blows to the heart does it take before that feeling died?*

Jenny was in the hall, portmanteaux and bandboxes at her feet and a battered hat box in her hands. 'What do you want this dirty old thing for, Miss Katherine?'

'I do not want it at all, I want what is in it.' There was an ugly hat resting on a bed of crumpled tissue paper. Katherine tossed it aside and reached under the paper. Her fingers closed over something as fluid and sinuous as a snake and she drew it out.

'Miss Katherine! Diamonds!'

It was a necklace, dull through neglect, but still sparking with the unmistakable watery fire of the true gems. 'This is my last thing of any real value and I have been saving it for a rainy day, Jenny.' She sighed. 'It belonged to my grandmother and it will have to be sold to be broken up, I am afraid, the stones are an old-fashioned cut and setting.'

'But, Miss Katherine, if you had this…'

'No, Jenny, it is worth a few hundreds, not thousands; see, there are not many stones and they are quite small. But I need it now—this is not a rainy day, this is a hurricane.'

John was ready and they piled their baggage into the old coach. 'Newman's of Lombard Street, please, John, and then the road to Aylesbury and Oxford.'

* * *

Mr Newman was courteous to Mrs Lydgate. He did not know her, or recognise the name, and her dress was two Seasons out of date, but he recognised Quality when he met it. What he had not bargained for was a steely determination.

'One hundred? I am sorry, Mr Newman, I have obviously been wasting my time and yours. I will find another jeweller with an appreciation of fine stones.' She let her eyes roam around the shop dismissively. 'You were recommended by Lady…er, well, perhaps I should not mention names. She will be so disappointed to hear she was mistaken in her advice.' Katherine rose and picked up the necklace, careful that the darn in her glove did not show.

Half an hour later she was hurrying out to the coach, her reticule bulging, a gleam in her eyes. 'Three hundred, Jenny, just imagine! I would have been happy with two, but I sneered so much at his lovely shop he gave me *three*.'

Her triumph lasted all the way to Hemel Hempstead. With money in her pocket they could afford a change of horses, and when they reached the town she indulged herself with two rooms in the Swan in the High Street. It was only as the three of them sat down to dinner in the private parlour she bespoke that the fear began to creep back. By tomorrow, four days left. Only four days.

If she failed, then Nick would hang. She would be there, although not where he could see her. He would hate that, his pride would revolt at the thought that she should see him choke and slowly strangle to death, kicking in front of a baying crowd. She had known him for only a few hours, but already she knew that his pride drove him, fed him with a sort of anger that had driven him into whatever life he had lived

on the continent and now gave him the grace to look an un-
just death in the eye with dignity.

'Are you going to tell us what we are doing here, Miss
Katherine?' John demanded after the waiter had deposited a
leg of mutton on the table and departed.

'Yes. Will you carve that, please, John? We are going to
prove Mr Lydgate innocent and to do that we need to meet a
highwayman called Black Jack Standon and a magistrate
whose name I do not know, but who probably has a new
watch and a scar on his head.'

'Heaven preserve us, Miss Katherine.' Jenny reached for
a glass of ale and gulped a mouthful. 'We'll be murdered in
our beds.'

'I doubt it,' Katherine responded tartly. 'We will have to
identify the magistrate, of course, but I need to find Black
Jack before I actually approach the Justice. Dear me,' she
added as John opened his mouth to begin what was obviously
going to be a lengthy protest, 'what melodramatic names
these highwaymen adopt. Quite unnecessary, I would have
thought. I am sure they are not as ferocious as they would like
everyone to believe.' She relented at the sight of their appalled
faces and retold Nick's story.

'That's a terrible thing if he is telling the truth, but do you have
to do this, Miss Katherine?' John asked sombrely. He appeared
to understand at last that she was not going to be discouraged.

'Yes, John, or I will always have it on my conscience.
Now,' she said briskly, 'how do you suggest we find the magistrate who was robbed?'

Jenny took another swig of ale, tossed her curls and said,
'I'll ask.' She got to her feet and with a swing of her hips vanished through the door into the taproom. Katherine looked dubiously at John.

'I'll keep an eye on her.' He followed the maid out, leaving Katherine sitting alone, her chin propped on her hand, her mind at last free of all distraction.

Last night she had slept in the arms of a man she scarcely knew, a convicted felon she had married out of hand for sheer expediency. Her conscience nagged her. She had not deserved to have found someone who treated her with respect and consideration, she told herself bitterly, but by some miracle she had done so. She might be innocent of men, but she had a very good idea of just what self-control it had taken to sleep with her scarcely clad in his arms. Katherine folded her arms on the table, bent her head down and tried to send some message of support. She dared not think of hope yet: it would be too cruel.

Back in his dank cell Nick rested his head on his bent knees and let his mind dwell on the warm, soft, trusting femininity he had spent the previous night cradling in his arms. He corrected himself: not so trusting, perhaps. She knew exactly what she was expected to have to do last night and had been prepared to go through with it out of a sense of honour that men liked to think only their sex possessed. What must that have cost? He had all too vivid a memory of himself in that mirror: filthy, dangerous, desperate. And yet she had sent him soap and soft towels and a book of poetry. What was she doing now? He breathed slowly, deeply, recalling her voice and the generosity of her innocent lips against his. *Kat. Kat, don't come back. Please.*

The next morning Katherine rose at seven, dressed with care in her best walking dress and left Jenny behind to discover the direction of Mr Highson, the outraged magistrate. Jenny had had easily extracted the tale of the magistrate and the highwayman from the crowd in the common tap the night before, even if she had had to be rescued by John from the somewhat over-amorous advances of her new friends.

John drove the gig they had hired and Katherine was thankful for his stolid bulk beside her. If she had realised he had felt it necessary to shove two loaded pistols into his belt, she would have felt considerably less sanguine. She tried to breathe deeply and calm herself. She had two days before they must return to London, surely that would be enough?

They crossed a bridge and she found herself looking out over water meadows dotted with grazing beasts. This must be Box Moor. What hope of being waylaid by Black Jack? she wondered. That would be a saving of time indeed! But nothing disturbed their journey and before many minutes had passed John was swinging the gig into a small stable yard.

Silence. The place appeared deserted. John shouted, 'House!' and finally a scruffy youth wandered out and squinted at the gig as though he had never seen one before.

'Yer?'

'Where is the landlord? My mistress requires refreshment.'

'Er. Inside. Master's inside.'

'Well, come and hold the horse, you half-wit, while I help my lady down.'

Katherine climbed down into the yard and looked around. It seemed harmless enough. She gathered up her skirts and trod across the cobbles, avoiding the worst puddles, and went in through a back door.

Someone was singing tunelessly in the back quarters, but the voice was male and not young and she wanted to find the barmaid. Clinking noises from the front sounded more hopeful. Following the sounds, she made her way through to the bar room. A young woman in a plain gown, low cut to show the edge of her chemise and kirtled up to keep her petticoats clear of the newly washed floor, was replacing tankards behind the bar.

She spun round at the sound of Katherine's tread and the flare of wariness and fear in her eyes gave Katherine hope. The woman collected herself quickly. 'Yes, ma'am?'

'A glass of your best ale,' Katherine said pleasantly. 'I will be glad of a short rest on my journey.'

'Yes, ma'am,' she repeated, turning to one of the great barrels propped up behind the bar.

Katherine took a table on the far side of the room and waited until the girl came and placed the tankard in front of her. She took a sip. 'Excellent. You brew here?'

'Oh, yes, ma'am. Famous hereabouts the Lamb and Flag is.'

'And for more than your ale, I hear,' Katherine said smoothly, dropping her hand over the girl's wrist to detain her. 'You have a notorious highwayman amongst your customers, so I hear.'

'Yes, ma'am.' The girl seemed unsure of how to deal with the detaining hand. 'But no longer, ma'am. The troopers took him near a month past.'

'Did they, indeed?' Katherine kept a firm grip of the slender wrist and pulled the girl down to sit beside her. 'Tell me all about it. Did you know this desperate villain well?'

Something in the quality of the air changed. Someone else was in the room. A powerful presence. Katherine's heart missed a beat.

'He'd come in from time to time, I s'pose,' the girl said sulkily. Katherine watched her eyes flicker to the doorway behind her. The air stirred. She watched the dust motes dance and offered up a silent prayer.

'So I imagine you were relieved that they got the wrong man?' she remarked conversationally.

'Yes… No! What do you mean?'

'That it was not Black Jack Standon they caught, of course. Fortunate for Mr Standon and his friends, a pity for the man they are about to hang.' Her ears strained for the slightest sound from behind her. 'Not what I would have expected from a man of Black Jack Standon's reputation.'

The maid's eyes flickered and she tried to pull her hand free. 'What do you mean?' she repeated dully.

'Black Jack has a certain fame for being a sporting man. A name for courage and being game. Not like him to let an innocent man hang in his place. Where's the pride in that?'

Now she could sense the presence directly behind her. He moved as silently as a cat. 'Good morning, sir.' She spoke without turning, before he could take another step. 'Please, will you not join me? Another tankard for the gentleman, if you will.' Katherine released the girl's wrist with a smile.

'I won't say no.' The big man who appeared by her side was so like Nick that she almost gasped. Then he sat down opposite her and she could see the difference. This man was perhaps ten years older; a good thirty-eight, if not forty. His nose had been broken and his face was rounder with less apparent bone structure. He picked up the tankard the barmaid put in front of him and tossed half of it back without taking his eyes off the woman before him.

'What do you know about Black Jack Standon, mistress?'

'Nothing, except for his reputation. I know the man taken up in his place: I am married to him.'

'Then tell the authorities who he is.'

'I cannot prove it. No one can. The only way to prove my husband innocent is for the real Black Jack to be seen again. I am sure if he knew of the situation he would want to help.'

The brown eyes looked into hers for a long moment then he grunted. 'Huh. What would be in it for Black Jack?'

'Pride,' Katherine said simply.

In the yard John did as he had been ordered and watered the horse, checked the harness, then sat in the gig. Every nerve quivered with the urge to disobey. He squinted up at the sun. Ten more minutes, fifteen at the most and he was going in, no matter what Miss Katherine said.

He was on the point of climbing down from the vehicle when the door opened and Katherine stepped out, speaking over her shoulder as she did so. 'Thank you. I will send word. I knew I could not be mistaken in you.'

In Newgate Nick paced back and forth in front of his bench, wishing he could stop thinking about Kat, returning to those very thoughts time and again as the only pleasant recollection he could conjure up. He felt uneasy about her and could not say why. Foolishness—she was safe enough in London now the risk from the bailiffs was gone.

The object of Nick's concern was experiencing a far more unpleasant time than she had during her encounter with the highwayman. With the freedom of an old family retainer, John was giving vent to his anxiety and his self-reproach at letting her meet the man at all, let alone by herself.

'And it's no good you telling me you're a married lady now, Miss Katherine, and can do what you want!'

'I haven't said that,' she replied mildly. 'But I must do what is necessary and I fear you are going to like the next adventure even less than this one. And I will need your help,' she added, gazing trustfully at him.

'Don't you go batting your eyelashes at me, Miss Katherine! It might work on some highwayman, but I know when you are up to no good.'

'Let us hope that Jenny has had as much success as we have and then we can all go home the day after tomorrow,' Katherine promised.

Jenny was waiting for them at the inn and positively bubbling with both the amount she had found out and her own cleverness in doing so.

'I went to Mr Highson's house, it's but a mile out of town. And I went round to the back door and started chatting to the kitchen maid; told her I was new to the area and looking for work and wondered what was this place like.'

'Jenny, that was brilliant,' Katherine said admiringly. 'Was she not suspicious?'

'Not in the least. Bored to death, cook's day off and she was left to make the day's meals for the master. I settled down and helped her with the vegetables and she told me all about the household. The magistrate is unmarried and has a valet, a rather elderly footman, the cook and herself. When she said she had to lay the table for his luncheon I said I'd help her so along we go, right through to the dining room.'

'Jenny!' Katherine stared in admiration. 'What else did you find out?'

'Well, I said wasn't it awfully exciting, her master being a Justice and all? Weren't desperate characters dragged there at all hours of the day and night? I wondered what his study must be like—did he have a great chair like a judge?'

'And?'

'She showed me his study. She says that when he's home he works there every day in the afternoon between two and four. It is on the ground floor and looks out on to the garden. See, I've drawn a plan.'

'You'd make a fair good spy,' John grunted with grudging admiration. 'But how to we know which days he'll be there?'

'Every day this week,' Jenny said triumphantly. 'Mary— that's the maid—said it was a nuisance because it made more work when he was home.'

Katherine sat back and closed her eyes against the sudden rush of relief. Thank goodness! Her biggest fear throughout was that they would not find the magistrate at home and she would have to persuade Jack Standon to travel to wherever he had gone.

Blinking, she pulled the plan of Mr Highson's house towards her and conned it. 'Now, this is what we must do. Listen carefully.'

Chapter Six

At three the next afternoon Katherine stood with her two
supporters in a small spinney a few hundred yards from Mr
Highson's front gates. Would Black Jack Standon come after
all? Was she placing her trust in the highwayman's pride and
arrogance too high?

Then there was a crackling of broken branches behind
them and he walked out of the trees, the reins of a handsome
bay gelding looped over his arm. *Nick's horse*, Katherine
thought. Now was perhaps not the best time to ask for it back.

'Good afternoon, Mr Standon,' she said as calmly as she
could. 'May I introduce you to John Morgan and Miss Pilgrim.'

'G'day.' He nodded to the others. 'You know what you're
doing, I hope, because if this is a trap I'm not going easily
and who's to say who will get in the way of these.' He pushed
back the edges of his greatcoat and Katherine saw the butts
of two large horse pistols.

John stepped forward belligerently, but she put a detaining hand on his arm. 'It is all right, John. Mr Standon, here
is a plan of the house Miss Pilgrim drew after her visit yesterday. Mr Highson will be in his study, John will be with me,

but will stop at the door so we are not interrupted. You have the article?'

The highwayman grunted and patted the pocket of his waistcoat. 'Pity to hand it back to him.'

'I have compensated you for it,' Katherine said firmly. 'We have a bargain, have we not?'

'You're a cool one,' he said grudgingly. 'What's your lay, then? Gentry morts aren't commonly found slumming with highwaymen.'

'*My lay*, as you put it, is simply to get my husband out of Newgate, Mr Standon. I find it surprising how cool one can be when an innocent life is at stake.'

'All right, all right, there's no cause to rub it in,' he grumbled, looking uncomfortable. 'How was I to know the cove had no way of proving who he was?'

'Then let us not delay. The sooner we do this, the sooner an innocent man will be free.' *It will work*, she told herself fiercely. It must work—the consequences of failure were too awful. 'Come along, Jenny, John. You, Mr Standon, need to be on the far side of the house.'

It was a distracted young lady who rang the bell at the magistrate's front door a few minutes later. Katherine found she did not have to act. Sheer nerves left her pale and trembling and her voice shook. The footman, somewhat grey and bent, admitted that Justice Highson was at home and might be willing to speak to the young lady who was so eager to report yet another outrage upon the King's highway.

He showed them through to a small, rather neglected salon, and returned a few moments later to announce that Mr Highson would be pleased to speak to Mrs Lydgate.

'Thank you so much,' Katherine said graciously, emerging from behind her handkerchief and bestowing a dazzling smile upon him. 'Come along, Jenny.'

She swept into the study, Jenny at her heels and, as the door closed, faintly heard John's voice announcing that he would stay just here outside the door in case his mistress needed him.

Mr Highson proved to be middle aged, rotund, somewhat choleric of complexion and neglectful of his dress. He brushed away a small cloud of snuff and surged to his feet as Katherine entered. 'My dear Mrs, er…Lydgate. How may I serve you? My man said something about a highwayman, ma'am. You must not alarm yourself, we laid the notorious rogue by the heels very recently; he is awaiting an appointment with the hangman even as we speak.'

'I fear…oh, dear!' Katherine waved her handkerchief somewhat wildly in front of her face. 'I fear I am about to faint! Some air, I beg of you…' She sank picturesquely into Jenny's waiting arms, carefully blocking the magistrate's route to his desk as he hurried towards the window. It was very possible he kept a pistol in the drawer. 'Oh, more, sir, throw it open, I implore you, I feel quite…'

She could feel Jenny's suppressed giggles and kicked her sharply as Justice Highson threw up the sash with an effort and stepped back. 'There, ma'am. What the devil!'

Jack Standon was over the sill and into the room before the outraged magistrate could do more than recoil from the window against Katherine. She threw her arms around him and clung.

'Never fear, ma'am,' he gasped, trying to disentangle himself. 'I will save you from this ruffian!'

Katherine felt positively guilty; the poor man was bravely shielding her from the threat she had brought into his house.

'Mr Highson, sir,' she said, 'do you not recognise this man?'

'Of course I do,' he snarled. 'It is that rogue Standon who held me up…' His voice trailed away as he stared at Black

Jack, then twisted to fix Katherine with a shrewd look. 'Black Jack Standon is in Newgate gaol. Just what are you about, young lady?'

'My husband is in Newgate,' Katherine said, clinging firmly to his arm. 'This is the real Black Jack, the man who held you up. Please, sir, may we all sit down and I will explain everything?'

Reluctantly the magistrate allowed himself to be pressed into a chair while Katherine recounted the story as Nick had told it to her. She explained how she came to be married to him, trying to ignore the look of shock on his face at the sordid story.

'Well,' he grunted at last. 'That is some tale, my dear. Now then, you, speak up. Is this the truth?'

'Yes, sir.' Black Jack dug into his pocket and laid a pocket watch on the desk. 'I've sold the rest, but I took a fancy to this. Pretty thing, as you'll remember I said to you at the time I took it.'

Mr Highson reached out his hand and picked up the watch. His fingers closed tightly on it. 'This was my father's,' he remarked in a neutral tone before tucking it into his waistcoat pocket. 'And what has this lady paid you to tell me this tale?'

Katherine stiffened indignantly, but Black Jack met the magistrate's eyes with equanimity. 'Just the price I put on the watch. No man goes to the gallows for Black Jack Standon. I have my pride. How was I to know the swell cove had no way of proving who he was?'

There was a long silence, then the magistrate said, 'When is he due to hang?'

'The day after tomorrow, sir.' Katherine could feel the room swimming before her eyes. She had convinced him, she knew it.

'Do not faint on me now, ma'am,' he said firmly. 'We have

a journey to make tomorrow and I must get some paperwork in order.' He turned a shrewd eye on the highwayman towering over them both. 'I presume you have no intention of surrendering to me?'

The dark man grinned, showing a set of blackened teeth. 'You have the right of it there, Mr Justice. I think I'll go and rob a coach or two, just to let them all know that Black Jack's back. Good day, ma'am—you tell your husband he's a lucky man.'

'You'll end on the gallows,' the magistrate prophesied grimly as the highwayman stepped over the sill.

'Happen I will, sir,' he responded equably and was gone.

'You believed me, Mr Highson?' Katherine demanded. 'You will come to London with us and clear my husband's name?'

'Yes, my dear. I will write a deposition and get it sworn in front of one of my colleagues in town and we'll be off tomorrow. Your young man will be glad to see you, I will be bound.'

'He is not my young man—' Katherine began, then broke off at the twinkle in Mr Highson's eye. 'I wish I could let him know now. He must be so—' She broke off again and took a moment to compose herself.

'Well, today is Sunday so he will have had the distraction of the Condemned Sermon,' Mr Highson said. 'That at least gets them out of their cells, although I doubt it could be characterised as light entertainment.'

'Sunday! Oh my goodness, I quite forgot. I must go to evensong.' Katherine gathered up her reticule and shawl, dropped when Black Jack had entered the room. 'What is the Condemned Sermon?'

'The Ordinary of the prison—that is the chaplain— preaches to the condemned awaiting execution, with a coffin in the centre of the chapel. It is intended to fix their minds upon eternity and to prompt repentance.'

'How horrible.' She shuddered, then resolutely pushed all thoughts of what Nick must be experiencing out of her mind. 'I cannot begin to thank you, sir. At what hour shall I call for you? I thought to hire a chaise for ourselves and my maid. My man can follow with my coach, for it is old and slow.'

'No need to hire. We will take my carriage. I have a good team and we will be in London by late afternoon, never fear. I will collect you at your inn at ten in the morning if you give me your direction.'

Katherine took a warm farewell of him and almost made it to the road outside before her legs gave way and she sank down on to the grass. 'We did it! Oh, John, Jenny, he is not going to hang.' And promptly burst into tears.

Nicholas Lydgate jerked upright on the hard pew where he had been attempting to doze and ignore the somewhat routine call to repentance the Ordinary was delivering. Sleep eluded him here as it did in his cell, but he had fallen into a pleasant half-sleeping dream involving freedom and Kat and broad acres under high moors. He straightened his back and looked coldly at the coffin lying in the centre of the chapel. Better not to dream, there was no hope to be had. To hope was to delude himself and he had never done that. The day after tomorrow his body would be tumbled into an open grave; he doubted that the prison authorities would go to the expense of providing a coffin.

If Kat was happy somewhere, so much the better. She would shed a tear for him, he knew. No one else would, and in a few years a better man than he would take what was his by birth. Robert would not disgrace the family name. He just wished he could be sure that Kat would be all right.

Katherine spent a sleepless night. What if the magistrate changed his mind or decided it was all some elaborate plot to free a guilty man? What if he was not believed when they reached London? What if the prison authorities changed the day of the execution and brought it forward?

As the clock struck three in the morning she threw back the covers, lit a candle and got out of bed to pace up and down the room. Her bare feet made little sound on the polished oak boards and the night was dark and still. Now she was moving, her frantic brain slowed and she felt calmer. Of course Mr Highson would not change his mind. He was a respected man of the law; even if Nick could not be freed on his word alone, it would be enough to halt the execution while further investigations could be made. And of course the date of the execution would not be brought forward, it was a public spectacle.

'And surely I would know if you were dead,' she whispered out loud. How strange that she felt so close to a man she had known for less than a day. But then they had shared an intense and strange experience—perhaps that had forged a bond.

Yet even before they had spoken, even while he had seemed a veritable ruffian, filthy and dangerous, there had been something as their eyes met. Katherine shivered and rubbed her arms. It might be mid-May, but three in the morning was no time to be out of bed wearing nothing but a thin night rail. She looked down and smiled. In her haste to pack and be gone from London she had thrown the same nightgown into her valise as she had worn on her strange wedding night.

'That is a devilishly pretty nightgown, Kat.' It seemed for a moment that Nick was in the bedchamber with her, his voice teasing with an underlying hint of sensual danger.

Katherine smiled again and climbed back into bed. She drew up the covers and blew out the candle flame, but stayed sitting up, her eyes unseeing on the darkness around her.

She was married to a very attractive man, she mused. Attractive in character as well as body and face. An honourable man. But for that sudden, hard kiss as they had parted he had treated her with respect and consideration. Katherine ran her fingertips over the swell of her lips. No one but family had ever kissed her, so she had nothing to compare it with, but somehow it had seemed that what he was wanting was not a simple sensual sensation but to imprint the memory of her upon his mind and body.

Had it given him what he wanted? It had certainly left a vivid impression upon her. She closed her eyes and the scent of him came back to her, the feel of his body hard under her spread hands, the taste of his mouth on hers. Katherine wriggled down under the covers and set herself to sleep again. Perhaps he too was lying awake, trying to distract his mind from the squalid reality around him by remembering that strange night.

It was torture to think of him there. Was that why she felt so strange inside? Unable to sleep, Katherine tossed and turned and tried to wait in patience for the morning.

Mr Highson was as good as his word, arriving promptly in a smart equipage somewhat at odds with his general appearance. 'Now I know you will be anxious, my dear young lady,' he said comfortably, helping Katherine into the coach, 'but we will make good time and your husband will be safely out of that place by tonight, never fear.'

She smiled and thanked him for his assurance, but something in her appearance must have betrayed her for Jenny slipped her hand into Katherine's and squeezed encouragingly. They set off at a brisk pace, leaving John and the old coach and pair far behind and, as King's Langley and then Watford were passed, Katherine began to relax and feel that after all she had succeeded in saving her stranger of a husband.

Unconsciously her lips curved in a smile. How ridiculous that she, Katherine Cunningham, should find herself married. She had put the slightest hope of that out of her mind three years ago when she realised the depths of Philip's fecklessness and the extent of his debts. Their acquaintances fell away as they were less and less able to go out into society and the few true friends that were left had gradually ceased to be frequent callers as Katherine sought to distance herself.

She could not endure their well-disguised pity, their attempts to include her tactfully in events where she might be able to afford to dress appropriately—and she dreaded any visitor coming across Philip in one of his drunken fits of moroseness. It was pride, she supposed, musing on it now. Strange that she had not realised it until she had recognised the same thing in Nick.

Well, she would not be married for long now, but she could not complain that it had been an uneventful experience.

'Where are we now, sir?' she asked, leaning forward to look out of the window.

'Not far from—'

The carriage lurched, jolted and then tipped suddenly on to its side with a rending noise of breaking timber and the shrill scream of a horse. Katherine grabbed frantically for the hanging strap, was knocked away from it by Jenny's helplessly tumbling body and then something came up and hit her across the forehead. The world went black with shooting white lights, then the noise faded away and all was still.

Chapter Seven

The jolt of the hammer on the anvil as the man struck off his irons jarred through Nick's body until it met the thudding ache in his head that had seemed to clench his brain in its grip since noon the previous day.

He sighed in relief as the leg irons fell away, then stooped to place his hand irons on the anvil. It was a temporary relief, for they would tie his hands behind his back before he left this room. Then it was the short walk out onto the gallows' platform along with his companions in death, who either huddled in front of him or who stood waiting their turn behind.

The stone-walled room was thronged with the condemned, the Ordinary, the Governor and Assistant Governor, the gaolers and the well-bred crowd who had paid to be admitted to this titillating glimpse behind the scenes. For perhaps the fourth time he let his eyes scan the room. No sign of her, thank God.

Not that Kat's absence here gave him much comfort. He had believed her promise to return, which meant that if she was not inside, then she was outside with the crowd. Nick stood to one side as the hand irons were removed and the next prisoner stepped up to the anvil. A woman—no, hardly more than a girl. She was thin and wretched, but a fierce anger burned in her eyes as they met Nick's and he nodded in recognition of another unbowed spirit.

His head thudded unmercifully and he put up a hand to rub where it hurt worst, over his right eye. Used to the weight of the shackles, he misjudged the gesture and hit himself a painful blow. Go home Kat. He tried to send the message but could sense no answering recognition. He hated the thought that she would see him die not some heroic death but merely a shameful, undignified, choking end.

The crowd of fashionable onlookers shifted, parted and he saw a face he recognised. It was that young lawyer. What was his name? Brigham, that was it. He seemed to be alone. His eyes met Nick's and he nodded, then made a strange gesture with his clasped hands as though tugging.

Nick understood him. He had one friend in this mob at least, one person who was prepared to stand at the gallows' foot and swing on his legs to make a merciful end come sooner. He raised a hand in silent acknowledgement and salute and the young lawyer nodded again, raised a hand in response and turned to burrow back through the crowd.

The ragged line of the condemned began to shuffle forward, the doors opening ahead. The roar of the crowd was suddenly loud in their ears. From behind he was suddenly elbowed in the kidneys and the thin young woman pushed past him. 'Ladies first!' she shouted in an unmistakeable East London accent. 'I'm not waiting around while you deal with all these 'ere coves. I'm going first while the audience is fresh-like.'

There were sniggers and the gaolers grinned, pushing her forward to the front of the desperate queue. Had no one but he seen the tears on her cheeks? Nick wondered. She was desperate to end the waiting, terrified of having to see what was happening before her, that was all.

The next twenty minutes passed in a daze. He fixed his eyes on the head in front of him and on nothing else as they slowly shuffled forward, stopped, waited uneasily, then moved again. What was happening in front he ignored, focusing instead on the grizzled hair, the scarred neck and the occasional flea on the man before him.

Then he was out in the sunshine and his turn was next. He looked up, over the heads of the mob, over the top of the gallows and concentrated on nothing but the memory of a trusting, fragrant, soft body nestled against his and the passionate intensity in a pair of brown eyes locked with his. *I promise.*

There was a thud, sickeningly familiar now, and the crowd yelled louder. He shut his ears to the noise. Minutes passed, then he was pushed forward. *Time to die,* he told himself. *Time to show them how a Lydgate dies.* The trap gave slightly under his feet as he planted them firmly on it. He dropped his gaze and scanned the crowd with an impassive face.

'Black Jack! Black Jack!' The shout was a chant, the upturned faces a blur.

The noose was hard and rough around his neck and he made himself not resist as the knot was jerked tight under his left ear. *Not long now, Kat.*

With a crack and a jolt the trap gave way under him and he fell, to be brought up with a sickening wrench. The pain was incredible, stars spun in front of his eyes, the world went red, black, then red again as he gagged for breath, but there was none to be had.

Arms wrapped themselves around his legs and dragged down as a woman's voice screamed 'No!' and another body hurtled through the trap beside him. The weight on his legs vanished and he was being lifted. Frantically he dragged air down into his lungs through his tortured throat.

The noose was jarring, moving, rasping at his neck, then suddenly gave way and he was falling, colliding with bodies. This was hell. He was dead and falling into hell. The blow as his head met the cobbles sent him spinning into darkness.

Darkness. Now they were trying to drown him. Nick coughed and spat as water trickled into his mouth and a voice he knew said, 'Is he breathing?'

Katherine struggled against Arthur's restraining arms, straining to see as the men clustered round Nick. 'Let me go! Is he alive?' She had been too late, too late by only minutes. Her lungs ached from the frantic race through the crowded streets, her head throbbed with pain and her throat was raw from that single scream which had been wrenched from her as she saw the trap open. *Nick...I failed you.*

John, who was bending over the figure sprawled on the table in the anteroom, looked up and nodded. 'Aye, Miss Katherine, he'll do. He'll have a powerfully sore throat for a while yet, though.'

'Thank God. Oh, thank God. Arthur, will you *please* let me go!' Katherine shook off the anxious lawyer's grip and ran to bend over Nicholas. She took his filthy hand in hers and rubbed it. 'Why does he not open his eyes?'

In response the limp figure stirred, coughed and said, 'Urgh.' He coughed, grimaced and tried again. 'Hell.' It sounded more like a statement than an oath.

'Nick, open your eyes,' Katherine urged.

There was a long moment of stillness, then, with an effort that was almost tangible, he dragged his lids open and stared up at her.

Katherine gasped; his eyes were red with broken blood vessels. 'Nick…'

'Kat?' He broke off, coughing desperately. 'Told you not to come.'

Katherine pulled off her pelisse, rolled it up and pushed it under his head. 'Do not try and talk. Someone, please fetch me water.'

'Katherine.' He was not taking the slightest notice of her words. 'I'm not dead?'

'Of course not,' she snapped, the nervous tension of the last few hours breaking down her control at last. 'Now be quiet, for goodness' sake, and lie still and we will…we will…' Suddenly she was shaking. Arthur started forward, John swore under his breath and elbowed the younger man aside and Nick, moving like a marionette with half his strings cut, lurched into a sitting position then on to his feet.

'Kat, Kat, don't cry.' She found herself gathered into his arms and held against a very malodorous frieze coat. It felt marvellous. 'Kat, what have you done to your head?'

She had forgotten it; now the pain over her eye returned with a vengeance. 'Carriage accident.' Justice Highson spoke. 'We would have been here yesterday evening if it had not been for that. But never mind that now. You, young man, should be in bed and your wife should not be in this place.'

Katherine pulled herself together. 'Oh, yes, please let us go home! Governor, will we be able to get out now?'

She found she was still clinging to Nick, although which of them was holding the other up she was not quite certain.

'John, help Mr Lydgate. Is the coach near? I can hardly recall where we got out and began to run.'

'Near enough, if the Governor can get us out away from the crowd,' John said stolidly. 'Come here, sir, you put your arm over my shoulders, we're much of a height. There we go.'

They made slow progress down the maze of passages. Katherine could not bring herself to look at Nick, to see more closely the purple swollen flesh of his throat where they had cut the noose away or the frightening bloodshot eyes. She just wanted them all out of this place. At the gateway she turned and held out her hands to Mr Highson.

'How can I thank you, sir? I feel so guilty for your injuries.'

'Nonsense, my dear.' The magistrate shifted his left arm, which was resting in a sling, and grimaced. 'A sore head and a dislocated shoulder are a small price to pay. Think how I would feel with an innocent man's life on my conscience. I'll be off now, you will want to get home. Goodbye, my dear Mrs Lydgate. Write and let me know how your husband goes on.'

Impetuously she put her arms around him and kissed his empurpled cheek. He smelt of snuff and Spanish leather and reminded her suddenly of her father.

'Now you just sit here a minute, sir.' John was propping Nick into a corner embrasure. 'I'll be back directly if that brat I left the horses with hasn't sold them.'

Katherine went to Nick's side and regarded him anxiously. He was leaning back against the wall, eyes shut. Should she take his arm? Or would he dislike that? She was still hesitating when a rumble of wheels announced John and the old carriage.

'Arthur, will you come back with us?'

Mr Brigham finished helping Nick into the coach and turned to offer his hand to Katherine. 'If I may. I hope I will be of some assistance, and I confess I cannot conceal my curiosity about how you pulled off this miracle.'

Katherine settled opposite Nick and watched him for a moment before answering. His eyes were closed, but he was responding to the shifting movements of the carriage, so he was conscious. She had a strong suspicion that he would react somewhat strongly to her story and she wanted him rested before he heard it.

'Yes, of course, I will tell you later, Arthur. But where is Philip? Was he not with you?'

There was an awkward silence. Katherine's heart sank— oh, no, not drunk again.

'Yes, where is my esteemed brother-in-law?' Nick enquired in a voice like a rusty saw. He had opened his eyes and was regarding Arthur's embarrassed face with sardonic interest.

'France.'

'*France?*'

'Well, he won't be there yet, I expect, but that's where he said he was going. He left the day before yesterday. I tried to stop him,' Arthur protested as she stared at him, appalled. 'I did try, Katherine, but he said he had had enough and couldn't stand it any longer.'

'*He* had had enough?' Katherine bit her lip to stop the angry words and tried to breathe deeply and calmly. 'How could he afford to travel?'

'He pawned some things,' Arthur said reluctantly. 'I said I would lend him the money, but he said he didn't want to be indebted to a friend.'

'Which things?' Katherine asked, suddenly all too afraid she knew what they were. 'The only things left of the slightest value are Grandmother Harrison's ormolu mantel clock and Mama's pearl ear-bobs.'

'There was a clock,' Arthur confirmed. 'And a small jewellery box.'

Katherine wrestled with hurt and anger. *They are only things*, she reasoned miserably. *You do not need them to remember the people who left them to you.*

'It appears Mr Cunningham has scruples about borrowing from his friends, but not stealing from his sister,' Nick rasped and Katherine wondered at how good that flash of anger on her behalf felt. 'Do you know which pawnbroker he used?' Arthur nodded. 'Do you have the tickets?'

'He left them in the study, I think.'

'Then will you redeem them for Katherine? You will be repaid.'

'Yes, of course,' Arthur said eagerly.

The exchange appeared to have exhausted Nick, for he fell back against the squabs, eyes closed again. Katherine sat watching him anxiously until at last they drew up in front of the house in Clifford Street.

Between them John and Arthur got the tall, unsteady figure out of the coach and up the steps to where Jenny was waiting. 'Jenny, run and set water to heat. When John has helped Mr Lydgate up to Mr Philip's room, he can carry the bath tub for you.'

The two women hovered anxiously outside the bedroom until first Arthur came out grinning, followed by John with a bundle of clothes held at arm's length. 'These need burning, Miss Katherine. Mr Lydgate says, begging your pardon, ma'am, that he isn't a bl—er, perishing child and can wash himself without the pair of us helping him. And do we have a back-brush?'

Katherine smiled, relieved. At least if Nick was capable of throwing out his would-be helpers he could not be feeling too dreadful. 'Fetch my back-brush, please, Jenny. John, what are we going to do about a nightshirt? Philip's will never fit, he is far too broad in the shoulder.'

'I'll get one of mine.' John turned to go downstairs, then looked back. 'Mind, I don't think he has any intention of going to bed.'

'As we've removed all his clothes, he had better,' Katherine said firmly. 'Especially as I intend to go in and bandage his neck and wrists.' She took the nightshirt when John returned with it and thrust both it and the back-brush into Arthur's hands. 'In you go, and make it quite clear he is to get into bed.'

Arthur grimaced, knocked and went into the bedchamber. No sound reached the listeners on the landing until eventually Arthur appeared, looking more than a little damp.

'What on earth have you been doing?' Katherine demanded.

'He threw the sponge at my head when I refused to bring him any clothes. I suppose it could have been the back-brush.'

'Has he gone to bed?'

'Yes, but only when I told him that if he did not, you would come in with your salves and bandages anyway.'

With some apprehension she tapped on the door and entered. The tub stood surrounded by sodden towels and Nick was sitting up in bed, looking pale and decidedly mutinous.

'Will you please ask John to lend me some clothes?' he croaked.

'Not until tomorrow,' Katherine responded calmly, setting her tray down beside the bed. 'You need sleep and quiet and rest. Tomorrow I will see. If you are not better, I will call Dr Wilkes; if you are better, then you may get up.'

'You are a very managing woman.' He broke off to cough and Katherine tried to keep the anxiety off her face.

'I have had to learn to be, certainly. Now, if you will just sit forward and let me fold your collar down—' She broke off at the sight of the empurpled flesh and swallowed. 'Is your neck very sore?'

Nick nodded and winced. 'Inside and out.'

'Then try not to talk. This may sting a little.' She smoothed the salve over the torn skin with as gentle a touch as possible, resolutely ignoring the indrawn breath that hissed through his teeth. 'There, I will just put a soft bandage round to keep it in contact with your skin. Now, let me see your wrists.'

Obediently he held them out, then, as she reached for them, caught her hands in his. 'Tell me what happened.'

'When you have rested.' She looked down at their joined hands and told herself that it would be undignified to start struggling. 'Let me go, please, Nick.' His pulse was strong where her thumb rested against his wrist and his hands were warm.

Slowly he freed her and she reached for the salve and bandages. 'These are much better than they were a few days ago. Did you manage to keep the bandages on under your manacles?'

Nick nodded as she tied the last knot, then recaptured her hands. 'Tell me now, Kat. Why am I not dead?'

Katherine met his eyes and read in them a will that was stronger than anything she could summon up. If she did not tell him now, he was quite capable of getting up and finding John or Jenny to ask.

'Very well, if you promise me you will stay in bed until tomorrow if I do. I went to Hemel Hempstead, found the magistrate who had you arrested—Mr Highson, he was with us today—and convinced him he had mistaken his man. Naturally, once he realised the truth he determined to have you released as soon as possible. We were travelling back yesterday and the wheel came off. Poor Mr Highson was knocked unconscious and put his shoulder right out of its socket and Jenny was badly shaken up.'

'And you?' Nick reached up and touched the bruise on her forehead. 'That gave you a headache. Are you hurt anywhere else?'

'No, just a few more bruises. I landed on Mr Highson. How did you know I had a headache?'

'Because I had one too,' he said simply.

For some reason Katherine was feeling quite flustered. 'Anyway, that was why we were so late. Mr Highson's carriage was badly damaged and poor Jenny was at her wits' end with the pair of us unconscious…I mean…' Botheration! She had not meant to let him realise she too had been knocked out.

'I see.' The rasp in his voice was even more pronounced. 'Perhaps you could tell me the whole story without editing out the bits that you consider would alarm me?'

Katherine flushed. 'John caught up with us, but Mr Highson's carriage was too badly damaged to repair quickly. We set out at five this morning in my carriage, which is slower, of course, but the crowds were terrible, we could not get through with the carriage and in the end John set us down and we had to run.' She could feel the colour draining out of her cheeks and broke off for a moment to compose herself.

'We could hear the crowd and every so often the noise would reach a crescendo and we realised another poor soul had been executed. We had no way of knowing whether we were already too late.' Her voice faltered and she bit her lip before continuing. 'It seemed to take an age to get to the Governor and for him to hear what Mr Highson had to say and then when we got to the scaffold… I am sorry to be so foolish. It is just that it was such a shock to see you there, to see the trap open.'

Nick reached out a hand and took one of hers in his gently. She felt his thumb caressing lightly over her palm. 'Shh. I should not have made you relive it so soon. Leave it now.'

'No, no, I am all right. I screamed and John ran forward and jumped down through the trap to hold you up. He found Arthur was already there and between them they managed to support you while they cut the rope above. The rest you know.'

They sat in silence for a while, Katherine content to let her hand rest in Nick's. Then he said, almost too low for her to hear, 'There was a young woman. Just a girl. She was behind me as they led us out, but she pushed through to the front. I think she was so afraid that she could not bear to wait and only wanted it all to be over.'

'Poor soul,' Katherine murmured, then the realisation of what he had just said struck her. 'You mean, if it were not for her, we would have been too late?'

'Mmm. Strange how lives can hang—literally—on such chances.' He fell silent. Katherine raised her eyes to Nick's and found that he had not begun to doze off as she thought, but that he was watching her, his dark, bloodshot eyes intelligent.

'You still are not telling me everything, are you, Kat? No, do not look so innocent and protest you have no idea what I mean.'

Chapter Eight

Katherine shut her mouth, only too aware that Nick was right and she had been about to say she had no idea what he meant.

'Come on, Kat. How did you convince that magistrate that I was innocent? He would not take your word for it, however charmingly you pleaded.'

Katherine stared back stubbornly. He would be furious if he knew what she had done, she knew him well enough already to guess that. On the other hand, he was not going to give up. If she did not tell him, John or Jenny would.

'I went to the Lamb and Flag and talked to the barmaid about Black Jack, and he was there.' Nick's eyebrows snapped together in an intimidating frown and she hastened on. 'I put it to him that to temporarily confuse the authorities was one thing, but to leave an innocent man to hang in his stead was not the action of a famous highwayman such as himself. I thought an appeal to his pride would work and it did.'

'Dear God.' Nick let his head fall back on the pillow. 'And he might just as easily have slit your throat.'

'Well, he did not. I rather liked him,' Katherine said, unwittingly adding fuel to the fire.

'Did you, indeed?'

'Yes, I did. He looked a lot less frightening than you did the first time I saw you.'

Nick merely rolled his eyes. 'And I suppose he wrote you a little note to take to the magistrate? Or did he turn himself in?'

'Neither. We went to Mr Highson's house. I pretended to faint and asked to have the window opened and Black Jack got in. Then we explained.'

'And instead of having you both arrested, he consented to listen?' Nick sounded incredulous. Katherine found she was becoming indignant. The more she thought about it, the more proud she was of her audacious plan.

'I was clinging to the magistrate so he had to listen, and John was guarding the door to stop the servants getting in. Mr Highson recognised Black Jack, who gave him his watch back and repeated something he had said when he stole it. So Mr Highson was convinced and was naturally anxious to have you pardoned as quickly as possible.'

'Let me be sure I have this right,' Nick rasped. He sounded absolutely furious. 'You travel into Hertfordshire, you beard a notorious highwayman in his lair, you assist him breaking and entering a magistrate's house, you assault the magistrate and, I presume, you help the highwayman escape again. Is that correct?'

'Yes,' Katherine said mutinously.

'And how did you pay for this excursion into crime?'

'I sold a hideous diamond necklace I had been hiding away for a rainy day, if you must know.'

She waited, a hot knot of misery inside her. She had not wanted him to be grateful, but she had expected him to be pleased, perhaps a little admiring of her enterprise and resolution. Now he seemed to be angry with her.

'You spent your last resources, you put your life and reputation in danger on the word of a complete stranger who you had every reason to think was a dangerous felon?' He was looking at her now, his eyes blazing, his hoarse voice no longer angry, but full of admiration. Katherine felt her heart thud. The tight knot of misery melted.

'I believed you. I had spent the night with you and you treated me honourably. And if you were innocent, then I had no choice but to help you.'

'Kat, come here.' He put up a hand to his eyes.

'Why? What is wrong? Is that bandage chaffing your throat?' Anxious, Katherine got to her feet and leaned over the bed. The next moment she was caught around the waist, pulled down against Nick's chest and was being thoroughly kissed.

He had kissed her once before. Once only as the prison clock struck eight with the turnkeys at the door. This was different. A slow slide of his lips across hers, a gentle pressure that tantalised, promised, stirred feelings inside her which burned and ached and made her arch instinctively closer.

Her lips parted and his tongue slid inside her to touch hers. Katherine gripped his shoulders as though she were drowning and tried to hold on to the remnants of rational thought. Those remnants were telling her that this was outrageous, that she should not be doing this, allowing this. Her self-control struggled briefly with the newly discovered wanton instincts that seemed to be rioting through her and finally got the upper hand. She opened her hands and pushed.

Nick released her immediately and she sat back panting on the edge of the bed. 'No! We should not!'

'I wanted to thank you, Kat, I just don't have the words, but perhaps I had better try if you will not let me kiss you.' His face was serious under the unruly tumble of damp black hair and Katherine caught herself before she could reach out and brush it back from his forehead. 'You saved my life, you put yourself in danger to do it and you gave up the last remnants of your financial security in the process. I do not deserve that and I can never repay it. I had resigned myself to dying, I felt it was probably a just return for the last six years of my life, for listening to my pride and not my duty and turning my back on my responsibilities.

'I had resigned myself, I thought, until I met you and found there were still some things I wanted.'

Katherine felt herself blush and he smiled wickedly at her. 'Not just that, although I have to admit that kissing you reminds me of why it is good to be alive.'

'I am glad,' she said simply. 'But we should not…not be alone, I think. After all, as soon as Arthur can arrange it, the marriage will be annulled.'

'How can it be? Have you forgotten why you married me in the first place? How will the debt be paid?'

Fear rolled back like a cold fog. 'I had not forgotten precisely,' she stammered. 'It just did not seem important under the circumstances. The last few days, all I have thought about was making sure you did not hang.'

'And by saving my neck you have resurrected the debt. The moneylenders will be interested to hear about this, I have no doubt. We had better leave town as soon as possible.'

'There is no "we" about it,' Katherine said robustly, fighting down the waves of panic. 'It is my debt, not yours.'

Nick grinned. He seemed invigorated by the dreadful mess they found themselves in. 'How can you smile about it?' she protested. 'I only married you because I thought the debt would make no difference to you. Neither of us has any money, for goodness' sake! You must disentangle yourself from my affairs.'

'Kat, you saved my life. Do you think I value that at less than a few thousand pounds?'

'Five thousand,' she said miserably. 'You might not be going to hang, but if you remain married to me *you* will end up in a debtors' prison.'

'I will not agree to an annulment, Kat.'

'Then I will go to the moneylenders and tell them the marriage was not consummated. That will do just as well.'

Nick sat up, the smile vanishing from his face. 'For one thing they will not believe you, and for another, if I really believed you would do that, I promise you I would make it a lie before you could leave this room.'

Katherine scrambled to her feet and backed off from the bed. 'No!' There was a very determined glint in his eyes. 'If I promise I will not go to them today or tomorrow, will you promise me you will rest now?' She received a reluctant nod. 'Would you like something to eat? No? Then I will bring you some lemonade.'

'Claret.'

'Lemonade.' She had reached the door and looked back, her hand on the knob. 'We have no claret.'

'Liar,' he observed amiably.

'Oh, very well, but it will do you no good whatsoever. In fact, I would not be surprised if you ended up with a brain fever!'

Katherine shut the door with a snap and went downstairs to find Jenny, feeling she had definitely come off worst in that encounter. She should have explained only what she had intended to about her adventures in Hertfordshire, she should have accepted Nick's thanks with dignity and decorum and she should have convinced him they should seek an annulment at the earliest opportunity.

What happened instead? she berated herself as she walked into the kitchen. *He knows every detail, you let yourself be kissed until you almost lost every shred of self-control and modesty and he is refusing to annul the marriage.*

'Are you all right, Miss Katherine?' Jenny asked anxiously, emerging from the pantry with a bowl of eggs.

'Perfectly, thank you. Could you ask John to clear the bath from upstairs when he has a moment? And if there is any left of that dozen of claret that Mr Philip thinks I do not know about, please will you take one up to Mr Lydgate?'

Jenny wiped her hands on her apron and went off to do as she was asked, leaving Katherine brooding at the kitchen table. *And there is still that debt and not the slightest hope of paying it.*

She was still deep in thought when the maid came back. 'I asked Mr Lydgate if he'd like a nice omelette and some ham and he said he thought he would, so that's good, isn't it, Miss Katherine?'

'He told me he was not hungry.'

'That's men for you.' Jenny reached for an empty bowl and began to crack eggs into it. 'They need tempting; I told him all about how good my omelettes are, though I say it myself. There's the front door, that'll be Mr Brigham and he'll be hungry too, I make no doubt.'

Need tempting! The last thing that Nicholas Lydgate needed was tempting, he appeared to take what he wanted quite easily without any such encouragement.

'Oh, hello, Arthur.' The young lawyer put his head round the kitchen door, saw Katherine and came in, his arms full of a handsome French clock.

'Here you are, and here are…where did I put them…? Yes, here are the earrings.'

'Thank you so much,' Katherine said gratefully, running a hand over the ornate metalwork of the clock. It brought back her grandmother so vividly she smiled as she touched it. 'What do I owe you?'

Arthur looked embarrassed, 'No hurry at all, don't think

of it. Anyway, I thought Lydgate was going to pay. You have other things to consider before that, it's a mere trifle; I told you I would have lent the money to Philip.'

'I do not borrow money and I have saddled Mr Lydgate with more than enough debt already,' Katherine said rather grimly. 'Please tell me.'

Reluctantly Arthur said, 'One hundred and twenty pounds.'

'Is that all? Honestly, you would think Philip would have the gumption to get a better price than that.' Katherine felt half-relieved—for at least she could repay Arthur from what remained of the necklace money—half-exasperated at Philip's foolishness.

She and Arthur ate with Jenny and John around the kitchen table, too tired and drained to worry about changing clothes or using the dining room. When Arthur took himself off home Katherine helped Jenny in the kitchen and sent John to make sure Nicholas had everything he needed. She had no intention of causing her emotions further turmoil by going up herself.

The sanctuary of her bed did not bring the rest she needed. The worry about the debt sat like a brooding vulture on the bedpost, and the presence at the other end of the landing of a mysterious half-stranger who was refusing to do the sensible thing and annul their marriage threatened to completely overset her resolution to do the right thing.

Consequently it was a heavy-eyed and depressed Mrs Lydgate who breakfasted alone and then set herself to establish the true extent of her financial difficulties. She gathered her own careful account books and the small pile of tradesmen's bills and went along to Philip's study.

The final demand from the moneylenders was easy enough

to find; it took longer to unearth all the other bills, dunning letters and scrawled vowels that littered the study or were jammed into drawers.

She had just drawn a line under a long and staggering list of figures when the door opened behind her and Nick said, 'There you are.'

Katherine pushed back the chair and stood up, scanning him with anxious eyes. He looked well enough in John's respectable jacket and breeches and the colour was back in his face. The edges of bandages showed under his cuffs and around his neck he had tied a loose spotted bandana.

He followed her eyes and said apologetically, 'Not perhaps the clothes to be seen wearing in St James's, but I can tell you the luxury of clean linen is priceless.'

'Should you be up?' Katherine asked. 'You do look much better, I have to admit, although your eyes are still red. Your voice sounds awful.'

'I slept like—I almost said the dead—like a log. Which is more, I think, than you did.' One long stride brought him in front of her and he ran the ball of his thumb gently under her eyes. 'You look tired.'

'After yesterday's excitements I found it hard to sleep.' Katherine tried not to shiver at the light caress.

'And what are you doing?' Nick reached behind her and picked up the paper she had been using to list Philip's debts. He let out a low whistle. 'Your brother's?'

'Yes.' Katherine took a deep breath. 'I have decided I cannot deal with those, he will have to, if and when he returns. I have added up my own housekeeping accounts and I can pay those with what is left from the necklace money. I paid Arthur for the pawnbroker last night. That leaves…let me see…just over thirty pounds. That will feed us and pay the housekeeping for a while, but it is not going to help with the big debt.'

'We need to leave town.' Nick turned and went to lean on the mantelshelf, apparently engrossed in the dead embers in the fireplace. 'If we go away, it will take them a while to find us, that's all I need, to buy a little time.'

'Where can we go?'

'Home,' he said simply. 'I will take you home.' Then he turned and Katherine saw the bitter frustration in his eyes before he dropped his gaze. When he looked at her again he had his expression under control.

'You do not want to go,' she stated, feeling miserably guilty.

Nick shrugged. 'No, but it is time I faced up to my responsibilities, swallowed my pride and made peace, I know that. Coming to London was only a way of delaying the inevitable.'

'Make peace with whom?'

'My father, and my brother perhaps, although Robert would forgive me anything, I sometimes think.'

'And where do they live?'

'Northumberland.'

Katherine stared at him. Northumberland. Why, that was almost Scotland. 'What will they say when you come home with a wife who isn't a wife and a debt of such proportions?'

'Robert will adore you. My father will be not in the least surprised at whatever I do. He and I have never seen eye to eye.'

'Is that why you left all that time ago?'

'Yes,' he said shortly. She waited, but he did not add anything.

What to do? Travel hundreds of miles to a family she did not know who would have every reason to resent her and the debt she brought with her? They must be happy to know she had helped Nick escape death, but the thought that this might somehow cancel out the debt she had saddled him with or the fact he had married without his father's blessing or approval was not one that sat comfortably with her. A life was not a commodity to be bought and sold.

'Very well, on one condition.' He raised an eyebrow and she added hastily, 'I know, I should not be making conditions when you are trying to help me, but you must promise me that we will have this marriage annulled as soon as possible.'

The quizzical eyebrow stayed up. 'Very well, if you still wish for an annulment by the time we have been in Northumberland for one month, then you shall have it.'

'One month?' Katherine regarded him, suspicious. 'Why one month?'

'To allow the charms of my family to grow upon you, perhaps.' He smiled and her heart did a little flip. 'Well?'

'Yes, I agree. I suppose it will take that long to arrange an annulment anyway, do you not think?'

'I should imagine so. It is not something I have any experience of.' His voice was sounding painfully hoarse again and Katherine poured brandy from the decanter that always stood on the end of Philip's desk.

'Try sipping this. I wonder if drinking it hot with lemon would be soothing.'

'This will be fine, thank you. Now, we must plan for the trip…'

'No, you must stop talking and sit down and rest. I will plan and you can nod or shake your head.'

With a flash of white teeth he sank obediently into an armchair and sat watching her with such an expression of meek obedience that she laughed. 'Oh, for goodness' sake stop looking so conformable! I know perfectly well that you only do what I ask when it suits you.'

'I am enjoying being ordered about,' Nick rasped, his grin broadening. 'Are you always so managing?'

'Yes,' Katherine said, somewhat shortly.

'Do you enjoy it?' He was steepling his fingers and regarding her over the joined fingertips. It made it hard to read his expression, but it drew her attention forcibly to how beautiful his hands were. Hastily she dropped her gaze to the desk and turned over the piece of paper she had been using for her sums.

'Not particularly, but I found I had no choice.' It sounded abrupt and rude, but she did not want to explain any more about the chaos her life would have been if she had not taken charge of the household.

'Then you shall manage me, Kat, and I will look after you,' Nick said amiably. 'You make your lists for the journey and I will add anything that occurs to me.'

Half an hour later they had a plan. 'So, tomorrow I pay off all the tradesmen's debts and Jenny and I will pack. John will check over the carriage and harness and the horses and you will rest.'

'I will buy some linen,' Nick interjected. 'Either that, or John and I between us will run through his stock of shirts within days.'

'Very well, but you need not purchase neck cloths for Philip has left some. Then we set out on Friday and go by easy stages to rest the horses. How long do you think it will take us?'

'It depends on the horses, but a week at least. We are going to have to balance the cost of rooms and food against the risk of pushing them too hard.'

'And John. It is a long way to drive.'

Nick got to his feet and stretched. 'Aah. It is so good to be able to do that.' He rolled his shoulders luxuriously. 'John and I can share the driving.'

'No, you cannot!' Katherine got to her feet too and marched over to stand toe to toe with him. 'Have you no sense? You should be resting, not driving a coach for miles.'

Rather too late she realised just how close it brought her to him. He smiled down wickedly. 'You do tempt me to show you how perfectly fit I feel, Kat. I have had my neck stretched for me a little, that is all. If I had been suffering from consumption or gaol fever, that would be quite another matter.'

Frustrated, Katherine fell back on another argument. 'You cannot sit on the box and drive a coach. You are a gentleman.'

'And I have been a common trooper for two years and a highwayman and felon for some weeks.' He pinched her chin and turned away to the door before she could retaliate. 'Now I really must go and lie down and rest or my managing wife will read me a lecture.'

'Insufferable man!' Katherine glared at the door as it closed behind him, then reluctantly smiled. Nicholas Lydgate was certainly proving difficult to manage. But it was intriguing to be matching her wits with a strong man and not a weak one.

She shivered. She was growing dangerously fond of him, she could recognise that fact only too well. What effect would being cooped up with him in a carriage for over a week have on her emotions?

It was rather too disturbing to think about. Katherine opened the door and walked briskly down the passage to the kitchen. 'Jenny! We have a lot to do, and only a day to do it in. We are going to Northumberland.'

Chapter Nine

Katherine regarded the sleeping man opposite her in the carriage with mixed feelings. Part of her was relieved that, after stubbornly refusing to rest all the previous day, Nicholas was doing so now; part of her was frustrated that, having anticipated the long journey together with mixed trepidation and pleasure, she now had no opportunity to talk to him. Was it exhaustion, or an excellent defence against questions?

He sleeps like a cat, she brooded. Nicholas had no sooner sat down, made sure the two women were comfortable and exchanged a few words with John, than he had simply closed his eyes and fallen asleep. It did give her the chance to study him unobserved, for Jenny, agog at the adventure of a long journey, had twisted round to watch the passing scene from the window.

He was certainly an elegant sleeper; his lips were parted slightly and his breathing was heavy and regular, compared to Philip's habitual slack-jawed snoring.

Katherine sighed inwardly and wondered where her brother was at that moment. Had he the sense to husband his resources and secure modest and respectable lodgings, or was he already seeking out whatever gambling and drinking dens the French coastal towns offered? Was he happy now there was no one to remind him of his obligations, no one to expect him to exercise self-control? Or was he lonely?

She blinked away a treacherous tear and resumed her study of her temporary husband. His colour was better, she decided, and he certainly looked very respectable now. His shopping trip the day before had produced not only a supply of shirts, but he had stopped at the barber and was sporting a positively fashionable Brutus cut.

So…she assessed the man in front of her. High cheekbones that gave him a slightly saturnine expression when he narrowed those dark eyes, a very decided chin, mobile and expressive lips and a straight nose. All very handsome, no doubt, although this perfection was disturbed somewhat by a scar that sliced across his right eyebrow, leaving a fine white line through the black hairs. He had been fortunate not to lose that eye.

Still, handsome looks were not so uncommon and doubtless she had seen men equally as good looking before now. Even some who combined looks with a fine physique. So why had none of them stirred any particular interest in her? Why did this one make her heart beat harder? And why, when he touched her or looked at her, did she feel that strange hollow ache inside?

Because you are not married to any of the others, the tart voice of common sense reminded her. *You have not slept with any of them and none of them have kissed—*

Nick's eyes opened suddenly without any clue from his breathing that he was awake. Katherine found herself staring straight into them with an absolute conviction that her thoughts must be plainly written all over her face. The blush that swept over her seemed to reach from her crown to her toes, but she could not unlock her gaze from his.

'I was just trying to decide whether you looked better,' she said finally. 'I think you do.' Concern for his health was the only legitimate excuse for a young lady to stare so at a man. 'You must be sleeping well.'

'As you can see,' Nicholas said with a smile. 'I must apologise for being such poor company, but my time in the army taught me to sleep when I could.'

It was a statement, not an invitation to discuss his service as a trooper. Katherine bit back the string of questions she had on that topic and smiled brightly. 'Very sensible. Jenny and I have been well entertained in watching the passing scene.'

'Where are we?' He leaned forward to look out of the window.

'Stevenage,' Jenny replied, having been the only one of the two young women who had actually been paying the slightest attention to the outside world.

'I thought we should stop at Baldock, rest the horses and have some luncheon,' Katherine suggested.

Nicholas nodded, settled himself more comfortably in his corner and slept again.

Four days later Katherine found herself sitting in exactly the same place and seething with suppressed indignation. The wretched man was purposely avoiding her, that she was certain of now. Not that it was not prudent to preserve a certain distance as they were soon to have their marriage annulled, but surely he could at least take the time to tell her about this unknown family she was about to be pitchforked into?

Nicholas had slept the first day and been politely distant and discreet at dinner time before he and John had departed for their bedchamber, leaving herself and Jenny to theirs.

The next day he had sat on the box with John and on the

third he had taken the reins. Every evening had been as quiet as the one before and on every occasion Nicholas had been as uncommunicative. And again today the two men were up on the box sharing the driving as the Midlands of England slowly gave way to the unfamiliar northern counties.

Tonight they would lodge in York and Katherine was absolutely determined that she was going to achieve some communication with Nicholas if she had to lock herself in his bedroom to achieve it.

'Are you all right, Miss Katherine?' Jenny was sitting regarding her with some concern.

'Yes, of course. Why do you ask?'

'Because you're scowling something dreadful,' Jenny responded frankly. 'You'll end up with terrible lines on your forehead if you carry on so.' She cocked her head on one side and waited patiently for her mistress to explain herself.

'Well, I am a little concerned about things,' Katherine began mildly enough. 'And I would like to discuss them with Mr Lydgate—who appears to be going to some lengths to avoid talking to me.' She felt her anger rising as she articulated what, up to then, she had only been brooding upon. 'I have no idea what to expect when we reach his family home. He just whisked me away from London—all I know for certain is that he parted on very bad terms with his father…'

'And you want to know all about his family and what his plans are,' Jenny soothed. 'Of course you do, Miss Katherine, 'tis only natural.' She fell silent, then suddenly remarked, 'I believe I have a headache.'

'There is some *sal volatile* in my reticule,' Katherine offered. 'Or we could bathe your temples with lavender water, if only I can recall where I packed it.'

'No, thank you. I know what I need, fresh air.' Jenny tugged the check string, and when the horses came to a halt jumped down without waiting for one of the men to open the door for her. 'John,' she called up, 'I have a terrible headache, I think I would be much better if I could sit up on the box with you in the fresh air for a while. Would it be a terrible inconvenience for you to change places, sir?'

A few minutes later, in a flurry of skirts and with a wink to her mistress, Jenny was settled on the box and Nick was climbing into the carriage. 'A decided young woman,' he remarked.

'Yes,' Katherine agreed, uncertain whether that remark held an element of criticism. 'She and John have both been wonderfully loyal to me since our situation became so bad. I have no idea how I would have managed without them, and half the time I was in arrears with their wages.'

'Devoted servants are—'

There was a gunshot from outside, then another. The horses plunged to a halt, throwing Katherine across the coach to land in Nick's arms. She scrambled back, only to find herself thrust firmly behind him on the seat when she tried to look out of the window.

'What is it?'

'Highwaymen—two, I think. Damnation, both pistols are on the box with John.' There was shouting from outside, the sound of John's voice raised in protest and another shot.

'Jenny…'

'Hopefully they'll both have the sense to do as they are bid and won't put up any resistance. Yes, they are both all right: they have just climbed down. Where's the money?'

'All over the place—some in my reticule, you have some, John the rest, I think. I never thought to hide it.'

Only minutes had passed since the first shot—it seemed like hours. 'Well, we must just put a good face on it and hand it over,' Nick began, then he grinned. 'Perhaps not. Kat, take off your pelisse. Good, now, get rid of that fichu or whatever it is and tug down the front of your gown a little.'

'What!'

'No, more, like this.' His fingers were warm on her skin. 'Off with that bonnet, far too respectable; unpin your hair— no, I'll do it. Good, now follow my lead.'

Katherine saw one of the highwaymen approaching the carriage door. The other had moved John and Jenny at gun- point to the side of the road. She glanced down and was shocked at the amount of swelling bosom Nick's cavalier treatment of her neckline had produced.

He threw open the door and jumped down before the man had a chance to reach it, then turned to swing Katherine down beside him, apparently unconcerned by the threatening long- nosed pistol being pointed at them.

'Good day, mate.' He grinned and Katherine realised with a shock that his voice had coarsened. 'This is a turn up and no mistake, eh, Katy?'

'What? Don't you try no nonsense, just hand over the dibs.' The man waved the pistol threateningly.

'Now then, cullies.' Nick raised his voice so it could be clearly heard by the second man. 'This is no way to treat one of your own.'

The nearest man squinted at Nick. 'What'yer mean? I don't recognise you and I know all the lads on the bridle lay round here.'

'Never heard of Black Jack Standon?'

Katherine stifled a gasp. Surely he couldn't hope to get away with it?

'Yeah, what of it? Everyone's heard of him; these last few days since the news reached here no one's talked of anything else in the taproom. Cut down from the gallows alive at New- gate, so they say. Don't say why... Bloody hell!'

Nick dragged at his neck cloth and pulled open his shirt. The vicious ring around his neck had developed more colours since the hanging, and if it was now less swollen it was certainly no less dramatic.

'You? You're Black Jack? How did you get off, then?'

'All due to my clever little Katy here.' Nick put an arm around Katherine's shoulders and pulled her to him. 'She found the clergyman who'd testified in court to my lifting his cash box and gave him a night to remember, didn't you, sweetheart?'

Chucked under the chin, Katherine managed a smile she only hoped looked suitably saucy.

'What, then he came over all soft hearted and told the court it was all a mistake?' the taller man scoffed.

'No.' Nick grinned wickedly. 'She told him she'd go into church and tell the entire congregation, including his wife and his patron all about it—right down to the birthmark on his left buttock. He couldn't get in front of the magistrates fast enough after that.'

'Gawd!' The man regarded Katherine with awe mixed with an unsubtle appreciation of her well-displayed charms. 'Left it a bit late, didn't he?'

'You could say so.' Nick rubbed his throat cautiously. 'Not an experience I would want to repeat.'

'Too right.' Both men stuffed their pistols in their waistbands and held out their hands to shake Nick's. 'Birthmark on the parson's bum!' The shorter one chortled. 'Pleased to have met you and proud to shake you by the hand, Jack Standon. I'm Will Buckley, they call me Will the Fly and this here's Long Harry Potts.' He leered cheerfully at Katherine. 'And if you want a change, sweetheart, you come asking for us at the White Horse.'

'I might at that,' she retorted, hoping her relief was not written plain across her face.

With a few more sallies at the unfortunate parson's expense the two highwaymen mounted up and vanished into the scrubby woodland that fringed the road.

'Jenny, John—are you all right?' They both seemed safe enough, walking towards the coach with relieved smiles on their faces.

'I've got a hole through my hat,' John grumbled, wriggling a finger through the crown. 'Still, a miss is as good as a mile. Bloody quick thinking, sir,' he added. 'I thought we were going to lose every farthing we'd got left.'

'Oh, Nick!' Katherine threw her arms round his neck and clung tightly. 'You were wonderful.' She had been far more frightened than she had realised while it was all happening, and certainly more so than when she had sought out Black Jack. Then nothing had mattered other than saving Nick; this time people she loved had been at risk for a few pounds.

With his arms full of warm, emotional and grateful young lady, Nick tightened his grip automatically. Something shot through him that blurred his vision and made the blood roar in his ears. It was like striking a spark on to tinder. He was scarcely aware of Jenny and John behind him climbing back on to the box in an undignified scramble to be tactful. All he was aware of was glorious curves pressed against him, the scent of femininity, the trembling of soft arms around his neck.

'Hrrumph. Are you going to be getting into the carriage, sir?'

Startled, Nick realised exactly where he was. 'Er, yes, John.' He swept Kat into the coach, slammed the door and sank back on the battered squabs.

Kat settled herself opposite him, flushed and laughing, apparently with relief rather than any emotional lightning strike as a result of his embrace. Nick dragged air into his lungs and looked at her. Her hair was in disarray, tempting his fingers to rake through it, her face was charmingly pink with excitement and the swell of her breasts, exposed by the neckline he had so roughly pulled down, rose and fell with her laughter. His wife.

Chapter Ten

Nicholas found he could not take his eyes off the woman opposite him. She was enchanting, absolutely enchanting—and she was his wife. He must have been mad to promise her an annulment. If he could just get her to change her mind before they reached his home and she discovered what he had been avoiding for six years, surely she would forgive him for the deception afterwards?

Something of his thoughts must have shown on his face, for Kat stopped laughing and glanced down. 'Oh, goodness, just look at this gown.'

'I am.'

'It is not funny.' She was tugging up the neckline in a manner that was utterly feminine, which made him smile. 'Please pass me my fichu. Thank you.' She tucked and pinned and, finally satisfied, began to search for hairpins on the seat. 'Goodness knows what those men thought.'

'Precisely what I wanted them to think, luckily.' God, the way she put up her arms to deal with her hair, the graceful line of her body… He shifted uncomfortably on the seat and found himself uncharacteristically lost for words.

Kat finished fussing with her hair, pulled on her pelisse and sat there regarding him with an air of expectation, which, as he continued silent, seemed to subside into something like resignation.

What could he say to her? Usually more than able to talk his way into, and out of, any situation, Nick sat and brooded on opening gambits. *Kat, my home is rather... Kat, I am a... My father... Kat, you may be surprised...*

Hopeless. He would just have to show her and trust that by then she was tied to him and could not escape. Many young women would not want to escape, he knew that. This one, exuding silent discomfort opposite him, undoubtedly would.

Kat appeared to cheer up as they approached the city and she exclaimed in interest as they caught glimpses of the imposing Minster tower rising over tiled roofs. Their carriage, guided by instructions he had given John that morning before they set out, made its way deep into the heart of York.

The familiar yard of the Crown and Anchor glimpsed through the coach windows was larger than any they had stayed at so far, and the ostlers hurried out to greet the new arrival with an alacrity that spoke of a degree of style in the establishment. Some things had not changed, then; he needed to forestall any betraying welcome.

Kat was frowning again as Nick opened the coach door and handed her down. 'Is it not to your liking?' he asked as she stood on the cobbles beside him, gazing critically around her.

'It looks expensive.' She was fingering her purse through the stuff of her reticule.

'More so than anywhere else we have stayed, I agree.' He had almost recovered his voice now, he realised, only a slight rasping edge when he was tired was left. 'But I had a yearning for a comfortable bed and a glass of good brandy.' *And to be somewhere familiar, to be amongst friends after all this time.*

He saw Kat shoot him a hasty glance to ensure that his neck cloth was back in place covering the betraying weal on his neck. No doubt she was expecting to be turned away from such a decent inn because he appeared to be some kind of felon.

'We haven't much money left,' she hissed, managing to smile graciously as the men lifted down their small amount of luggage. 'How many more nights will it take?'

'After this? Two if we are lucky, three if the weather turns or the roads are bad.' He regarded her expressionlessly. 'You think I am being profligate with your money. We have enough to get…to get home and then you will have nothing to worry about.'

Kat looked mutinous as Nick took her arm and steered her firmly towards the inn door. 'See how you fare trying to get lodgings at a smart inn like this,' she hissed. 'You are wearing a coachman's clothes, driving an old-fashioned coach yourself—we will be lucky to be given a garret if they are busy.'

Being turned away was the least of Nick's worries at that moment; being welcomed with open arms was more of a threat. 'House!' He strode forward into the entrance to intercept a tall, heavily built man who hurried forward, wiping his hands on a voluminous white apron.

'Excuse me, sir, I was just in the tap and didn't see you come in.' He broke off and stared at Nick in the shadowy hall. 'My…' His voice trailed away.

'Your inn was recommended to me,' Nick said, cutting across the rest of the sentence. He kept his back to Kat and gestured with his hand. The abrupt signal was enough; old Summerhays was no fool. He managed with aplomb to suppress his surprise at seeing a man who had vanished six years ago.

'I require a room for my sister and her maid and one for myself and my man. Just the one night, if you please, landlord.'

Summerhays nodded briskly, concealing entirely natural speculation about exactly where Nicholas Lydgate might have acquired a sister. 'Yes, sir. And a private parlour, sir?'

'Of course.'

The innkeeper turned to summon a boy to take their bags. 'Here, lad, the two rooms at the side with the parlour, and then get Molly to bring some hot water up for the lady.'

'You had better go up,' Nick turned to Kat. 'I will bespeak some dinner for you.'

Kat paused with one foot on the step. 'For *me*? Are you not hungry?'

'John and I will be going out to dine. I will see you in the morning.'

'Out? While Jenny and I are cooped up for yet another interminable evening? I want to come too!'

'That would not be suitable,' Nick said smoothly, taking her arm again and turning her firmly back to the stairs. 'Not suitable at all. Now run along, Kat, while I speak to the landlord.' She might be furious now—she would be even more angry if she overheard the conversation that was about to take place.

'You...' Katherine subsided, fuming, and marched upstairs with her chin up and her back rigid. This was not the place to make a scene. *Not suitable* indeed. They were probably planning to visit some low ale houses or a cock fight. Perhaps even acquire some friendly female companionship.

'Mr Lydgate's very forceful, is he not?' Jenny observed as the door closed on the pot boy.

'That is not the word I would choose,' Katherine retorted. 'Arrogant and overbearing would fit better. How he managed to keep his pride in check and his tongue between his teeth during two years as a trooper I cannot imagine.' Her voice softened. 'But he was wonderful when we were held up—so resourceful and quick thinking.'

'What happened in the coach? You know, when you were hugging him and your dress was half off?'

'Jenny! It was not half off, simply somewhat low. And I was only embracing him in relief, nothing more. Nothing happened at all in the coach. I put myself to rights and he brooded as though the cat had got his tongue.'

'Probably worrying about what sort of reception he's going to get when he reaches home,' Jenny said sympathetically.

'If we have enough money to get there after tonight's extravagances. I suppose the only consolation is that they do not have enough money to get seriously drunk on.' Katherine unpinned her hair and began to brush it out.

Jenny, who was lifting night things from the valise, looked up with a grin. 'John took his savings out from under the floorboard in the kitchen before we left. They've enough to give themselves sore heads in the morning, I'll be bound.'

Whatever the state of the men's heads come breakfast time, Katherine's was throbbing with the effects of a restless night and worry. It would be simply too feeble to give way to all the anxieties racking her; she had too much self-control to take out her feelings on her maid and her husband appeared set on staying well out of her way.

When she emerged, blinking irritably, into the morning sunlight after breakfast, it was to find the luggage strapped on and John just giving Jenny a hand to climb up on to the box.

'Jenny! What are you doing?'

'I thought I'd have some fresh air again, Miss Katherine,

if that's all right with you,' the maid responded with a wink and a jerk of her head towards the door where Nick could just be glimpsed paying their shot. 'I enjoyed it yesterday.'

'Oh! Oh, well, all right Jenny. You are looking a little pale.'

Footsteps behind her approached and halted at the sight of John and Jenny already on the box. Katherine bit her lip to suppress her laughter and waited.

'I will drive, John.'

'Begging your pardon sir, but I get sick in the stomach if I travel in a closed coach. Always have to sit on top when I take the stage, sir. Miss Katherine wouldn't like it, sir. And Jenny's got a headache again, like yesterday.'

Katherine could feel the icy stare behind her and watched appreciatively as John looked bland and Jenny gazed round the yard, apparently entranced by what the stable boys were up to.

'Very well.' Katherine stepped up to the coach and waited modestly to be handed into it. She kept her eyes down to hide the amusement in them and waited for what Nick would say next.

Nothing, appeared to be the answer. She flickered an upward glance through her lashes and saw him regarding the passing street scene from under lowered brows. Her amusement died as irritation returned.

'Why are you avoiding me?' she asked abruptly.

That seized his attention at least. The dark eyes fixed hers and she saw a flash of anger in their depths. 'I am not avoiding you, Kat. I could not leave John to drive day after day.'

'And you could not be bothered to speak to me in the evenings?'

'Bothered?' Nick's face cleared and he leaned over and took both her hands in his. Her pulse fluttered and raced. 'It was not that, Kat; I am sorry if it seemed so. I have been...preoccupied and not good company. And you looked tired.'

As he said it, Nick realised that telling any woman that she looked tired was not a remark likely to pacify her. The hands he had trapped in his stiffened, her chin rose and the pansy-brown eyes hardened.

'I can assure you that I have felt nothing more than the usual slight fatigue to be expected after sitting for hours on end in an uncomfortable coach. Certainly nothing that would have prevented me holding a conversation.'

Rebuked, he fell back on part of the truth. 'This is an unconventional journey, I thought it wiser to keep my distance during it. After all, you are a well-bred young lady; I imagine that a long journey in the enforced company of a man would not be to your liking. Especially as we have been staying in inns that are not of the first respectability.' Except last night. That had been a risk. Kat was going to find out the truth soon; he acknowledged that he was not looking forward to her realisation of just what she had married into.

'You are my husband,' she pointed out, her eyes downcast. Nick regarded her narrowly, unable to read her mood.

'For a few weeks only,' he reminded her and was unprepared for the flash of anger in her eyes as she looked up.

'So what you really mean, and are tactfully circling round, is that it is better if we keep our distance in case anything occurs that prevents our marriage being annulled?' she said sweetly. 'I really have no fears that you are likely to be making assaults on my virtue and thus jeopardise our release from a situation which I am persuaded is as distasteful to you as it is to me.

'Especially,' she added with a flash of fire, 'when you have been entertaining yourself last night in much more conge-nial company than that of a *well-bred young lady.*'

Nick sorted through his emotions, discovered that amuse-ment was predominant and grinned, apparently infuriating his already angry wife further. 'I can assure you, my dear Kat, that John and I indulged in nothing more carnal than a large beefsteak pie, rather too much Yorkshire ale and a disap-pointing cock fight. I have to admit that John did wink at a comely redhead, but that was as far as our encounters with the fair sex went.' With a pang he noticed a sudden bright-ness in her eyes and added fatally, 'There is nothing for you to be jealous of.'

'Jealous?' The icy hauteur in her voice would have frozen water. Nick sat back, abruptly releasing her hands and found that this new Kat was every bit as intriguing as all the others he had encountered. An aloof cat who any minute was likely to spit and claw, he decided appreciatively.

'I have no reason to be jealous of what you do, sir—we are, after all, nothing to each other.' That hurt, an unexpected swipe of her claws. 'We have nothing emotional between us,' she cor-rected meticulously. 'Naturally I am deeply grateful to you for your help with my debt, but that does not mean I wish to ar-rive on your father's doorstep after having had to spend two or three nights sleeping in this coach because you have spent our resources on expensive inns and gambling on cock fights.'

Now he was beginning to sense what was upsetting her. 'We have enough money,' he assured her. 'The inns north of here are far from luxurious and I do not gamble on cock fights. I bet little these days,' he added, meeting her disbeliev-ing stare. 'Real life produces more interesting games of chance.' And he recalled only too clearly the time when his entire livelihood depended on his skill with cards to want to repeat the experience for amusement.

Kat produced the enchanting sound he thought of as her infuriated kitten noise. 'Will you not tell me what is really upsetting you?' he pressed.

'Very well.' The sparkle in her eyes was more anger than unshed tears now. 'I am about to arrive—penniless—on your family's doorstep, knowing not the first thing about them other than that your return is likely to be difficult for all concerned. Not only have you married without your father's blessing to someone completely unknown to him, but I bring with me a vast debt and the prospect of disgrace and scandal. However delighted he will be to see me gone from your family, he can hardly welcome the prospect of an annulment.'

Her eyes on his face were stormy with what he realised was not only anger, but fear. Her fury was not with him, but with herself for not being able to overcome it.

'Kat.' He tried to take her hands again but she batted his away.

'And I have absolutely no idea how I am going to support myself and my servants, let alone pay off this debt.' Nick opened his mouth to speak, but she was before him. 'And I do *not* mean I want you to help me. This is *my* problem and *my* debt. All I meant was that I would have welcomed discussing it so that I have some plan to lay before your father. I would not have him thinking I will be a burden upon him for the world.'

'You do not think that saving his son's life entitles you to some support and assistance?' Nick enquired mildly.

'I did not help you because I wanted a pension! And to accept being a burden simply because of an act any Christian person would see as their duty…'

That was another swipe from her claws, and one she did not even realise she had delivered. 'So you rescued me simply out of a sense of duty?'

'Of course.' Her head was averted now, but her chin was

still up. 'I believed in your innocence and you had treated me much better than my foolish actions deserved.' Suddenly she moved to face him, reaching out her hands to take his. 'I am sorry to subject you to my megrims. But I feel better for that outburst, I have to confess. Nick, please tell me *something* of what to expect.'

Her ungloved hands in his were small, soft, vulnerable, yet, as his fingers closed over them, he felt their strength and determination too. He sought for some words to satisfy her that would yet leave all the difficult matters untouched. Soon he was going to have to sacrifice his pride and confront the past, but not yet, and by then he hoped she would have given up this nonsense of an annulment.

'My father married twice,' he began slowly. 'His first marriage was childless and his wife died when he was forty. He married my mother a few years later and he was forty-five when I was born.' He watched her attempting to calculate his own age and did the addition for her. 'He is now seventy-three. Not possibly the most flexible of ages for dealing with prodigal sons. I have a younger brother, Robert, who was obedient where I was rebellious, dutiful where I was arrogant, sober where I was a rake.'

'Were you?' She was leaning forward, engrossed in his story, her hands still trustingly in his, her eyes alight with interest. 'I've always wanted to meet a rake.'

'Well, you are married to one,' he responded somewhat grimly.

'And your father? Has he lands? Or an occupation? The church perhaps?'

Katherine was entranced by the sudden flash of humour that transformed Nick's face, the first real smile she had seen for days from him. She smiled back, not in on the joke, but happy that he was amused. 'What is so funny?'

'The thought of my father in the church. Now Robert would make an excellent cleric, that I can believe. No, my father…farms.'

'A large farm?' He was telling her so much she did not want him to stop now.

Again, that flash of amusement. 'Yes. Large. But up in Northumberland that is the way of things. The land is less fertile and the climate hard, so you need more land.'

She thought she was beginning to understand. 'And you did not want to be a farmer?' She could believe that; all that energy and pride and courage would not sit well with the need to worry about the spring sowing or the routine of stock raising. 'He will be glad to have you back,' she said gently. 'He is an old man now, he will need your help. What would have happened if you had never gone back?'

'If I had dangled for a few more minutes from that rope, you mean? Or simply continued on my undutiful way?' There was the darkness back in his eyes and unconsciously she tightened her grip on his hands. 'After seven years of no news I could be presumed dead in law—Robert would become the heir. Doubtless he would make a much better fist of it than I.'

'Do you not like your brother?' His voice had been bitter.

'Like him? I love him, no one could fail to. I was not being sarcastic—he truly should have been born first. He was a good boy, he will be a good man now.'

Katherine's heart twisted. So much bitterness, so much pride. '*You* are a good man,' she said impulsively, lifting her hands so they brought his up against her cheek. She met his eyes, dark and intent on hers, saw the harsh twist of his mouth soften and the sensual lips curve into a smile.

'You are a sweetheart Kat,' he said softly, opening his fingers so they spread on her cheek, cradling it gently. 'So sweet.'

Something inside her slipped, moved. She felt dizzy for a moment—surely her heart should not be beating like this? Then she turned her face instinctively into his caressing hand and met his eyes. It hit her with the force of a blow. She was in love with Nicholas Lydgate. In love with her husband who was no husband and who must never be.

Chapter Eleven

Katherine knew she should move away from those gentling hands, break contact with those expressive eyes. Nicholas must not know how she felt or she was certain he would feel honour bound to their strange marriage.

She broke eye contact with an effort that left her breathless and sat back in her seat, releasing his hands as she did so. 'They will be so happy to see you again,' she said firmly with a bright smile. The feel of it on her lips reminded her of the determined smile she used to use to assure her younger brother that he had nothing to fear from a visit to the tooth-puller. Inside she had an unpleasant feeling that it was just as false a hope that Nick's homecoming would be painless.

Nick raised one brow quizzically; he was obviously not convinced either. 'I am putting all my reliance upon my father being so charmed by my beautiful wife that he forgets my numerous sins.'

Katherine blushed. She was not beautiful, she knew that. Her chin was too pointed, her eyes too big, her hair was too dark to be truly fashionable and her manner far too independent and forthright to appeal to an elderly patriarch. That is, if he managed to look beyond the staggering debt she had brought to the marriage.

'There is no point in flattering me,' she said briskly. 'I do not believe you, and in any case your father is going to have far too much on his mind to notice anything about me except the manifest disadvantages of the situation.'

Nick settled back against the battered squabs and regarded her seriously. 'I have told you before that you are beautiful. Why do you not believe me?'

'You told me I resemble a cat,' she pointed out. 'And I know I am not in the slightest in the fashionable mode; I am far too used to having my own way…'

'Surely not,' Nick interrupted. 'Your life recently, if I may say so, appears to have consisted of anything but self-will and indulgence. You have no close friends that I am aware of, no money, no life of your own. You have been an unpaid house-keeper for years and somehow you seem to have remained meek and dutiful in the face of your brother's outrageously selfish behaviour. If that is having your own way, then our definitions of it must be very different.'

'I am too managing, then,' she amended, trying not to let him see how his ruthless description of her life affected her.

'A most useful attribute in a wife. I am sure my father will entirely approve of it.'

'Will that be before he learns of my debts and the annulment, or afterwards?'

'There is no need to worry about the debt, I told you. And we agreed to leave the annulment for one month after we arrive in Northumberland, did we not?'

'But we must tell your family,' Katherine protested.

'Why?' he asked, infuriatingly bland.

'Because…because they will be very shocked to learn of it if they have begun by accepting me as your wife. And will they not expect us to…to share a bedchamber? I mean…' The colour was rising in her cheeks again, she realised, furious with herself.

'That is another thing you need not worry about.' Nick's smile was obviously intended to reassure; all it did was infuriate her.

'How can I not worry?' she demanded. 'I would be an idiot not to worry about things.'

Her temper appeared to amuse Nick. 'Now you are a married lady, you should surrender all your worries to your husband,' he remarked, obviously intent on provoking her.

Katherine directed a smouldering look at him. The temptation to retort was strong, but she could sense his enjoyment at sparring with her. Self-preservation told her that the less pleasure he found in her company, the safer her feelings for him would be.

'Very well, Nicholas,' she said meekly, folding her hands demurely in her lap.

Unfortunately this uncharacteristic behaviour produced the opposite effect to the one she wanted. Nicholas roared with laughter and leaned forward to pinch her chin affectionately. 'Do you know what you look like now?' he demanded. 'The kitchen cat with her eyes on a chump chop, just waiting until Cook is out of the kitchen.' The shift in position brought him closer to the window. 'It has started to rain, I had better let Jenny back inside and take a turn with the reins. Will you pull the check strong?'

Torn between relief at not being alone with Nick any longer, and anxiety about the two men becoming drenched up on the exposed box, Katherine greeted Jenny somewhat distractedly.

'Did you enjoy the fresh air?' she asked as the maid shook the first raindrops off her cloak and draped it over the seat beside her to dry. 'I wish I could ride outside, but I fear it is not even worth suggesting that to Nicholas.'

'It is good to be outside,' Jenny commented, 'but, my goodness, that box seat is hard, I declare that my backside is quite benumbed.'

'Jenny! What a thing to say. You should have asked John to stop and come inside much earlier.'

'I wanted to give you a good chance to talk to Mr Lydgate,' Jenny said, shrugging off the reproof. 'Did it help? Has he confided in you?'

'Not a great deal. He told me a little about his father—who is somewhat elderly—and his younger brother. His father is a farmer, I gather.'

'A prosperous one by all accounts. The master didn't get that way of speaking or those manners at the plough's tail or the village dame school.'

Katherine blinked, then decided to ignore Jenny's turn of phrase. She had never once in Katherine's hearing referred to Philip as 'the master', only as 'Mr Philip'.

'No,' she agreed. 'He is probably a prosperous squire, well able to give his sons a tutor and send them to university.'

'So you've come to an understanding, then? There won't be any more talk of ending the marriage?' Jenny asked brightly.

'No, of course not! Whatever are you thinking of—naturally we must have the marriage annulled.'

'Despite the way you feel about him?'

Katherine met Jenny's shrewd eyes and struggled to keep the truth out of her own. 'What *do* you mean?' she demanded. 'Naturally I admire Mr Lydgate's courage and his sense of honour in helping me. And naturally I cannot impose upon his good will a moment longer than is necessary.'

'I mean you are in love with him,' Jenny retorted, presuming ruthlessly on years of intimacy. She watched Katherine struggle wordlessly for a crushing phrase to contradict her. 'I knew it, the way you look at him—or half the time *don't* look. What does he feel about it?'

'Nothing at all! Really, Jenny, you quite mistake the matter. Mr Lydgate's feelings are simply those of a chivalrous gentleman attempting to help a lady in a difficult situation. Now, please, stop trying to put me to the blush.' So Jenny had already seen something, seen it before she herself had acknowledged how she felt about Nicholas. She could only trust that no one else was so perceptive.

They made good time, despite the rain that afternoon. The next night, as Nick helped her down from the carriage, his news released both a sigh of relief from her lips and a cold sinking in her stomach at the thought of the confrontation to come.

'We have only a short drive tomorrow—an hour at most. I thought you would prefer to arrive rested and in daylight.'

He appeared to have taken her strictures about the extravagance of the York inn to heart, for since then their stopping places had been humble, although clean and well kept. This last was no exception; it sat sturdy and ancient in a fold of the hill beyond the small town of Marlowe Beck. They had pressed on past the fine Duke's Arms in the main square and, despite her earlier protestations about money, Katherine had watched it go with some regret. Although too well bred to utter the words, her anatomy was suffering as much as Jenny's was from the long hours sitting, and the thought of a fine goose feather bed and a hot bath was deeply tempting.

But thoughts of the smart inn vanished as John helped her down from the coach. The evening sun was setting behind the hills, sending long shadows over the rolling green of the fields and making dark mysteries of the endless stone walls and the occasional copse of twisted trees.

Nick had vanished into the inn and emerged again with the landlord, who had a beaming smile on his face. Katherine caught a snatch of the man's words, but, what with the breeze blowing them away and his unfamiliar accent, she could not catch the whole sentence.

'…back parlour, Mr Nick, and no fear…anyone will…big house. It's a great day, that's for sure.'

Nick ushered them all firmly through into the room the innkeeper indicated and opened a door in the panelling at the rear. Katherine glimpsed the foot of a narrow flight of stairs. 'Up there are the rooms, choose whichever you wish for yourself and Jenny.'

'You sound as though you know this place,' she observed, only to interrupted by a hearty chuckle from the inn keeper.

'That he does, hinny, that he…I mean to say, ma'am, we remember Mr Nick from years back. When he was just a lad,' he added hastily with a glance at Nick. 'I'll just take your bags up, I expect you ladies would prefer the back room, it being quieter, like.'

'Hinny?'

'You are lucky he didn't call you hen or flower.' Nick smiled, suddenly looking five years younger. 'It's good to hear the accent again.'

The old inn was like a haven before a storm, Katherine thought two hours later as she curled into the corner of the settle in front of the fire after dinner.

Nick and John were playing cards with an ancient pack Nick had somehow known to find on the mantelshelf and Jenny was leaning over John's shoulder, egging him on to wild bets with the broken pieces of spill they were using for gaming counters.

From the public taproom across the hall came the sound of a fiddle and an instrument the like of which Katherine had never heard.

The windows were snug behind curtains apparently made from a cast-off chintz gown and the fire flickered and glowed, casting hot light over the flagged floor and gleaming off the old polished oak of settles and tables.

Candles cast more intimate pools of light on the hands of the card players and made strange masks of their faces. Under-lit, John's double chin was exaggerated, Jenny's brown hair gave off red glints and Nick's face was unguarded as he fanned the cards in his hand, his head slightly cocked, his underlip just caught by sharp white teeth as he considered his bet.

'I will meet you and raise you ten.'

Suddenly she saw the young man of six years ago, straightforward, untried, proud and hot at hand. He must have sat here on many an evening with friends, perhaps with the sons of local farmers and squires, learning to keep their faces straight whether they held good hands or bad, flirting with the barmaids, boasting of their horses. Her mouth curved in an unconscious smile.

John folded with a groan, tossing his hand on the table. 'You're bringing me no luck at all,' he chided Jenny. 'Go and jinx the master's hand, why don't you?'

Nick laughed and reached out long fingers to gather up the pile of spills. His eyes met Katherine's and suddenly he was still. The smile faded from his lips and his shadowed eyes seemed to speak straight to hers. The room went quiet, so quiet that the crackle and spit of the fire and the tic-toc of the battered mantel clock sounded louder than the music from across the way.

'You can't afford to lose any more, John,' Jenny said brightly. 'I want to hear the music—they might be dancing.'

'They will be,' Nick told her, scooping up the cards and tapping them back into one pack. 'Why don't you go on and tell me what you think of the Northumberland pipes?'

Jenny needed no further urging. She tugged John grumbling out of his chair and out of the room. The volume of the music swelled, diminished and swelled again, marking their progress through the doors into the tap.

Katherine swallowed. She knew perfectly well what Jenny was up to, wretched chit. She had some romantic idea of throwing her mistress together with 'the master' and confounding all talk of annulment.

Nick got up lazily and wandered over to replace the cards where he had found them and toss the handful of spill fragments on to the fire. He stood gazing into the firelight, one foot up on the high fender seat, his forearm resting on his bent knee.

Katherine was so jumpy she felt sure she could feel the nerves crawling under her skin. If only he would say something. She had a careful store of unexceptional subjects for conversation: how much later the season was up here, how much smaller the lambs were than in the south, how surprised she was not to find great mountains, how far were they from the sea?

Nick straightened up and came to sit beside her on the settle, propping his feet up on the fender and falling into a relaxed slump that somehow managed to look elegant. Still he did not speak. Katherine clamped her teeth firmly together to prevent herself beginning to babble of nothings.

'You look very comfortable.' His remark was so sudden she almost jumped.

'Doubtless you are about to make a cat-comparison,' she grumbled, attempting to inject a note of humour.

'Well, you are not quite purring, Kat. What would it take to make you purr, I wonder?'

You could listen only to the teasing, she realised, or you could listen to the sensual undercurrent in his voice. 'Oh, cream and a feather cushion and a mouse to catch. This is a very comfortable room.'

'It is, is it not?' He seemed pleased with her appreciation. 'I have always thought so. What do you like about it, Kat?'

She considered, head on one side in thought. 'I like the entire inn. I like its size—it is so snug and homely. I love the way it sits here in the shelter of the hill, half-hidden, its back protected from the wind. I like the faded old fabrics and the deep glow on the furniture.' She thought some more, letting the comfort and security of the old house sink into her bones. 'Yes, homely. Perhaps I can find somewhere like this to live.'

'Ah.' Nick seemed momentarily disconcerted and Katherine had a qualm that she had been tactless. What if his home was like the bleak foursquare farmhouses and manors they had passed so frequently? 'You would not prefer something just a little larger?'

'Well, perhaps just a little.' Somehow his arm had crept around her shoulders and she was curled more against his side than the settle cushions. How had that happened?

'Kat.'

'Hmm?' She looked up, having to tilt her head back against his shoulder to do so, and his mouth found hers.

This was not the desperate last kiss of a condemned man, nor was it the first sensuous celebration of a reprieved one. This was an assured, deliberate claiming, a determined attempt at seduction by a man who appeared to have no doubt he would succeed.

He held her, not brutally but firmly, so that she could not escape without fighting; that, somehow, did not seem to be an option. He held her with those long, strong fingers while his mouth systematically removed every trace of resistance.

Her own lips had no choice but to part under the pressure

of his, her own tongue seemed to know just how to meet the challenge of his as it touched, flickered, tasted, then plunged and took quite ruthlessly.

She was bent back over one imprisoning arm, her breasts crushed achingly against his chest and suddenly he left her mouth and began to nibble the length of her throat, down the delicate, tender curves, down to where the pulse raged in the angle of her collarbone.

Katherine moaned, part in protest that he had abandoned her mouth, part in exquisite agony at the havoc he was wreaking now with his teeth and lips.

She was so hot, so…needing. She wanted him to touch her everywhere and did not know quite why. Her body arched against him, untutored, innocently demanding. He growled deep in his throat in response and his mouth was suddenly on the curve of her breast, impatiently pushing aside the modesty of the fichu she had tucked in around her shoulders. She moaned, whimpered.

'Purr for me, my Kat.' His voice was husky, muffled against the taut swell of her breast. And then he had swung her up into his arms. It was several confused, giddy moments before she realised he had one foot on the bottom step of the stairs to the bedrooms.

Where did the strength to resist come from? Or was it simply common sense reasserting itself the moment his drugging mouth left her hot skin?

'No! Nick, put me down!'

He paused, still halfway through the doorway, then bent to find her mouth.

'No!' Katherine twisted her head away and instantly he set her on her feet. She found herself standing on the second step, high enough to meet him eye to eye. 'Nick, what do you think you are doing?'

'Making love to my wife.' He was breathing hard, but somehow he kept his voice light.

'But you cannot! We will never get an annulment if you do—what are you thinking of?'

He raised one hand and twisted an errant lock of her hair between his fingers. 'Do you want an annulment so badly?'

'Of course I do!' Katherine stared at him as though he had lost his senses. 'You cannot want to be tied to this sham of a marriage any more than I do.'

'You were willing to be a true wife to me in Newgate.' His voice was still light and in the gloom she could not read his face.

'But we had a bargain and I could not break that, it would have been dishonest,' Katherine protested. 'And anyway, you were—' She broke off, appalled at where that train of thought was leading her.

'Going to be hanged, so that would have drawn a convenient line under the whole messy business?' Now he sounded angry.

How dare he? she thought, *I did not start this.* 'That is not what I meant and you know it. You promised me an annulment in a month's time. What you were about to do would have made that impossible.'

'I promised you that we would get an annulment if you wanted one. I thought perhaps that after tonight you might not want that.'

'Oh! You arrogant...' Katherine fought for words. 'You thought you would seduce me, did you? I am sure you would succeed with many women—after all, you appear to be very good at it, doubtless as the result of much practice.'

'And why would I want to seduce you?' He shifted slightly so the light from the room struck his face. His voice was dangerously calm, but his eyes were hard with anger.

'Other than simple carnal desire? Presumably you would feel humiliated by having to tell your family that your marriage was about to be dissolved.'

'More humiliated than living with the thought that I had seduced an unwilling woman? I thought we understood each other, Kat. It appears I was quite out.' He stepped back from the stairs and took the edge of the door in one hand. Kat found her eyes unable to leave the long finger where the mark of his signet ring still showed white against the tanned skin. On her own hand it seemed to burn with its own heat. 'I suggest you go to bed before we start hurling the fire irons at each other like a real married couple.'

He reached out and picked up a chamber stick from the side table. 'Here, madam wife, a candle to light you to bed. I wish you a goodnight. It will doubtless be better than the one I anticipate.'

Chapter Twelve

Katherine passed a night of restless wakefulness interspersed with dream-racked snatches of sleep. She kept trying to push away the memories of Nick's caressing hands and demanding lips, but whenever she tried her strangely aching body recalled her to the recollection of every touch, every *frisson*. Their furious exchange of words at the end she simply refused to recall.

In an effort to distract herself, she attempted to rehearse how she should greet his father and brother the next morning. What should she wear? What would Mr Lydgate senior expect of his unexpected new daughter-in-law? And when would Nick reveal the true state of their marriage and the news that his sham wife had saddled him with a vast debt?

Unfortunately the image she conjured up of her father-in-law closely resembled Nick in forty years' time and in the throes of an icy rage. This was not comforting, and the knowledge that her in-laws would be utterly justified in being appalled and angry on discovering her existence did nothing to help.

Tossing and turning uncomfortably in an effort not to disturb Jenny's untroubled slumbers, Katherine tried to plan for what she should do once she had obtained her annulment. Somehow she would have to earn her own living.

Gloomily she reviewed her talents. She was an adequate, but not exceptional, needlewoman. Setting up in a millinery or dressmaking business was not therefore to be thought of. She had an excellent grasp of languages, but no talent with any musical instrument so becoming a governess was beyond her reach. Her earlier confident assertion to Jenny that she could earn her living teaching French and Italian now seemed hopelessly over-confident. Housekeeper or companion appeared to be the only options for a living wage, however modest.

Neither was likely to pay so much that she could hope to discharge her debt. All she would be able to do was salve her conscience by sending what little she was able to save each year to the moneylenders under her own name, but concealing her whereabouts. Goodness knows what the effect of the interest would be upon the total. *I am going to go to my grave in debt*, she thought despairingly, struggling not to think harshly of Philip, heedlessly pursuing his own pleasures somewhere on the Continent.

When the clock downstairs struck three the treacherous voice of temptation began to whisper in her ear. *Let him make love to you*, it murmured insidiously. *You love him, you want him. He knows what the consequences are, he will pay your debt and you will never have to worry again.*

Katherine lay still, wrestling with herself until her conscience won. No, she could not do it, not and live with herself afterwards. And at last she dropped off to sleep.

The next morning they breakfasted in their rooms and Nick went down with John to pay their shot. The effusiveness of

Paul Carson, the landlord, made him feel uncomfortable, as though he was back under false pretences, as indeed an inner voice told him he was. Banished, he had sworn never to come back; now he wrestled with the uncomfortable thought that he was using Kat as an excuse to do the right thing and return.

That was considerably less uncomfortable to his peace of mind than the memory of last night and the recollection of the vivid anger and betrayal on Kat's face as they had stood, eye to eye, on the inn stairs. How had he misjudged her so badly? He was not inexperienced with women, he thought ruefully as he strolled out into the yard to see if John needed any help hitching up the team. With Kat it seemed that every instinct was awry.

Without a word spoken he took the head of the wheeler and backed it into the shafts while his mind raced. She had seemed yielding, aware of him. In his arms she had responded with an innocent passion that turned his bones to water even as it fired his blood. But she was having none of him, it seemed, however dire her circumstances.

With a shake of his head he cinched the girth and turned to see what else needed doing. But he was too near home now for physical effort to distract him from his circling thoughts.

And what would his father say to Kat? One word of disparagement and he would turn on his heel and leave, he resolved grimly. She might be determined to free herself from him, but his honour and his instincts would fight her every step of the way. Never mind that he had married her expecting to be dead days ago; now she was his first concern over family and all other duties.

'That's all right and tight,' John said, twisting the reins around the brake. He regarded Nick with an uncomfortably intelligent eye. 'And where do we go now? Sir.' The last word was an afterthought, not a disrespectful one, but a clear indication that John had still not made up his mind about the man Jenny was happy to refer to as 'the master'.

Nick leaned against the nearside shaft and began to explain the route that was as familiar to him as the back of his own hand. John's eyes became round, then narrowed and then finally round again. He asked one question, which Nick answered with a curt nod. There was a moment's silence, then John remarked laconically, 'Miss Katherine will have something to say about that when she realises.'

'Indeed.' Nick thought she would have rather more than 'something' to say, but he preferred that it was not said in the inn courtyard. Not that she was likely to be saying anything at all to him after the way they had parted last night. On that thought Kat appeared, Jenny at her heels.

Nick conjured up all the sang-froid at his disposal and opened the carriage door. She was wearing what must be her best day dress, he realised. Her bonnet was smart whilst being restrained and her hair was rigorously constrained beneath it. All in all, the perfect new daughter-in-law. His heart ached at the effort she was making.

Katherine nodded in the general direction of Nick as she climbed into the coach. She found she could not meet his eye and neither could she find any word of greeting. It was as though a pane of glass had descended between them and all they could do was gesture at each other through it.

The glass shattered as he entered the carriage on Jenny's heels. Katherine stared at him, aghast. She had not expected this, none of her defences were in place to deal with him.

'Good morning,' he said pleasantly, settling back opposite the two young women. 'I hope you slept well.' The query was directed straight at Jenny, who smiled unaffectedly and nodded.

'Oh, yes, sir. Good feather beds they have here, sir.'

'I passed an indifferent night,' Katherine remarked and was surprised at the fire in the dark eyes as they focused on her.

'Indeed? So did I. Perhaps our unrest had a similar cause.'

She had hoped to discommode him; now he had thrown the challenge straight back to her. 'I have no doubt it did,' Katherine agreed warmly, aware that her temper was showing in her eyes, but uncaring of the fact.

'To what do you attribute it?'

Damn him. And damn him for making her use bad language, even in her thoughts. She smiled sweetly. 'I am nervous of meeting my new family, and I am sure you feel some apprehension after all these years, Nicholas.'

Her husband made no attempt to reassure her about his family and her heart sank. This was going to be every bit as difficult as she feared. They both fell silent. To Katherine, completely at a loss as to how to pierce his armour, it seemed that Nick simply retreated into his own self-contained world. What he was facing could not be easy, yet he was not going to let her glimpse the slightest sign of inner turmoil.

Pride, she thought resentfully, then wondered. Was last night's outburst of passion some glimpse into an inner turmoil?

She had hardly formulated the thought when Jenny remarked, 'What a long wall.'

Katherine leaned forward to look out of the window. On the nearside of the carriage stretched a high freestone wall, neatly mortared, regularly buttressed and apparently endless. After ten minutes, when there was no break in it, she remarked, 'The park of a great estate, one assumes.'

'Yes, the Duke of Marlowe's.'

'A family with which you are acquainted?' That might give her some clue as to his family's local standing.

There was a pause, then Nick replied evenly, 'I was close to the younger son at one time.'

They drove for perhaps another two miles in silence. Katherine found the monotony of the uniform wall cast an almost hypnotic spell over her and she could do little other than gaze at it. Then the carriage slowed. Glancing at him, she saw the sudden alertness in Nick, the way his eyes darkened. Expecting John to turn left, away from the wall, Katherine was taken by surprise as the carriage made a right turn and passed between high gateposts.

Off balance, she swayed against the movement of the carriage and was thrown forward. Nick caught her forearms and settled her back on the seat. The incident was over in a moment, but it was enough for her to miss whatever John called down to the gatekeeper as the great gates swung open and the carriage was all at once bowling through parkland.

A herd of fallow deer browsed under the spreading branches of a coppice of sweet chestnuts. They raised their heads to regard the passing carriage with great soft, incurious eyes and bent to the short grass again.

'Miss Katherine—' Jenny began, then stopped abruptly as Katherine's hand closed tight on her wrist. She met her mistress's wide eyes and read the unmistakable message of silence on them. As one the young women turned and stared at Nicholas Lydgate.

He was not watching them. Instead, his face unreadable, he was gazing out of the carriage window as the acres of parkland unrolled before them. His eyes were wide, dark and bright with unshed tears.

Katherine caught her breath, yearning to lean forward and touch him, terrified of disturbing his fragile control. This…this great estate must be home.

She found her mind was prey to theories and questions

tumbling one after another. What were they doing apparently driving up to the mansion of the Duke of—what did Nick say? Marlowe? Was his father the steward to the Duke? Or perhaps as he was the greatest landowner Nick felt it incumbent on him to call upon the Duke first? No, surely not... The questions trembled on her tongue, but the look in Nick's shadowed eyes warned her to keep silent. Inside the cold knot of apprehension grew and burgeoned.

Then the house appeared, reflected in its lake like a mirage, and all the questions disappeared. 'Oh, how beautiful!' Katherine was not aware of speaking aloud.

'I have always thought that from this view across the lake it seems more like a dream than a real building.' Nick cleared his throat and spoke dispassionately, only his right hand balled into a fist on the ledge of the window betrayed emotions he would not display. Katherine glanced at his face—his eyes were dry again.

Cold greyish-white stone, turrets and towers, a shifting pattern of roofs as the carriage moved—it was like a fairytale castle at one moment, a palace the next.

'It is vast.' Katherine heard the shake in her own voice and stiffened her spine. It seemed that this was their destination and that Nick must be some connection with the family who inhabited this awe-inspiring dwelling. Not a younger son, that she knew. She turned to him, suddenly agitated out of her usual calm self-control at the answer that was forcing itself into her mind. 'Nick, why are we here?'

'Because this is where I live,' he said simply as the carriage drew to a halt at the foot of a great double sweep of steps. They rose gracefully to a balustraded platform in front of the doors.

Nick got up and threw open the door before John could climb down. Katherine found herself handed out, a gaping

Jenny at her heels. 'Follow the drive round to the side, you will see the stable block,' he called up to John, then took Katherine's arm and began to climb the right-hand branch of the steps.

Stunned into silence, she let herself be guided. The hand under her elbow was steady and, glancing up, she saw his face was calm, severe and quite unreadable. With a sudden flash of insight she realised this was the face he would have shown to the mob at the hanging. They arrived on the wide flagged platform and, as if at a signal, the doors swung open.

Katherine did not know quite what to expect. This seemed to be a dream so fantastical that if the great Chan of China or the Prince Regent had emerged she would not have been surprised. The reality was more prosaic. Firstly a liveried footman and then, stepping primly in his wake, a thin, elderly man in dark clothing, unmistakably the butler.

'Good day sir, madam, I regret that his Grace is not—' He broke off and stared. 'Mr Nicholas! My lord!' His face turned white. For a moment Katherine thought he would faint, then Nick had him by the shoulders and the colour ebbed back as he slowly shook his head in wonderment. 'Heavens be praised, my lord, we thought you must be dead for sure. Six years...' His voice shook.

'Heron, if you break down, it will quite unman me,' Nick said roughly. Katherine could hear the affection in his voice and recognise the shake of emotion he was trying so hard to suppress. 'I was relying upon you to maintain a little decorum and restraint at the return of the prodigal son. Now, do not let me down.'

'No, my lord, of course not. It is merely a little breezy out here, it must be making my eyes water.' He rubbed hastily at his eyes and was once more the impassive butler. 'We must not detain the lady out here, my lord, if I may say so.'

They passed into the hall, the footman closed the doors behind them and Katherine found herself gaping like a tourist at an exhibition. The ceiling was high above them, the room a double cube of white marble, watered blue silk walls and massive paintings. A tall man was coming down the stairs. He stopped at the sight of the new arrivals, then, with a cry of 'Nick!', flung himself down the remaining flight.

There was no mistaking who he was. Younger than his brother by perhaps five years, brown haired where Nick verged on the raven, lanky where his equally tall brother was hard with muscle, he was still unmistakably the brother Nick had spoken of with such affection.

'Robert!' Katherine drew back as the two men embraced, a torrent of questions and half-completed sentences tumbling from Robert's lips.

'I beg your pardon, madam.' It was the butler. Hernshaw? No, Heron, that was it. 'I am afraid their lordships will be somewhat preoccupied for a few minutes. Have you luggage, madam? This will be your abigail, I assume?'

She pulled herself together. Few things in any house of rank were as important as to make a good impression on the upper servants and she was not going to let Nick down, however much she trembled inwardly at the shocking surprise he had sprung upon her.

'Thank you, Heron. Yes, this is Pilgrim. My man has taken the carriage with the luggage round to the stables.' She drew a deep breath, then said with a pleasant smile, 'I collect that my husband's message did not arrive to warn of our coming?'

The poor man had received more shocks that morning than were fair to inflict upon an elderly family retainer and she admired the manner in which he kept all traces of his reaction from his face. Only his eyes widened perceptibly. 'My lady. Welcome to Seaton Mandeville. I deeply regret that we could not assemble the full staff as is only fitting to receive the new marchioness.'

There, he had said it, the thing that she had been refusing to think ever since the dreadful certainty of who Nick was had come to her on the steps. She was, it seemed, a Marchioness. A temporary Marchioness. Somehow she must keep this bizarre conversation going until Nick was able to rescue her. 'Under the circumstances that is quite understandable. I shall look forward to meeting them all later.' Could the butler see the terror in her eyes? How many staff could this palace possibly require? Hundreds, she supposed. Around them other staff were gathering, ostensibly to assist the new arrivals, but quite obviously agog at the unexpected return of the heir of the house.

Mercifully Nick was turning, his arm still across his brother's shoulders. 'Robert, I have the honour to present you to my wife. Katherine, my brother, Lord Robert Lydgate.'

She kept her eyes from Nick's face, knowing it was unlikely she could hide the mingled reproach and fear in them. Instead she dropped a neat curtsy to his brother. 'My lord. I have heard so much about you from Nicholas.'

'Robert, please, and I hope I may call you Katherine.' He strode forward, suddenly so like Nicholas that her breath caught in her throat. 'And I trust I may kiss my new sister.'

The kiss was a firm but chaste pressure on either cheek and Katherine found herself smiling up at him gratefully as he held her at arm's length to study her. In the same way as Nick had made her feel safe in Newgate, this young man, so like him, was making her feel less unsure in this equally frightening new environment. 'Nick always had the best of good taste. Welcome to our home. I hope—'

The voice that cut across Robert's was calm, beautifully modulated and reduced the small crowd to immediate silence. 'Heron, it appears that I have received visitors of whom I was unaware. How could that be, I wonder?'

'Your Grace, I was just coming to announce them.' Katherine saw the stain of colour on the butler's cheeks and turned to regard the newcomer from under level brows. It did not take Heron's words to tell her who was standing in the open doorway regarding the scene, a book in one hand. She had imagined her new father-in-law as Nick in forty years' time and had not been mistaken. But this was not the patriarchal farmer she had imagined.

Nick himself had gone quite still, except to reach out a hand and take hers. She squeezed his fingers briefly and drew her hand away; she needed all her wits for this encounter and the touch of Nick's warmth was more a distraction than anything.

Robert appeared immune to the prevailing atmosphere. 'It is not visitors, Father, it is Nick, safe and sound at last.'

Around them servants were melting away, leaving only Heron and Jenny standing behind Katherine.

'We will retire to the library. Heron, some refreshments, if you please.' The Duke turned on his heel and re-entered the room behind him, leaving Katherine with an impression of immaculate and fashionable tailoring and an air of precise elegance.

'Kat,' Nick began, 'I will explain later...'

Katherine regarded him levelly. 'You certainly will,' she said with feeling, then put up her chin and concentrated on making her entrance through the door, which Robert was holding for her, with as much poise as she could conjure up.

She found herself standing directly in front of the Duke, who regarded her with no sign of emotion. 'Good day, madam. You are welcome. No doubt one of my sons will have the grace to introduce you presently.'

'Sir, I have the honour to present to you my wife, Katherine.' Nick addressed his father for the first time and, to her lasting admiration, managed to sound both unapologetic and perfectly polite.

'Your Grace.' Katherine dropped her very best curtsy and rose to meet the older man's eyes calmly. It appeared that she had met with some approval, for he bowed slightly in acknowledgment and stepped forward to take her hand. To her amazement he kissed her cheek, a chilly touch to be sure, but still more than she had expected.

'Then I must welcome you both to the family and to this house,' he said gravely. 'Am I to thank you for my son's return?'

'Thank you, your Grace. I understand that Nicholas was already planning to return before we met.' She should say something about the status of their marriage, she knew it, but a cowardly reluctance dragged at her tongue.

'Please, sit, Katherine. Have you had a long journey?'

'Your Grace, you are most kind.' No, she could not sit, could not be accepted by this terrifying old man under false pretences. 'But I must tell you that you should not be welcoming me to your family.' Beside her she heard a sharp hiss of indrawn breath from Nick and hurried on. 'I married your son because he was gallant enough to do so to save me from very difficult circumstances. We intend to seek an annulment at the earliest opportunity.'

'Indeed?' The dark brows, so in contrast to the steel grey hair, rose in exquisitely controlled surprise. 'Am I to understand that my son is unable to perform his marital duties?'

Chapter Thirteen

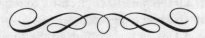

Katherine felt the hot blood rise in her cheeks and bit the inside of her lip. She was *not* going to be cowed by this terrifying old man.

'Sir!' At least she now knew what it took to break Nick's control.

Her blushes under control, Katherine shot him a quelling look and sank into the chair the Duke had offered her, glad of the moment's distraction to recover her poise. 'I have no information on that subject, your Grace,' she replied icily. 'From the beginning this has been a marriage of convenience and one intended to be of short duration. *Very* short. You will, doubtless, wish to know with whom Nicholas has made this temporary contract; my name is Katherine Cunningham. My late father was Philip Cunningham of Ware, in Hertfordshire.'

'I see. My son appears to have exercised a surprising degree of good judgement in his choice, however temporary. You are naturally most welcome to remain here for as long as it is convenient to you to do so, Katherine.' He appeared as unsurprised by the news of the annulment as he was by that of the marriage. Katherine began to realise where Nick had learned his formidable self-mastery.

The Duke swung round to study his elder son. The sight did not appear to afford him any great pleasure. 'So, Nicholas, you have decided to return after—what is it?—six years?'

'You dismissed me. Sir.' Released from the duke's steely regard, Katherine relaxed enough to watch Nick. Under the circumstances he was maintaining an admirable composure. But it was news to her that he had been dismissed by his father; the impression she had received was that he had walked away after a disagreement. Her anger with him at having concealed his true identity began to wane and in its place returned the unwelcome, uncomfortable tug of love at her heartstrings. It must be so hard, so very hard, to come back to such a cold reception.

'So I did. How amazing that for once you chose the path of obedience.' The Duke sat in the chair opposite Katherine and studied his sons. 'Robert, stop hovering and sit.'

Robert did as he was bid and, to Katherine's surprise, Nick followed suit so that the four of them formed a circle. It was far from a cosy conversational group.

'Now, let me see, why *did* I tell you to remove yourself?' the Duke mused. 'Ah, yes, the final straw, that highly unsuitable woman.'

Wide-eyed, Katherine looked at Nick. He stared back haughtily at his father and she was suddenly put in mind of two stags she had once seen in Richmond Park. The old stag, his head heavy with antlers, his muzzle white; the younger, with a less impressive spread, but all the stature and arrogance of powerful youth and the pair of them at a stand, eyeing each other for advantage.

'You made little allowance for young love,' Nick said eventually, his tone light, and the older man laughed shortly, a harsh note of grudging acknowledgment.

'I did not, you have the right of it. And it seems I made little allowance for youthful pride. I expected to see you back within a month or two.'

Nick shifted in the chair, crossing his legs and making himself more comfortable and his father's hard gaze sharpened. 'Come here.'

'Sir?'

'Come here.' Katherine froze, for she too had seen what that shift of position had revealed: the edge of the fading mark of the noose on Nick's neck. She put up her hand to her own neck in an attempt to warn him, but he was watching his father, a frown between his eyes.

Slowly Nick uncrossed his legs and stood, then took the two steps which brought him before his father's chair. The Duke rose and reached out long fingers to push aside the neckcloth around his son's neck. 'And what is this?'

'You told me I was born to be hanged.' Nick was rigid with some emotion that Katherine could only assume was anger at this chilly interrogation. 'As always, sir, you were correct.'

'And how did you escape?' The Duke flicked back the ends of the neckcloth with fastidious fingers and resumed his chair.

Nick took his time to walk back to his own seat. 'I was in Newgate, condemned to hang as a highwayman. Katherine saved me, at no little risk to her own life.'

'Then we are in your debt, my dear.' The old man twisted in his seat to look at Katherine. 'Your timing appears to be exquisite—late enough to teach a sharp lesson, not so late that it is fatal. I am agog to hear this entire tale, it appears positively Gothick. However, I believe Heron will soon be announcing luncheon—if this event has not thrown the entire household into total disarray—and I am sure you will wish to retire to your room beforehand.' He stretched out a hand to the bell pull and Katherine recognised the same long fingers that made Nick's hands so graceful.

He regarded his elder son from under hooded lids. 'No doubt Heron will be able to decide which is the most appropriate suite of rooms for Lady Seaton under the circumstances. If you will excuse me, my dear.'

The silence that was left when the door closed behind him appeared to fill the room. Katherine yearned to go and put her arms around Nick, but his very control told her that would be unwelcome. At least she now knew what her own title was. *Lady Seaton, the Marchioness. This is a nightmare.*

At last, when she felt on the point of screaming at the men to provoke some reaction, Robert said, *'Hanged?'* His brother nodded. 'As a *highwayman*?'

To Katherine's relief a wry smile twisted Nick's lips. 'As the notorious Black Jack Standon, no less.'

An inelegant whistle escaped Robert. 'You weren't, were you?'

'Certainly not. I was most elegantly entrapped by Black Jack and his doxy and haled off to Newgate where I had no means of proving who I am.'

'But you look nothing like a highwayman,' Robert protested. 'I mean, I know your clothes are hardly what one might expect—'

'They belong to my groom,' Katherine interjected. 'And Nick does look very like Mr Standon. Younger, but very like.'

'How do you know?' Robert swivelled in his chair to regard Katherine with fascination.

'Because my wife took it upon herself to go to find him and to persuade him to show himself to the magistrate in the case.'

Robert's eyes opened wide, making him look even younger than his years. 'But why was Katherine not able to prove who you were without having to do that? As your wife—'

'I married Nicholas—'

'Kat!'

Katherine shot her husband a defiant look. He wanted to shield her and protect her and part of her loved him for it, but she was not going to pretend to her terrifying new family. 'I married him in Newgate because I was—I *am*—heavily in debt.'

Robert whistled again. 'Well, that's not a problem for you any more. Nick's as rich as Croesus; old Wilkinson, our man of affairs, has been squirreling his income away in all sorts of interesting ways ever since he left. Nick, for goodness' sake, are you not going to tell me where you've been?'

Katherine cleared her throat. 'Before this goes any further, let me make my position quite plain. I will have this marriage annulled and I will look after my own debts.'

Robert's gaze flickered from one determined face to another and this time his whistle was silent. *You've met your match with this one, Nick.* It was a pity, he was rapidly becoming very attached to his new sister-in-law.

'We will discuss this later,' Nick began as the door opened and Heron entered.

'My lord, I have taken the liberty of opening your old rooms and her ladyship's woman is unpacking her ladyship's things in the Lake Suite. I have ordered hot water sent up in case her ladyship would care to retire before luncheon, which will be in half an hour.'

Katherine got to her feet with a smile. 'Thank you, Heron, if you would show me the way.' Nick made as if to join her, but she smiled coolly at him. 'I am sure you and Lord Robert have much to discuss, my lord.'

The door closed behind them, leaving Nick conscious of a strong desire to kick the furniture and very aware of his brother's fascinated gaze.

'What?' he demanded.

'You want to annul the marriage?' Robert sounded incredulous. 'She is enchanting.'

'No, I do *not* want to annul it, but Kat does and she's as proud as they come and the most stubborn woman I have ever met. She married me in sheer desperation because of the mess her scapegrace brother had got her into and in the expectation that the debt would die with me. I had the devil's own job getting her to agree to come here in my company.' He dug his hands into the pockets of his coat and began to pace up and down the room. The emotions that were flooding through him were too complex to untangle, but most of them hurt damnably.

Robert's uncritical affection he had always been assured of, but he should not have been surprised at his father's chilly reception. Nor should he have been surprised at the feelings that had gripped him as the landscape had become more and more familiar. Affection, memory, pride and the dragging knowledge that one day all this would be his responsibility. All the acres, all the possessions, all the people inescapably his until the day he died. And then the shock of seeing his home again. The rush of water to his eyes had startled him; perhaps he loved the place more than he had ever realised.

And now he had one more responsibility to worry about— Kat. He remembered the way her eyes had widened and darkened with the dawning knowledge of what she was about to discover of the man she had married. Unconsciously he smiled at the picture of her as she stood in the Great Hall, chin up, back straight, making appropriate conversation with Heron, determined to let neither of them down.

'I did not tell her who I am—she had no idea until Heron called me by my title,' he confessed, unpleasantly aware that he was going to be expected to explain himself once Katherine had him alone.

'No wonder she looks so coolly at you! Why do you want to stay married if she does not?' Robert asked.

'Because I owe her my life. I can never pay that debt.' *And because making love to her is rapidly becoming an obsession.*

'And you will persist whether she wants it or not?'

'Whether she wants it or not,' he agreed harshly.

A cough announced Heron's reappearance. 'My lord, I have asked Lord Robert's man to lay out a suit of clothes for you from his lordship's wardrobe. What you are wearing may, of course, be most suitable for travelling, but I fear his Grace will not look kindly upon a frieze coat at the luncheon table.' He looked pointedly at the clock and both brothers made for the door with alacrity.

'I remember all too well our father's views on unpunctuality,' Nick observed as they parted on the upper landing. 'I have no wish to render today any more hideous by being three minutes late.'

Robert grinned and slapped him affectionately on the shoulder. 'Welcome home.'

Katherine stood and looked helplessly out across the parkland to the lake.

With her hands full of folded garments, Jenny was chattering happily as she moved between portmanteau and highboy drawers. 'A Marchioness! Who'd have thought it? And I've just realised—that puts me top of all the female servants excepting the housekeeper. Oh, Miss Katherine, just when things looked so black, this is a miracle.'

'Well, do not get too used to it, Jenny.' Katherine tossed a fine linen hand towel on to the washstand and gave her appearance a distracted glance in the mirror. 'We have no choice but to stay here until the annulment, but after that I must be earning my own way.'

'But, Miss Katherine, the master's a *lord*, the heir to a dukedom. You don't need to worry about the debt—he must make more money than that in a week. And you lo—' she caught Katherine's eye, bit her lip and continued carefully '—you *like* him.'

'You are talking nonsense.' Katherine twitched at her hem. In a minute she was going to have to go downstairs, face the three men again. 'Lord Seaton is heir to a dukedom. For that reason alone he must marry well.'

Jenny bristled in her defence. 'You are well bred, a lady.'

'Oh, Jenny, a duke is going to be looking for an heiress for his oldest son. He will expect a young lady of lineage and land, someone whose family has connections at Court and in society. Not, of course, that I would not be seeking the annulment in any case, however good my birth,' she added hastily. *Could the heir to a dukedom marry for love? Stop it,* she scolded herself, *He is not in love with you, that is an academic question.*

Somewhere far below her a gong sounded, reverberated. Luncheon was obviously served. *Now all I have to do is find the correct dining room in this labyrinth, sit through a meal with a terrifying duke and a man I love and from whom I must hide every tender feeling…*

'I must go. Jenny, have they looked after you? Do you know where to go and have you a chamber to sleep in? And what about John?' she added distractedly as Jenny pushed her firmly out of the room.

'I have a very nice room to myself, as befits my new station, and so has John, I believe. And I know the way to the servants' hall. Now go, Miss Katherine, or you'll keep the Duke waiting.'

She made her way downstairs slowly, taking the time to compose herself and wishing that for the last few years she had not been so out of society. Not that she would ever have been in a position to make conversation with dukes.

Heron was waiting in the hall and steered her towards, 'The panelled dining room, my lady. It is the smallest of the dining rooms.'

'Thank you, Heron.' She was pleased with the calm way she smiled at him as he opened the door. It was, indeed, a small chamber; Katherine had been envisaging glossy yards of mahogany and having to attempt conversation around gleaming épergnes.

Her relief was abruptly terminated when she realised that the only other occupant was the Duke. His smile, unexpected, was all too reminiscent of Nick at his coolest and she felt her back stiffen as she returned it.

'You are very prompt, my dear. You found your way with ease, I surmise. Are you comfortable in your suite? Ah, my sons are at your heels.'

Katherine avoided looking at any of the men as she nodded acknowledgement to the footman who pulled out a chair for her and took her place at the table.

'Most comfortable, thank you, your Grace.' Acutely conscious of the rigid footmen at the buffet, Katherine was profoundly grateful that he made no comment on the choice of rooms that Heron had assigned to her. Doubtless it would be all over the house in no time that the Marquis was not sharing his wife's bed. She felt a flush of embarrassment, then thought of how much more Nick would feel it.

'Has your journey taken you long?' She pulled herself together and concentrated on making conversation. Naturally the Duke could not ask her where she had come from in front of the servants; he would be endeavouring to make this surprise arrival seem as normal as possible. She set herself to give him as much information as she could without appearing to.

'We took several days over it, your Grace. Nicholas needed to rest, of course, as he has not been well.' Katherine ignored the suppressed exclamation from her husband's lips. 'The weather in London was very clement when we left.'

'And your family is well?'

'My brother is travelling in France, your Grace. Since my parents' deaths, he has little business, and no family other than myself, to keep him in this county. He left shortly after the wedding.' Doubtless the Duke's first recourse when he had returned to the library had been to the *Peerage* and the *Landed Gentry*. He would know by now that she had no relatives other than a brother and that their birth, while respectable, was as nothing compared to his.

The meal passed with a rigid formality, which left Katherine dreading dinner. Conversation was measured, general, and left her quivering with tension. The weather, the news of local events, the prospect of a touring company of players at Newcastle and the latest London *on-dits* served to fill the time unexceptionally. Katherine decided that if it went on much longer she would scream.

Cautiously she glanced at Nicholas while accepting a plate of bread and butter or passing the salt. He appeared calm and relaxed, but she could sense a suppressed emotion in him; doubtless he wanted to have the interview with his father for which he had been bracing himself and this mannered inaction was chafing his nerves as the shackles had chafed his wrists.

Finally the Duke sat back and regarded his family ranged on either side of him. 'Nicholas, I would speak with you. Robert, perhaps Katherine would care to be shown around the house.' It was an order, not a suggestion, and Katherine smiled politely.

'Thank you, your Grace. That would be delightful if Lord Robert can spare the time.'

They all rose and Katherine found Nick at her elbow. He kept his face straight, but the message his eyes sent her was warmly reassuring. However, all he said was, 'Do not let Robert bore you with every picture in the Long Gallery.' He bent and kissed her cheek fleetingly and stood aside for her to precede the men from the room.

Nick found himself watching her straight back as she walked away with his brother. Elegance, pride, dignity—he found himself smiling just to watch her.

'A charming young lady, and one who is disguising with great courage the fact that this household is entirely beyond anything she has experienced before,' his father remarked drily. 'Perhaps you can explain to me why you are so intent upon an annulment.' He strolled towards his study without a backwards glance.

Nick unclenched his teeth, told himself firmly that this was only to be expected and followed.

'So,' the Duke continued, 'I deduce that you did not marry your Clarissa—or was it Annabelle? The objects of your youthful affections are somewhat blurred in my mind after all this time.' He tugged a cuff slightly. 'The penalty of old age, no doubt.'

'I believe you require little reassurance on your memory, Father. You are correct, there were enough young women for you to have easily forgotten Arabella. And, no, I did not marry her; despite the aspersions you cast upon her breeding and up-bringing, she was shocked at my suggestion we should elope and for all I know has now married some worthy gentleman.'

'But you took me at my word and left?'

'Yes, sir. I understood it to be a command.' He was damned if he was going to explain now how Arabella's refusal to give up everything for him had hurt. He had been prepared to estrange himself from his family for her; now he could hardly conjure up the memory of her face. But at the time, to return home a rejected suitor was too hard for youthful pride to swallow.

'Most dutiful.' The sceptical expression on his father's face showed that he had read the situation aright at the time and his next words confirmed it. 'I expected you to return after a week or two.'

Nick did not rise to the implied question and to his surprise the older man continued. 'I confess to being less than pleased with the news that my son and heir was keeping himself in London as a Captain Sharp.'

'I never fuzzed the cards,' Nick said flatly. 'I did not need to—you taught me too well.'

'Gratifying that something I endeavoured to educate you in remained with you. And after two years you disappeared. Why?'

Nick shrugged. 'I was bored. I moved around the country for eighteen months, then I joined the army on a whim and found I liked it.'

'Which regiment? Why did I not hear of this?' The old man stared at him from under levelled brows. 'What rank?'

'Private,' Nick replied, expecting an outburst.

'A private? My God—' the Duke threw back his head and gave a bark of laughter '—someone to teach you discipline at last.'

'It certainly taught me self-control,' Nick agreed pleasantly. The old devil, outflanking him as he so often did in the past!

'And between that and your career as a highwayman?'

'Nothing, sir. I was discharged after Waterloo.' He saw the flash of some emotion in his father's eyes and pressed on. 'I returned to England and was on the road to London when I found myself in a country inn. I was drugged and, when I woke, found myself in the guise of the infamous local high-wayman Black Jack Standon. I could not prove who I was, so I ended up in Newgate awaiting my execution.'

'Why did you not send to me?'

'I really am not sure.' Nick thought back to those confusing first days after his capture. 'Too proud, perhaps—and uncertain whether you would acknowledge me. Soon it was too late in any case.'

'Not acknowledge you!' The old man was on his feet, his face thunderous. Nick sprang to his and they confronted each other for a long moment before the Duke dropped heavily back into his chair. 'Damn it, you are my heir, Nicholas.'

'Robert would make a better one.'

'He is a good man, too good in many ways—but you are the elder and, whatever your sins, I will do everything in my power to see you step into my shoes when the time comes.'

There seemed to be no answer to that, or at least none that did not carry the risk of giving his father an apoplexy.

'So how did Katherine come to rescue you from the gallows?' the Duke enquired finally.

'Her brother, a spineless young pup, managed to gamble away the family assets, then tricked her into signing the papers for a loan. She found herself confronted with pressing creditors and her lawyer and brother persuaded her that marriage to a condemned man was her only escape from debtors' prison.'

'And she agreed? I find that hard to believe.'

'Very reluctantly, that was obvious. And when I consider how I appeared when she saw me, I can only be astounded that her resolution held. Once she had heard my story, she made up her mind that I must be cleared and set about it. The entire story still makes my blood run cold, but to summarise, she sold the last thing of value she possessed, bearded the real highwayman in his den, convinced him to meet the magistrate in the case, persuaded the magistrate of my innocence and dragged him to London where they arrived, despite a carriage accident on the way, in time literally to cut me down from the gallows.'

'A remarkable and courageous young lady,' the Duke remarked. 'I confess I am not quite clear why you wish to end your marriage to this paragon.'

'I do not.' Nick got to his feet and walked across to look out of the window on to the wide and somewhat old-fashioned parterre that the Duke insisted on preserving, despite the best endeavours of his landscape gardener. In the distance he could see Robert, who had Kat's hand tucked into his elbow and was pointing out something in the view to her. She turned and laughed up into his face and Nick felt a sudden pang inside; she would not be amused when he was finally alone with her, he was quite convinced.

'I owe her my life. I am honour bound to marry her. I am aware she has not a great name and brings nothing but a debt with her, but…'

'But I entirely agree with you. The family can cope without the necessity for you to marry an heiress and the girl is obviously of respectable birth. The problem appears to lie in her quite understandable reluctance to marry you, a sentiment with which I can heartily sympathise. You are staring at me, Nicholas—do try for a little more decorum. Now I suggest you go and find her or you may discover that your brother has cut you out.'

Nicholas shut his mouth with a snap. 'I believe that would be within the prohibited degrees of marriage, sir.'

'Surely not, if your marriage is annulled?' his father said gently. 'Oh, and, Nicholas, if you intend to stay, I trust you intend to work. Witherspoon will be delighted to take you under his wing. He is always politely intimating that he wishes I would concern myself more about the estate.'

Nicholas bowed his head respectfully, managed a smile with tight lips and retreated. 'Rolled up—cannon, cavalry and infantry too, the old devil.' He laughed suddenly, unaware that the two footmen in the hall started nervously, believing the old Duke was about to appear. He let himself out on to the terrace and scanned the gardens for Kat and Robert. 'Made me feel seventeen, never mind the twenty-two I was when I last saw him, damn him.'

He grinned. He had been braced for a rare scene; what he had experienced was his father's remarkable ability to catch one wrong footed whatever the circumstances. But he liked Kat, that was a relief. Nicholas realised that a good part of his apprehension had been the expectation of having to protect Kat from his father's opposition to the marriage.

He rounded the corner of the house into the rose garden, the grin still on his lips as he remembered his father's neat attempt to make him jealous of Robert. Robert, for goodness' sake! There they were, sitting in the far arbour, Kat with her hands in Robert's, the pair of them gazing deep into each other's eyes.

With a muffled oath Nick strode across the lawn.

Chapter Fourteen

'I think you would make an excellent clergyman,' Katherine said firmly, catching Robert's hands in an effort to convince him of her sincerity. 'Surely your father can have no objection now that he knows Nicholas is safe?'

Her brother-in-law returned the comforting pressure of her hands with an answering squeeze. 'I suppose so. It is cowardly of me, I confess, but I have suppressed the very idea for so long that it is hard to talk of it now, let alone believe it would be possible.'

'It is not so hard—you are telling me,' Katherine said encouragingly.

'And I hardly know you. I should be showing you around the house, not pouring my troubles out into your ears.'

'Well, I am scared of the house and quite comfortable with you, so I would much rather hear about your ambitions. I have heard of many members of the nobility in the church. You will become an archbishop—I can tell you are destined for great things.'

'And I can tell you are a darling,' Robert said warmly, planting a kiss on her cheek.

Katherine laughed, quite at ease with him. 'Thank you, but you flatter me. Oh, look, here is Nick.'

He must have had a difficult interview with his father, she realised, seeing the black fire flickering dangerously in his eyes. 'Nick! I was a complete ninny and had to confess to being totally confused by the house within minutes, so Lord Robert brought me out here to enjoy the gardens.'

'So that is what he is doing, is it?' She saw Nick glance at his brother and felt a sudden qualm. Surely he did not think…?

It appeared that Robert also recognised danger when he saw it. 'I was confessing my secret ambitions to Katherine and she has taken it upon herself to encourage me.'

One dark brow rose and Robert added hastily, 'I wish to enter the church.'

'Good God!'

'Do not blaspheme, Nicholas,' Katherine said sternly. 'Your brother is perfectly serious. I am sure he would make an excellent clergyman. Now you are home safe, should he not speak to your father as soon as possible?'

The darkness had left Nick's eyes as he regarded his brother with affectionate amusement. 'Father should jump at the chance of elevating the moral tone of this family.' Katherine sent him a reproving look and he added with the seriousness that always made her suspect he was teasing her, 'However, he may not want you committed to this course of action until he sees me married and setting up my nursery.'

'You are married,' Robert pointed out.

'And I have made it quite clear that is a temporary state of affairs!' Katherine interjected hastily. Nick *was* teasing, the wretch. Katherine schooled her face and added, 'But I am sure we can have everything tidied up before next Season and you can find yourself an eminently suitable bride.' She turned to

Robert. 'I still think you should speak to his Grace sooner rather than later.'

'Did I mention that I have an exceedingly managing wife?' Nick enquired.

'Er, no.' Robert was watching her face with some amusement and Katherine suspected that she was betraying rather more of her emotions than she was prepared to. She stood up and brushed down her skirt.

'Delightful as the garden is, I think I should not disregard his Grace's wishes and should resume my tour of the house.' She looked expectantly at Nick. The Long Gallery sounded an admirable place to have a private discussion and she very much wanted to speak to him alone.

'I am so sorry, Kat,' he replied with a charming smile. 'But Father has asked that I speak to Witherspoon, our estate manager. I received a clear hint that I am expected to apply myself to learning all those things which I shirked in the past. I am sure Robert can continue to escort you—after all, I hardly feel it would be tactful to deliver a second shock to Father in one day.'

'Grr.' Katherine watched his retreating back, wishing that her attention was not drawn quite so forcibly to the breadth of his shoulders or the easy length of his stride.

'I beg your pardon?' Robert was also watching his brother. 'Did you speak? I was just thinking that Nick really must get to a tailor before he goes out into society; we are much of a height, but he is definitely wider in the shoulders than I. It will have to be Newcastle, I suppose. I wonder why he did not stop to order some clothes while he was in town.'

'Because he had no money and I had hardly any and we were outrunning the bailiffs.' Katherine began to stroll with him across the grass back to the house. If she only looked at one wing at a time it was not too bad, it was when she looked at the entire extent of the place that she began to feel as though she had strayed into a fairy tale. 'How much interest do moneylenders charge?'

'I have no idea.' Robert looked startled. 'An extortionate amount, I imagine. But you do not have to worry about that, Nick will pay off the debt. Here, we can go in through this door.'

'That would stop the interest, of course, but I am sure he will not let me repay him.' Katherine allowed herself to be guided up a narrow staircase.

'Why repay it at all? From what I understand, it is your brother's debt.'

'I know, but I signed the papers, so it is my responsibility. It will be a lesson to me to read everything first,' she added ruefully as they stepped out through a jib door into what must be the Long Gallery.

One wall appeared almost to be made of glass divided by slender mullions. The other wall was covered with crimson damask and on it were hung what seemed like hundreds of paintings, nearly all portraits.

'Behold the family, rogues most of them.' Robert waved a hand at the rows of gilded frames. 'You will observe the Nose, and in a few unfortunate individuals, the Chin. Now this one is— What is it, Jenkins?'

The footman bowed. 'My lord, I am sorry to disturb you, but Durren sent up from the stables to say the farrier is here and he was worried about the shoeing of his Grace's bay hunter. I cannot find his Grace to ask.'

'I had better have a word with the man myself. Tell Durren I will be down directly and the farrier is to do nothing until I get there. Katherine, will you excuse me for a little while? The bell pull is over there if you need anything.' He grinned ruefully, suddenly so like his brother that Katherine's heart flipped. 'It is more than our lives are worth to risk anything going wrong with that animal.'

'Of course, please go. I shall enjoy just strolling here.' Katherine began to pace slowly down the room, standing back to admire some large groups and full-length portraits of former dukes in ermine-trimmed robes, coming in close to peer at tiny dark paintings, which seemed to her untutored eye to be Jacobean or Tudor.

Nick was unmistakeably a Lydgate; his face looked back at her from countless paintings: dark eyes, straight nose, sensual mouth. Some depictions gave their sitters a familiar haughty look, a few had the spark of mischief she had come to watch for. All had the expression of proud intelligence that she had come to expect of him. One or two had the chin Robert had referred to, not such a handicap for the men, but a definite disadvantage to the ladies on whom a square, determined jaw did not sit prettily. *I hope our daughters escape that,* she thought, then caught herself with a horrified little gasp. *What am I thinking of? Fantasising, that's what you are doing, you foolish creature. Loving him is no excuse.*

Shaken, Katherine continued her examination of the pictures, ignoring her aching neck as she tipped her head back to take them all in. The discomfort was a penance for such undisciplined daydreaming. Suddenly she came upon a group of relatively recent paintings, judging by the hair and clothes. That must surely be the present Duke with a small, fair lady in clothes perhaps half a century out of date. His first wife? Yes, it must be, for here he was again standing behind a different, seated, lady with a baby on her lap and a small boy by her knee.

The child must be Nick. Smiling, she stepped closer to study it.

'A pretty group, that,' a voice said dispassionately behind

her. She jumped. 'I am sorry, my dear, I had no intention of startling you.'

Katherine turned hastily. 'Your Grace. I was quite absorbed by the portraits.'

'Have both my sons abandoned you?'

'Nicholas is with your estate manager. Lord Robert left a few minutes ago because of an urgent message from the stables. Something about the farrier and your bay hunter, your Grace.'

'Indeed? In my young day it would take rather more than a horse to distract me from a charming young lady.'

Katherine's lips twitched. She was beginning to take the measure of the formidable old man. 'I believe it was the thought of your displeasure rather than the needs of the horse that animated Lord Robert.'

'That is as it should be,' the Duke remarked gravely. 'I see it falls to me to exhibit the rest of the collection, unless you are bored with an unending succession of Lydgates?'

'No, your Grace. I find it fascinating.'

'Then let us see if we can find any other depictions of your husband. Ah, yes, rather over-dramatic, perhaps.'

He had stopped in front of a full-length study of a rearing horse against a stormy sky. Holding its reins, his attention fixed on the animal as it fought for its freedom, was a young man, hardly more than a youth. 'Two wild animals,' Katherine said without thinking.

'And each as stubborn as the other,' the Duke agreed. 'Nicholas's temper was as free as that stallion's in those days. He appears to have governed it now.' It was a question.

'I would say he has quite remarkable self-control,' Katherine said as judiciously as she could. 'And remarkable courage. To see him in prison, bearing those dreadful conditions and the certainty of death with such dignity and even humour—that was very impressive.'

The old man said nothing, but Katherine sensed his pleasure. He was not going to admit to his pride in his son, had still not forgiven him, but that pride ran deep and to hear it justified could only gratify him.

All he said was, 'Nicholas has told me nothing about the conditions in the prison except that he was amazed that, having seen him, you still consented to marry him.'

Katherine chuckled. 'Well, your Grace, I *was* desperate. He was filthy, bearded, his hair in rats' tails and as for the prison smell… But there was something, I am not sure what, something in his eyes that made me feel safe. And his wrists were raw under the shackles.' She broke off, suddenly finding herself emotional and appalled to be revealing so much of her feelings. She swallowed and said lightly, 'I sent him soap.'

The Duke laughed, apparently genuinely amused. 'An admirably practical thing to do. Now, come and see this glass case in the window. There is an excellent series of miniatures that you may like.'

Katherine allowed herself to be drawn into the deep bay formed by an oriole window and they bent over a glass-topped table that contained a dozen or so exquisite miniatures. As she was studying them, there was the sound of doors opening and voices from either end of the Long Gallery.

'Robert! Where's Katherine?'

'I left her here. I had to go down to the stables.'

'For goodness' sake, if she has wandered off she will be lost in this maze of a house—we'll have to turn all the footmen out to look for her.'

The voices were coming closer as the brothers converged on the centre of the Gallery. 'I am sure if she is lost she will simply ring the nearest bell,' Robert said placatingly.

'Fortunately Katherine has not been put to that expedient,'

the Duke remarked drily, emerging from the embrasure, his hand firmly under Katherine's elbow. 'Come along, my dear, I will show you the way back to the main hall so you can get your bearings.' A clock struck and he added, 'Doubtless your woman will be waiting to help you change for dinner.' He regarded his two sons as he passed. 'We have been having a comfortable cose,' he remarked blandly. 'Such a pleasure for an old man.'

He shut the door behind them and caught Katherine's eye. 'You wish to say something, my dear?'

'Only that I think neither of your sons regards you as "old," your Grace.' She saw the glint in his eye and added daringly, 'I think you enjoy teasing them.'

'It is a relief to have two of them to tease,' he said. 'Not that you will repeat that to them, I trust.'

'No, of course not,' she assured him as they parted company at the foot of the main stairs.

What was it that Nick had said so lightly when she had asked him why he wanted a month to elapse before the marriage was annulled? *To allow the charms of my family to grow upon you, perhaps.* She had liked Robert on sight, now she found herself unexpectedly liking the formidable Duke himself.

In fact, she suspected that after a few weeks she could well find herself very fond of both of them. Which was no reason not to annul the marriage; in fact, liking them, she felt more than ever that she must not impose upon them.

In her room Jenny was ready waiting with hot water and hair brushes, the best of Katherine's limited choice of evening gowns laid out on the bed. Light was fading over the park and, as Katherine washed, the maid went round the room closing the heavy blue curtains across the windows.

With the outside world shut out, she looked closely at the

bedchamber for the first time and shivered. The room seemed glacial to her eyes, used as she was to a bedchamber as a sanctuary, a warm retreat where she could create a feminine, private world.

The walls were lined with ice blue watered silk, the polished boards were largely obscured by a vast Chinese rug in shades of blue and ivory and the high ceiling and plasterwork seemed to enclose her like the sugarwork on an elaborate cake. Even the bed did not offer much promise of comfort. It was so high she would need a footstool to get into it, the covers were a mass of white lace and the hangings more chilly blue silk.

The pictures played their part in her discomfort—a full-length portrait of an exquisite young lady in a lavish gown and marvellous parure of diamonds regarded her with disdain and, on another wall, a classical scene showed maidens being dragged to a sacrificial altar.

Jenny followed her mistress's gaze and pulled a face. 'Nice thing to have in a bedchamber, I don't think! Enough to give a body nightmares. Here's your pearl ear-bobs, Miss Katherine.'

Katherine hooked them into her lobes with the sinking feeling that she was the maiden on the way to a sacrifice. The prospect of the meal filled her with dread. She would be surrounded by servants who, if they did not know it already, would soon be aware of the strange nature of the Marquis's marriage.

Luncheon had been an ordeal, how much worse was a formal dinner going to be? She would have to make polite and appropriate conversation with three men, two of whom she hardly knew and one of whom she loved and could not have. And, to crown it all, she must hope that with her limited experience she did not commit some breach of etiquette in this ducal household and embarrass both herself and Nicholas.

But it was none of those things that made her want to order Jenny to throw everything into their portmanteaux, to send for John to harness the team and to flee back to the shabby comfort of last night's inn. A creeping unease was coming into her heart, a feeling that she was out of her depth already and into a situation where she had no control. Whatever happened she was going to be hurt, she knew that, but now it was no longer just herself and Nick involved.

The men were gathered in what Heron informed her was, 'The Chinese Salon, your ladyship, it being more comfortable for small family gatherings.'

Remembering some of the bewildering succession of apartments through which Robert had led her that afternoon, Katherine could only be thankful for that information. She swept into the room with her chin up, telling herself that if she could beard a highwayman in his den she could face a Duke in his palace.

The men looked up as she entered. They had been gathered around a table with a paper spread upon it and, as Katherine came closer, she saw it was a large map. She bobbed a curtsy and looked up to meet Nick's eyes. He smiled and without calculation she smiled back, relieved to find his warmth in the middle of the cold formality. Then Robert greeted her and the Duke stepped forward, gesturing her to look at what they had been studying and the chill, lonely feeling ebbed away.

'I was just showing Nicholas this map which Mr Crace, our archivist, found recently in the Muniments Room. He is unable to join us for dinner, as he is dining with Reverend Rossington, our chaplain, at the Bishop's palace.'

Katherine swallowed a small gasp. Of course, a Duke would have an archivist and a chaplain and of course they normally joined the family for dinner. Was it ever possible to be private in this vast house?

Nick was poring over the map again, one long finger pointing to what seemed to be a house towards the edge of the park. 'Is Cousin Wilhelmina still in residence in the Dower House, sir?'

'No, she died three years ago,' the Duke replied. 'The place is empty now.' He regarded his elder son sharply. 'Have you a use for it?'

Nick shrugged, 'Possibly, sir, if you have not. I shall need to be setting up my own establishment.'

'You can have the east wing here to your entire use should you wish,' the Duke remarked. 'Why do you wish to move out of the house?'

'Because, with respect, sir, I think we would deal better together if we are not in each other's pocket. And my wife informed me last night that she prefers a smaller home. Something snug and cosy were the words she used, if I remember aright.'

'Nicholas!' The word was forced out of Katherine with more emphasis than decorum and she blushed. 'Excuse me, your Grace. I meant no disrespect, I had no idea where Nick lived when I spoke.'

'So, he had not told you.' The Duke smiled thinly at their discomfiture. 'You could not have guessed what you would find. And in any case, you would expect the marriage to have been ended long before the Dower House is fit for habitation, would you not?'

'Yes, of co—'

'No.' It was Nick, cutting emphatically across her response. 'No, that is by no means agreed.'

Chapter Fifteen

As soon as he spoke he regretted it. Not the sentiment, but the abrupt way he had spoken, for Katherine's eyes meeting his held not the defiance and anger he expected, but a sort of blank tiredness. He felt as though he had raised his hand to strike an already beaten animal.

'Kat…'

'Dinner is served, your Grace.'

The Duke stepped forward to offer his arm to Katherine and Nick wondered if he had imagined the expression in her eyes. Now they were bright, attentive on his father, and she was already asking a thoughtful question about the Chinese wallpaper which extended from the Salon into the dining room.

The table was reduced by most of its leaves and conversation would be easy, he thought, taking the foot of the table while Katherine was seated on his father's right and Robert took the opposite place. It did mean he was sitting at right angles to her, which made it difficult to examine her face more closely.

Still, he mused while mechanically disjointing the capon

set before him, the view of Kat's profile was charming enough to keep any man occupied over dinner. The dark lashes swept her cheek, fluttering modestly in contradiction to the set of her firm little chin. Her nose was straight and when she smiled, as she was doing now at Robert who was offering her fish, there was a hint of a dimple in her cheek.

But despite the smile, he could not read her mood and he had become used to being able to do that on the long journey together. It had seemed she was not used to dissembling, to hiding her feelings; when she was angry her chin came up, her eyes flashed and she said what she thought. When she was happy her laughter was infectious and her whole body relaxed into a fluent softness that had an alarming effect on his own.

But now she was on society manners, listening attentively to her father-in-law and interposing a sensible question from time to time. She seemed to be sharing her attention equally between his father and brother. Nick tried interjecting a question.

'Do you ride, Katherine?'

She turned to look at him and he was struck by how refreshing she looked in her simple gown in that exotic room. Her expression was serious and when she smiled the warmth did not reach her eyes. 'No, I have never ridden.' The smile became rueful. 'We never lived in the country after I was twelve and in town it was difficult enough keeping the carriage and pair without adding riding horses.'

'Would you like to learn?' Her eyes came back to his reluctantly, he could swear. What was wrong? Surely something more than pique over having been kept in the dark over his title and circumstances?

'Thank you, but I am sure you will be too busy while I am here. And I will have no use for such a skill—it would be a waste of your time.'

'I do not intend to keep Nicholas chained to the estate manager's side,' the Duke interjected drily. 'He will catch up on affairs here soon enough. And possibly he has plans of his own.' He regarded his son blandly and Nick acknowledged the remark with a movement of his head.

Now what was the old devil up to? Calling his bluff seemed the easiest way to find out.

'Indeed I have, sir. Naturally I must devote some time to Witherspoon and to whatever I may do to assist you. Then there is the Dower House to set to right, a hunting lodge to acquire in the shires—I think I will rent at first—and the question of a house. In town. None of that should stop me spending time teaching Kat to ride.'

She did not rise to the bait, merely toying with the timbale of rice before her. The Duke remarked, 'The town house is entirely at your disposal, I visit only when the Lords are sitting, and these days, not always then.'

'Thank you, sir. However, I was wondering whether to take something smaller for the time being.'

The footmen cleared the table and for a moment the room was emptied of staff while the second remove was collected from the adjoining pantry.

'But surely,' Kat observed mildly, 'the family house would be more suitable for your purposes next Season?'

'Why so?'

'It will impress fashionable mamas, and that is so important when entering the Marriage Mart.'

Robert stifled a gasp of laughter with his napkin, earning himself a look of mild reproof from his father, and a glare from his brother.

'I am not intending to enter that particular circus.'

'Well, not quite yet, of course, it would not be proper, but you did say something about the need to set up your nursery, did you not?' Kat remarked with maddening affability. Heron returned with the footmen and she asked the Duke, 'Is that delightful view over the fireplace the park here?'

The next course passed with conversation on neutral topics, relieved only by Robert remarking that, whatever else Nick did, he must take himself off to Newcastle as soon as possible and see a tailor. 'For my coats will not stand the strain on their seams for much longer.'

There was general laughter at Robert's mock indignation at the fate of his clothes, but Nick was watching Kat. Her hand trembled as she lifted her glass and she set it down hastily. The graceful line of her shoulders drooped slightly and he thought her laughter sounded forced.

Nick watched her chase a little curd tart round her plate until she could hide the remains neatly under her spoon and realised what was wrong: she was exhausted.

Should he say something? What would she expect to happen in this all-male household? But he had underestimated Kat's poise. She caught his father's eye, stood gracefully and smiled as the men got to their feet. 'If you will excuse me from presiding over the tea table this evening, your Grace, I would like to retire, if I may.'

'But of course, my dear. Sleep well.'

Nick moved to come to her side, but she shook her head slightly and he dropped back into his chair as she left the room. He felt guilt that she was obviously too tired even to want to berate him for his deception, hurt that she did not need his company. She seemed more comfortable with his formidable father than with him, she was certainly more relaxed with Robert. With an effort of will he dragged his eyes from the door and listened to what Robert was saying.

Kat was met in her suite by Jenny, bright eyed and excited. 'Oh, Miss Katherine—my lady, I should say—it's a palace here! The servants' hall is so grand, and I've a room all to my-self like I told you, and they've given me a girl to look after my things. And it runs like some great machine, they sent for me to say you were on your way, and a footman brought hot water, and another the warming pan, all without me having to ask…'

'Please don't call me "my lady",' Katherine said, sinking wearily onto the dressing table stool. 'I am glad you are en-joying yourself. Is John all right?'

'Oh, yes, my…Miss Katherine. A nice room to himself in the stable block and a lad at his beck and call.' She unpinned Katherine's hair, picked up a silver-backed hairbrush from the dressing table and began to brush out the brown curls in steady, soothing strokes.

Wearily Katherine closed her eyes and surrendered to the comfort of the nightly ritual. After a few minutes she reached up and unhooked her ear-bobs, eyes still closed. 'I'm fright-ened, Jenny.'

'Why?' The rhythm of the brushstrokes hesitated, then re-sumed. 'Because of his Grace? I'd be frightened of him and no mistake.'

'No, Jenny. Because Nicholas—Lord Seaton—does not want to annul our marriage.'

'Well, and why should he?' the maid queried stoutly, un-clasping Katherine's necklace and beginning to undo the but-tons down the back of her gown.

'He should because of all the reasons I have already told you,' Katherine said wearily. 'And he will not because this is now a matter of pride with him.' She stood up and stepped out of her gown, then sighed with relief as Jenny untied her stay laces. Finally draped in her negligee, she went to wash in the great bowl of steaming water on her washstand. 'This is such luxury—we must not get accustomed.'

'No, Miss Katherine.' Jenny sounded unconvinced as she shook out a nightgown and passed it to Katherine. It was the pretty, flimsy one she had worn that night in Newgate. Katherine opened her mouth to protest, then shut it again. If she was tired, then so must Jenny be. He maid did not need her megrims.

'Thank you, Jenny, now you run off to bed and try to get a good night's sleep.'

As the door closed behind the maid, Katherine eyed the glacial chamber. It seemed vast now she was alone, the light from the flickering branches of candles hardly reaching the frosted detail of the ceiling, the shadows in the corners moving unnervingly.

She climbed into bed, a difficult manoeuvre involving a footstool, and found herself sitting up against a bank of pillows.

'I am tired, that is all,' Katherine told herself, her voice echoing round the room. It seemed to be quite out of scale to her solitary figure, as though it belonged to a giantess who would return at any moment and claim it.

She should wriggle down and go to sleep, she knew. The effort of will seemed beyond her.

The clock that was somewhere on the landing outside struck, time passed, it struck again, and again. This was ridiculous, she was fixed there like a rabbit mesmerised by a stoat. Now she was so tired she knew she could not sleep, she seemed to have passed beyond exhaustion into some kind of dream state.

A book, that would help. Katherine threw back the covers and slid out of bed, jolting herself painfully as she forgot the height she was at. But the room revealed not a single item of reading matter. She knew where the library was—dare she go down and find a book?

Defiantly Katherine shrugged herself into a wrapper. Anything had to be better than sitting sleepless in this ice cavern of a bedchamber, and no one would be about at this time of night. Her slippers appeared to have vanished, so with chamber stick in one hand she opened the door and slipped out into the corridor.

It seemed she had much to learn about life in a ducal home. Candelabra stood lit at each turn of the corridor and she saw a soft-footed servant making his way methodically along them, trimming wicks. Presumably just in case his Grace or one of the household decide to take a night-time stroll. Katherine blew out her own candle and drifted silently along the tortuous way to the stairs in the wake of the footman. He continued on and she ran lightly down, only to freeze at the bottom at the sound of light snores. A pair of legs protruded from the deep cowled porter's chair by the front door, its occupant unstirring as she made her way across the hall and through the library door.

Even here there was a branch of candles on a side table by the fireplace and the fire itself was alight, banked up behind a wide brass screen. The great winged chairs on either side looked warm and inviting, the most homely sight she had seen since she set foot in the mansion.

Books were everywhere, filling the shelves, in piles on the floor and heaped on tables. She began to turn over one pile, delighted to find it consisted of novels, and recent ones at that. She took two at random, then went to curl up in the nearest wing chair, tucking her feet up under her with a little sigh of pleasure; books had always been a refuge when having to think about, and face, reality became too much.

Katherine flicked open the first book and found it was Scott's *Waverley*. Good, she had missed that last year. She leaned forward to set the other volume on the table next to the candlestick and almost dropped both in shock.

'Hello, Kat. Is the fire warm enough for you?'

It was Nick, leaning back in the shadowed depths of the other wing chair, enveloped in the dark folds of a silk dressing gown, a glass of brandy cupped in his hands.

'Oh! You... I had no idea you were here, that anyone was.' She swung her legs down and began to get to her feet. 'I am sorry, I will go.'

'No, sit down, please, Kat. I did not want to scare you away. What brought you down here? If the fire in your room has gone out, you only have to ring.'

'I wanted a book to read, that is all. And I would not dream of disturbing the staff at this hour of the night.'

Nick shrugged. 'Someone is always on duty.'

'It seems ridiculous, on the off chance that someone might want something at two in the morning—I am sorry, that was rude of me, of course his Grace must order his household as he sees fit. This is his home, your home.' Home sounded a hopelessly inadequate word for this place. 'Palace,' she corrected herself.

'Does it seem like one to you?' Nick sounded amused. 'I suppose I just think of it as normal. I was brought up here, played in the corridors, fought the suits of armour, climbed up the ivy. Fell off the ivy,' he added with a grin. 'And into the lake.'

'It is magnificent,' Katherine said. 'It is not that I do not appreciate it, just that tonight I needed somewhere cosy.'

Cosy, she chided herself. *What a ridiculous word to use.*

'Was our cell cosy?' Nick asked, the smile still in his voice.

'Our cell?' Katherine laughed. 'How wonderfully domestic that sounds. I should imagine no one has ever thought of a Newgate cell with any affection before.'

'Do you think of it with affection?' She was becoming used to the flickering firelight now, could see the lines of his face etched by the light and shadows.

'Yes,' she said, then caught herself, surprised. 'Yes,' she repeated slowly. 'It was so…safe. I was so frightened before—of the debt, of what Philip had done, of what was going to become of us.'

'Of me?'

'No, never of you. Never from the moment I saw you,' she said vehemently.

'Why ever not?' Nick twisted in his chair so he could look directly into her face. 'I must have looked terrifying.'

'Your eyes were not. And you are…big. That is reassuring. And I just felt that if anything threatened me you would stand in the way and whatever, whoever it was, would never get past you.' She sat back, alarmed at her own frankness.

'Then let me keep you safe!' He was on his feet in a swirl of rich, dark silk, the firelight glinting off his hair, raising red lights in it. He looked magnificent, angry, barbaric and Katherine's heart missed a beat. 'Forget this nonsense about an annulment and let this marriage stand.'

'No.' She stayed in her chair; it was too dangerous to get closer to that male energy, that powerful force. 'It would be wrong. I take marriage very seriously. I have the example of my parents to guide me and I will settle for nothing less than a love match and a marriage of equals.'

'You are a stubborn woman.' He came to a halt in front of her, silhouetted against the flame so she could not make out his face as she stared up. 'I could, so easily, ensure you could never get your annulment.'

'And you would never force me. We discovered that last night,' Katherine said, keeping her voice steady with an effort that hurt.

Nick threw himself down in his chair again and eyed her ominously. 'It seems we have a stalemate.'

'No, we have an agreement,' Katherine said. 'And in twenty-five days you are going to honour it.'

Silence. Then Nick let out a huff of frustrated breath. Katherine curled up more tightly in her chair and waited.

Eventually he said, 'Why could you not sleep? Are you worried about Father?'

'The Duke? Why, no, I like him.'

'You do?' His brows slanted up in surprise.

'Yes, of course. You are very like him. And Robert, of course, I like him too.'

'Then what is it?'

Katherine bit her lip. 'Oh, dear, this sounds so rude and ungrateful. But it is my bedchamber. It is so…so chilly.'

'Then we must have a fire rekindled, fetch you some warmer bedcoverings. Tomorrow I will have the sashes checked, there must be a draught—'

Terrified that he would ring for servants on the spot, Katherine stammered, 'No, it is not the temperature. Oh, this is so foolish of me.'

Nick was on his feet. 'Come along, let me see for myself.'

'But, Nick, we cannot walk about the house together at this time of night!' Katherine let herself be pulled to her feet because struggling did not appear to be of much use, but she quailed at the thought of being seen walking about the corridors at two in the morning in her nightclothes in company with her…with Nick.

'Why ever not?'

'But the servants!'

'Yes?' His eyebrows rose with all the unconscious arrogance of a marquis in his own home. 'You are my wife. Why should I not walk where I wish with you?'

He was already halfway to the door, her hand held firmly in his. 'And when they find out about the annulment? What then?'

'They will assume I am insane,' he said grimly, stepping out into the hall. 'Provided they keep that opinion to themselves, that is their privilege.'

The snores from the porter's chair ceased with a grunt, and a tousled grey head emerged around the edge, rapidly followed by a shaken-looking man in livery, scrambling to his feet. 'My lord!'

'Goodnight, Grimshaw,' Nick said cheerfully as they passed. 'Time for your rounds, I imagine.'

'Yes, my lord. Er, goodnight, my lady.'

Katherine found herself being towed remorselessly back to her own chamber. Nick threw the door open and walked around, touching a candle to the various branched candlesticks that stood on surfaces round the room. In the flickering light of perhaps thirty candles, the Lake Suite stood revealed in all its icy magnificence.

He rotated slowly on his heel, staring around him, then went to peer more closely at the painting of the virgin sacrifice. 'Hmm. A tactless choice of subject, one cannot but feel. I had forgotten this room—like being inside an ice sculpture is it not?'

'You think so too?' Katherine asked in surprise. 'I thought perhaps it was just that I am not used to grand apartments and was being foolish.'

'Well, I would not care to sleep in it if I had the choice.' Nick was striding around the room, snuffing out candles as he went. 'I will talk to Heron tomorrow.'

That was a relief, she could surely manage to sleep one night in this room, knowing she could move tomorrow. Nick blew out the last candle. 'Oh, now I have nothing to see me to bed,' she protested.

'You have me.' He bent, hooked on arm neatly under her knees and the next thing Katherine knew he was shouldering open her door and carrying her off down the corridor.

Chapter Sixteen

'Nick!'

'Shh, the servants will hear.' He was so obviously teasing her that Katherine gave a gasp of outrage before she found herself being set neatly on her feet just inside a room.

She stared round, instantly wary. It was a bedchamber, a dark, rich masculine room of simple lines and polished wood, heavy crimson hangings and comfortable, well-used furniture. A fire, almost down to the ashes, still fed a few flames in the hearth and one branch of candles stood on a dressing table, its light cast back by silver and cut glass.

'Cosy?' Nick asked, leaning back against the door panels.

'Comfortable. Very masculine. I like it. Is this your bedchamber?'

'It is.'

'I cannot possibly stay here. You know I cannot sleep with you, Nick.'

'You already have, once. If you mean that we cannot make love if you want an annulment, then that is quite correct. However, I have no intention of making love to you.' He paused, those dark eyes resting on her like a caress. 'Not tonight.'

Taken off balance, Katherine snapped, 'And why not, pray?' then blushed crimson.

'Because I do not enjoy making love to very sleepy and thoroughly argumentative women.' He was beginning to untie the sash of his dressing gown. Katherine was seized by a sudden terror that he was wearing nothing beneath it.

'And you have such a wide experience,' she commented bitterly. Thank heavens! He was wearing a perfectly respectable nightshirt.

'Now, Kat, get into bed and stop trying to provoke me into ungentlemanly bragging,' he said sanctimoniously. He began to snuff candles, leaving only the single light by the bed.

Reluctantly Katherine untied the knot of her wrapper and slipped out of it before scuttling into bed with more speed than dignity. She burrowed across to the furthest side and regarded Nick nervously over the edge of the sheet.

'Is that the same nightgown?' he enquired, lifting the bedclothes and getting in beside her.

'That I wore in Newgate? Yes.'

He made no comment, but his low hum of appreciation was as real as a touch. Katherine closed her eyes. 'Goodnight, Nicholas.'

'Goodnight, Kat.' He was smiling, she could hear it in his voice. She sensed by the sudden total darkness against her lids that the last candle was out and stiffened. Now he would touch her, hold her. The mattress shifted, the bedding over her moved, there were the sounds of someone making themselves comfortable, then only the faint sounds of the dying fire settling in the grate and Nick's steady breathing.

Katherine lay there, stiff with what she realised, in a burst of honesty, was disappointment. She expected him to have held her, cradled her in his arms as he had done in that prison cell. But he had had no choice in that narrow bed, she reasoned with herself: in this great four-poster there was room and to spare. Comforted by the sound of his breathing and the warmth of his nearness she turned on her side, pulled the sheets around her ears and slept.

Nick waited until the regular breathing on the far side of the bed settled down and then cautiously stretched, allowing his own breathing to resume its normal waking rhythm. This was an indulgence his peace of mind could ill afford, he told himself severely, then smiled as Kat murmured in her sleep.

So sweet, and so trusting, despite his error of judgment last night. He had sensed that her feelings towards him had changed subtly and that his advances would not be unwelcome; it seemed he was wrong. Her instincts were quite correct—he would never force her, never seduce her against her will. But how could he move that will, make her see that the course she was set on was madness?

He turned over cautiously, trampling on the urge to reach out and pull her soft, warm body against his so they curved together as they had in that prison bed.

He had kissed her three times now; each time had been different and each time she had answered him with an innocent passion that shook him to his core. She obviously had no idea of her own power to move him and that was powerfully erotic. Nick shifted uncomfortably and reminded himself that this purgatory was self-inflicted.

Why had he done it? Kat would have slept tonight in that chilly white bed, consoled with the thought of a new bedchamber the next night. But she would not have been comfortable, and he wanted to do whatever he could to make up to her for the situation she found herself in. Cautiously he turned over, moved closer to her until his body curled around hers without touching. She would not be cold tonight.

Katherine blinked awake and lay watching the play of sunlight over the crimson bed hangings. She was warm, comfortable, rested—and in the wrong bed. The source of the warmth, the long male body curled around hers, one arm flung over her waist, appeared oblivious of her wakening. Somehow she had to get out of bed without rousing Nick and make her way back to her own chamber without being seen by any of the servants. Which was easier thought than done, she realised. The route by which they had arrived here last night was a complete mystery to her.

Carefully she inched towards the side of the bed. Nick's arm slid over the fine lawn of her nightgown easily enough. Just another wriggle and she could lower his hand on to the mattress and slip out of bed. She reached round, took his hand and found her own held very firmly.

'Mmm?' Nick enquired, pulling her back so that she arrived in a tangle of bedclothes nose to nose with him. His eyes were shut. 'Mmm… You smell so good Kat.'

'Please let me go, I must go to my room.'

Nick opened his eyes slowly, regarding her from under relaxed, half-closed lids. 'Why?' One brow quirked. 'I thought you were a lie-abed, Kat—think of the trouble I had to get you awake and out of bed last time.'

'That was different,' she said slowly, trying to ignore the fact that when he spoke his breath tickled her nose, he was so close. 'I did not want the morning to come; there was too much reality to face.' There still was, but at least this reality was not life and death. She hesitated, then, 'Nick, I know your father will have much he wants to discuss with you, and you will have many duties, but please, I must talk to you.'

'We are talking,' he pointed out, obviously intent on teasing.

'A *serious* talk. Out of bed. Dressed.' He smiled and she found herself staring at the flecks of gold she had never noticed before in his eyes. 'This is very distracting,' she complained.

'Good.' Nick leaned forward and kissed her lightly on the lips. 'You think altogether too much. Stop managing, Kat, and relax.'

Kat jerked back as if he had bitten her. 'You said you wouldn't make love to me!' She scrambled backwards and out of bed.

'I said I wouldn't last night. And that was simply a good morning kiss for my wife: perfectly chaste.' He hauled himself up against the pillows and regarded her silently until she began to fidget with embarrassment.

'What is it?'

'I was thinking that for once I agree with my father. He remarked that you make a most unusual Marchioness—'

'Well, of course I do!' Katherine broke in before he could finish. 'His Grace is quite amazingly forbearing not to add impossible, ineligible and utterly unsuitable to that description! If you would only stop teasing me for just one minute, you would realise what a totally impossible position I am in unless you agree to this annulment.

'Why did you not tell me, Nick? Why did you let me come here without telling me that your father was a duke? How can I trust you?'

She threw on her wrapper, wrenched open the door and ran down the corridor before Nick could untangle himself from the bedclothes and get out of bed.

A door started to open as she rounded a corner; Katherine skittered past it and round another bend before whoever it was emerged, and subsided panting on a window seat to scan the view. No sign of the lake, so she was not even on the correct side of the house, although she did seem to be on the right floor.

Her wrapper was not fastened. Katherine drew it close, tied the cord and walked briskly down the corridor again. Surely if she kept going long enough she would eventually see the lake from the windows? She walked on, round another corner—still only endless parkland, no hint of water. With a little sob of frustration Katherine broke into a run again. The corridor narrowed and began to curve: she must be in one of the turrets. She was just racking her brains to recall how many there were and on which façade when a door opened and she collided hard with a tall figure in riding dress: gloves, whip and hat in one hand.

'Your Grace!' Katherine fought back the instinctive curtsy. It would look ridiculous to curtsy wearing night attire. 'I am…I got…lost,' she finished lamely.

'Good morning, Katherine, you are a very early riser.' Not by a flicker of an eyelash did he betray any surprise that his daughter-in-law should be running along the corridor *en negligée*. 'I was just going for my morning ride before breakfast. Neither of my sons could ever be persuaded to join me at this hour, perhaps one morning you would care to. Ah, no, I forget, you do not ride yet, do you?'

'No, your Grace. Your Grace…'

'You want the way back to your room? Of course, this way.' He offered her his arm and began to stroll back the way she had come, through a door she had missed in the white panelling and into the Long Gallery. Katherine was convinced that every portrait figure in the room swivelled in their frame to regard this hoyden with horrified condemnation.

'I know the way from here, your Grace, please, do not let me keep you from your ride any longer.' She freed her hand, shot him a tentative smile and hastened down the endless room, her knees knocking.

'I will see you at breakfast, Katherine,' he called after her, but when she turned he had gone.

She arrived at her bedchamber door at the same moment as Jenny, who was carrying a cup of chocolate. The maid's eyes opened wide with surprise, then her face broke into a broad smile. 'You spent the night with the master! Oh, Miss Katherine, that's wonderful, I knew it would be all right.'

'Oh, shh!' Katherine bundled Jenny through the door and shut it with a thud behind them. 'It wasn't like that at all.' She took the cup of chocolate and began to sip thirstily as she recounted the story.

'The Duke? Oh, my goodness.' Jenny stared, horrified. 'What did he say?'

'He behaved as though we had met in the middle of the morning and I was fully dressed. Goodness knows what he must think of me, not that it could be much worse than what he doubtless thinks already.' She put down the cup and cupped her chin in her hand, gazing blankly across the room.

'But he is so polite to you,' Jenny pointed out.

'It is part of his style to be imperturbable, I think. And very courteous. And I suppose he does not care to show me the door after learning that I had saved Nick from hanging.' The two regarded each other miserably, then Katherine shook herself, got to her feet and announced, 'Ring for hot water, Jenny. I am going to get dressed, be on my best behaviour—and do my utmost to make Nick see reason today.'

There was a peremptory knock on the door. 'Please see who that is, Jenny.'

The voice made it quite clear. Jenny pushed the door to. 'Lord Seaton, Miss Katherine.'

'Please tell his lordship,' she said, making sure her voice carried clearly, 'that I will see him at breakfast.'

'Yes, Miss Katherine. My lord…'

'I heard, thank you.' Nick sounded furious. Katherine suddenly found the humour in the situation. He must have imagined her lost goodness knows where in this great pile and had set out to rescue her. Unfortunately for him, she did not need rescuing.

Katherine made a leisurely *toilette*, paying particular attention to her hair and her choice of a gown. She felt she should spare the Duke any further shocks to his system that morning. She also felt, but would not admit to herself, that looking as elegant as possible would disconcert Nick.

His Grace was just entering the breakfast room as she approached the door and his two sons were already there, engaged in what sounded like a vigorous argument. 'If you do not tell him, I will,' Nick was saying.

'Good morning. Ah, Katherine, good morning my dear. Will you not sit here, and perhaps be so good as to take charge of the coffee pot? And who, might I ask, is the person apparently being kept in the dark?'

Robert shot a darkling look at his brother and said, 'I had something I wished to discuss with you, sir, but it can wait. Should wait.'

Nick sat back in his chair. 'Robert desires to tell you, Father, that he wishes to read for the church, but he perceives that my own domestic…difficulties might create too much of a stir to raise the matter at present.'

'Damn it, Nick! I am sorry, Katherine. Yes, Father, I would wish to enter the church, but this hardly seems the moment.'

'I cannot say I am surprised.' The Duke smiled at Katherine, who was handing him a cup of coffee. 'What do you think, my dear?'

Startled to be asked her opinion, she said honestly, 'I believe Lord Robert would go far in the church, your Grace.'

'You had better speak to the Bishop, Robert.' The look he sent his younger son held, to Katherine's hopeful eye, a faint hint of approval. 'We will talk about it later.' He swivelled to look at Nick. 'And what are your plans?'

'For today? To speak to Wilkinson to establish exactly how my affairs stand and then to ride over to the Dower House with Katherine to discover if it meets with her approval.'

'You are set on that as a residence, then?'

'With your permission, sir.'

The duke gestured with an elegantly long-fingered hand. 'It is at your disposal. As you know, it always reverts to the heir when it is not required by the dowager of the day.'

Katherine tried to catch Nick's eye. Had he forgotten that she had told him she could not ride? She had no habit either.

'Philpott.'

The footman went to Nick's side, received a low-voiced instruction and went out. Katherine mused for a moment on the resources that could muster so many footmen, all over the desirable six foot in height, then decided that the thought of so much money made her dizzy.

She found her husband was looking at her and mouthed, 'I cannot ride.' He merely smiled and mouthed back, 'Time you learned.' Katherine picked thoughtfully at her ham, not at all certain she wanted to be any closer to a horse than the interior of a carriage. They were large and she suspected she would be quite unable to convince one to do anything she wanted. Then she realised she had no riding habit, there were no other ladies in the house to borrow one from, and so she was safe. A small smile curled her lips; his lordship had not considered that little detail.

She poured more coffee, found she had an appetite for her breakfast after all and decided to slip away afterwards to a sunny window seat in the Long Gallery, which had the double advantage of being somewhere she could find her way to, and removing her from her husband's disturbing proximity so she could try and think what to do when she had left Seaton Mandeville.

But when Nick rose, he stopped beside her chair. 'Have you finished?'

'Yes, thank you, but please do not trouble about me, I will be perfectly all right.'

'But we must talk to Mr Wilkinson,' Nick said, still waiting.

Kat bit her lip and regarded him cautiously. Why should he want her to meet Mr Wilkinson, who, if she remembered, was his grace's Steward and man of business? She studied his face for signs of the anger she had heard in his voice earlier, but he appeared quite sanguine. One could not, of course, make a fuss with the Duke within earshot, calmly eating his toast.

She stood up, smiling at the two men who rose courteously, and allowed Nick to usher her out.

'Why do I need to speak to Mr Wilkinson?' she hissed as they made their way along yet another corridor, this one panelled in handsome oak wainscoting. There were too many servants about to allow for a proper, blazing, argument, which is what she was longing for.

'Because he has information you will wish to hear.' Nick paused before a door and opened it. 'Wilkinson, good morning. My dear, may I introduce Mr Tobias Wilkinson, who has been our steward and much else here for many years. Wilkinson, the new marchioness of Seaton.'

The steward was tall, thin, slightly stooping and of indeterminate age. Sixty, Katherine guessed, liking the quiet humour in his eyes and the genuineness of his smile as he shook hands.

'Many felicitations, my lord! And, Lady Seaton, may I wish you every happiness in your new estate.'

Katherine responded appropriately and sat where Nick showed her, prepared for a boring wait while he discussed business.

'I have summarised how your affairs stand, my lord.' Wilkinson passed over two sheets of foolscap and folded his hands together on the table while Nick read.

Katherine watched as Nick's eyebrows rose and his lips pursed in a soundless whistle. 'You have done well by me these past years, Tobias, I can only thank you for your care and diligence.'

The other man smiled modestly. 'If I may say so, my lord, achieving a good return on investment is always easier if the principal is not in a position to spend the capital.'

Nick gave a snort of laughter. 'Not spending it on gambling, women and racehorses, I assume you mean? No, do not answer that. We will talk over detail later. Meanwhile, have you been able to deal with that other matter?'

'Yes, my lord, I have sent details of the loan to our London agent with instructions to pay both the principal and the interest in full.'

That was her debt paid; Katherine tried to catch Nick's eye, but he was attending to the steward. How did she feel about it? Part of her was distressed and embarrassed that Nick had been put in a position where he felt he must pay it, part was relieved that the interest was no longer accumulating. Now all she had to do was to convince Nick that she should repay him. Not an easy task, she acknowledged ruefully, forcing herself to listen to Mr Wilkinson again.

'And the other bills and dunning letters I sent as a summary to the agent, asking him to settle those as well, with all speed.'

Katherine was aware of Nick's sudden movement, swiftly suppressed, and saw from the arrested expression on the steward's face that this was a subject not intended to be discussed in her presence. For a moment she was puzzled, then light dawned. *Nick had paid Philip's debts as well.* She had left them behind in London, knowing she could never hope to pay them and feeling that, finally, her brother must acknowledge his own responsibilities. Nick must have taken them, brought them with him to Northumberland.

Why? she puzzled, ignoring Mr Wilkinson's rapid change of subject. Then, with a wave of shame, she realised. Philip was Nick's brother-in-law now; he must have decided that no connection of the Lydgates must be in a position to be publicly exposed for his debts.

She could say nothing here, not in front of the steward. Feeling sick, she forced her attention back to the conversation between the men.

'...the Settlements,' Mr Wilkinson was saying. 'I have drawn up something based on the usual provisions—widowhood, remarriage, children and so forth. If you would care to scrutinise it, my lord, and make any notes of changes you wish made, I will have it notarised as soon as possible.'

Katherine opened her mouth, realised this was another argument it was impossible to have before an audience and shut it with a snap. *Children!* The thought of Nick's children made her feel slightly dizzy. There was nothing, other than hearing him tell her he loved her, that she wanted more, she realised. And all she had to do was to stop protesting, give in and allow the marriage to stand.

Chapter Seventeen

'And her ladyship's allowance,' Mr Wilkinson continued, unaware that one of his audience was fighting a battle with her conscience just the other side of his desk. 'I have made arrangements with Coutt's bank as you directed, my lord. I have a portion of the first quarter here, my lady, and I have put in a note with details of how you may draw on the balance at your convenience.' He handed a fat packet to Katherine, who took it with an automatic murmur of thanks.

Conscience won. Katherine pushed the thought of children with Nick's eyes out of her mind with a pang and thought about the money instead. Another debt. Her instinct was to hand it back to Nick the moment they were alone. Common sense told her that she must pay Jenny and John and that was more important than her pride. She must buy some clothes for the time she was here, for she could not fail to present a seemly appearance in a ducal household. And when she left she must leave vails for the servants. None of this common sense made the slightest difference to the way she was feeling. Katherine realised she was angry, but who with—herself, Philip or Nick—she could not analyse.

Finally Nick was standing, thanking the steward again, holding the door for her. Katherine said all that was proper, managed a pleasant smile and swept out into the passage. The moment the door closed behind them she rounded on Nick.

'You have paid Phil's debts! How could you do such a thing?' Her voice broke and she fought to get a grip on her feelings. 'And a settlement! The marriage is going to be annulled—why is there a settlement?'

'We cannot speak out here.' Nick took her arm and guided her through a door into an empty room, which appeared to be part of the estate office, for stacks of dusty ledgers stood on the tables and shelves of dockets and bundles of papers lined the walls.

'I had not intended telling you about your brother's debts yet,' he admitted.

'Indeed?' Katherine managed to instil a certain icy quality into her voice. 'Did you ever intend telling me?' He opened his mouth to speak and she swept on, 'I know why you feel you must pay them, of course: the embarrassment of a debtor as a brother-in-law. Please do not think I do not understand. Do you think I am not as ashamed of it as you, to know that I risk bringing scandal to a household such as this?' Her anger began to fail her and her voice shook. 'I think that perhaps I could have borne anything, even his deceit over the loan, better than the humiliation of this.'

Nick stared at her, his face appalled. 'Kat, never say that. Sweetheart…' Then she was held against his chest and he was stroking her hair. 'Kat, think. He does not know who you married—no one in London knows my true identity. I have no need to protect the family against the small scandal he might evoke, even when the connection is known. For goodness' sake, Cousin Hereward has been in debtors' prison three times, my great-uncle believes himself to be the Tsar of all the Russias, and I have earned my bread playing cards and taken the King's shilling as an outcast. And that is just a sample of our family scandals. Your brother's foolishness is nothing against that.'

It was seductively pleasant to be held by strong arms against a broad chest and to be reassured. Katherine tried to tell herself that under the circumstances anyone offering comfort would be welcome but she could not deceive herself. This was the man she loved holding her, resting his cheek against her hair, gently stroking the nape of her neck. All she wanted was to turn up her face to his, to kiss and be kissed.

Resolutely she disentangled herself from his arms and moved away. 'What is a scandal in a family of lower degree is merely eccentricity in a ducal household, I understand that,' she pointed out. 'But I feel so ashamed.'

'But why? To be angry and disappointed with him, that I can understand, but to be ashamed?'

'I am his elder sister,' Katherine said helplessly, recalling the hours she had spent agonising over how to help Philip break away from his self-indulgence, make him face up to reality and his obligations. 'I should have been able to influence him for good.'

'Impossible,' Nick said firmly. 'Nothing you could have said or done would have helped. An elder brother might have been able to steer him right.' He stopped abruptly and Katherine saw his eyes darken. 'I should have been here for Robert; it is my good fortune that he has a goodness of character I never had.'

Arguing against that was not going to help, Katherine saw quite clearly. Nick was going to have to deal with his guilt at staying away so long in his own way. 'He had your father,' she said encouragingly.

'Er, yes.' Nick grinned. 'Fortunately Robert appears to

have exhibited none of the tendencies that would cause our father to deal with him as he did me.'

'Do you mind very much?' she asked, distracted from her own preoccupations.

'No, if you mean do I resent it. I was hot at hand, thoroughly wild, thought I was in love—which, coming on top of a fairly convincing showing as a rakehell, must have seemed highly improbable. Father, not unreasonably, put his foot down and I was in no mood to accept it.' He shrugged. 'It was an interesting six years. Now, shall we go riding?'

'Not until you explain these settlements,' Katherine said firmly, planting herself between Nick and the door.

'Well, Wilkinson will explain them better than I—'

'I do not mean that and you know it, Nick! Why have you settled anything on me when we are getting the marriage annulled?'

'*We* are doing no such thing. *You* may be if I cannot persuade you otherwise. And what would happen if I fell off my horse and broke my neck?'

'Exactly what would have happened if you had fallen off a scaffold and broken it,' Katherine said crisply. 'I will go and earn my own way in the world.' She regarded his rueful expression and fought against letting her feelings show on her face. 'But I suppose I need the pin money at the moment, so I will simply add the allowance to the amount I already owe you.'

She expected a fight the moment she mentioned repayment, but her infuriating husband merely nodded amiably and reached round her to open the door. 'I think, if you come with me, you will find that your new bedchamber is ready and that you will be able to change so we can have your first riding lesson.'

Katherine meekly allowed herself to be shown the way to

her new rooms, refraining from pointing out her lack of suitable garments. She tried to pay careful attention to the route. Some paintings and a large Chinese vase looked familiar. 'Is this near your rooms?'

'Yes, Kat, next door.'

Her gasp was cut off as he flung open a panelled door and let her step through. 'Less modern than the lakeside wing where you were before; this is an older part of the house and you should be more comfortable here until we can move into the Dower House.'

Restrained by the discovery that not only Jenny but another maid were in the room, Katherine could not retort that neither sleeping next door to him nor the prospect of moving into the Dower House made her feel the slightest bit comfortable.

Both young women were sitting on the bed, a garment with long flowing skirts spread out between them. The unknown maid was industriously whipping stitches along the hem and Jenny was just biting off her cotton, having done something to the waist.

They both jumped to their feet and Jenny said, 'I think it will be a very tolerable fit, my lord, now we have taken the skirt up an inch and narrowed the waist.'

Not only was a very handsome riding habit being shaken out before her eyes, but a pair of boots and a dashing veiled tricorne hat were also on display.

'And where did these come from?' Katherine enquired dangerously.

'Cousin Augusta. I thought there was sure to be something somewhere in the house, but I did not expect anything quite so *à la mode*.' Nick flicked the intricate frogging with one finger. 'Gussie apparently had this made, convinced that, even after presenting Lord Pickforth with a *petit pacquet* six months ago, she would still retain exactly the same waist measurement. Apparently this was not the case and she discarded it while visiting last month. The boots might be a little large, but nothing to worry about. I will see you in the front hall in an hour.'

It was tempting to pick up the boots and throw them at his retreating back. Instead Katherine smiled pleasantly at the maid. 'I am sorry, I do not yet know your name.'

'Eliza, my lady.'

'Well, thank you, Eliza, it seems that you and Jenny have done an excellent job. You may go now.'

The minute the girl had shut the door behind her Katherine swept across the room, tossed the tricorne off the dressing table stool on to the bed and sat down with a thump. 'Oh...*bother* the man!'

'Who, Miss Katherine?' Jenny caught Katherine's smouldering eye. 'Ah, the master.'

'Everything I want to do he forestalls and everything I don't want him to do he just goes ahead and does,' Katherine grumbled. 'He has paid my debt, and Philip's debts and given me an allowance. At least I can pay you and John. And now he says I must learn to ride, if you please.'

'That'll be nice, Miss Katherine,' Jenny said, a quaver of what sounded suspiciously like laughter in her voice. 'You'll see John then, I expect he's down at the stables.'

Katherine allowed herself to be buttoned into the habit, which, although a little large over the bust, was a tolerable fit. It was certainly a flattering colour. The boots, as Nick had predicted, were slightly large, but the hat was delightful. Jenny bundled her hair into a coarse net at the nape, set the tricorne at a rakish angle, secured it with a large pin and lowered the veil.

Katherine stood up and practised walking up and down with the long skirt looped over her arm. 'Cousin Augusta,

whoever she is, certainly has excellent taste.' She was looking forward to discovering what Nick thought of this fine outfit; it was almost enough to distract her from thinking about
having to get on to a horse.

He was certainly appreciative as she walked down the
great staircase. 'You look very dashing, Kat.' He walked
round her, studying the effect, which made her blush. 'Come
along and meet your new mount.'

The stable block was magnificent with carriage houses,
rows of loose boxes, its own farrier's shop and numerous
open doors through which Katherine could glimpse racks of
saddles and bales of hay. Horses were standing looking over
the doors of many of the boxes and Nick stopped at one of
them.

'My father's new bay hunter, if I'm not mistaken.'

'Aye, my lord, and his Grace's pride and joy,' the groom
who was just sliding the bolt across the door confirmed.

'He always had a good eye for a horse.' Nick leaned on the
door for a moment, running his eye over the animal. 'What
have you got for me and her ladyship, Durren?'

'Lightning for her ladyship.' Katherine swallowed hard.
'Her ladyship's man is saddling him up. His Grace thought
you might like to try Xerxes, my lord. He's a bit of a handful.' He nodded towards a large grey in the middle of the yard,
which was attempting to bite the unfortunate stable lad who
was holding him. 'He likes to see how far he can go with a
rider,' he added laconically.

'Hmm.' Nick eyed the animal, who was now rolling his
eyes and lashing out with his hind legs at the stable cat who
was crossing the yard. 'I see his Grace has not lost his sense
of humour. This looks like your mount, Kat.'

John was leading out a middling-sized blue roan, which,

much to her relief, appeared to be content to follow him placidly. 'John!'

'Miss Katherine—your ladyship, I should say.' He waited until she reached his side, then added quietly, 'You all right, Miss Katherine? Jenny says you're in clover, but I wanted to ask you myself.'

'I am fine, at least for a week or two. How are you? Have they given you a comfortable room? And I have your wages at last.'

'I'm suited fine, don't you be worrying about me. Now, what's all this about you learning to ride?'

'His lordship is set on teaching me, so I thought it churlish to refuse.'

'You'll be all right with this beast, then.' John slapped the roan on its neck. 'It's like a sofa with legs.'

'Good,' Katherine breathed, then followed John's gaze to where Nick had mounted the grey, which was doing its level best to unseat him. 'He's a good rider, isn't he, John?'

'That's an understatement,' the groom agreed. 'Bloody hell... sorry, Miss Katherine, but did you see what that brute just tried?' They watched in silence until the grey subsided and stood, its neck flecked with sweat, its ears flicking back to listen to what Nick was saying to it.

This appeared to be a lively description of its habits and character, delivered in a style that had the audience of grooms cackling in appreciation. Katherine closed her ears firmly to the several choice adjectives that her husband was employing and waited patiently. Hopefully he would feel he had had sufficient challenges for the day and would decide against teaching her to ride. But no. Nick swung down, tossed the reins back to the reluctant stable boy and walked over.

'John.'

'My lord.'

'Will you have a word with Durren and get me something else saddled up? That's not a safe animal to take out with her ladyship.' He watched the groom make his way across the yard and remarked, 'Good man, that. Now, then, we'll get you up.'

Katherine managed a bright smile. 'How?'

'I'll give you a leg up. Now, stand like this, and hold the reins like that...' He patiently sorted the reins out for her, then cupped his hands. 'Right foot in here. One, two, three, up.'

Katherine found herself seated sideways on a moving, slippery surface. 'Now, then, you put this foot in the stirrup. Hold on, just let me lengthen it a little.' Competent hands moved against her leg, doing something, then her foot was pushed into a stirrup. 'Now, the other leg goes here, over one pommel and under the other. Yes, like that. Now shift so you are sitting square on the saddle: from the back it ought to look as though you could have a leg on each side.'

How she was remaining on top of the horse and not on her back on the cobbles Katherine had no idea. The horse was moving, just a little, but enough to make her feel quite unsettled; the saddle was slippery under the folds of cloth and the position Nick's hands were turning her into felt completely unnatural.

'Is the habit smooth between you and the saddle? It will be uncomfortable otherwise. Just stand in the stirrup and let me tug at the skirt. Good.' He broke off and looked at her face. 'Kat, what is it? You are stiff as a board. Is it that I am touching you? I'm sorry, I did not mean to put you to the blush, only it is very difficult to explain without doing so.'

'No, not that. Oh!' The horse shifted, apparently taking the weight off one hind leg and Katherine lurched. Nick grabbed her and thumped the horse, which straightened up with an affronted snort. 'It is so high up,' she finished lamely.

'High up? We've got beds that are higher up than this.' Realisation dawned and Katherine saw his face relax into rueful apology. 'Kat, are you scared of horses?'

'Yes. I am very sorry.'

'Why did you not say?'

'I thought you would think me very feeble.' If only he
would stop looking like that: so understanding and gentle
and...

'I know how brave you are, Kat, I would never think you
feeble. Would you like to get down now and I will have a carriage put to instead?'

Suddenly that was the last thing she wanted. 'No. Not if
you think I can do this.'

'Very well. Now sit up straight, hold the reins as I showed
you, keep your heel down and off we go.' He was leading the
horse around the yard. Katherine held her breath, but it did
not break into a gallop, rear, buck or do anything that the grey
had done. In fact, it plodded. 'Good. You see? Quite safe. Now
just wait there and I'll see what Durren has found for me.'
Nick let go of the bridle and strode off to where the head
groom was waiting with a leggy black gelding.

Katherine gave a squeak of alarm, but the misnamed Lightning merely stood where he had been left.

'Lift your hands a little,' Nick said, bringing the black up
alongside. 'Just so you can feel his mouth and he knows you
are in charge.' He spoke without any apparent irony. 'Then
press your heel back into his flank and say "walk on".'

Convinced that the horse was about to bolt, Katherine tentatively did as she was told and to her amazement the roan
began to walk sedately forward. 'Oh,' she said, pleased, then
'Oh!' as she began to slip sideways.

'Press down in the stirrup, sit up straight—there, good
girl!'

They walked out of the yard and down the carriage drive, Nick maintaining a steady flow of reassuring comment and instruction. Katherine had expected him to be demanding, perhaps critical of her lack of skill, but his good-humoured encouragement reminded her of the way he had dealt with her in the prison cell.

She risked looking at him and met his eyes. He was smiling and it suddenly seemed the most natural thing in the world to smile back.

'Enjoying yourself, Kat?'

'Why, yes,' she admitted, surprised. 'I thought I would be terrified—for the three seconds it took me to fall off. We are not going to go any faster, are we?'

'Not unless you want to,' Nick said.

'Doesn't your horse want to?' Katherine eyed the twitching ears and the playful sidle the black kept employing.

'He wants to gallop and it will do him good to learn to walk when he's told to.'

Just how Nick was managing to stop the animal taking off and doing exactly what it wanted seemed a mystery. Katherine watched him, seeing the almost invisible shifts of leg, tightening of thigh muscle, movements of long fingers that appeared to work this magic. 'Did you ride in the army?' she asked, greatly daring.

'Yes.' He seemed to think better of his abruptness and added, 'Yes, I was a trooper. You get all sorts to ride. On a battlefield you can pick up some good beasts whose owners have no further use for them.'

Katherine shivered. 'And you rode at Waterloo?'

'Yes.' This time he showed no inclination to expand on that curt response.

'Your father will be very proud when he learns you fought there,' Katherine ventured.

'We have not discussed it. I mentioned it in passing, that is all.' Nick's voice was quite dispassionate, but his body betrayed him. The black tossed its head and broke into a trot for a few strides before its rider could rein back. Obediently the roan started to trot too. Katherine grabbed for the pommel, the mane, her reins, missed them all and found herself tumbling over the horse's shoulder. It seemed a very long way down, and the ground, when she met it, much harder than she could have imagined.

'Ough!' she gasped inelegantly.

'Well done!' Nick had swung down and was kneeling beside her, helping her to sit up.

Katherine took a painful whoop of breath. 'Well done?'

'You are still holding the reins. That is very important.'

'It is?'

'Of course. You don't want to fall off miles from home and see your horse vanishing into the next county. Now, just wriggle everything, make sure nothing is strained—'

He broke off. Katherine found herself supported against his knee. Nick had one arm around her shoulders, the other was resting on her ankle. She was cradled in such a way that their faces were very close, close enough for her to see the gold flecks in his eyes, the sweep of his lashes, the scar over his eye, the way his pupils contracted seconds before his mouth covered hers.

The kiss was leisurely, exploratory, quite undemanding. Katherine was well aware that she only had to move away and to push against his chest for him to stop. But she did not want this to stop. She summoned all her small experience and kissed him back, fighting to keep herself from betraying everything she felt for him with the pressure of her mouth, the way her fingers moved restlessly through his hair. With a sigh she closed her fists on the linen of his shirt and surrendered to the heat that his knowing mouth was evoking.

How long that sensuous caress would have gone on she had no idea. She had not the slightest idea how long it had already lasted when a wet, warm, soft muzzle pushed firmly against her ear.

Chapter Eighteen

'Ahh!' Katherine struggled to sit up from what had become a shockingly prone position on the grass and met the reproachful eye of her mount.

Nick rocked back on his heels and began to laugh. 'I have never,' he managed between gasps of mirth, 'never, been chaperoned by a horse before. I have, however, seen uglier chaperons.'

Katherine found herself giving way to giggles. 'He looks so shocked,' she managed to gasp, hugging her sides. Lightning gave her a disgusted look and began to crop the grass, apparently resigned to the stupidity of humans. She looked around her, finding that they were close to the lake and that tall red chimneys were rising over a small copse ahead of them.

'Is that the Dower House?'

'Yes. Kat, you wanted to talk, this is probably as private as we can be.'

'What I really want to do,' she said warmly, 'is box your ears for deceiving me so! How could you not tell me you were a marquis, that your father was a duke?'

'In Newgate? Would you have believed me?' Nick sat up

and clasped his arms round his knees. 'This view—I would dream of it sometimes, when I actually managed to sleep.'

'Of course I would not have believed you then.'

'I did tell you my real name, you could have looked it up.'

'Naturally, that should have occurred to me,' Katherine said with sarcasm. 'I meet a highwayman and should immediately assume it would be sensible to check on his parentage and titles.' She picked a daisy, slit its stem with her fingernail and plucked another to thread through it. 'You should have told me afterwards, when you were free.'

'Would you have believed me?' He was watching her, not the view.

'Yes, of course.'

'And what would you have done?'

'Refused to come with you, naturally.'

'You make my point for me.' Nick unclasped his arms and fell back on the grass with a deep sigh. 'Bliss. The last time I lay on my back in a field I had just had my second horse shot from under me and I was lying in a pool of mud.'

'Waterloo? Was it dreadful? I'm sorry, that is a stupid question, of course it was.'

'It was perfectly bloody. Literally bloody. It is not easy to speak about. Kat, you're the only person I have ever talked about it with.' He fell silent.

'Any time you want to tell me more, I will listen,' she promised. They remained without speaking for a while. Katherine threaded more daisies and, finally satisfied with the length of her chain, linked it into a circle and leaned over to drop it on Nick's dark head.

'What?' He opened his eyes and reached up to feel what she had done. 'Baggage. I suppose if I had not realised, you would have let me put my hat on top and ridden off.'

'Possibly. Nick, how did you know how I would react

when I discovered the truth about you? I might have had hysterics on the spot.'

'No, not you. I knew you would be angry with me—you had every reason, even though I did it for the best. You would never have left London with me if you had known. I expected you to give my head a washing the moment we were alone, but I had every confidence that you would deal with a duke with every bit of the courage and aplomb you showed in dealing with a highwayman.'

'I was too tired, too overawed to do more than accept what was happening, I suppose.' She tucked his praise away into some secret part of her mind to take out and look at later. 'And between you, you and your father made sure I spent much more time with Robert than with you. It is too late now to shout at you and throw the china.' She began a second daisy chain. 'I like you brother very much.'

'Father remarked that when you are no longer married to me you could marry Robert.'

'What!' The fragile links of flowers tore in her hands. 'Marry *Robert*?'

'I believe he was trying to pique my jealousy.'

'Oh.' Katherine subsided, too shaken by the very thought to absorb the implications of what Nick had said. To think of marrying anyone, anyone at all, after Nick was impossible. How could she when she loved him so much and always would? Then her mind caught up with her hearing. 'Jealous? Why should your father believe that suggestion would make you jealous?'

Nick shrugged. 'He likes to tease us, to pink us neatly with the point of his wit and watch us dance a little. He very rightly assumes that I do not relish being reminded that my wife does not wish to remain my wife and that I am frustrated in my efforts to provide for her.'

Yes, not jealousy so much as pride, she realised. Possessiveness and the rivalry that must always exist between healthy young males, even when they are devoted brothers.

'I am growing very fond of Robert,' she said primly. 'But as a brother. I would as soon marry the Duke as him.'

As she had intended, this provoked a gasp of laughter from Nick. 'Now that would create some talk! A May and December match indeed. You are teasing me, wife; I suspect my father is a very bad influence on you.' He got to his feet with the elegance that characterised his movements and held out a hand to her. 'Stop sitting on that grass, which is doubtless damp, and come and tell me what you think of the Dower House.'

Katherine waited to see if he would remember the daisy chain. He did, hooking it out of his dark hair and holding it dangling from his fingers for a thoughtful moment. 'I should be giving you jewels, Kat.'

'No, you should not,' she retorted, gathering up Lightning's reins and concentrating on holding them as he had shown her. 'I do not want to be indebted to you for anything more than I can possibly help.'

Nick boosted her up into the saddle, checked her seat was secure and went to mount the black gelding. 'I know. I do wish you would let me look after you Kat.'

'You are doing so, very well. At least,' she added doubtfully as Lightning pricked up his ears and started to take more of an interest in the open parkland in front of them, 'at least you will be if you can stop this animal going any faster than a slow crawl.'

'You just have to show him who is in charge,' Nick said encouragingly.

'That is the trouble, he knows.'

Nick laughed at her gloomy tone. 'Never mind your fierce steed, what do you think of that?'

That was a perfect little gem of a house, all soft grey stone and sparkling windows, nestling in a fold in the hillside, protected by a grove of trees and with its own miniature lake reflecting it back to itself.

'Oh, Nick, it is enchanting!'

'I think so,' he agreed gravely. 'I am glad you like it. Wait until you see the inside.'

'Are there staff in residence?' There was no smoke rising from the tall chimneys.

'No, I sent to have it opened up this morning, but it is completely unoccupied now.'

Katherine stared as they approached, trying to absorb every detail. Something about the little house tugged at her. Was it just that Nick was so obviously in love with it?

He halted in front of the portico and swung down from the saddle, looped his horse's reins over the railings and came to lift her down.

Katherine slid out of the saddle as his hands clasped her waist. She expected to be set on her feet, but, instead, no sooner had her boots met gravel than he swung her round and into his arms.

'Nick! What on earth are you doing?'

He strode up the two shallow steps to the front door and applied a shoulder to the panels. It opened smoothly on to a sunny hall with a gracious staircase winding upwards and dove grey and white tiles on the floor.

'Nick?' He was holding her very tightly. Katherine considered wriggling, then decided it was undignified. The fact that being held like this gave her a delicious sense of danger, of being mastered, she fought to ignore.

'I am carrying my wife over the threshold; a good old English custom that I fear would have caused an uproar if I had attempted it at the House. And, in any case, this is my home.'

'Yes, but we are over the threshold now,' Katherine felt compelled to point out.

Nick simply ignored this observation and strode across the marble and up the staircase. Any gently bred young lady should be protesting at this point, remonstrating with the gentleman and, if necessary, struggling; Katherine was quite well aware of that. On the other hand, any young lady who did not revel in the fact that the strong arms of the man she loved were carrying her as if she was as light as a feather was devoid of all romance. Beside, to struggle on the stairs was an unsafe thing to do.

He would stop and put her down on the landing, she told herself, only to gasp as Nick simply pushed open another door and walked into a bedchamber. It was deliciously, sensuously feminine, a confection of amber silk and cream lace, warm old panelling and pretty furniture apparently gathered together with an eye to comfort and charm, not formality and status.

Nick lowered his burden reluctantly until Kat stood in the circle of his arm, gazing round at the room.

'I thought—' He broke off, surprised to find his voice husky when he had imagined it had recovered. 'I thought you would like this as your bedchamber.'

'Oh.' What was she feeling? Her eyes were wide, the pansy-brown depths of them reflecting back the amber light. She moved back against him as she half-turned to look around her, the unexpected contact affecting him as even the feel of her in his arms just now had not. He felt his body tighten with desire and made himself breathe deeply to contain it. He must not frighten her at this moment, too much hung in the balance.

'Nick, it is lovely, so very lovely. Look at the view!' Kat half-ran to the window, heedless of the swirl of green skirts that followed her. He stayed where he was, looking at her.

'I am.'

'But you can see better here.' Then she turned and saw his eyes on her and blushed deliciously. But she had become self-conscious now, and watchful. 'It is all quite lovely, but of course I cannot stay here, Nicholas.'

So, he was 'Nicholas' all of a sudden. 'Why not?' Nick made himself lean against a bedpost rather than yield to the temptation to cross the room and show Kat precisely why she should stay.

'Because of the annulment,' she said, wearily. 'How will it look if I live with you here, in such an intimate household?'

Nick refrained from pointing out that a few days ago she would never have dreamed of referring to a Queen Anne Dower House boasting fourteen main bedrooms as intimate. 'How is your virtue any more at risk here than it is up at the house? All the servants will know by now that you slept in my bed last night; you cannot keep that sort of thing secret. And you were going to rely upon medical evidence if necessary, I recall.'

'Yes.' She winced. He could imagine just what an ordeal it was even thinking about that.

'Let me show you round some more,' he coaxed. 'We will have a full household of servants, there will be room for John and Jenny…' She was through the door into the dressing room, then through another door and into the master bedroom without baulking. Nick eyed the green brocade of the bedcovering, imagining white limbs against it, before he put a hard hold on his imagination and ushered her out on to the landing. The tension that vibrated from her was tangible, he felt it on his skin like the approach of a summer thunderstorm.

'It would be kind if you would help me with the refurnishing,' he said as they descended the stairs. Kat was visibly more relaxed away from the bedrooms and talk of furnishings seemed to help.

'Of course,' she agreed. 'Oh, Nick, all these rooms are so lovely! They only need the lightest touch, but perhaps they are a little over-furnished and some of the hangings are rather heavy.'

Watching her moving gracefully around the salon, her fingers trailing over the backs of sofas, adjusting the position of an ornament, twitching a curtain, he began to relax. He had caught her with the charm of the house. *Love my house, love me.* He froze, eyes focused painfully on the green-clad figure. *Love me.* Is that what he wanted? Her love? Was that what he felt for her? Not just liking, not just desire—certainly not gratitude.

It had crept up on him so gradually he had not noticed, had not recognised it from that long-ago attack of calf love that had led to his exile. And he had managed to fall in love with one of the few women in the kingdom who could recoil at the thought of marrying the heir to a dukedom, a woman who fought tooth and nail for the right to bear her own burdens, however heavy and unfair and however easy it would be to surrender them.

Kat had stopped exploring and came back to stand in front of him, a frown between her brows. 'But twenty-four days is not long if I am to order fabrics for you.'

'Twenty-four days?' He blinked at her. 'Ah, until you leave.' *Over my dead body.* 'There is probably no need to order anything, just take what you want from the House. If you talk to Mrs Arbuthnot, the housekeeper, she will show you hoards of treasures, I am sure. I will ask Father which staff we can borrow for the meantime. I see no reason why we could not move in tomorrow.' He watched the play of emotions on Kat's face and decided to keep things light. 'I am certain Mrs Arbuthnot will be over here with a positive army of maids to set about airing the bedchambers if that is what is worrying you.'

'No, that is not what is worrying me,' she retorted with that sudden flash of kitten claws that always enchanted him. 'Although naturally the thought that you may succumb to rheumatics is a concern. Nick, I have never been in charge of more than six servants in my life—how am I going to manage however many this house will require?'

'Appoint Jenny housekeeper.' It was the first thing that came into his mind and it worked magic.

'Oh, yes, Nick, how clever of you. Between us we can manage, I am sure of it.' Suddenly she was relaxed and happy again, threading her hand through the crook of his elbow and urging him towards the front door. 'We must go back now, I have so much to think about.'

Nick let himself be hustled out, suppressing the grin that was threatening to break out. It was a secret, dangerous delight being managed by his wife. The trick was to ensure this lasted a lifetime and not a mere twenty-four days.

'Jenny!' Katherine whirled into her bedchamber, causing her maid to jump and to drop a pile of freshly laundered chemises.

'Look what you've made me do now, Miss Katherine,' she grumbled, stooping to pick them up again. 'I'd just folded them all as well... What is it? You look so happy.'

'I have seen the Dower House and we will be moving in there tomorrow. Oh, Jenny, it is delightful. And I would like you to be housekeeper. Will you do that? On an appropriate salary, of course.'

Jenny made a little flapping movement with her hand, dismissing the money. 'For how long, Miss Katherine?'

'Oh,' she said flatly. 'Oh, just the remainder of the time I will be here—twenty-four days.'

Jenny was refolding underwear with an exasperated snap

and slap. 'But that's how long the master said you must wait before he would agree; it will take goodness knows how long after that. Where will you go then?'

'I do not know,' Katherine said wearily, all the fizzing excitement of her ride and the Dower House ebbing away. 'I must think of something. And, Jenny, I do not know how I will be able to keep you and John on either. I am so sorry. I will quite understand if you want to start looking for a new position right away.'

Curiously Jenny flushed a rosy pink. 'Don't you worry about that, Miss Katherine, we'll be all right. Now, let's get you out of that habit. Did you have a nice ride?'

Katherine was still subdued and preoccupied when she came down to dinner. Earlier she had waylaid Heron and enquired which newspapers the household received. '*The Times,* the *London Recorder* and the *Leeds Intelligencer*, my lady. Plus, of course the various journals to which his Grace and Lord Robert subscribe. Would you wish me to place an order for some ladies' journals, my lady? *La Belle Assemblée*, perhaps?'

'No.' Katherine hesitated, then recalled what Nick had said about the extent of the servants' knowledge of what was going on. 'Heron, I would like to take you into my confidence.'

The butler bowed slightly. 'I would be honoured, my lady. Might I suggest we step into the Blue Salon?'

Once in private, Katherine clasped her hands together and sought for words, feeling far more like an errant chambermaid than the lady of the house. 'Heron, you are aware that his lordship and I are seeking an annulment?'

He inclined his head, but did not comment.

'When I leave here I must seek employment as I have no resources.'

Now he did look shocked. 'But, my lady, his lordship will naturally provide for you.'

'I know that, but I do not wish him to, Heron. Now you understand why I need to see the newspapers; I wish to scan the employment vacancies.'

'I will secure the daily papers as soon as his Grace has finished with them, my lady. I will also place an order for the local newspapers that we use when advertising for staff. Those, that is, which advertise positions of a genteel nature.'

'Thank you, Heron, I appreciate your assistance.'

'My lady, I can assure you that anyone in this household would do their utmost to be of help to your ladyship.' He bowed stiffly and went out, leaving Katherine somewhat taken aback.

Now, entering the Chinese Salon, a further uncomfortable thought struck her. Could she hide her marital history from a potential employer who would very likely consider it shocking? And what about references? She could hardly ask Nick or the Duke for a recommendation. A sudden bizarre notion flashed into her mind and she could imagine Nick penning a letter to some elderly lady who had wanted a companion.

I can recommend Miss Cunningham most highly as an accomplished pursuer of highwaymen. She is skilled in assaulting magistrates and is capable of conversing with such varied members of society as the Governor of Newgate prison and Will the Fly...

'You are looking very cheerful, my dear Katherine,' the Duke remarked as she entered.

'Good evening, your Grace. Just a foolish thought that entered my head.'

'Not so foolish if it can bring a smile to your lips. Now, my dear, allow me to introduce you to two members of our household who have been away from home visiting the

Bishop. Mr Crace, our learned archivist…' Katherine exchanged polite bows with a tubby little man who beamed at her '…and the Reverend Rossington, our equally learned chaplain.' A large, rather shambling man with bushy eyebrows and bulging pockets.

'Mr Crace, Reverend. I do hope you had a pleasant journey back from Bishop's Auckland.' She smiled, inwardly wondering what, if anything, his Grace had told the two men about her position in the household.

The Duke took her elbow and steered her towards a chair by the fire, murmuring, in uncanny echo of her thoughts, 'Mr Crace is also our lawyer and Mr Rossington will be able to advise on the ecclesiastical aspects of your proposed course of action, Katherine. I have already apprised them that you are considering an annulment, and they stand ready to advise you and Nicholas at any time. I thought you might be more comfortable knowing exactly what the extent of their knowledge was.'

'Thank you, your Grace,' she said. That at least solved the problem of seeking legal advice, which had been exercising her greatly. If Nick chose to be difficult, she shrank from the thought of revealing such a sensitive matter to a strange lawyer.

Nick and Robert entered on the thought, both of them with the vaguely guilty air of schoolboys late for dinner. After greeting the other men, Nick made his way over to her chair. 'And what, madam wife, is causing you to smile your *cat at the mousehole* smile, might I ask?'

Katherine tipped back her head to look at him. 'You and Robert looked about fourteen coming in just now, as though you had been out playing and had come in late for dinner.'

He grinned. 'True enough. One of the things that can still fill me with a healthy dread is Father's wrath at unpunctuality. And, yes, the two of us have been out schooling that grey horse, Xerxes.'

'Did you enjoy yourselves?'

'Very much. Robert fell off three times, I fell off—'

'I have been thinking,' the Duke announced with a sublime confidence that every other conversation in the room would cease. 'And I have decided that, to announce to local society that my elder son has returned, I will hold a ball.'

Chapter Nineteen

'A ball?' Nick echoed his father icily. 'And exactly how do you expect to introduce my wife to society at the moment, sir?'

'As Miss Cunningham,' his Grace suggested with equal *froideur*. 'That leaves all Katherine's options open, I believe.' He smiled benignly at her.

'And how do we account for the fact that an unmarried lady is living unchaperoned in an all-male household? Sir,' Nick enquired with a politeness that did not convince Katherine for a moment.

'I will simply not appear at all,' she said hastily.

'You are my wife, I will not have you skulking like some demi-rep I am ashamed to produce!' he thundered, making her jump. The chaplain and archivist began an earnest conversation in a far corner about ecclesiastical Latin, obviously used to effacing themselves while the Lydgates robustly exchanged opinions.

'Cousin Fanny,' the Duke announced, ignoring Nicholas's bristling indignation. He continued to address himself to Katherine. 'Lady Fanny Craven, a cousin of somewhat straitened means who enjoys a visit to Seaton Mandeville now and again. I am sure she will be delighted to oblige and, as she lives in Durham, I foresee no problems with her travelling here in time.'

Katherine cast a hasty glance at Nick, who was still looking far from appeased. 'Thank you, your Grace. That would be most kind, if Lady Fanny is able to spare the time.' The idea of a ball in the great house, the thought a dancing in Nick's arms, was powerfully tempting.

'I am damned if I am having her living in the Dower House,' Nick stated.

'Of course not. Fanny shall have her usual rooms. I wrote this afternoon,' he added, with sublime disregard to the effect this high-handed approach was having on his son and heir. Katherine, silently musing on how much like his father Nick could be, kept her counsel.

'When do you plan to hold the ball, your Grace?' she ventured, deciding it was time to intervene before Nick exploded.

'In ten days' time.'

'Dinner is served, your Grace.' Heron appeared at the door as Nick and Katherine said in unison,

'What the devil am I supposed to wear?'

'But I have no ball gown!'

'You will both have to take yourselves off to Newcastle tomorrow and see to it,' the Duke announced calmly, offering Katherine his arm and proceeding to take her into dinner.

Behind her she heard Nick's sudden laugh and loved him for it. He was never a poor loser, despite, she suspected, rarely finding himself in that position.

The next day Katherine went in search of John. She had every intention of getting him to drive her and Jenny into

Newcastle and not going with Nick, as she was quite certain her husband intended.

On her way out she pressed a letter into Heron's hands. 'His Grace has been kind enough to frank this for me.' It was a brief account of her whereabouts for Arthur, and a plea to keep her present circumstances a secret. She was reluctant to commit anything to writing, but Arthur had been a good friend and she hated to think of him worrying. And now he knew her direction, he could let her know if he heard anything about Philip.

When she reached the stable yard, the grooms were polite but somewhat vague about John's whereabouts. He might be in the tack room, or on the other hand he and Durren had been seen talking to the corn chandler. Would her ladyship like the boy sent to fetch him?

'No, that is quite all right,' Katherine assured them. 'I will find him.' She recalled Jenny telling her where John's room was, so she made her way from the main stables into the quieter secondary yard and climbed the flight of external stone steps that led up to the room above the hay store which Jenny had described.

The door stood open, but inside all was silent. Just in case, Katherine looked round the door and froze in incredulous silence.

Her groom and her maid were locked in each other's arms in what she could only describe as a passionate embrace. Katherine stole backwards as quietly as she could, but her very presence must have alerted the lovers for Jenny looked around.

'Miss Katherine!'

'I am sorry, I should have knocked, excuse me…' She was already backing away down the steps when John appeared at the top.

'Miss Katherine, please—may we speak with you?'

Flustered, Katherine climbed the steps again. She was definitely not of the school of employer who believed they should order their servants' private lives for them, and, even if she were, John and Jenny would soon be independent of her.

'I beg your pardon,' she said stiffly as she re-entered the room. 'I had no intention of—'

'We are going to be married, Miss Katherine,' John said bluntly.

'Congratulations! I am so happy for you.' Katherine embraced Jenny, then threw John into considerable confusion by kissing him on the cheek. 'I am so sorry that our ways are going to have to part soon. But perhaps you have plans?'

'We have that.' John pulled out chairs and they found themselves grouped round the small table that served as John's dressing table and desk. 'My father owns a carter's business down in Devon. He's in a small way of trade and things are getting a bit much for him now. He's been on at me to take over for a few years now and I reckon this is the time.'

'And we also reckon,' Jenny put in, 'that we can make it more than just a small, local concern. We reckon that with a bit of hard work and some ambition we could have a network of haulage all over the West Country. And that's not all.'

John picked up the tale with the ease that told Katherine this was a well-rehearsed discussion between them. How long had this romance been going on under her unsuspecting nose?

'My mother has been running a shop. A haberdashery shop mainly; again, nothing flash, just a little business. But if we have a distribution network we could supply several shops, bring in good London wares to stock them—'

'Serve the fashionable trade, or at least the merchant class,' Jenny chimed in.

'But that is a wonderful plan. You will go far, I can see it now.'

'The thing is, Miss Katherine…' Jenny met John's eye, he nodded and she said tentatively, 'If things really don't work out for you here, Miss Katherine, we wondered if you'd like to come and stay with us while you work out what to do.' She hurried on, almost gabbling before Katherine could speak. 'I know it'd be a come-down, but—'

'It would be anything but,' Katherine said warmly. 'I am touched that you should ask me. I hope I would not have to impose upon you, but if I did I insist on working for my bread and butter. Perhaps your new business would need a book-keeper? It is about my only skill.' It was a tempting vision of life with friends, an honest job of work to do, the challenge of building a business. If she could not be with Nick, then this was the next best thing. But however generous the offer, she knew it would have to be the last resort; she could not risk being a burden on the two people who had shown her un-swerving loyalty.

'That's a good idea,' John said with enthusiasm. 'I reckon we could make a go of that. Now, you think on it, Miss Kather-ine. If it don't suit—and heaven knows we hope it doesn't come to it for your sake—you just say so, and no bones bro-ken.'

'John, you have to think about this…'

'We have been,' Jenny said. 'And we've talked and talked. We wouldn't say anything unless we were sure.'

'Then thank you, both of you, I accept, but I promise I will not impose upon you unless I have absolutely no choice.' The relief was almost overwhelming, and with it came the deso-lation—now, with a safety net below her, she had to accept that she was leaving Nick, there was no possible excuse not to. 'When will you be married?'

'When we get down to Devon,' John said with a fond look at Jenny. 'Jenny's got no folks living, so that'll be best.'

'I'll leave you in peace, then,' Katherine said, getting to her feet and wondering if she was going to make it out of the door before she gave way to tears. *What am I crying about?* she wondered as she stumbled down the stairs. Happiness for John and Jenny, of course. A pang of jealousy? Yes, that too. Relief? Definitely relief. And heartache…

'There you are.' It was Nick. She could not retreat and it was too late to hide the tear tracks on her cheeks. 'Kat? What is wrong?'

'Nothing.' She forced a smile on to her lips; it was not so very hard after all. 'I am simply being foolish and sentimental.' She tucked a hand under his elbow and walked away from the stairs. 'You'll not say anything yet, please, but John and Jenny are getting married.' She chattered on, telling him all about their plans and omitting anything of her proposed part in them.

'That is good news indeed.' He stopped just before the arch into the main yard and took her by the hands. 'I would have offered them places here, however things turned out, but this is best for them.' He released one hand and fished in his pocket, producing a large white handkerchief. 'Do not cry, Kat.'

The gentle pressure of the linen under each eye as he dabbed made her want to weep more, throw herself into his arms, confess her new plan to escape him, be comforted and persuaded that she was wrong, she could stay and that was the right thing to do.

'Stop it,' she ordered lightly, conjuring up a watery smile. 'I am being foolishly sentimental and you are encouraging me in it. Now, were you looking for me?'

'I have ordered the carriage to be brought round to the front in half an hour—we cannot waste any time in ordering clothes for Father's confounded ball. In any case, I have to visit a tailor soon or all Robert's coats will be out at the seams.'

'But I need to find a Newcastle *Directory*, otherwise how am I going to find a *modiste*?'

'I know just the one for you, and I have checked that she is still in business. Madame LeBlanc will be able to recommend a milliner and so forth.'

'French?' Katherine enquired, interested despite her worries about paying for all this. 'I have never been able to afford a French dressmaker, even when things were much better at home.'

'She is probably from Wallsend,' Nick said cynically, 'but she knows her business. Where are you going?'

'To fetch Jenny. I cannot possibly go shopping in town without a maid, think what an appearance that would present!'

'I was rather hoping I would be adequate company,' Nick said with a grin.

'And you know perfectly well what that would look like,' she scolded, walking back towards John's room. 'We will be in the hall in half an hour.'

It did not occur to her to wonder exactly how her husband had acquired such a knowledge of Newcastle *modistes* until the three of them were standing outside Madame LeBlanc's chic establishment.

'Very smart,' Jenny approved, eying the green paint picked out in gold and the tasteful window display.

The lady herself swept forward to greet the new arrivals, a smile on her lips. 'Good day, madam, sir. How may I be of assistance?' Then the smile changed to one of warm recognition and she cried, 'Lord Seaton! Why, it must be five years at least since you have visited us.'

'More like seven. Your memory is excellent, Madame. This lady is Miss Cunningham, who is a guest at Seaton Mandeville. Unexpectedly the Duke has decided to throw a ball and Miss Cunningham has no suitable wardrobe for such an occasion.'

'But of course, I perceive this is a matter of the utmost urgency, my lord. When is the ball?'

'In nine days' time. Are we setting you an impossible task, Madame?'

'For you my lord…' she cast him a look which could only be described as coquettish '…for you we will contrive. Please, be seated while I fetch some pattern books and samples.'

'Nicholas,' Katherine said with a deceptively sweet smile, 'how, exactly, does Madame know you so well?'

'Not because we have had a liaison, which is what I suspect you are most improperly assuming. In my younger, wilder days I paid for a number of charming barques of frailty to be dressed by Madame.'

'Really, Nicholas, I wonder that you tell me such a shocking thing.' Katherine tried to sound outraged and failed.

'I did tell you I had been a rake, Kat. But of course, that is now all behind me as I am a sober married man.'

Jenny, who had been correctly sitting to one side appearing not to listen, let a giggle escape her. Katherine gave both her companions a severe stare. 'Shh! Madame is returning.'

Madame returned with a veritable train of attendants bearing fashion plates, pattern books and swatches of fabrics that made Katherine's mouth water just to look at.

After almost an hour of flicking, pondering and discussion Katherine said, 'This one.' It was a charming gown, very simple, but given distinction by elegant bell sleeves and a graceful neckline. It also had the advantage of appearing relatively cheap compared to some more ornate offerings and simple enough to be made in a rush.

'But, yes, you have excellent taste Miss Cunningham—'

'No.' Nick tossed a fashion plate on to the table. 'This one.'

'But Ni…Lord Seaton, surely this could not be produced in time.' It was breathtaking, a slender, sleeveless column of a gown with a scooped and twisted neckline, given a touch of drama by the way the skirt was cut at the back to form a demi-train. The hemline was heavily beaded, as was the bodice, and Katherine could almost feel how the weight this would give to the fabric would make the gown hang and move.

'It is not suitable for an unmarried lady,' she said regretfully, letting her finger trail down the line of the drawing.'

'Not in that strong colour with the jet beads, no.' Madame flipped back a pile of silks and produced one with a flourish. 'But in this and with crystal beading, what could be more refined and suitable?'

This was a silk of the softest primrose yellow. Madame urged Katherine to stand in front of the mirror while she draped a length of it over her shoulder. 'You see? Over a white satin underskirt and with slippers and gloves of kid a few shades darker—enchanting.'

Katherine turned from the glass with a pang. 'That fabric, that colour, but in the style I picked out first, if you please. The other is delightful, but I can tell it will cost considerably more and I had not budgeted for this expenditure,' she said firmly.

'There is no time to lose,' Madame announced, scribbling in a notebook. 'If Miss Cunningham and her attendant would be so good as to accompany Hortense to the fitting rooms, measurements may be made.'

Nick stood up. 'Madame, will you be so good as to give Miss Cunningham directions to suitable shops for her slippers, gloves and so forth? Miss Cunningham, I will meet you back at the Lamb and Flag at three o'clock, if that will be enough time? And I will order a late luncheon.'

He smiled inwardly. Kat already had that focused look, which, in his wide experience, women always acquired on a serious shopping expedition. She might be acting most sensibly about her choice of gown, but he did not delude himself that by the time she and Jenny arrived back at the inn they would have subjected Newcastle's most eligible emporia to a thorough pillaging.

'Yes, thank you Lord Seaton, that will be delightful,' she said over her shoulder, already halfway through the door. Then suddenly the focused look vanished and she smiled at him, excited and enchanting, and his heart contracted painfully, startling him. It seemed this business of being in love took some getting used to.

'Madame!' He pulled himself together and lifted the second design, the one he had chosen. 'This gown, if you please. There is no need to say anything to Miss Cunningham until the first fitting. And, Madame, send the account to me.'

The knowing black eyes narrowed and he smiled at her. 'No, Madame, this is absolutely not what you suspect.' As he opened the door on to the street he added, 'Quite the opposite, in fact.'

Nick was not surprised to find himself still alone at the Lamb and Flag at half past three and congratulated himself on his foresight in ordering a cold collation. When the door finally did fly open to admit two flushed and chattering young women, he rose to his feet, nobly forbearing from a pointed glance at the clock on the mantelshelf.

'Have you had a successful expedition?' he enquired, pulling out chairs.

'Just look!' Kat gestured at the pile of bandboxes and parcels that a sweating inn servant had deposited on the settle. 'And I congratulate myself on exercising the utmost economy. We found the equivalent of the Soho Bazaar and made some fine bargains, I can tell you.' She attacked the cold meats with admirable appetite.

'How did you get it all here?' Nick asked, fascinated.

'Madame LeBlanc lent us a footman. It was most kind of her, considering I am only buying one quite modest gown and she cannot expect any further patronage from me. Would you like some of this pickled salmon? It is excellent.'

For a few minutes they were quiet, enjoying their very belated luncheon, then Kat asked, 'Did you succeed in finding your tailor still in business?'

'And my bootmaker, and my hatter,' Nick said with some satisfaction. 'And my equivalent pile of incidental shopping is in the carriage. Goodness knows how we are going to get it all home; I expect to have to sit on the box.'

He watched Kat affectionately as she found the sweetmeats and pounced on them. 'This is an interesting new experience for me, shopping with my wife,' he said, forgetting to guard his tongue. Instantly the shutters came down behind her eyes. He could have kicked himself. How was he ever to persuade her to give in and to let the marriage stand?

Attempted seduction had not worked and had only driven her further away; persuasion had failed, even hard common sense had broken on the rocks of her resolve. Perhaps courting her would work. There was the ball, after all—what more romantic setting could there be than Seaton Mandeville *en fête* for a ball, moonlight on the towers, music and flowers and wine working upon the senses? Nick absently peeled an apple, the peel curling over long fingers, and plotted.

Chapter Twenty

Lady Fanny Craven proved to be a vague, amiable person who accepted everything her awe-inspiring relative told her as gospel. The fact that she had been summoned to act as chaperon to a young lady who was married to Cousin Nicholas while pretending to be still single and was yet living with him at the Dower House did not appear to disconcert her in the slightest.

'You must think this all very irregular,' Katherine ventured shortly after Lady Fanny's arrival. The entire household was gathered in the Chinese Salon to take tea.

'Irregular?' Lady Fanny was blonde, wispy and perhaps forty years of age. Her single status could be explained by the fact that she had, she explained, been a Support to Poor Dear Mama for many years. That lady having now passed away, she found herself only too happy to assist Cousin Lionel, as she somewhat nervously termed the Duke, whenever he called upon her. 'This seems to be a perfectly usual time to take tea. Have I missed some irregularity?'

'No, not the tea, Lady Fanny,' Katherine explained, fighting the urge to wave frantically at Nick for rescue. 'The fact that you are chaperoning me under these circumstances.'

'They may be a trifle unusual,' Lady Fanny murmured, nibbling like a voracious vole at her third macaroon, 'but if Cousin Lionel approves, then it must be perfectly correct. Cousin Lionel is *always* right.'

Just like his elder son, Katherine brooded, watching the two Lydgates lounging elegantly one each side of the fireplace. Nicholas was engaged in persuading his father that he should replace his main carriage with one possessing the latest in patent springs, the Duke in arguing that what he had was perfectly adequate. They seemed, despite the fact that they were disagreeing with each other, far more in harmony than they had at any time since Nick's return home. Was the old man thawing, and was his son letting his hackles down at last?

'Would you care for the last macaroon, Lady Seaton?' Katherine blinked and recalled herself.

'No, thank you, please do have it, Lady Fanny.' Where did she put all that food? She was as thin as a rake. 'And please call me Katherine; no one but the family knows of the marriage, remember, and it would not do to let it slip during the ball.'

'Oh, my goodness, what a shatterbrained thing that would be, to be sure,' Lady Fanny tittered. 'Dear Cousin Nicholas *would* be annoyed with me. And he has moved to the Dower House, I understand? I wonder how he can live there instead of in all this splendour.' She gazed myopically at the exotic wallpaper and the Aubusson rugs and sighed wistfully.

'This is very splendid, I quite agree,' Katherine said, wondering compassionately exactly where Lady Fanny lodged since her mother's death, 'But I must confess to having fallen in love with the Dower House; it is quite charming and I never get lost, which I do all the time here.'

'And you too are living there now?'

'Yes, just for a while, since yesterday. I am helping Nicholas with some renovations he is planning, that is all.' Was her new chaperon going to comment on this highly peculiar arrangement? It appeared not. Katherine just hoped that she was not going to think it her duty to move into the Dower House too.

To her relief, for she had to confess that she was finding conversation with Lady Fanny somewhat hard going, Nick came over to join them. 'Have you persuaded the Duke to buy a new carriage?' she asked.

'No.' He smiled ruefully. 'I shall just have to buy one myself and lend it to him so he is convinced. I will order it next time I am in Newcastle. What colour would you prefer for the upholstery? Burgundy, dark blue?'

'Forest green, I think,' Katherine said, then caught herself. What was she thinking of? 'But naturally, you must choose, I do not know what would be best for a gentleman's carriage. Will you place the order when we go into Newcastle for the first fittings for our new clothes?'

'No need. Madame LeBlanc and my tailor will come out here for the fittings, the day after tomorrow. My bootmaker will send my shoes; he still has my lasts, so fitting is no problem.'

'They will come here?' Katherine queried. This was life as she was totally unused to living it, that was obvious.

'But of course, Katherine dear.' Lady Fanny looked astonished. 'This is the Duke's household, no local tradesperson would dream of doing anything else.'

'Would you excuse us for one moment, Cousin Fanny?' Nicholas took Katherine's hand and led her to a quiet corner of the room. 'Is she driving you demented?' he asked sympathetically.

'Certainly not, what an improper thing to say,' Katherine

said reprovingly. 'She is perhaps a little difficult to make conversation with…'

'She is an amiable peahen,' Lady Fanny's unsympathetic relative commented, 'but she will serve the purpose.'

'Are you still annoyed at the Duke's decision to hold the ball?'

Nick regarded her thoughtfully. 'No, I have come to the conclusion that it was an admirable idea.' Now why did she suspect him of a hidden meaning behind that gracious acknowledgment? 'And it has inspired me to suggest that we hold a dinner party at the Dower House.'

'Us? A dinner party? At the Dower House?'

'Kat, I have to tell you, you sound every bit as bird-witted as Cousin Fanny. Yes, us, a dinner party. Just for the household here.'

'When? Why?' If she was still sounding bird-witted she could not help it.

'Three days after the ball, I thought. And why? Because I have a desire to entertain in my own home.'

'Would it not be better after I have gone? I can hardly act the hostess…'

'Why not? Or do you think I should ask Cousin Fanny to take that role?' He hesitated. 'Please, Kat, it would give me so much pleasure.'

Nick had never asked her for anything in that way before and it made her feel guilty. She had put him in a position where his homecoming was overshadowed by his sham marriage; surely the least she could do was to agree to a dinner party where all the guests were known to her.

'Yes, of course, if you would like it. We had better stop talking apart, and I must rescue poor Mr Rossington, who appears to be receiving an account of the set of church kneelers Lady Fanny is producing.'

'No harm in that,' Nick said heartlessly. 'He is, after all, supposed to excel in Christian charity. Ouch!' he added indignantly as his wife gave him a sharp jab in the ribs with a forefinger and went to the chaplain's assistance.

As she joined the discussion on the minute details of the kneelers, Katherine looked back and caught his eye. 'I am sorry,' she mouthed.

'I forgive you,' he mouthed back with such a gentle smile that her heart contracted sharply. Constant contact with him was such a torment, such a deliciously anguished reminder of just how much she liked her husband, how much she loved him, how much she was coming to desire him. She tried to work out how many days were left before the month was up, before he would permit her to begin the annulment process, and realised she had lost track of time. This would not do, she must pull herself together, stop playing at being Lady Seaton and make her plans before her feelings for Nick seduced her into abandoning all principle.

'And all edged with laurel leaves in gold, how lovely,' she said serenely to Lady Fanny. 'You must tell me how you chart your patterns.' And in the meantime there was no excuse for not behaving as a lady should.

Two days after Lady Fanny's arrival, Madame LeBlanc and her entourage arrived at the Dower House. Katherine peered around the edge of the screen in her bedroom as Jenny undid her morning dress and helped her out of it. Madame herself carried nothing. Behind her two girls struggled with a vast box from which a foam of tissue paper emerged and behind them came the senior seamstress with a basket of threads, pincushions and extra lengths of silk.

'This is exciting,' Jenny whispered, peeping round the screen.

'I know, I cannot wait to see it. Can you pass me my wrapper, please?'

Katherine emerged, fumbling for the ties of her wrapper, but too eager to see the new gown to wait and tie them properly. 'Madame, good morning. You seem to have made excellent progress.'

'I believe so Miss Cunningham. I expect there to be few changes necessary, in which case, if a room can be made available, my girls can finish the gown here today.'

'But of course.' Katherine turned to the box as layers of tissue were removed, revealing the pale primrose silk. Pale silk and an intricate pattern of crystal beading across a bodice with a twisted neckline and no sleeves. 'This is the wrong gown! Madame, this is not the gown I chose.'

'No, Miss Cunningham, but his lordship countermanded the decision…'

'We will see about that.' Wrapper flying, Katherine stalked over to the connecting door that led to Nick's dressing room. She had never tried it to see if it were locked, considering that to check on such a thing showed little confidence in him. Now it jerked open under her hand.

The dressing room was deserted, but the door into his bedchamber stood ajar. Furious, Katherine palmed it open and swept into the room. 'Nicholas! Will you kindly tell me what is the meaning of—?' and found herself confronting her husband in his shirt and apparently little else and a pair of dark-clad men, one clutching a pair of satin knee breeches, the other with his mouth full of pins.

Nick stared, enchanted and aroused at the sight of Kat, colour high, storming into his bedchamber in her stockinged feet, unfastened wrapper flying, bosom heaving above a very fetching set of stays.

The tailors whipped round and beat a hasty retreat. 'We

will wait outside, my lord,' one mumbled dangerously through the pins. Nick ignored him, scarcely registering the sound of the door closing behind them.

'Kat, darling…' All he wanted to do was sweep her up, toss her on to the bed and make ruthless love to her until her anger turned to gasps of passion.

'Don't you darling me, you deceitful man! Why did you tell Madame LeBlanc to make the other gown? I did not agree to it, I cannot afford it and I do not want it!'

'Now that last is a fib and you know it, Kat. You *did* want it, you were just too proud to let me buy it for you.'

She responded with a hiss of fury. God, but she was lovely! He had never seen her lose her temper, and suspected it was a rare event. Rare or not, it was powerfully erotic, and would have been even were she fully clothed. He was thankful for the voluminous cut of his shirt, which hid just what an effect she was having on him.

'So why did you buy it when you knew it would upset me?' she demanded, hands fisted on her hips.

'To give me the pleasure of seeing you wear it.' That effectively took the wind out of her sails, he noted. 'So it is a gift I make to myself—all I ask is that you enjoy it for the night.'

'Oh.' Katherine watched him, obviously undecided how she now felt. 'It would give you pleasure if I wear it?' She seemed suspicious, claws retracted, but not sheathed.

'Everything you wear gives me pleasure, Kat,' he murmured, taking a step forward. 'This, for example, is a very fetching ensemble.' He let one finger trace the swell of her breasts, pushed up by the stays Jenny had laced tight in anticipation of the ball gown.

Her skin was like hot satin under his caress. For a long moment she was still, only her tumultuous breathing moving his hand as it rested on her. Nick was not conscious of breathing, of anything but the feel of her, the scent of her rising hot and heady with her anger. Anger that was turning into something else as he held her eyes.

Then she blinked, as though waking from a trance and looked down. 'My…look what I am wearing!'

'I am.' His voice felt as husky as it had in the days following the hanging.

'And you…' She backed away, the hot colour of temper replaced by a vivid blush. 'You…'

'If you will burst in on a gentleman when he is trying on his breeches,' Nick said, knowing his reasonable tone was enough to provoke her into another stimulating outburst, 'you must expect him to have removed his old pair first.' He managed, with an effort, to look faintly shocked. 'I do trust Cousin Fanny does not take it into her head to come over and exercise her role as chaperon.'

'Oh, you are impossible!' Kat stamped her foot. All he wanted was to take her in his arms, kiss that temper off her face, replace it with yielding, pulsing passion. Dare he risk it, or was it too soon? Kat took the decision out of his hands. 'Men!' she said with withering scorn. 'You are all the same.' And marched back through the dressing room door.

'Phew.' Nick let out a deep breath and walked to the window, which he threw wide. A little fresh air and some calming thoughts about porridge, or the Hearth Tax or Cousin Fanny's church kneelers were necessary before he let the tailors back in. He leaned out and looked towards the windows of Katherine's suite. At least, hopefully, she was now too flustered to do anything but accept the ball gown of his choosing.

Katherine paused in Nick's dressing room and tied the sash of her wrapper. The tender skin below her collarbone seemed so sensitive that it might have been scalded. She stared, wide-eyed, into Nick's dressing mirror and could only hope that her tumultuous breathing and flushed face could be put down to her outburst of temper just now. With a deep breath she pushed open her own bedchamber door and walked back in with rather more decorum than she had shown leaving it.

Madame LeBlanc turned from where she had been making polite conversation with Jenny. The sewing girls kept their heads down. Doubtless, she thought bitterly, only strict discipline kept them from giggling openly.

'I beg your pardon, Madame,' she said coolly. 'I remembered something I needed to say urgently to his lordship.'

'Of course, Miss Cunningham,' the *modiste* said graciously just as Katherine realised that she had admitted storming, in her undergarments, into a gentleman's chamber. She saw Jenny rolling her eyes in despair at such a *faux pas*. Oh, well, there was nothing to be done about it, she could only hope that Madame was discreet. There would be no doubt just what she was thinking.

'Now, Miss Cunningham, if you could just slip this on.' Madame advanced, her arms full of silk, and Katherine gave up thinking about anything except her ball gown.

But, after the final pin had been placed and the confection lifted tenderly away by the seamstresses to one of the bedchambers where they were going to work on the final adjustments, Katherine realised that there was a very good chance that she would soon find herself alone with Nick. And after that stormy encounter in his bedchamber she was not at all certain how she was going to react to that, or how she wanted him to. The feeling that had throbbed between them for those few seconds had been so intense, so...*carnal* that it had shaken her out of the feeling of safety she had slipped into. It had been a tense and unhappy sort of safety, but now even that had vanished.

She would certainly be dining alone with him, for they had agreed to stay at home that evening. Still, the presence of two footmen would ensure the conversation stayed on strictly impersonal lines and perhaps by the end of the meal she would be feeling a little more composed.

But that left luncheon and the whole of the afternoon. Katherine glanced at the clock. It was noon. If she went to the House she could eat there and that would give her the opportunity to ask the Duke if there was anything she could do to assist with the preparations for the ball. Not that she had ever had to plan such an event, or even attended anything that might approach the magnificence of a ducal entertainment. Still, she was a guest and it behoved her to make the effort to be useful.

'Jenny, please lay out my riding habit and ring for Paulson.'

The senior footman who was doing duty as butler until Nick engaged his own staff received with some concern his mistress's request to have her pony saddled and a groom standing by to accompany her to the House.

'Without his lordship, my lady?' he queried, shooting an anxious glance in the direction of Nick's rooms.

Katherine hid her amusement at the contrast between Paulson's nerves and Heron's imperturbable approach. 'Certainly. And would you tell Cook that I will be taking luncheon there.'

'Yes, my lady.' He backed out and Katherine was seized by a sudden qualm that he might ask Nick for his opinion before obeying her orders. But when she hurried downstairs in her flowing habit the groom was waiting patiently, Lightning and his own hack by his side.

He gave her a careful lift into the saddle with cupped hands under her foot and waited while she settled herself. Katherine felt a momentary stab of nerves: was she really ready for this without Nick?

'We will walk the entire way, please,' she said, missing the look of relief on the groom's face. He did not want to be the man in charge when the mistress fell off, that was for sure.

In the event the ride was completed successfully and Katherine toyed with the idea of asking Nick to teach her to trot soon. When they were talking again, that is.

Heron assured her that it would not be the slightest inconvenience if she partook of luncheon and ventured that he expected his Grace downstairs at any moment. Katherine hastened along to the small dining room, concerned not to be late and irritate the Duke. In the event she arrived at the same time as virtually the entire household, including Lady Fanny and a pale young man she did not recognise.

'My dear, you are joining us. Delightful.' His Grace seemed pleased to see her.

'Thank you, your Grace.'

Robert pulled out a chair for her on the Duke's right hand and beamed at her. 'I have not seen you for what seems like an age. Where has Nick got to?'

'He is at the Dower House with his tailor,' Katherine helped herself to bread and butter. 'I rode over with a groom.'

'Then the riding is going well?'

She wrinkled her nose. 'Very well, provided we only walk. Although I have to confess to thinking I might venture to trot soon. The reason I came over today is because I wanted to ask if there is anything I can do to assist with the preparations for the ball.'

'Not a thing, my dear, but it is good of you to ask.' The

Duke nodded in the direction of the pale man who was sitting silently beside Katherine. 'Jeremy has everything entirely under control as usual. Ah, perhaps I have been remiss—can it be that you have not yet been introduced to Mr Greene, my secretary? Jeremy, Lady Seaton.'

'Ma'am,' he murmured, blushing.

'Are you resident here?' Katherine asked. He was very self-effacing, but surely she would have noticed him before?

'No ma'am. I live in the village with my mother, who is widowed, and his Grace is good enough to allow me to come in daily—'

He broke off with a start as the door opened and Nick strode in, looking thunderous. 'Katherine! So here you are.'

Chapter Twenty-One

'**W**hat the devil are you doing, jauntering about the countryside by yourself without a word to anyone?' He appeared to become aware of the other occupants of the room, but his frown did not abate. 'Cousin Fanny, I beg your pardon. Well, Kat?'

A swift glance in the Duke's direction warned her that he was about to take exception both to his son's entrance and his speech. She said brightly, 'Oh, did Paulson not tell you I was riding over here?'

The Duke relaxed and sat back in his chair; Katherine had the distinct feeling that he was amused.

'You could have broken your neck!' Nick was not about to be appeased.

'I had a groom with me,' Katherine riposted with sweet reasonableness.

'And what good would he be if you fell off?'

'He would have helped me up, I trust. And I am pleased I came over today, for I have just met Mr Greene.'

The shy secretary appeared to be attempting to wriggle backwards out of his seat. Katherine favoured him with a warm smile that made her husband's eyes narrow. He said abruptly, 'May I join you, sir?'

'Please do,' his brother begged, before their father could speak. 'You are giving me acid indigestion fuming just behind my shoulder. Here, have some sirloin and stop lecturing Katherine, we do not want you putting her off coming to see us.'

'Have your tailors gone?' Katherine asked with what she hoped might be seen as a proper wifely concern.

'Yes, we were slightly delayed as one of them thought he had swallowed a pin. I cannot imagine why.' He was teasing her; obviously he had forgiven her—whether she was quite ready to be easy with him was another matter.

'Extraordinary,' Katherine agreed solemnly, biting her lip so as not to smile at the teasing twinkle in his eyes: it was quite impossible to resist Nick when he looked like that. 'Perhaps he had a shock?'

'Katherine,' the Duke remarked to his elder son, 'has been dutiful enough to come over especially to offer her assistance with the preparations for the ball: a courtesy that neither of my sons has seen fit to extend.'

Robert did not rise to the bait, merely dropping one lid in the ghost of a wink to his sister-in-law. Nick too had his own way of dealing with provocation. 'Sir, unless things have changed greatly since I have been away, any attempt to interfere with your plans to present Seaton Mandeville *en fête* would be spurned.' He passed the secretary the mustard. 'Naturally, had I known you wished me to, I would have hastened over and ordered flower arrangements, or decided on the order of dances…'

Surely the Duke would respond in kind, make some light remark? Instead his eyebrows rose haughtily and he said, 'As it happens, your assistance is not required.'

Katherine felt the set-down as acutely as if it had been directed at her, and she felt her cheeks colour. She glanced under her lashes at Nick, but he seemed unmoved, only the ironic twist of his mouth telling her that he too had felt the touch of ice. But of course, he must be used to it, expect it. This was the way relations between father and son had always been.

Biting her lip, she continued making conversation with Mr Greene and listening with every appearance of fascination to Lady Fanny recounting how amazing it was that she had thought to put in her ball gown. 'Quite a miracle, so providential because of course I had no reason to suppose…and I only put it out by accident. Such a scatterbrained thing to do, was it not?'

It was difficult to answer that without discourtesy. Katherine said warmly, 'But providential, as you said.' Her mind was somewhere else entirely. Could she do anything, say anything, to help reconcile Nick and his father in the days she had left at Seaton Mandeville? And what influence could an embarrassment of a daughter-in-law, one who was soon to be set aside, have in any case? The Duke had been kind to her beyond her deserts, but he would not welcome presumption, of that she was convinced.

The days before the ball passed for Katherine with a sense of unreality. Nick appeared to have recovered from whatever alarm her riding without him had produced and taught her to trot. Katherine was very proud of herself, once she had stopped falling off, and her husband had not laughed at her once.

She had also forgiven him for the ball gown, sensibly realising that it was the most beautiful garment she would ever wear and to spurn it would be ungracious and, at this late stage, impractical.

Nothing was said about that moment when they had stood in his room, her anger transmuting into sensual awareness, and she began to wonder if, after all, he had felt it too. And anyway, she scolded herself, what if he had? Feelings of physical desire were far removed from love, and love was the only possible reason she could think of for a marquis to stay married to a nobody who had wed him out of her own extremity.

On the afternoon of the ball Nick's new valet Cuthbertson and Jenny transported their burdens of carefully wrapped evening attire, accessories, brushes and colognes and installed themselves in Nick's suite and the adjoining rooms at the house. Nick had announced that it would be much simpler if they dressed for the ball there and spent what would remain of the night as well.

'That should make it easier for Lady Fanny to appear to be chaperoning me,' Katherine remarked. 'It will appear to those who are staying over that I am simply another guest.'

'Yes, that too,' Nick said vaguely, surprising Katherine, who had imagined that would be the main reason behind his decision.

She shut herself away with Jenny after luncheon, turning the key firmly in the lock in both the outside door and the door that led from her dressing room into Nick's; she wanted no interruptions, and certainly she did not want Nick to witness any stage in the transformation she was hoping to achieve.

'I shall have a rest for two hours, if I can sleep,' she decided, feeling as though she would never be able to close her eyes. 'Then I will have my bath and wash my hair—that should give it long enough to dry, do you think?'

Jenny calculated. 'What time is dinner?'

'Seven tonight. Lady Fanny thought I had better go down

at about half past six with her. I do not want to give the impression I am one of the family; simply a guest.'

'That should give us plenty of time,' Jenny decided. 'I'll take the gown to press now and make sure we get a bath and hot water brought up in two hours—there is sure to be quite a demand!'

She helped Katherine out of her gown and stays and under the coverlet, drew the curtains closed and bore off the precious gown in a rustle of tissue.

Left alone, Katherine shut her eyes and tried to compose herself to rest, but sleep proved elusive. She was not used to dozing in the middle of the day and the morning had hardly proved so tiring that she needed a rest. Her mind was buzzing with excitement, apprehension and anticipation.

Would Nick think her beautiful in her new gown? Would he dance with her? As the elder son of the house, his duty would be to dance with the most senior ladies and with the most eligible young ones and not to spend his time with unknown and obscure girls under the wing of his cousin. Anything else, she resolutely told herself, would draw the sort of attention to her that she most hoped to avoid.

Would anyone ask her to dance? Surely someone would, she thought doubtfully, speculating about the sort of guests who would attend a ducal ball. She had seen the pile of acceptances that had flooded in despite the short notice; surely amongst them would be some young gentlemen who would not be so high in the instep as to ignore humble Miss Cunningham?

Her eyelids began to droop and she fell into a state that was half-doze, half-nightmare. Nick, looking distinguished, handsome, every inch the marquis, was dancing with a succession of well-dowered, haughty, exquisite young ladies, while their titled parents looked on with delight. Meanwhile, Miss Cunningham sat with the other wallflowers, grateful for an occasional country dance with a shy youth or possibly his Grace's archivist.

She woke with a headache, feeling utterly cast down. Miserably she kicked back the covers and rubbed her forehead. Jenny would be back in a minute, it would never do to be found moping like this.

What was the matter with her? She tried to rally her spirits. *You are perfectly respectable, presentable and socially adept,* she scolded herself. *You can run a household, cope with debts, confront a highwayman. Have a little courage!* But deep down she felt out of her depth, uncertain…

'Whatever's the matter, Miss Katherine?' Jenny was back in the room without her noticing. 'Why such a Sad Susan! Anyone would think you were going to the dentist, not to a great ball!'

'I am terrified,' Katherine confessed, startled into frankness. 'I will not know anyone except the family and a very few of their professional advisers—and I cannot reveal how well I know *them*. I have never been to any occasion so lavish or with such grand guests.'

'And your lord must pretend he hardly knows you,' Jenny said, shrewdly getting to the heart of the matter. 'Do not worry so, he will not let you sink, nor will Lord Robert, nor his Grace, come to that.'

'What if I let them down?' Katherine said anxiously.

'This is beyond anything foolish,' Jenny scolded. 'You are equal to anything—look how you saved the master.'

'I did not have to do it under the critical gaze of dozens of society ladies,' Katherine retorted with a rueful smile, beginning to feel better.

'Look,' said Jenny, peering out of the window. 'Carriages

are arriving; it must be the guests who are staying over. There are two very plain redheads, a portly gentleman, and—oh, Miss Katherine, look at him!'

The man in question, as Katherine saw as she very reprehensibly joined her maid at the window, was tall, broad shouldered, and, so far as one could see from the first floor, extremely personable.

'Stop staring,' Katherine reproved hypocritically. Now, if that gentleman were to ask her to dance, it could not fail to stir a pang of jealousy in Nick's breast. She made a decision: tonight she was not going to think common-sense thoughts, she was not going to be sensible, she was going to enjoy every moment, savour every opportunity to shine in her husband's eyes.

'And never mind tomorrow,' she said mutinously just as there was a tap on the door.

'That'll be the bathtub, Miss Katherine,' Jenny said, shooing her behind the screen before letting in two perspiring footmen with the tub and a procession of chambermaids with hot water. 'In there,' she directed, waving towards the dressing room.

On the other side of the connecting door, Nick paused and put down the knife with which he was paring his nails. The sound of cascading water reached him through the thick panels and he listened, head cocked on one side, to the muffled sounds.

Jenny's voice, a rumble of answering male voices—the footmen. Silence, then swishing, more pouring. *Adjusting the temperature*, he thought, closing his eyes to better follow the unfolding scene just feet away. Jenny's voice again, then Kat's. Silence, then a laughing protest and more pouring—the water was too hot or too cold. A splash and Jenny's voice, suddenly perfectly audible,

'You've got it all over the floor, Miss Katherine! This tub is far too shallow.' She was answered by laughter and another splash.

The image the words conjured up of Kat sitting, quite naked, in a shallow bath tub just feet away was so erotic that Nick found himself on his feet, one hand on the door handle, before he caught himself.

With a rueful shake of his head he turned on his heel, picked up the paring knife and retreated into his bedchamber, shutting the door softly behind himself. Control, that was what the situation demanded, he reminded himself as his new valet advanced ominously with a towel and a pair of scissors. 'Just a little at the nape and behind the ears, my lord.' Cuthbertson did not approve of his lordship's liking for letting his hair grow.

'As you will.' Nick surrendered himself to his valet and pondered on just what it was about his provoking wife that made him want her so badly. And more than want her physically. True, she was beautiful, whatever she said to disparage her looks—but then he had experience of diamonds of the first water. True, she was brave, intelligent, resourceful and devastatingly unconventional when circumstances called for it—was that enough to make him lie awake at night wondering how to make her laugh, how to please her?

She had shared his bed twice, lain in his arms and left him as innocent as she had joined him. That, certainly, was provoking enough of sensual longings. But there were women aplenty to take care of inconvenient physical urges. Startled, Nick realised that the thought of being with any other woman was not so much repulsive as utterly impossible to conceive of. It was as though he was thirsty and someone had suggested he drink sea water. A shiver ran through him with the realisation that nothing was ever going to be the same again, whether he lost her or made her his.

'My lord! I beg you to be still.' Cuthbertson, flustered by almost taking a snip out of his new employer's ear, stepped back hurriedly. 'I beg your pardon, my lord, it was my own—'

'No, I moved. Have you finished? You may shave me when I have had my bath.'

'That will be the footmen with the water now.' The valet put down the scissors with a tremulous hand and hastened to the door. To send a marquis to a ducal ball with a cut ear! He would never have lived it down, never.

Chapter Twenty-Two

Katherine started nervously as the clock struck the half-hour, to be followed by a tap on the door. 'It is only me!' Lady Fanny called coyly.

'Um…'

'I had better let her in,' Jenny said, rolling her eyes heavenwards as she went to open the door. 'You'll have to go down some time, you know.'

'I know.' Katherine took a steadying breath and stood up as her chaperon fluttered in. Lady Fanny was wearing a surprisingly elegant, if subdued, gown of dove-coloured silk and a headdress that clearly proclaimed by its ruching and feathers that she was amongst the chaperons and dowagers for the evening.

'My dear Katherine!' She stopped in the middle of the room and threw up her hands. 'Oh, my goodness!'

'Is something wrong?' She should have known—something was unsuitable, or insufficiently elegant or…

'You look *ravishing*, Katherine, positively ravishing. Oh, to be twenty again.'

'Thank you, although I have to confess to being rather

more than twenty.' Cheered, Katherine managed to smile despite the cloud of butterflies in her stomach. 'Your gown is lovely, Lady Fanny.'

The spinster patted the silken folds tenderly. 'I have to confess to a weakness for evening gowns and treat myself to a new one *every year*.' She made it sound as though she were revealing a serious addiction to gaming. 'But truly, my dear, that gown is quite inspired. Is it only from a Newcastle *modiste*?'

'Yes, one Nicholas recommended.' Katherine began to pull on her long kid gloves, holding out her arms in turn for Jenny to fiddle her way down the row of tiny pearl buttons.

'Well, I never.' Lady Fanny looked positively roguish. 'Of course, he would know all the most fashionable establishments.' She fluttered a little under Katherine's startled gaze. 'You must know he was quite the rake as a young man—so good looking too, although I have to confess he has grown even more so. All the girls were after him, and not just the respectable ones, if you follow me. Still, he sobered up when he fell for that Somersham chit—not that that lasted long when Cousin Lionel came to hear of it. Still, that is all in the past now and here he is home to become respectable again.' She beamed happily, apparently forgetful of Katherine's ambiguous position in Nicholas's redemption.

'Why was she so unsuitable, the Somersham girl?' she asked curiously.

Lady Fanny shrugged. 'The family was well to do enough, but not good *ton*, you understand—gentlemen farmers for the most part. And her father was always in and out of debt; apparently a fatal tendency to gaming of all kinds.' She handed Katherine her reticule and twitched her own skirts into order. 'Now, where did I put my fan? Oh, yes, here it is. A very pretty child though, Annabelle, or Arabella, I cannot recall exactly.

Big blue eyes, golden curls and she always looked helpless. Men seem to like that.'

There was plenty in that to digest, Katherine thought grimly as Jenny fussed round her. 'Will you come back up after dinner, Miss Katherine?'

'Yes, thank you, Jenny,' she agreed absently. *So, the Duke had disliked an alliance with the daughter of a gamester and had disapproved of a girl from a gentry family. That could be me, if one substitutes brother for father,* she acknowledged. It was as she had known all along, her instinct that this marriage could not stand was well founded. *But this evening I am not going to remember that and I am going to make very certain that Nick is going to recall more about a brown-eyed, practical lady than he does about a blue-eyed helpless one.*

'Shall we go down?' she suggested, following one step behind her chaperon as an unmarried girl should.

Nick was standing in the Crimson Salon, the main reception room that led into the larger of the dining rooms, parrying the questions, subtle and not so subtle, that old acquaintances, neighbours and almost-forgotten friends were asking.

It was not an easy task to reveal very little while at the same time not creating an air of mystery that would provoke even more gossip.

'Yes, indeed, Lady Jarvis, I have to confess to fighting as a common trooper; a most instructive experience.'

'Brave man,' the dowager barked, rapping him painfully on the forearm with her fan. 'Eccentric, but at least you weren't gadding about like so many young officers seem to. At Waterloo, were you? Bad affair that, for all that we won. What does the Duke say about it, eh?'

'I believe he would agree with you in categorising my be-

haviour as eccentric, ma'am.' Nick smiled and passed on to
greet another guest.

'Lady Fanny Craven, Miss Cunningham,' the footman announced as Nick turned to look at the door. At first he did not
see her; several of Fanny's old friends had turned too and
moved to greet her.

Then the space between him and the doorway cleared.
There was Kat and he was back in the Assistant Governor's
office in Newgate with the force of that first impression catching the breath in his throat. And as he had seen then, she was
beautiful. Huge brown eyes, wide cheekbones tapering to a
pointed chin, a mass of dark blonde hair caught up into elaborate coils in a gilt net—lovely, terrified, brave.

He doubted anyone else could see the fear she was controlling so firmly, but he knew his Kat. At least, he corrected,
staring at the slender figure in its exquisitely simple gown,
he knew several Kats, but not this one. Not this poised, lovely
young lady who was following her chaperon obediently over
to greet his father. He had seen a cheetah once: beautiful,
sleek, apparently passive to its handler's leash, until it had
stood up and walked towards him with a grace that spoke
eloquently of its power and its danger.

It was not the domestic cat, the docile single miss that she
was pretending to be that he saw, but a strong, resolute, unconventional wild version. Could anyone else see it? He
glanced around and met Robert's startled look.

His brother edged over. 'Is my mouth open?' he hissed.

'No,' Nick assured him. 'Not now. Spectacular, is she not?'

Robert's low whistle was answer enough. 'I'm off to ask
her for the first waltz.'

'You can't have it, and neither can I. We cannot risk drawing attention to her by neglecting our duty dances in her favour. We will both have to wait until after supper. Stay here,

it will not do for both of us to descend on her the moment she appears.'

Nick strolled off, following a meandering path through the chatting guests until he appeared, as if by chance, where Katherine was being introduced by Lady Fanny to the Gunton sisters. They broke off, wide eyed, and curtsied to him.

'Lord Seaton.'

'Miss Gunton, Miss Amelie, good evening. I hope you had a safe journey over the moors? I see Cousin Fanny has introduced you to her friend Miss Cunningham.'

Kat turned to him with calm composure and dropped a slight curtsy. 'Good evening, Lord Seaton.'

God, but she was lovely. Her skin looked like milk against the soft primrose of the gown; the crystal beads in her bodice shimmered with the rise and fall of her breathing and the subtle scent of lily of the valley and fern rose from her warmth. 'Ladies, if you would excuse us, I have been asked to introduce Miss Cunningham to Lady Foxe.'

'Why?' Kat hissed as he took her arm and steered her back across the room.

'Because I wanted to talk to you. Lady Foxe is not even here yet.' He bowed to a small knot of gusts talking animatedly and strolled on. 'You look breathtaking, Kat.' He let his fingers caress the crook of her arm where he held her and felt her shiver.

'Thank you, but it is this lovely gown. I am sorry I was ungracious about it.'

'Kat, you would look lovely in a sack. The gown simply shows off the loveliness that it sheathes.' He watched her blush, saw the pearl eardrops tremble and wondered how he was managing not to bend down and nibble the delicate lobe it was suspended from.

'You should not be spending time with me.' She sounded

anxious and he saw she was watching his father, alive for any sign of disapproval.

'I know. I will leave you here with Mr Crace. Kat, I cannot dance with you until later, after supper. Keep your card free after then.'

She smiled, a genuinely amused flash of humour. 'I do not think that humble Miss Cunningham is going to have any problem doing that, Lord Seaton.'

Nick smiled too, at her ridiculous modesty. Was she really unaware that male eyes were following her from all corners of the room? And this was simply the fifty dinner guests.

'Mr Crace, might I leave Miss Cunningham in your care? I believe you will be taking her in to dinner.' He freed her arm and turned away abruptly, suddenly all too conscious that if he did not, he was going to find it impossible to leave her side.

'Miss Cunningham, may an old man be permitted to say that you are in great beauty tonight?' Katherine was startled out of the breathless state Nick's sudden appearance, and as sudden departure, had left her in by the archivist's gallant observation.

'Why, thank you, sir.' The tubby little man beamed at her.

'Now, who can I introduce you to, I wonder?' he mused. 'Not the young men, they will find you quite of their own accord.' He chuckled. 'Let me see…ah, yes, Lady Laithwaite and her daughters. Charming girls, and not so plain that they will mind your company,' he added wickedly. 'Over here.'

Katherine accompanied him, reminding herself that this avuncular figure was also his Grace's lawyer and therefore perfectly *au fait* with her scandalous secret. The whole scene was quite unreal, she felt, glancing round to find Nick. There he was, talking to an uncommonly handsome young lady with copper-red hair and a very lovely bosom. *Which she is displaying to good advantage,* Katherine thought cattily, reluctantly admiring the graceful shoulders and daringly low neckline displayed.

'Who is that?' she whispered to Mr Crace, who appeared to have lost sight of his quarry. 'The tall, red-headed lady talking to Lord Seaton.'

'Lady Camilla Wilde. A striking young lady, is she not? Niece and heiress of old Lord Polkington. Dotes on her and intends to dower her royally, they say.'

Katherine was saved from any further questions that might have revealed the jealous pangs she was experiencing by Heron throwing open the double doors into the dining room and announcing, 'Dinner is served, your Grace!'

As a single girl, Katherine found herself midway down the table, Mr Crace on one side and on the other the handsome young man she and Jenny had spied from the bedroom widow. Mr Crace introduced him.

'Mr Roderick Graham, Miss Cunningham. Mr Graham is a cousin of the Bishop of Durham.'

Close to, Mr Graham proved every bit as personable and attractive as the glimpse from the window had suggested. Katherine soon found herself engrossed in conversation with him about his recent impressions of London which, as a native of Edinburgh, he had visited this year for the first time.

'I have only just returned, in fact,' he explained. 'My cousin was good enough to offer me his hospitality at the Bishop's Palace for the summer. It is already proving as interesting an experience as my visit to London.'

'Is it truly a palace?' Katherine enquired. Mr Graham had explained that as a younger son he had been studying law and she gathered that his home was far more modest than that of his exalted relative.

'Indeed it is,' he agreed, smiling, 'although not so deserving of the name as this edifice.'

'I know,' she replied with feeling. 'I keep getting lost and I suspect that our entire London home would fit easily into this room.'

His speaking look around them encompassed the soaring ceilings, the mirrored walls, the length of silver-laden mahogany and Heron with his army of footmen, and was so comical that Katherine laughed.

As she did so, her eyes found Nick's at the far end of the table. His brows rose, apparently in reaction to her animation. *Good*, the little voice of mischief whispered. *Let him see me having a good time.* She turned back to Mr Graham.

'Have you lived in London all your life?' he asked, listening attentively as she explained how they had moved from the country and how she and Philip had been left alone on the deaths of their parents.

'My brother is travelling abroad at present,' she explained. 'Which is why I find myself here. Lady Fanny has been so kind,' she added, telescoping events ruthlessly to give the impression her chaperon had invited her to stay. 'What did you do in London, Mr Graham? Did you find society to your taste?'

'I did not mix in very exalted circles,' he admitted. 'But I had secured some introductions and had a most pleasant time. I enjoyed visiting galleries and the museums as well, and attended scientific lectures. Out of professional interest I attended several trials at the Law Courts. I even went so far as to attend a public hanging at Newgate.'

'You did?' Katherine enquired faintly.

'Yes. A most barbaric spectacle,' the young lawyer said severely. 'I was soon regretting my error of judgment in being there, but the crowds was so vast that I found myself effectively trapped.'

'Horrible.'

'Your sensitivity does you credit, Miss Cunningham. However, my ill-judged expedition did allow me to witness a most remarkable event: one felon was actually hanged and then cut down at the last moment and pronounced innocent—' He broke off, looking alarmed, 'Miss Cunningham, ma'am—please take a sip of wine. I do beg your pardon, it was most thoughtless of me to speak of such matters to a lady...'

Katherine was faintly aware of him pressing a glass into her hand and took a distracted sip. 'Thank you, no, please do not concern yourself, Mr Graham, I am quite all right.' The dizziness passed. No one else around seemed to have noticed the blood leaching from her face or the slight sway she had given that so alarmed Mr Graham. No one, she realised, except Nick, who from half the table's length away was watching her with a frown. He had put down his knife and fork and his palms were flat on the table as though he were about to rise. She shook her head slightly, saw him relax, and turned back to her concerned neighbour.

'It was nothing to do with the topic, Mr Graham,' she fibbed, the eyes of the hanged felon in question seeming to bore through her. 'I was just feeling a little faint with the heat. I have to confess to being more than a little nervous this evening. I think that your feelings on such spectacles as you describe do you credit, and no one should shrink from discussing such barbarity. How else can we see things improved?'

The passion with which she spoke appeared to make an impression upon the young lawyer and she was startled by the warmth of his regard as he said, low-voiced, 'I would like to discuss other matters of public policy with you, Miss Cunningham, if such things are of concern to you.'

'But certainly, Mr Graham. However, if you will excuse me, I must not neglect Mr Crace.'

She turned to the archivist with a worrying feeling that she had perhaps over-encouraged Mr Graham's interest. The rest of the meal passed uneventfully, even when, with the last remove, conversation became general and she found herself speaking to him again. With relief Katherine told herself that she was imagining things, only to have her hand pressed warmly as the ladies rose to leave the table.

'I hope you will save some dances for me, Miss Cunningham.'

'Of course, sir, I would be delighted.' She smiled up at him and turned to find herself, once again, the focus of Nick's attention. Or, to be more accurate, it was Mr Graham's hand, just releasing hers, that seemed to be attracting his interest. Katherine smiled serenely, deliberately not meeting Nick's eyes as she followed her chaperon out.

Instead of congregating in a withdrawing room, the ladies at once dispersed to their rooms and the attentions of their maids to repair whatever ravages dinner in a warm room had wrought.

Jenny, dabbing Katherine's temples with cologne and whisking a hare's foot dipped in rice powder over her face, professed herself satisfied. 'It's a mercy you don't get all flushed up with the heat like some ladies,' she said chattily, checking hairpins and patting Katherine's glossy coils of hair into place. 'I'll be in the ladies' retiring room all evening in case you need me.'

'Are you sure?' Katherine queried, concerned. 'There will be maids on hand, and you have worked so hard all day. Have you had any dinner yet?'

'Yes, thank you, Miss Katherine. But I am not going to miss this for all the world! And I am certainly not going to risk you not looking your best all night either. Now then, fan, reticule, dance card.' She tied the card by its ribbon to Katherine's wrist and checked that the little pencil was sharp. 'I'll wager it is full already, is it not?'

'Mr Graham, that handsome gentleman we saw from the window, has asked me to dance,' Katherine admitted.

'Now that'll make his lordship jealous,' Jenny concluded smugly.

Katherine was guiltily aware that those were her sentiments too, so she could hardly reprimand Jenny for repeating them. 'Mr Graham was in London and attended the hangings at Newgate,' she said, sombre now that shock was recalled.

'No!' Jenny sat down on the edge of the bed with a thump. 'Did he recognise you?'

'Oh, no. I think there would be no danger of that. All eyes were on the hanged man, I am sure, and the Assistant Governor held me back. But it is a disturbing coincidence, is it not? Thank goodness Lord Seaton's beard had grown, else he could hardly fail to be recognised.'

'Has his neck healed?' Jenny asked. 'Is there still a scar?'

'I have no idea,' Katherine said with dignity. Even the other day when she had burst into his dressing room, disconcerting the tailors, Nick had an immaculate neckcloth in place. He would have to take great care for quite a while, she surmised, wondering what he had told his new valet.

The reappearance of Lady Fanny instantly ended all conversation on dangerous topics and Katherine once more found herself descending the stairs in her chaperon's wake.

'I do hope I have the duties of my charge right,' Lady Fanny confided as they entered the ballroom, bypassing the receiving line where those not resident or dining were being greeted. 'I have never been a chaperon before, you know.' She looked anxious. 'Should I perhaps have warned you about not dancing more than twice with any gentleman? And not drinking champagne?'

'I expect so,' Katherine said gravely. 'And I think you should also warn me that you must give your approval before I waltz, that I must not romp during country dances and I must not go out on to the terrace unless you are with me.'

'There, you know it all as well as I do,' Lady Fanny said gaily, unfurling her fan. 'Now, let us sit over there next to Mrs Cartwright—the general's wife, you know—and their daughters. *Such* a nice family—' She broke off with the approach of Mr Graham.

'Ma'am, I have come hoping to solicit the favour of a dance with Miss Cunningham, if you will permit.'

Lady Fanny beamed. This was her idea of a well set-up young gentleman. 'Of course, sir.'

'Miss Cunningham? Might I hope for a waltz?'

Katherine received an encouraging nod and opened her empty dance card. 'The choice is yours, Mr Graham.'

'The first?' He took her nod for assent and carefully wrote his name in the tiny space. 'And a cotillion?' Again he wrote, then bowed and effaced himself.

To her surprise, Katherine found her card filled rapidly, although she kept the latter part free, mindful of Nick's words. Still, it seemed odd. He could not, obeying convention, ask her for more than two dances, nor could Robert.

The ballroom filled up rapidly, the band ceased playing light airs, paused to retune and then Katherine realised that the Duke with his sons had entered, were taking partners and sets were forming for the opening cotillion.

Nick, she felt predictably, was leading out the eligible redhead; Robert was with a middle-aged lady who was chatting to him in animated fashion and the Duke, looking extremely distinguished, had offered his hand to a formidably handsome lady.

'Baroness van Elvestein,' Mr Crace murmured, arriving to

lead her out. 'The ambassador's wife. Now, this set appears to have a space for us.'

Soon Katherine was lost in the magic of the ball. It was not so terrifying after all, she soon realised. True, the setting was magnificent, the tone lofty, the company distinguished, but she had the satisfaction, regularly reinforced by compliments and admiring glances, of knowing that she looked well. Her upbringing and natural charm stood her in good stead with even the highest sticklers amongst the *grande dames* she encountered, and her full dance card was most gratifying.

The first waltz was next, she realised, glancing round from her position seated meekly beside Lady Fanny. She need not have worried, Mr Graham was at her side, bowing punctiliously to Lady Fanny before taking her charge by the hand and leading her out.

'I am not a very experienced waltzer,' Katherine confided, her cheeks slightly warm with the daring pressure of his hand at her waist.

'What a relief! Neither am I,' Roderick Graham admitted. 'We will just take it carefully and hope your toes will be safe.'

In the event it was a pleasure. Mr Graham had a natural sense of rhythm and was too considerate to try any fancy steps, so Katherine circled the dance floor feeling perfectly at ease.

Mr Graham's new-found expertise was not, however, up to timing his movements so as to deliver Katherine neatly back in front of her chaperon as the music stopped and they found themselves on the far side of the floor.

'Do not worry,' Katherine reassured him as he apologised for them having to circle back. 'I was intending to sit this country dance out in any case.'

'Miss Cunningham.' It was Nick, firmly in front of them and looking, to Katherine's appreciative, and somewhat nervous eye, distinctly saturnine.

Chapter Twenty-Three

'Graham.' Nick nodded to the other man.

'Seaton.' Mr Graham's voice was equally pleasant, equally unyielding.

'If you will excuse me, I will escort Miss Cunningham back to her chaperon.'

'Unnecessary, Seaton, I was just escorting her myself.'

'But I insist.'

'And so do I.'

Oh, Lord. Now what to do? The two were bristling at each other in the most perfectly polite manner imaginable. 'Mr Graham?'

'Yes, Miss Cunningham?'

'I would be most grateful for a glass of lemonade, if you would be so kind.' Katherine opened wide brown eyes at the Scotsman and smiled.

'But of course, Miss Cunningham. I will bring it to where Lady Fanny is sitting immediately.' There was the slightest emphasis on the last word, then he turned on his heel and began to weave his way through the onlookers watching the dancing.

'Honestly, Nick,' Katherine hissed as he took her arm and began to walk in the opposite direction. 'I was feeling like a bone between two dogs.'

'That Scotsman is paying you altogether too much attention.'

'He is not *that Scotsman*,' Katherine retorted. 'He is a perfectly pleasant young lawyer who has simply been courteous enough to talk to me at dinner and to ask me for two dances. If you did not want me to talk to him, you should not have placed me next to him.'

'I had nothing to do with the seating plans.'

'I can see that. If you had, I doubt you would have placed me next to a man who saw you hanged.'

'*What?*'

'He was at Newgate. Somehow I do not think he will recognise you.'

'Is that why you suddenly looked faint at dinner?' She nodded and Nick steered her neatly into an alcove. 'That is better, one can hardly hear oneself think out there.'

'It is certainly a difficult environment in which to have an argument in whispers,' Katherine agreed tartly.

'Is that what we are doing?' He smiled and took her chin between long fingers.

'I do not know how else to characterise it. You pounce on me when I am in the company of a perfectly unexceptionable gentleman, you lecture me on associating with him, for no good reason—oh!' Her complaint was silenced by Nick simply leaning down and kissing her, very firmly, very calmly and with a complete disregard to whatever was happening just the other side of a silk curtain.

'Nick!' Katherine freed her mouth and took a hasty step backwards, coming up with a bump against a pillar. 'People will see.'

'Please be assured, Miss Cunningham, that if I have placed you in a compromising position I am only too ready to do the honourable thing…'

With a suppressed squeak of outrage Katherine swept out of the alcove in what was dangerously close to being a flounce. Nick did not attempt to follow her and she made her way back to Lady Fanny feeling more than a little flustered. Mr Graham was waiting patiently with her drink. He had obviously brought one for her chaperon as well, and was politely attempting to follow one of Lady Fanny's more discursive commentaries.

'Miss Cunningham.' He leapt to his feet and looked behind her with furrowed brow. 'Where is Lord Seaton?'

'I…we…quarrelled. I think.' Katherine took the lemonade and drank it thirstily.

'If he has—' The lawyer was on his feet, hands clenched.

'No, no!' Katherine urged him to sit again. 'Nothing of that sort. It is a…family matter which causes some tension, that is all.'

'You will allow me to escort you in to supper?' He still did not seem easy with her explanation.

'Thank you, yes, that would be most kind.'

Lady Fanny gave an approving nod, then smiled as another tall man approached. 'Cousin Robert, have you come to ask Miss Cunningham to dance?'

'Well, yes.' Robert smiled cheerfully at Katherine. 'Do you have any waltzes free after supper, Miss Cunningham? I'll have done my duty dances by then. But I was hoping you'd let me take you in to supper.'

'You are just too late, Lord Robert. Do you know Mr Graham?'

The men exchanged greetings and Robert suggested they all go in together. 'Cousin Fanny?'

'No, Robert dear, I am joining Lady Willington's party.'

Katherine looked around her for Nick, but there was no sign of him. She bit her lip: quarrelling with him was far from what she had dreamed of doing on this fairytale evening.

Everything was as magnificent as she had imagined, yet light-hearted, almost whimsical in tone. The flowers were massed banks of wildflowers mixed with hot house blooms, the lights twinkled behind shades of different coloured glass, the luxury and attention to detail was laid on with a light hand. It made her smile and think of Nick. She had not expected it of the Duke and wondered if, despite their exchange at lunch the other day, Nick had had some hand in it. Or perhaps he had inherited yet another characteristic of his father.

Then they entered the supper room and there he was, sitting very much at his ease, conversing over a plate of shaved ham with the redhead. What was her name? Clarissa? No, Camilla. Katherine fixed a glittering smile in place and allowed Robert to guide her to a table in full view of his brother. She sank gracefully on to the chair Mr Graham pulled out for her and allowed the two men to bicker politely over who was going to serve her.

'I will fetch the champagne and you fetch the food, then,' Robert concluded, making off towards the table spread with black bottles.

Champagne? Lady Fanny had expressly said no champagne. A few feet away Nick was pouring a wine into Lady Camilla's glass. *Well, if she can, I can. I am not going to be a provincial mouse,* Katherine decided.

Nick looked over and she smiled sweetly at him and waggled her fingers in the kind of coquettish gesture she had always despised in other women.

Nick saw the little wave, correctly reading it for the sarcastic gesture it was meant to be. He bowed in return, lifting his glass in a silent toast that was not lost on his companion, who turned a haughty stare on Kat.

'And who is she?' she enquired coolly. 'A tolerably pretty girl, I must admit, she can certainly dress.'

'A friend of Cousin Fanny. Would you call her pretty?' Nick enquired lazily, trailing one finger around the top of his wine glass. *Good, Robert had recalled his instructions and was bringing champagne. Why the devil he had also brought that prickly Scottish lawyer, goodness knows, unless he had not been able to dislodge him.*

Camilla was preening slightly at his apparent criticism of Kat. She was quite obviously expecting that, as the most eligible lady in the district, he would be making her a declaration before long. Even if he was free, such an assumption irritated him. 'No, definitely not pretty.' Camilla smiled. 'I would call her beautiful.' The smile vanished to be replaced with a pout. *Kat never pouts.*

'Look,' Camilla said brightly with an edge that revealed her anger with him. 'There is Jack Waterfall and my sister Lucy. Jack! Jack, come and join us.'

Nick stood as the others reached the table. 'Will you excuse me a moment?'

Kat was still alone. Across the room Robert was juggling a bottle and three glasses while Graham was apparently undecided on the best way to convey food for three people back to the table.

'Kat?' She was quite well aware he was there, but her start of surprise was masterly and his lips twitched.

'Oh. My lord?'

'Have you saved me a dance, Kat?'

She flicked open the card that dangled from her wrist. 'As instructed, I have kept my card free, awaiting your pleasure.' *Oh, no, Kat, awaiting your pleasure…*

'That one.' He picked up the pencil and wrote his name against a waltz halfway through the remaining dances.

'Just the one?' She sounded piqued, and then frowned, annoyed at herself for revealing it.

'Just the one, Kat.' He smiled and went back to his table. *One is all I need.*

Katherine drank two glasses of champagne, amazed at how it made even the haughtily averted profile of Lady Camilla less annoying. It did not, however, make her husband's behaviour any less mysterious. Was he teasing her? Punishing her for some offence she was unaware of? Flirting?

Flirting? She was not very experienced with such an activity, but surely that was a very strange way to go about it? A footman came up with a message for Robert, who scrambled to his feet with a muttered, 'Oh, lor'. Cousin Timberlake is in his cups again. Please excuse me, Ka…Miss Cunningham.'

Alone with Roderick Graham, and emboldened by the two glasses of wine, Katherine said, 'Mr Graham, if you were to flirt with me, how would you go about it?'

He almost choked on a lobster patty and took several moments before he could reply. 'You would like me to flirt with you, Miss Cunningham?'

'Oh, no, I am sorry. No, it is just that I am very inexperienced with things like that, and I am sure I would not notice if a gentleman were to flirt, and, naturally, one should be awake to that sort of thing.' Now she had embarked upon this, Katherine was not at all sure how she was going to extricate herself. 'And, naturally, one cannot ask a man who one would not trust,' she finished in a rush. Possibly respectable Scottish lawyers, however youthful and good looking, were not the right type of man to ask. She misjudged Mr Graham.

'Well.' He cleared his throat. 'Firstly I think I would fill up your wine glass and hand it to you, like this—and let my fingertips touch yours, like that.'

'Oh.'

'And then I would raise my glass in a toast to you, like this, and hold your eyes while I did so.'

'Oh.' Katherine swallowed. 'And then?'

'I would tell you what very beautiful eyes you have. And what very long eyelashes you have.' He paused. 'Would you like me to continue? I have to say, it is a pleasurable employment, but Lord Seaton appears to be becoming enraged, and whilst I—'

'No! No, thank you very much, Mr Graham; that was most instructive.' Well, if that was flirting, then Nick was certainly not indulging in it. On the other hand, if he was annoyed by Mr Graham—and she was most certainly not going to give him the satisfaction of looking in his direction—then that was interesting in itself.

She refused offers of another ice and left the supper room with her escort. There seemed to be only one explanation for her husband's behaviour: possessiveness and a strong protective instinct. Which was depressing, for she did not want to be regarded as a possession to be guarded or a feeble woman to be protected.

But such melancholy thoughts were banished by a gratifying stream of requests for dances, to the point where she had to refuse the two before her waltz with Nick in order to escape and see Jenny.

Her maid clucked over a torn hem and made Katherine stand stock-still while she knelt and whipped the seam hastily. 'And just look at your back hair.' She relieved her feelings by jabbing in pins enthusiastically. 'When do you dance with the master?'

'The next dance. Jenny, am I flushed?'

'Just nicely,' Jenny pronounced, head on one side. 'Bite your lips a little. There, now off you go.'

A quadrille was in progress and Katherine stayed where she was rather than make her way round to where Lady Fanny was deep in gossip with a bosom friend.

'Another glass of champagne?' It was Nick, standing right beside her, a glass in each hand.

'I have had two,' she said realising how gauche it sounded.

'Another will not hurt.'

'Very well.' Katherine took the glass, startled to find that Nick's fingertips touched hers. She looked up and found herself gazing deep into black eyes that seemed to burn hot.

The quadrille came to a close, the dancers clapping and walking off the floor. Nick retrieved her half-empty glass and set it down. 'Now, Kat.' And took her in his arms.

She was reminded of how he had held her the morning she had left him in Newgate; that fierce intensity. She looked up, but only his eyes betrayed any emotion beyond a pleasant social smile.

The music started and she was swept into the dance. This was nothing like Mr Graham's carefully executed steps or the cautious and proper approach of the other gentleman she had waltzed with that evening. This was a very different experience indeed.

Her head whirling, she was conscious that she was improperly close to Nick's body. When he whirled her round their thighs brushed, his hand tightened on her waist. She was so close that when she tried to look up she had to tip her head. It would be much more comfortable just to move closer and rest it against his waistcoat.

It was very strange, the music seemed to be getting softer, the floor harder, the air cooler. Hazily Katherine realised her eyes were closed and her head was, after all, resting on Nick's chest as he swept her round and round and round. And there was no more music, only Nick humming softly in her ear.

'Nick?' It was far too difficult to open her eyes.

'Mmm?'

'Where are we?'

'On the terrace. Look.'

He came to a halt and reluctantly Katherine opened her eyes and gasped. They were standing on the edge of the terrace, looking out towards the lake. Instead of it being merely a darker smudge in the dark parkland, it was illuminated with lanterns all around the edge and on what she realised must be boats on the surface.

'Nick, it is magical.' It came out as a whisper. Had anyone seen them come out here? It was a very fast thing to be doing, yet here, now, in his arms, prudence fled.

'Look at the house.' He turned her within the shelter of his arm to look at the fairytale palace the Duke had conjured up with light. Flambeaux blazed along the frontage, lanterns flicked and danced on every balcony and, amidst the urns and containers of white flowers that seemed to be everywhere, more lights glowed silver.

'Come this way, let me show you a secret.' She was almost unaware of his arm around her waist, drawing her to him. All she was conscious of was enchantment, a feeling of safety and warmth, and a stirring deep in her veins as though her blood was turning to liquid silver, flashing and running through her.

In a dream she let Nick guide her slowly along the broad terrace and round the corner of the great house. On this façade too the flambeaux blazed and the lanterns glowed. Nick stopped at the foot of one of the turrets. One flaming torch was thrust in a holder by a small door. In the breeze the flame snapped and flared, colouring Nick's face with red light. He looked unfamiliar, but not frightening.

'Kat, look at me.'

'I am.'

'Kat…' His mouth took hers in a hot, fierce claiming that swept her away instantly. There was nothing to do but yield to it, arch her body into his, open her lips to the pressure of his, ignore the voice of common sense that was battering away at her mind like a moth at a lighted window. *Stop this now, before it is too late…*

It's a kiss, only a kiss, her yearning, loving, heart argued back. *I can stop any time I want to… I love him, he will never hold me like this again… It is only for a moment, then we can go back and no one will know.*

His mouth was kissing, nibbling a hot path down her throat, up again to the lobe of her ear. One hand held her hard against him, the other strayed down caressingly to circle her breast.

Katherine gasped, stunned that the touch could send fire deep into her belly, set up an ache that could find no relief in either his touch or his mouth returning to hers. The earth moved, the stars and the looming bulk of the tower above her shifted. At first she thought dazedly that she was fainting, then she found she was in Nick's arms and he was shouldering open the tower door.

No. Her voice was not working; she mustered all her strength of will now, while his caressing hands were stilled and his mouth had left hers, and tried again. 'No. Nick, stop, this is madness. What are you doing?'

'Carrying you upstairs to my bed where I intend making love to you.' His voice was calm, not even breathless with the climb; if she had not been pressed against his chest, able to feel the thud of his heart, she would have thought him unmoved.

'No!' she said again. 'You *promised* me that I could have the marriage annulled. How can I if we make love?'

'I would never break a promise to you, Kat.' He had reached a landing on the spiral stairs and shifted her in his arms so he could open the door. 'I did not say *we* were going to make love. I said I am going to make love to *you*. There is a difference.'

'I…I do not understand.'

'I know.' They were at his bedchamber door. Katherine knew she should struggle, but the same trust that had filled her when she had looked across that prison room into the eyes of a filthy, unshaven felon possessed her now.

They were inside the room. Candles burned steadily, there was a fire in the grate and on the washstand steam rose lazily from the jug. Someone had only just left. Nick set her gently on her feet and reached behind him to turn the key in the lock. 'The key is in the door, Kat—you can walk away if you want to.'

Chapter Twenty-Four

'I do not think I do want to leave,' she said with difficulty, searching his face. 'I should, I know. Nick, why?'

'I asked you to wait a month before you made your decision. I have shown you my family, my home, the house you can make our own. I just wanted to give you a glimpse of one of the other benefits of married life.' He was smiling at her reassuringly, but the dark fires were in his eyes and she knew that, whatever he was feeling at this moment, it was not calm, not restrained. And yet he was holding all that back for her.

She knew she was blushing and suddenly did not care. 'Yes, Nick.'

'You trust me?'

'I have always trusted you,' she said simply and was rewarded by the flare of emotion in his eyes.

'I think we had better dispense with this very beautiful gown extremely carefully,' he said thoughtfully, letting his hands rest on her shoulders. 'I look forward to seeing you wearing it again. Now, how does it fasten, I wonder?' His hands drifted, explored while she held her breath. 'Ah, I see, little buttons: one, two, three…four.' The narrow shoulders of the gown slipped down under his palms. 'If I hold it and you step out—or is the approved method over your head?'

'Over.' It was so hard to speak. She was suddenly blind in the rustling silken darkness, then blinking again in the candle-light.

Her petticoats were slipped off, then Nick was turning her in his arms, nuzzling softly at her nape while his fingers tangled with the laces of her stays. 'These are tight. How do you breathe?' Then the stays fell away and she took a deep breath, cut short as Nick's hands came up to cup her breasts.

'*Nicholas.*'

'Mmm?'

'You…oh!' His thumbs were flicking lightly at her nipples through the thin fabric of her chemise. She wriggled against him and found herself turned again.

'Do…not…wriggle like that.' He seemed breathless and Katherine suddenly experienced a soaring, liberating sense of power. She had thought her body and will were reacting blindly to his knowing hands and mouth, but now she knew she could have as powerful an effect on him. And it was a power she would do well not to exercise, she realised. Which was easier thought than done, given her complete lack of experience with men. She slid her feet out of her kid slippers, then stood quite still, her heart hammering, wondering what he was going to do next.

With an expression of great concentration Nick was undoing the ribbons that secured the shoulders of her chemise, and with a little shiver she realised his fingers were shaking, just very, very slightly. And this was a man whose hands had been steady in the condemned cell, on the gallows, facing an armed highwayman.

She was so rapt in the thought that it was a second before she realised that she was naked except for her silk stockings and her long evening gloves. Instinctively her hands flew to cover herself. Nick was looking at her with an expression that took her breath away. There was desire there—however inexperienced she was, she could recognise that—but there was something else, something almost reverent.

'Are you not going to take anything off?' she ventured, anxious to break the silence that was racking her nerves.

Nick kicked off his shoes, tossed aside his jacket and waistcoat and tugged loose his neckcloth and the top three buttons of his shirt.

'Is that all?' Katherine was uncertain whether to be relieved or disappointed.

'I told you I would never break a promise to you, Kat, but I have no intention of making it any harder than it need be.' He took a step towards her, then another. With a squeak Katherine backed away until the edge of the bed caught the back of her knees and she sat down. 'Am I frightening you?' He stopped.

'No. Yes. I do not know.' She was wittering, she realised, and pulled herself together. *How am I feeling?* 'Yes, I am scared,' she admitted. He took a step back. 'And I think I rather like it,' she finished in a rush of honesty.

Before she knew quite what had happened she was flat on her back on the bed, her hands caught above her head in the grasp of one large, gentle fist, her legs, which she tried instinctively to curl up protectively, were trapped under the weight of his leg and Nick was looking down at her with a gleam in his eyes that made her swallow hard.

'Brave, honest Kat. May I take off your stockings?'

He was asking permission to take off *stockings* when everything else had been so ruthlessly disposed of? She nodded. As soon as her hands were free, one arm flew to cover her breasts, the other hand spread palm open, protectively across the dark tangle of curls.

She had a lot to learn, she realised as his fingers began to play with her garters. Apparently it was possibly to make removing a pair of stockings last not seconds but long, long minutes, and to make the act one of exquisite, pleasurable torture.

Stunned, she wriggled up against the pillows so she could watch his dark head, bent attentively over the task of removing two ribbons and two scraps of knitted silk. How could the straying fingers following the slow descent of the stockings as he rolled them down create such shivers of sensitivity? Why, when he bent to kiss her knee, did she have to bite her lip to stop crying out? Why, when his long fingers reached her ankle and then her instep and stopped to trail slowly up and down, up and down, did she have not the slightest urge to giggle, to protest that she was ticklish? Why was she lying back against the pillows, her eyes closed, her breath short?

His mouth replaced his fingers; kissing, nibbling, licking its way up to her knees, which she instinctively drew together. His hands pressed them apart, open, and his mouth began to torment the soft flesh of the back of her right knee. She gasped, felt her body arch with some instinct she did not understand and he murmured, 'Too soon.'

The mattress shifted and Katherine blinked and found he was lying beside her again, propped on one elbow. Everything inside her ached, yearned, needed...what? She had no idea. Nick had promised she would remain a virgin, so what could her untutored body be expecting?

He took her hand in his and bent over the tiny pearl buttons that fastened her glove from wrist almost to shoulder.

Removing her evening gloves with a button hook and great care took Jenny five minutes. Hazily trying to keep track of the passing of time Katherine thought it had taken Nick that long to undo five buttons, exposing enough of her wrist for him to kiss it with soft, nipping kisses. Slowly he worked his way up one arm, then the other, then peeled off the soft kid and threw the gloves aside.

Silence. Her eyes closed, arms thrown back on the pillow, Katherine waited, all thoughts of modesty utterly vanquished. Her body felt heavy, languid, yet her heart was beating like a mill wheel in the race and her breathing was short.

'Look at me, Kat.' She dragged her eyes open and found Nick was looking down into her face while the palm of his hand moved slowly down the swell of her breast until it was over the nipple. Her eyes fluttered closed.

'Look at me, Kat.' With an effort she opened her eyes again and his hand skimmed lower until it caressed the soft swell of her stomach, then down again until his fingers tangled with the curls beneath.

'Shh,' he whispered even as her lips parted in protest, then stayed parted in a gasp of shocked pleasure as one finger slipped through the curls into the secrets they hid.

It slipped, moved, teased until her body was tossing restlessly, her eyes wide and unseeing and her breath coming in short desperate gasps as she struggled to find whatever this aching frenzy was promising her. Then he closed her desperate mouth with his just as the tormenting pleasure burst in a shower of lights and spiralled her into darkness.

'Kat.'

'Mmm?' It seemed that she was not drifting through space, but was being held, very gently, against a long hard body that smelt familiarly of limes and sandalwood.

Her cheek was resting on warm linen, her legs curled up against satin. 'Come back, Kat.' Nick was gently kissing his way along the sensitive line where hair met forehead.

Seized with shyness, she buried her face against his chest,

curling her naked body against his clothed one. 'I had no idea,' she said shakily when she thought she could command her voice.

'I am glad to hear it,' Nick said so drily that she laughed and looked up at him.

'You told Robert to give me champagne,' she accused, suddenly seeing his tactics clearly. 'You did not...'

'Tell him why? Of course not.'

'Then why should he do as you ask?'

'Because I am his elder brother,' Nick said with unconscious arrogance. 'Forget Robert,' he added callously. 'Are you cold? Sleepy?'

'No.' Katherine shook her head. Did he want to send her back to bed? Her entire body was soft, glowing, alive with a new vibrant awareness. She wanted to touch him, explore his body as he had explored hers, and she knew that was impossible, forbidden.

'Good.' He bent over her, his lips and then his tongue fretting at her nipple.

'Nick!' The sensations her body had only just learned surged back, differently nuanced now with her newfound knowledge, every bit as overwhelming. He moved down her body, slowly tasting and savouring while Katherine, shocked, shy and in thrall all over again, surrendered to him.

His tongue flicked teasingly at her navel, making her laugh, then trailed down with an intent that turned the laughter into a gasp of protest, then a low moan of pleasure as Nick kissed her intimately, his hands caressing her flanks, his breath heating her already hot flesh into shuddering arousal. She knew now what that aching, building tension was leading to, but when it broke she broke with it into a thousand sparkling shards of pleasure, falling, drifting down into velvet blackness.

Nick lay watching the morning light build outside his windows, the discomfort of his unsatisfied body at odds with the deep contentment of his mind.

Kat was curled up against him, her head on his chest, one hand tucked confidingly in his, deeply asleep. He smiled, his mouth buried in the soft tangle of her hair. The most difficult thing had been not to tell her he loved her. Every instinct had urged him to do so; his mind had urged caution. Caught up in the emotional tumult of her first sexual experience, could she trust her own responses in the cold light of day? Could he?

No, best to let her think, to ponder on what his own abstinence might mean, wonder about his motives a little. On the night of the dinner party he had planned, that was when he would tell her and hope that she had fallen just a little in love with him—enough to agree to give up her desperate independence and take on what he realised, if his father and Robert did not, must seem an even more daunting responsibility.

She liked him, trusted him, that he had always known. She seemed, by her innocent responses to him, to find him attractive, but none of that would be enough for Kat. She wanted love and he had to make sure she saw it as genuine, not a trap to hold her to this marriage that was not a marriage.

The sun was edging higher: time to move. He slid carefully out of bed, hardening his heart against the small grumble of protest she made. With the care of a ladies' maid he picked up discarded petticoats, hunted for stockings and garters, found an errant glove and began to ferry all of Kat's clothing back to her own dressing room.

Then he returned to the big bed, reached under the covers and picked Kat up. She turned in his arms, half-waking, and her mouth found his neck just below the fading marks of the noose. Her lips moved slightly as if tasting and the caress almost undid his will power. Nick stood with her in his arms, breathing deeply until the urge to lay her down and rip off his clothes ebbed a little, then strode into her bedchamber and tucked her into her own bed, pulled the covers up snugly around her, turned on his heel and walked away.

He went and looked out over the park, shining in the early morning light. The chilly waters of the lake beckoned as a cure for his aching loins and overheated imagination. His mouth curled at the thought of what any early-rising guest might think if they saw him striding across the dew-soaked grass in the full splendour of a Chinese silk dressing gown and diving into the lake. That would be taking eccentricity a little too far.

But there was Grandfather George's plunge pool, which the previous Duke had had constructed in the aftermath of his Grand Tour in imitation of a Roman bath house. Nick pulled on the heavy dressing gown, snatched up a towel and padded off along the corridors in the direction of the Duke's suite.

The pool was concealed with heavy drapes further down the corridor from his father's bedchamber. Nick slipped in and saw that it was full of clear, doubtless cold, water with a stand of towels by the side. It was a rectangle with a curved end set within a small pillared room with some of the statues the Duke had brought back from Italy and marble inlays on the floor. He remembered it as being perhaps four foot deep and just long enough to take two strokes from end to end, with a submerged bench all around the edge.

Too shallow for the dive he was hoping for to shock his system into some semblance of calm, but he cast off his robe, stepped down into the pool and ducked under the water. It was as cold as he expected and wonderfully effective. With a sigh of relief Nick struck out and took two plunging strokes to the apse end, turned and dived under the surface to glide back again.

As he surfaced, tossing the wet hair back from his face, the curtain opened and his brother and Roderick Graham appeared. They were still in evening dress, more than a little owl-eyed and dishevelled, and Robert had a champagne bottle by the neck.

'Hello, Nick,' he said amiably. 'Didn't expect to see you here.'

'You are drunk,' Nick observed. 'If you're coming in, for heaven's sake get undressed first.'

'What? Oh, yes, good idea. We're a bit tired, that's all,' Robert announced, shedding clothes on to the marble with a fine disregard. 'Not drunk, just a bit on the go.'

'Aye, that's the way of it,' Graham announced, suddenly sounding extremely Scottish. He tossed his waistcoat on to the pile of Robert's clothes and peered hazily at Nick. 'Hurt your neck?'

Nick slid further down on the submerged bench until the water reached his chin. 'Leather military stock,' he said lightly, 'Damn things chafe like the devil at first, I've never lost the mark.' He choked as a slapping wave of water hit him with Robert's uncoordinated tumble into the pool, followed by the lawyer's slightly more graceful descent. 'Will you have a care, you clumsy oaf?' He slapped his brother lightly over his soaked head and suddenly found himself seized in a wrestler's hold. The two of them struggled, laughing and spluttering in the cold water, all at once boys again. Graham fended off one, then another, and finally managed to duck both of them, at which they turned on him and pushed him under.

Nick surfaced, almost weeping with laughter, to find himself regarding the toes of a pair of Morocco leather slippers and the hem of a sombre red silk robe. 'Oh, God.'

'Inaccurate and blasphemous,' his father observed frigidly. 'Might I hope that one of you will be good enough to knock on my door and inform me when my bath is available? If, that is, there is any water left in it.'

From the swirling water Nick realised that the other two had taken cowardly refuge behind him. 'Yes, sir. I mean, we are just about to get out now, sir.'

'Then I will remove myself from what will doubtless be a thoroughly unedifying sight.'

The curtain swished closed and Nick hauled himself out of the pool with a rueful chuckle. 'And how old did that make you feel?' he enquired of Robert, who was clambering out the other side.

His brother considered carefully. 'Fourteen,' he hazarded. 'Damn it, I wish I had his tongue—or is it that left eyebrow?'

'I have no idea, they are both lethal.' Nick finished a brisk towelling and pulled on his robe, which he had had the foresight to hang up. 'How do you two intend to get back to your rooms?' He prodded a saturated pile of cloth, then shook out the pile of towels. 'It will take more than one of these to cover your blushes. I suggest you hurry before the upstairs maids are about.'

Katherine swam up out of a dream where she was floating in a mass of black velvet, sipping champagne while Nick caressed her body with peacock feathers. 'Tickles,' she murmured faintly and woke to find her own tumbled hair was tickling her nose.

'Are you awake, Miss Katherine?' It was Jenny, who stopped tiptoeing around the room and drew back the curtains with a swish. 'It's a lovely day.'

Katherine struggled up sleepily against the pillows, her brain fuddled by the incredible dreams that had filled her night. Then she saw Jenny's expression as the maid waited impatiently at the end of the bed. 'What happened?'

'Happened?' Katherine blinked at her.

'After supper. The master told me I could go up to bed any time I wanted because he would look after you.'

'He said…' Katherine was suddenly very awake indeed. It had happened, it was not a dream. Nick had made love to her last night.

Jenny was positively fidgeting with impatience. 'Is it all right now? You are staying married to him?'

'No. No, nothing happened that meant I could not get an annulment,' she said firmly, ignoring Jenny's downcast face while she wrestled with last night's events and what they meant.

Had anyone seen them leave? Had they been missed or had Nick's timing been perfect? And if they had been seen, what then? Nick already had a reputation as a rake, possibly his actions would provoke nothing more than some tuts of disapproval. *As for me*, she reflected ruefully, *I'll soon be gone so they can think what they like of Miss Cunningham.*

Nick had done everything he could to seduce her into staying short of breaking his promise to her. Why? Presumably because she had made it clear she was not going to change her mind because she liked his family or he had offered her a home less overwhelming than the house. But the only thing that was going to persuade her to stay was if he told her he loved her. And surely, Katherine thought, hugging the memory of last night to her, surely if he was ever going to say it, that would have been the time.

Even if he had, they would have had to consider long and hard whether it would be right to stay together. She could never forget Nick's position, his inheritance and his father's expectations.

But although he did not love her, he had given her a night she was never going to forget, a night filled with tenderness and ecstasy and trust fulfilled. Leaving him was going to hurt his pride, if not his heart, and she had so much to thank him for. How was she ever going to repay that?

Katherine swung her legs out of bed. One thing was certain, she had no intention of facing Nick over the breakfast table, so the sooner she went down the better. 'What time is it?'

'Half past seven, Miss Katherine. Surely you are going to have breakfast in bed?'

'No, I will go down.' She felt too restless, too unlike herself to stay in bed. Nick was not one of life's early risers if he had any choice, so, if she was down by eight, she should be safe. 'The dimity gown will be perfectly all right.' Probably none of the other guests would be about either and she could escape to a corner of the Long Gallery after breakfast and try to think.

Nick was not in the breakfast room, but to her surprise both Robert and Roderick Graham were, both of them looking somewhat the worse for wear. They got to their feet as she came in and out of respect for their heavy eyes and sallow faces she helped herself quietly from the chafing dishes arranged on the sideboard and did not attempt to make conversation once the conventional greetings had been exchanged.

Then they were on their feet again as the Duke stalked in, looking as fresh as if he was fifty years old and had spent the previous evening reading by his fireside before retiring to bed at ten.

'Good morning, Miss Cunningham. Mr Graham. Robert, where is your brother?'

'Breakfasting in his room, I imagine, sir.'

'Hmm.' The old man's inimical stare fixed on Katherine.

'Possibly Lord Seaton is not a natural early riser, your Grace; some people are not,' she ventured.

'Modern affectations. I do not hold with them.' The Duke sat down with his plate and engaged a nervous Mr Graham in meticulously polite conversation. That gentleman's relief when the Duke finished his frugal breakfast was patent and he made his escape with Robert without a backward glance.

Katherine watched the Duke from under her lashes. His back was upright, his shoulders set, his expression calm and haughty. But under it she thought she could glimpse an old man. A tired, sad old man. Something caught inside her and she realised it was a pang of pity and compassion. But what could she do to help the Duke?

Chapter Twenty-Five

Katherine was visited by a sudden, terrifying idea. If she could, in some small way, reconcile Nick and his father, surely that was the best way she could possibly repay him for everything he had done for her? It was the only way she could express her love, even if he never knew what she had done, or why.

'Sir.' She got to her feet as the Duke did. 'May I speak with you, sir?' As soon as she had thought it, she knew how foolish it was to be afraid. He was just a man, an old man she had grown fond of.

'Of course, my dear. Would you care to come into the library?' When they reached it he pulled forward a chair for her and she sank into it, searching for words she wished desperately she had had the opportunity to rehearse. 'Katherine, is anything wrong?'

'Sir...please forgive me if this is presumptuous, but I have to speak with you about Nicholas.' He still seemed receptive, so she carried on in a rush. 'Sir, he loves you so much, he is so proud of you and I believe you feel the same about him, but neither of you show it. He is hurting, although he hides it, and I know it cannot be easy for you either.'

The old man's mouth twisted suddenly and Katherine held her breath, convinced she had either distressed him or had simply overstepped the mark, but all he said was, 'Go on.'

'He left all those years ago because he was hurt and angry. From what he has told me, I am sure he offered you ample cause for anger. But you knew where he was in London, you knew what he was doing and you did not send for him, or go to him. He was very young, very proud, with a pride he learned from you. And that pride has hardened now to the point where it is difficult for him to take that first step, even though his conscience tells him he should.

'Sir, you were so cool, so ironic when he came back. My father died ten years ago, but what I remember most of all about him was his warmth, his forgiveness, even when we had hurt or disappointed him.'

'I find it hard to imagine that you were ever a disappointment to your parents, Katherine.' It was said gently without any of the mocking edge the Duke's voice so often held.

'Of course I was,' she said, half-laughing at the memories. 'All children are, surely, from time to time. But if they know themselves to be loved, then they try harder next time.' It had worked with Philip while her parents were alive, but since then it seemed her own influence was never enough.

'I love both my sons, and I am proud of them both.'

'I know that, but do they?' She was growing in confidence now she knew the old man would not snub her efforts. 'Did you know that Nicholas fought at Waterloo, that he had two horses shot out from under him?'

'I knew he fought there, he let that much slip.' The Duke hesitated, then said slowly, 'I felt such dread that I could hardly speak, such pride I thought my heart might burst with it. I saw him standing there, so correct, so controlled, so obviously unwilling to share with me what must have been a devastating experience, and there were no words.'

'He is a fine man,' Katherine said, unaware of how her expression betrayed her. 'And a brave one. It hurts him to speak of that battle and he will say little to me because I am a woman and he wants to protect me. He would speak to you, if you only ask. Has he told you that we were held up by highwaymen on our way here?'

The Duke's eyebrows rose. 'He has not.'

Katherine giggled, despite the tension she was under. 'He was wonderful. He climbed out of the carriage, told them he was Black Jack Standon and showed off the marks of the noose on his neck. He thinks so fast and has such courage.' She hesitated. 'I saw him on the scaffold in the moments before the trap dropped. No one there knew who he was: but he did. He knew he was a Lydgate, and he knew how a Lydgate faced death. And he learned that at your knee.'

The Duke suddenly dropped his face into his hands and Katherine, without thinking, fell to her knees beside his chair and put her arms around him. 'Oh, sir, you are both so proud—please do not let that separate you from your son.'

After a moment he looked up at her and she saw his eyes were wet with tears. 'Thank you for that, my dear. I imagine I am not an easy person to approach in such a way, am I?'

That, if ever she had heard one, was an understatement.

'No, sir.'

'I rather think your courage is a fitting match for my son's. I will do as you ask, I promise. Perhaps, when he does bestir himself, you would be very kind and ask him to join me here. There is no need to tell him why. And Katherine,' he added as she reached the door, 'you have heard the expression, *The pot calling the kettle black*?'

'Yes, your Grace.' She regarded him, puzzled.

'Might I humbly suggest you apply it to yourself?'

Even more puzzled, she walked back slowly into the Long Gallery. What could the Duke mean? She was so absorbed in speculation that when she bumped into her husband she spoke to him without the slightest self-consciousness.

'Oh, there you are, Nick. Your father asked me when I saw you to request that you join him in the library.'

'Yes, of course. Kat, are you…?'

'Go on, he is waiting.' She pushed him firmly in the direction she had come from and walked on until she found her favourite window seat and curled up in it.

She had had the temerity to chide the Duke for letting his pride stand between him and the son he loved. Was that what he meant? That she was letting her own pride stand between herself and Nick? It was a chastening thought. All the time she had been fighting his pride, the honour that she felt must be driving him to maintain this marriage, and all the time it was her own pride that was opposing him.

To see her motives in such a light was not very comfortable. And if the Duke was encouraging her to examine her feelings, did that mean he was not opposed to the match? What other way could she read it?

And if the Duke was not opposed, and Nick was doing everything in his power to stop the annulment— *Why am I fighting? I love him. He cares for me. To turn from him cuts at his sense of honour and what is right. I might not be the bride he would have chosen, but…* Her thoughts baulked for a moment, then continued. *I can make him happy and, one day, he might grow to love me.*

Dizzy with a sort of terrified happiness, Katherine got to her feet and ran down the Gallery. She would wait outside the library, close enough to see when Nick came out. And then she would tell him that she would agree to let the marriage stand if he still wanted it.

There was a seat just past the library door that would be ideal. She slowed to a decorous walk and came level with the library door, which stood ajar.

Nick's voice came clearly through the opening, then faded. He was obviously walking up and down.

'…honour bound to marry her. How could I do anything else?…trapped…make the best of it…' She froze, uncaring that she was eavesdropping.

The voices within dropped to a murmur. It seemed both men were pacing. Then the Duke's voice came to her.

'A nice enough girl… but in no way fitted for the role of your wife. Such a marriage…disastrous, and I think you knew it…from the beginning, but once…your honour would not let you turn away from her…'

Katherine walked blindly on down the corridor. The Duke had spoken of her with pity but also with a finality that made any idea of giving in to Nick's persuasions quite ineligible. Under no circumstances was she going to be the cause of a new estrangement from his father. How could she have so misinterpreted the Duke's parting words to her? Perhaps they had simply been a subtly worded rebuke.

'My lady?' It was Heron, a salver balanced on his white gloved hand.

'Heron, I am sorry, I did not see you.' She blinked back the moisture in her eyes and forced a smile.

'This note has just arrived for you, my lady. The lad from the Durham Ox delivered it.'

Curious despite her distress, Katherine lifted the proffered note, then froze as she saw the direction—it was unmistakably Philip's handwriting. All other thought fled. Thank goodness, at least he was alive and in England. Oblivious of

Heron's presence, she broke the seal and scanned the single sheet.

Katy, I am here at the Durham Ox, please come, I badly need to see you, Your loving brother, Philip.

He was back in England! Was that good news, or bad? Part of her hoped he had come to his senses and decided to return and reform his life, but bitter experience and the desperate scrawl of the writing made her fear the worst. How did he know where to find her? Arthur, she supposed. She had asked him to keep it a secret, but presumably he considered she could not have meant to hide from her own brother.

'Heron, I need a gig and a groom to drive me to this inn directly.'

'My lady, his lordship—'

'My lord is with his Grace and must not be disturbed. My bro…there is someone whom I need to see at once.'

'Very well, my lady.'

Katherine did not trouble to ring for Jenny. Her bonnet was on its block, her pelisse and gloves were laid out on the bed and it was a matter of minutes to make ready. Katherine scooped up her reticule and hesitated; the stocking purse within had just a few coins in it after her extravagances for the ball. With a grimace she reached into the dressing table drawer and withdrew the last of the money Mr Wilkinson had given her. It would be a miracle if Philip were not short of funds.

Heron was hovering in the hall when she got there. 'The gig is outside, my lady, but are you sure you should not wait for his lordship?'

'Quite certain, thank you, Heron,' Katherine said with a confidence she was far from feeling. She wanted to see her brother again; no day had passed without her worrying about him and how he was faring, but this unannounced arrival did not bode well.

'Very well, my lady. Durren, drive her ladyship to the Durham Ox. And wait *inside* for her,' he added with some emphasis.

Her first glimpse of the hostelry explained much about Heron's concern. It was the antithesis of the inn they had stayed at on the last night of their journey from London. This place was stark, shabby and, to Katherine's anxious eye, sinister.

Durren handed her down from the gig with an air that spoke clearly of his own feelings about the place.

The landlord, when he finally appeared, was surly until confronted by Katherine's coldly raised eyebrows and firm request to be taken to Mr Cunningham. 'Back parlour, miss,' he admitted with a shrug and a jerk of his thumb.

'I'll wait in the tap,' Durren said, eyeing the man with disfavour. 'Unless you wish me to accompany you, ma'am.'

'No, thank you, Durren. I will call if I need you,' Katherine said and laid her hand on the door to the parlour.

'Go and find Katherine.' The Duke laid a hand on his elder son's shoulder and let it rest for a moment. 'It is time you ended this farce of a marriage.'

Nick looked at his father and met the dark eyes, so like his own. He could remember feeling this churned up inside, this unsure, only once before. And that was six years ago when he had made the decision to walk away from his home, his family, his inheritance without even the woman he had thought he loved by his side.

He put up his own hand and let it rest on the older man's for a moment. Whatever else happened he had this now, this warmth and understanding that he had never shared with his father before. And he was all too aware he had Kat to thank for it. 'I will go and find her now,' he said.

Heron appeared as if by magic as he came out of the room. 'My lord, might I speak with you?'

'Later, Heron, I must find her ladyship.'

'It is about her ladyship that I wish to speak my lord. She has left.'

'*Left?* When?'

'About thirty minutes ago, my lord. Without her maid.' He hesitated. 'A letter arrived for her, hand-delivered from some-one staying at the Durham Ox.'

'From whom?' Who the devil could be writing to Kat, and who, staying at the Ox, could possibly know her?

'I could not say, my lord.' The butler hesitated. 'It seemed to worry her, my lord, although as she already appeared to be somewhat distressed I cannot be certain it was the letter that had that effect.'

'Lady Seaton was distressed? Do you know what caused that?' What could have upset her enough to leave so abruptly?

Heron looked embarrassed, an unusual phenomenon. 'I was coming to look for her and saw her approaching down the corridor. I do not think she was aware of me, as I had just come around the corner and this end of the corridor is some-what shadowed. She stopped abruptly at the door of his Grace's study, hesitated and appeared to listen. She only stood there a moment, but she put up her hand to her mouth, as though in distress, and when she came up to me I saw she had tears in her eyes.'

Nick stared at the butler blindly. The door had been ajar, he had noticed it just now as he left. What had they been say-ing that she could have overheard? Then he realised just how their conversation about Arabella could have been misunder-stood, especially if only partly heard.

What had he said? Something about having realised that Arabella was not the right wife for him, but feeling honour bound—feeling trapped—into asking her to marry him. His father's words came back clearly. *A nice enough girl, Miss Somersham, but in no way fitted for the role of your wife. Such a marriage would have been disastrous, and I think you knew it in your heart from the beginning, but, once committed, your honour would not let you turn away from her, I know that.* If the name had been inaudible, as indeed it might, for the Duke had been pacing up and down the room as he spoke, then Kat could well have believed everything he said applied to her.

'Her ladyship began to say something,' Heron ventured. 'I thought it might have been her brother who had written.'

'Hell,' Nick said softly. He had always felt confident that Kat would not take it into her head to simply leave him and try to obtain an annulment at a distance because she had no one to go to and no resources. But her brother, however unsatisfactory, was at least a male protector. 'Thank you, Heron.'

He strode towards the hall, taking the stairs two at a time and burst out of the front door just as Robert rode past on the grey stallion Xerxes. The animal shied violently, then reared, almost unseating Robert, who got it under control with an effort and the use of language most unfitting to a candidate for the church.

Nick grabbed the rein. 'Off, Robert. I need him.'

'What for?' Robert dismounted. 'Is something wrong?'

'Kat.' Nick swung up into the saddle and reined in hard while he found the stirrups. 'She's run off.' He was not wearing spurs, but the grey did not need them; with a snort it gathered its haunches under it and set off at the gallop.

'Phil, you look so thin!' Katherine put her arms round her brother and hugged him, appalled at how the ill-pressed coat hung off his frame. She released him and stood back to look at him anxiously. 'Have you been ill? Or not eating properly.'

He shrugged sulkily. 'No money. France ain't all it's cracked up to be, Katy. The inns are the devil of a price, the food's awful unless you pay through the nose and the gaming's crooked.'

'Then why play?' she asked despairingly.

'How else was I supposed to live?' he demanded petulantly. 'It's all right for you—you've been living in your palace with your marquis, dining off gold plates, no doubt.'

The sheer unfairness of it stung her into retaliation. 'I had no idea who he was until we got here! You left without even waiting for the execution, without a word to me other than that you had gone to France—and you stole my clock and earbobs.'

He looked shiftily ashamed, but continued to whine. 'I couldn't stand it, I told you that. You do not know how bad it was for me.'

'*For you?* I faced debtors' prison, marriage to a man I thought was a common felon, the prospect of widowhood—and you could not stand it? There are times, Philip, when I despair.'

He shifted around the room, fidgeting so as not to meet her angry eyes. 'Well, I'm back now, and you've fallen on your feet. Your marquis will have to do something for me.'

'Oh, no, he will not,' Katherine said vehemently. 'I am getting the marriage annulled, so do not think you can sponge off Nicholas.'

'Annulled?' Her brother's face broke into an unpleasant grin. 'After you spent a night in a cell with him, goodness knows how many on the journey up here and have been living with him ever since? I know all about the Dower House—the goings-on at the big house are the main topic of gossip hereabouts.'

'I will rely on medical evidence,' Katherine said stiffly.

Philip sneered. 'Virginities are restored daily in every brothel in the land, no one is going to believe—'

He did not finish the sentence. The door slammed back on its hinges and a tall figure took one stride into the room and hit him square on the jaw.

'Do not,' said Nicholas, Marquis of Seaton, massaging his grazed knuckles, 'do not ever speak to my wife like that again. Get up and apologise.'

Philip struggled to his feet and backed away. 'Katy, you know I didn't mean it…'

'Apologise.'

'I am sorry, Katy.'

'Now, listen to what I have to say, and listen to it well.' Nick pressed Katherine gently down into a chair and smiled reassuringly. The caressing look was strangely at odds with the cold anger in his voice. 'Tomorrow you will come to Seaton Mandeville and you will ask for Mr Wilkinson, the steward. He will arrange a quarterly allowance for you and will advance you the first quarter.' He named a sum that made Katherine start in surprise and a slow smile to spread itself over Philip's pasty features.

'If my wife feels able to receive you tomorrow, she will tell Mr Wilkinson so. If not, you will leave the district immediately. If you attempt to visit Katherine without her express permission, the allowance will be stopped. If you try and run up debts using my name, it will be stopped. If you say or write anything to Katherine that causes her the slightest distress, it will be stopped. Is that clear?'

Philip nodded dumbly.

'My wife, your sister, is a lady whose only fault is her loyalty to you and her persistent love for a man who has let her down, betrayed her and insulted her. You may believe she will forgive you and indulge you, but understand this: I do not for-

give you, I do not trust you and, if I have to, I will break you.'
He turned on his heel without looking further at the shaken
man. 'Come, Kat, it is time to go home.'

Katherine held out a hand to her brother. 'I will see you
tomorrow, Philip, I promise.' Then she was out of the door
and being walked firmly downstairs. This was the crowning
humiliation in a day of humiliation. Katherine managed to
keep her expression calm as Nick spoke to Durren who was
waiting outside, warily holding the grey horse.

'How did you drive here?'

'In the gig, my lord, it is in the yard.'

'Very well, I will drive her ladyship back, you can ride
Xerxes.'

'I'll lead him, if it's all the same to you, my lord,' the man
said with some feeling. 'Shall I get the gig, my lord?'

'No, we will walk round. Thank you, Durren.'

Katherine got up on to the leather seat and sat silently
while they drove out of the yard, past Durren and on to the
road that led to Seaton Mandeville. *What can I say to him?*
she wondered miserably. *How can I apologise?*

'Kat, I am so sorry.' He took the reins in one hand and
clasped the other over hers. 'That must have been so distressing for you. I should have handled it better, but I am afraid I
lost my temper.'

'You are sorry? Nick, I was wondering how I could start
to apologise. That you should feel you have to give Philip an
allowance.' Her voice faltered and she stiffened her spine. 'Tomorrow I will speak to him. He must understand that of course
he cannot accept what you have offered.'

'I am not going to have my brother-in-law in and out of
debtors' prison. This seems the best solution,' Nick replied
calmly.

'But he will not be your brother-in-law!'

'Kat.' He tightened his grip on her clasped hands. 'You have been eavesdropping.'

'I know,' she admitted shamefaced. 'I did not intend to. But it was a good thing that I did.'

'Because you now know that I feel I have to stay married to you and my father opposes the match?'

'Yes.' She was not going to cry, not out here in the middle of the public highway.

'And like many eavesdroppers you misunderstood what you heard. We were discussing my ill-fated romance with Arabella. My father is entirely in favour of my marriage to you—and we are both in your debt for what you said to him this morning.'

Unsure she was hearing aright, Katherine asked, 'You are reconciled?'

'I do not think we were ever in a state of conciliation to be returned to!' Nick chuckled. 'This harmony is strange for both of us, I rely on you, Kat, to act as ambassador and make sure we stay in such a condition.'

'But you cannot wish to be married to me,' she said, trying to keep her voice steady and not sound as though she were pleading.

'Why should I not wish to be married to a lady I love?' Nick turned the gig through the gates of the park and drove off the roadway under a spreading grove of chestnut trees. He looped the reins around the brake and shifted in his seat to look at Katherine.

'You…you love me?' *No, it was not possible.* 'Why did you not tell me?'

'Because you would think I was trying to hold you to the marriage and because, then, you did not want to be held. I rather hoped you might grow to wish it. I was going to tell you after our dinner party when you saw for yourself what a fitting hostess you made.'

'I always wished it,' she whispered.

'*What?*'

'Ever since the journey up here. I knew I loved you, and I knew I could not be your wife.'

'Because of who my father is?'

She nodded. 'And because I could not hold you to a marriage begun in such circumstances.'

'My father points out that I have no need to marry for fortune and that in you I may, against all my deserts, have found a woman who will be the making of me.'

'Oh, Nick.' She found she was in his arms, not quite certain how she got there. 'I could not bear to come between you and your father, not after you had been estranged so long.'

Nick pushed her gently back from him until he could look into her face. The dark eyes that had so affected her across that stark prison room held hers. 'In effect, you proposed marriage to me, Kat. Now I propose that we stay married. What do you say to that?'

'Yes, Nick. Oh, yes.'

'Then there is but one act left to make it so.' His long fingers caressed down her cheek. 'Your bed or my bed, Lady Seaton?' He gathered up the reins and turned the gig in the direction of the Dower House.

With the mid-day sun streaming over the amber silk of the coverlet, Katherine opened her arms and her heart and her body to her husband, her eyes wide, drowning in the dark fire of his as he possessed her, joining them.

'I love you, Kat,' he murmured as she cried out his name, arching to meet him, match him, envelop him. 'I love you,' and his beautiful, brave Marchioness drew him down to her heart and gave him back love for love.

* * * * *

REGENCY
Collection

*Let these sparklingly seductive delights whirl
you away to the ballrooms—and
bedrooms—of Polite Society!*

Volume 1 – 4th February 2011
Regency Pleasures by Louise Allen

Volume 2 – 4th March 2011
Regency Secrets by Julia Justiss

Volume 3 – 1st April 2011
Regency Rumours by Juliet Landon

Volume 4 – 6th May 2011
Regency Redemption by Christine Merrill

Volume 5 – 3rd June 2011
Regency Protectors by Margaret McPhee

Volume 6 – 1st July 2011
Regency Improprieties by Diane Gaston

12 volumes in all to collect!

MILLS
BOON

www.millsandboon.co.uk

REGENCY
Collection

*Let these sparklingly seductive delights whirl
you away to the ballrooms—and
bedrooms—of Polite Society!*

Volume 7 – 5th August 2011
Regency Mistresses by Mary Brendan

Volume 8 – 2nd September 2011
Regency Rebels by Deb Marlowe

Volume 9 – 7th October 2011
Regency Scandals by Sophia James

Volume 10 – 4th November 2011
Regency Marriages by Elizabeth Rolls

Volume 11 – 2nd December 2011
Regency Innocents by Annie Burrows

Volume 12 – 6th January 2012
Regency Sins by Bronwyn Scott

12 volumes in all to collect!

&MILLS BOON

www.millsandboon.co.uk

HISTORICAL

Regency

LADY FOLBROKE'S DELICIOUS DECEPTION
by Christine Merrill

Lady Emily Longesley married the love of her life and hoped that he would learn to love her. Instead, he upped and left! Confronting her errant husband three years on, she sees that Adrian, Earl of Folbroke, has been robbed of his sight! If she plays his mistress by delicious deception, can he finally learn to love his wife?

Regency

HOW TO MARRY A RAKE
by Deb Marlowe

Heiress Mae Halford has mended her heart after her friend Stephen Manning's rejection. She's ready to find herself a husband, but the first man she bumps into at a Newmarket house party is Lord Stephen himself!

BREAKING THE GOVERNESS'S RULES
by Michelle Styles

After being dismissed from her post as governess for allowing Jonathon, Lord Chesterholm, to seduce her, Louisa Sibson has rebuilt her life. She lives by a rulebook of morals—and will not allow the devastating Jonathon to break them again!

On sale from 4th March 2011
Don't miss out!

*Available at WHSmith, Tesco, ASDA, Eason
and all good bookshops*

www.millsandboon.co.uk

0211/04a

HISTORICAL

HER DARK AND DANGEROUS LORD
by Anne Herries

Exiled Lord Stefan de Montfort rescues Englishwoman
Anne Melford from the sea and takes her to his château
in Normandy. Anne fires within Stefan a disturbing,
forbidden desire. Could such a lady ever marry a dark
and dangerous scoundrel like him?

SIERRA BRIDE
by Jenna Kernan

Wealthy Sam Pickett is used to getting his way. So he is
baffled when Kate Wells, a feisty little hellion who steps
between him and a bullet, isn't interested in becoming
his wife. If he can't make her his bride, then he'll
most certainly make her his mistress!

BREATHLESS
by Anne Stuart

Ruined beyond repair and shunned by London society,
Miranda Rohan rebelliously embraces the freedom of having
nothing left to lose. This dangerous course throws her under
the power of the darkly enigmatic Lucien de Malheur—
known as the Scorpion...
The House of Rohan

On sale from 4th March 2011
Don't miss out!

*Available at WHSmith, Tesco, ASDA, Eason
and all good bookshops*
www.millsandboon.co.uk

04a

0211/04b

Tainted with
dishonour, undone
by passion

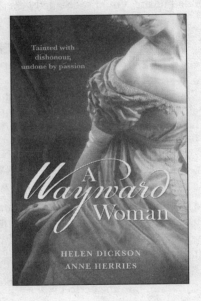

Two women destined for ruin, but can
they be rescued by love?

Available 18th February 2011
www.millsandboon.co.uk

"*The rules of the ton are
made to be broken...*

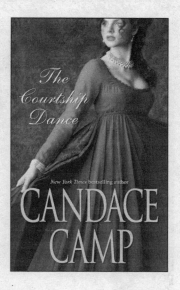

Lady Francesca Haughston finds passion in making
desirable matches for others. So it seems only fair,
after breaking her own long-ago engagement to
Sinclair, Duke of Rochford, that she now help
him find the perfect wife.

But soon Francesca finds his lessons in love
scandalously irresistible – and a temptation
that could endanger them both.

"The arrogance! To think that they can come here with their town bronze and sweep some heiress or other to the altar."

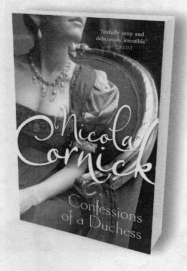

When a feudal law requires all unmarried ladies to wed or surrender half their wealth, the quiet village of Fortune's Folly becomes England's greatest Marriage Market.

Laura, the dowager duchess, is determined to resist the flattery of fortune hunters. Young, handsome and scandalously tempting Dexter Anstruther suspects Laura has a hidden motive for resisting his charms…and he intends to discover it.

www.mirabooks.co.uk

"I promise that I will release you tomorrow – when the hour of the wedding is past."

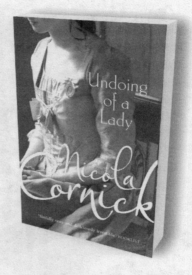

Nat Waterhouse must marry an heiress.
Lady Elizabeth Scarlet vows there is just one way
to save her childhood friend from a loveless
marriage: kidnap him!

When her inexperienced attempt flares into intense
passion, Lizzie is ruined...and hopelessly in love!
Now the wild and wilful Lizzie must convince Nat
that they are a perfect match – in every way.

www.mirabooks.co.uk

England's Forgotten Queen

Anne Neville is the heiress and daughter of the greatest powerbroker in the land, Warwick the Kingmaker. She is a pawn, trapped in an uncertain political game.

When the Earl of Warwick commits treason, his family is forced into exile. Humiliated and powerless in a foreign land, Anne must find the courage and the wit to survive in a man's world.

www.mirabooks.co.uk

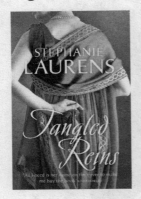

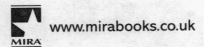